"Make no mistake, Hall is an accomplished wordsmith. The novel's prose is meticulous." —Lionel Shriver, *Financial Times* (London)

"Both uplifting and enthralling, *The Wolf Border* is as much a hymn to the rugged beauty of the Cumbrian countryside as it is an exploration of the nature of wilderness and of the durability of the human spirit. Beautiful and quite stunning." —*Mail on Sunday*

"[A] wonderfully assured page-turner. . . . Worth reading for its style, wisdom, and narrative pull, as well as for its exploration of wildness in many forms, human and lupine." —*Literary Review*

"Her sense of place is visceral, the changing of seasons as dramatic as any of the plot's set pieces." —*Aberdeen Press and Journal* [Scotland]

"I was swept along by the stunning prose and compelling story." —*Woman & Home* (UK)

"Regeneration in a multitude of guises is the mainstay of the novel; but rather than overworking the metaphor, Hall organically incorporates each and every instance into the narrative, adding a tensile strength to the base architecture upon which the story hangs. . . . One of the fiction highlights of this year." —*The Observer*

"Compelling . . . [a] gripping last third." —*New Statesman*

"A sumptuous study of truth and trust. . . . A magnificently metaphorical novel: an extended exploration of myth and motherhood—indeed the myth of motherhood. . . . A feast of the finest fiction: a captivating and cannily crafted character-focused showcase of one of Britain's most promising young novelists." —Tor.com

THE WOLF BORDER

THE
WOLF BORDER

A Novel

Sarah Hall

HARPER PERENNIAL

NEW YORK • LONDON • TORONTO • SYDNEY • NEW DELHI • AUCKLAND

First published in Great Britain in 2015 by Faber & Faber Limited

FIRST HARPER PERENNIAL EDITION PUBLISHED 2016.

Library of Congress Cataloging-in-Publication Data has been applied for.

ISBN 978-0-06-220848-4 (pbk.)

16 17 18 19 20   OFF/RRD   10 9 8 7 6 5 4 3 2 1

For Fiona

Susiraja (Finnish) – Literally 'wolf border': the boundary between the capital region and the rest of the country. The name suggests everything outside the border is wilderness.

O, thou wilt be a wilderness again,
Peopled with wolves, thy old inhabitants!

Henry IV, Part II

OLD COUNTRY

It's not often she dreams about them. During the day they are elusive, keeping to the tall grass of the Reservation, disappearing from the den site. They are fleet or lazy, moving through their own tawny colourscape and sleeping under logs – missable either way. Their vanishing acts have been perfected. At night they come back. The cameras pick them up, red-eyed, muzzles darkened, returning from a hunt. Or she hears them howling along the buffer zone, a long harmonic. One leading, then many. At night there is no need to imagine, no need to dream. They reign outside the mind.

Now there is snow over Chief Joseph, an early fall. The pines are bending tolerantly; the rivers see white. In backcountry cabins venison stocks and pipes are beginning to freeze. Millionaires' ranches lie empty: their thermostats set, their gates locked. The roads are open but there are few visitors. The summer conferences and powwows are long over. Only the casinos do business with tourists, with stag parties and addict crones, in neon reparation. Soon the pack will be gone, too – north, after the caribou – the centre will close for winter, and she is flying home to England. Her first visit in six years. The last ended badly, with an argument, a family riven. She is being called upon to entertain a rich man's whimsy, a man who owns almost a fifth of her home county. And her mother is dying. Neither duty is urgent; both players will wait, with varying degrees of patience. Meanwhile, snow. The Chief Joseph wolves are scenting hoof prints, making forays from the den. The pups have grown big and ready, any day now they will start their journey. The tribal councils are meeting in Lapwai to discuss scholarships, road maintenance, the governor's hunting quota, and protection of the pack. The Hernandez comet is low and dull in the east, above survivalist compounds.

The night before Rachel leaves Idaho, she does dream of them, and of Binny. Binny is sitting on a wooden bench in the old wildlife park outside the bird huts, wearing a long leather coat and smoking a rolled cigarette. She has dark, short hair under a green cloche hat. It is Rachel's birthday. This is her birthday wish – a day at Setterah Keep: the ruined Victorian menagerie in the woods of the Lowther Valley. They have walked round the boar enclosures, the otters, the peacocks, to the owls. Binny likes the eagle owl. She likes its biased ears, the fixed orange tunnels of its eyes. She sits quietly and smokes, watches the bird beating its clipped wings and preening. She is all bone and breasts under her coat: a body better out of clothes, a body made to ruin men. Not yet pregnant with Rachel's brother. Her green nylon trousers tingle with static when Rachel leans against them. The stocky, haunched bird prowls across the pen towards its feed, gullets a mouse whole, up to the tail. Rachel hates owls. They are like fat brushes – a ridiculous shape for a thing. They sweep and swivel their heads and have sharp picky beaks. When she goes inside the hut to see the lunar white one, the darkness hurts her head. The bird shed stinks of lime and feathers and must. Back outside, she sits on the bench with Binny and kicks the ground. *Are you bored, my girl?* Binny says. *You wanted to come. Go and see the otters again. You can take some ice cream.* Binny likes freedom. She likes the man in the sweet kiosk. He makes her laugh by asking if they are sisters. She holds his eye. *Off you go, my girl*, she says, lighting another cigarette. *Be brave.*

Rachel walks to the otter pool, unwraps the mint choc chip and licks the gritty dome. The pool has a green-stained moat that moves like a river. The otters paddle round it on their backs, eating fish heads. Their fur snugs the water. They chitter to each other. Under the ice cream is a malty cone. She goes into the snake house, where there are bright insects clinging in glass tanks. The snakes move slower than forever.

Binny is still talking at the kiosk, leaning in. Rachel is allowed to go quite far – she knows all the ways around the village where she lives, the lonnings, the drove-tracks over the moors. She walks past the netted parrots squawking at each other, past the gift shop and toilets, over a bridge over a stream, to a burnt creosoted gate, on which there is a sign, made of red writing. She can't read it because she's not yet in school. Through the gate and into the trees. The trees smell of mint too. Wooded pathways with arrows pointing, corridors of shadows either side. *Be brave.* It is very quiet. Brown needles stream between trunks, and her steps make tiny silky squeaks. Fork to the right. Fork to the left. Into the dark, filtering green. At the bottom of the cone there's a chocolate stub. Once that's gone she's more aware of where she is.

Here. Beside a fence built tall and seriously, up into the trees. The wire is thick and heavy, knotted into diamond-shaped holes. Pinned to it is another sign. Maybe it's the end of the park. What is on the other side? *Hello?* She reaches up and takes hold of the wire. She slots the tips of her shoes through and lifts herself off the ground. Beyond are bushes and worn earth. A bundle of something pinkish, with bits of ragged hair and buzzing flies. She leans back, bends her knees, sways and rattles the metal. Emptiness beyond. Flickering leaves. *Hello?*

It comes between the bushes, as if bidden. It comes forward, mercilessly, towards her, paws lifting, fast, but not running. A word she will soon learn: *lope*. It is perfectly made: long legs, sheer chest, dressed for coldness in wraps of grey fur. It comes close to the wire and stands looking at her, eyes level, pure yellow gaze. Long nose, the black tip twitching, short mane. A dog before dogs were invented. The god of all dogs. It is a creature so fine, she can hardly comprehend it. But it recognises her. It has seen and smelled animals like her for two million years. It stands looking. Yellow eyes, black-ringed. Its thoughts nameless. She holds the fence but the fence has almost disappeared; she is hanging in the air, suspended like a soft offering. Any minute it will be upon her.

In sleep, Rachel has stopped breathing. Snow is falling on the cabin roof, through acres of blackness; the computer in the office is winking slowly, storing emails and data; elk season is open. The Chief Joseph den has been abandoned and the pack is moving single file through the Bitterroot terrain, winter nomads. Her British passport is in her jacket pocket and her mother, no longer hale or able, is dying, a long way away. *Go on, my girl.* In the dream, the wolf stands looking at her. Yellow-eyed and sheer. A mystic from the Reservation once asked her to describe the feeling of communion seeing a wolf that first time. What did her heart feel? There was money in it for him he'd hoped – she had only just arrived, maybe she would buy one of his sachets of fur, a leather charm, a tooth. *I don't believe what you believe*, she'd said.

How does it feel? Pre-erotic fear. The heart beneath her chest jumps, smells bloody. She unclutches the wire and steps to the ground. Its head lowers: eyes level again, keen as gold, sorrowless. Then it releases its extraordinary jaw. Inside is a lustre of sharpness, white crescents, ridges, black pleated lips. A long, spooling tongue. In her brain an evolutionary signal fires. What a mouth like that means. She steps back, turns and walks carefully along the fence, her hands clenched. The wolf crosses paws, folds round, and walks parallel behind the wire. A blur of long grey, head tilted towards her, one eye watching. She stops walking, and it stops. She turns slowly and walks the other way. It crosses paws, turns, and follows. An echo, a mirror. She stops. *What are you doing?* Its ears prick up, twitch forward. She begins to run along the wire, over the slippery forest floor, needles and branches. She is fast. But it is there, running at her side, exact, switching direction when she does, almost before she does, running back the other way. It turns as she turns, runs as she runs. She runs hard through the Setterah woods, along the fence, and it runs with her. Through the trees. To the very corner of the cage, where she stops, breathing hard, and it stops and stands looking at her. *What are you doing?* she says.

But already she knows. The layers of sleep are falling away. The radio alarm is blaring, KIYE station, a rock song from the eighties. Her shoulder is cold outside the heavy covers. Her brain is restarting. That creature of the outer darkness – of geographic success, myth and horror, hunted with every age's weapon, stone axe, spear, sprung-steel trap, and semi-automatic – was playing.

5 a.m., Mountain Time. Kyle will drive her to the airport before daylight to catch the hopper to Spokane. She lies under the blankets and listens to snow dispatching softly from the roof and the

branches. Setterah Keep: a lost world. She had loved going there for birthdays as a child. Until, in 1981, the Licensing Act brought an end to many of the parks and it closed down. Even a century before, they must have known the enclosures were too small, pens, dementing places. After coffee and a shower, when she is properly awake, she phones Binny and reminds her what time she will be arriving. *Yes, Thursday. Yes, by dinnertime, if the traffic isn't bad.* Then, unusually, she tells her mother about the dream. *No,* Binny says. *No. That wasn't a dream. There were wolves in the park for a while. Don't you remember? You kids used to torment them. One of them got out, created havoc.*

*

The Earl is not at home when Rachel arrives at Pennington Hall. She was warned by his secretary that he is unreliable, that he keeps only some of his appointments. The prerogative of wealth and eccentricity. The drive from London has taken eight hours: congestion around the airport and the north orbital, an accident south of Kendal, all lanes halted until the air ambulance could set down on the carriageway to collect the shattered motorcyclist. As ever, the county's interior routes move sluggishly: compact dry-stone lanes and dawdling sightseers. A landslide on one of the mountain passes has resulted in road closure, so she must turn back at the barrier and take the longer lakeside road into the western valleys. The fells rise, carrying dead bracken on their slopes the colour of rust. Granite juts through, below gathering cloud. She sets the wipers to intermittent, but the rain is either too heavy or too fine; the rubber blades screech or the screen blurs. The GPS recalculates, asks her to turn round, go back the way she has come. She switches it off and buys a map from a village shop. This is not a part of the district she knows – her home village is on the other side of the mountains.

She is extremely tired by the time she reaches the gate into the estate, nauseous with jetlag and service station coffee. But she's alert enough to notice the beauty of the place – September's russet fading in the trees, wet, glistening light on the hills – and to note that the lake would be a good territorial boundary, were this still wilderness. It has not been wilderness since the primeval forest was felled. The gate into the estate is an elaborate wrought-iron affair, bearing a coat of arms. She pulls up next to the intercom, lowers the window, and inhales. Moorland, peat, ferns, water and whatever the water touches: the myrrh of autumn. She's become used to spruce and sagebrush, the rancid vegetable smell of the paper mill downriver from the Reservation. Cumbria's signature aroma is immediately recognisable: upland pheromones.

She reaches out to press the button, but the gate opens silently. She is being watched on the CCTV. The drive is long and newly gravelled, oak-lined. She passes a tree so old and obese with bark that its lower branches are sagging almost to the ground. Wooden struts have been built underneath to prop them up. Beside the drive a handful of roe deer graze. They raise their heads as she drives by and do not move. In the rain, the red-stone manor looks patched and bloody. Ivy is growing shaggily up the facade, but for a building of its size and age it is far from dereliction. The crenellations are intact; the windows expensively replaced. Thomas Pennington has not suffered hard times, death duties, or insurmountable taxes, it would seem. The building is clearly not a casualty of democratic change like so many of the country-side's aristocratic behemoths. Perhaps the garden and house are open to the public, or a lucrative tearoom is hidden somewhere behind the maze, bulbs and plant cuttings for sale, wedding hire, the usual schemes. Or perhaps the Earl's business portfolio has been skilfully updated and he has accounts offshore. Rachel parks at the side of the tower, next to a little blue MG and a utility van, gets out, and stretches. The air is damp and cool. Rooks clamour in the nearby trees. The mountains behind could have been built for aesthetic purposes – it is an incredibly beautiful view.

The main door of the hall is a dense medieval affair, shot through with bolts: siege-proof. On either side sit two stone lions, lichen mottling their manes. It seems wrong to use such an entrance, but there is no other way, no tradesman's signpost. She pushes the bell and a ferrous donging sounds within. A woman answers: middle-aged, plump inside her navy suit. She is auburn-haired, unadorned by jewellery or cosmetics, with winter-rose skin. Extremely English-looking; from an England seventy years gone. She would suit a rabble of hounds at her feet, Rachel thinks, a shotgun crooked over her elbow – the complete incarnation has probably at some stage existed. The woman introduces herself as Honor Clark, the Earl's secretary. Rachel shakes her hand.

Really sorry I'm late. The flight was delayed. Snow in Spokane. We were sitting on the runway too long – they had to re-spray the plane. I almost missed the connection. Then the drive up . . . I hope he hasn't been waiting long.

The apology is irrelevant. *He* isn't here.

I don't know where he is at the moment, Honor Clark tells her. The Land Rover's gone, which doesn't bode well, but it does mean he's on the estate. I'm leaving in an hour. Do you want to come in?

Rachel checks her watch.

Ah. Yes, OK. Thank you.

She follows the woman across the threshold, into a large, temperate reception hall, then down a corridor hung with portraits of stags, Heaton Coopers, and a few tasteful abstracts. She is shown into a vast drawing room containing an elaborate suite of furniture, a Bauhaus chair, glassware cabinets, bookcases, and an immense stone fireplace. The grate is un-laid but the room is warm, free of medieval draughts. The secretary holds her hands up as if fending something away.

Look, I can't offer you dinner, I'm afraid. Thomas has an event in Windermere tonight so he's dining out. We don't have guests this week – the chef's off.

I'm fine.

As I say, I doubt he'll be available before he has to go out.

OK. But I did have an appointment. I should probably wait.

The secretary nods and lowers her hands.

You said you didn't need a hotel so I haven't booked one.

No. I'm staying with family.

You're local? I don't hear an accent.

I've been away quite a while.

I see.

Honor Clark ushers her across the room, and Rachel sits on the chaise longue near the empty fire. Lambent Chinese silk, in near-perfect condition. Her trousers are badly creased. The sales tag inside the waistband is irritating her lower back but she has failed during the course of the flight or the drive to tear it out. She has not worn slacks for over a year, not since the Minnesota conference, at which she delivered the keynote speech, drank too much in the hotel bar with Kyle and Oran, argued with the chairman of the IWC, slept with Oran again, and left a day early.

Not disgraced exactly, but en route. In the bars and restaurants of Kamiah, which the centre workers frequent at weekends, the dress code for both men and women extends no further than boots and jeans. She hasn't showered since leaving the centre; any trace of deodorant has gone. She has never been received at this level of society before, in any country. Even beyond the warp of altered time zones and the déjà vu of coming home, the event feels deeply uncanny. Honor Clark moves to the sideboard.

OK. Well. I'll set you up and then leave you. Would you like a sherry?

Yes, alright.

Sweet or dry?

Dry?

The secretary lifts one of the cut-glass decanters, unstoppers it, and pours out a viscous topaz liquid. The rugs under her heels are intricately woven, plums and teals, each one no doubt worth thousands. Rachel's cabin in the centre complex has flat-pack cabinets and linoleum floors. There are fading plastic coffee cups with the Chief Joseph logo stamped on them. Her entire cabin would fit, if not into this capacious, silk-wallpapered room, then certainly into the wing. It feels as if a kind of Dickensian experiment is taking place, except there will be no charitable warding, no societal ascent. Her intended role has not yet been defined. A consultant? A named advocate? A class of specialist suddenly called upon in times of extravagant ecological hobbying? A delicate, bell-shaped glass of sherry is placed in her hand. Honor Clark heads for the door.

I'll come back before I go. Have to make a few phone calls and finish up. If he arrives I'll send him to you. But, as I say, it's unlikely. You'll be alright in the meantime?

Yes. Fine. Thanks.

And the woman is gone, back into the panelled opulence of the manor corridors, back into whichever chamber of the hall she inhabits while arranging the abortive comings and goings of the Earl. The sun shifts from behind a cloud and the drawing room is filled with moist Lakeland light. Rachel sips the sherry, which is crisp and surprisingly enjoyable. Not a trace of dust or mouldering cork. She finishes the drink quickly, then stands and crosses the room.

Beyond the tall windows, the estate extends for miles. It is now the largest private estate in England. Little of the acreage has been sold off. In fact, quite the opposite. Thomas Pennington owns most of the private woodland in the region, farmsteads, mostly empty, all but the common land. On the horizon, the fells roll bluely towards bald peaks. At the bottom of the sloping lawn, at the lake edge, is a wooden reiki structure – one of the Earl's alternative hobbies, perhaps, certainly safer than flying microlights, which famously almost killed him, and did kill his wife.

The lake's surface reflects complicated weather. On an island near the opposite shore is a red-stone folly, a faux architectural match for the hall, and towards this a tiny boat is rowing, leaving a soft V on the cloudy surface. The west coast is fifteen miles away, ugly and nuclear. Somewhere between, behind the autumn trees, is the enclosure.

Maps of the estate have been sent to her. Spatially, the argument is easily made; it is one of the few tracts of land where such a project is viable. The new game enclosure bill has given the Earl licence for such a project. No doubt he pulled strings to have it passed. Work is underway on the barrier. The money seems limitless. What he does not have, what he wants, is her – the native expert.

She takes her phone from her jacket pocket. Binny has rung but left no message. There are two texts from Kyle. *Left Paw radio transmitter kaput, possible dispersal. Trustafarian volunteer quit owe you 50.* Then, off duty: *How's merry old England had any warm beer?* He will be out trying to track Left Paw, whose disappearance is not unexpected. The young male has been making solo excursions, preparing to go and find a mate. Still, such events are not without worry. There's a text from one of the local rangers, married but persistent. A mistake over the summer. Another white night. She deletes it without reading.

The light outside the windows remains bright, but hanging over the lake are fine slings of rain. The boat has made it to the island and has moored. Rachel walks the circumference of the room, pauses at an adjoining door, then opens it. A library. Assuming no intrusion – is she not somehow entitled while she waits? – she goes inside. There's another fireplace, deeply recessed with seats inlaid, classical scenes painted on the tiles. On every wall shelves are fitted, floor to ceiling, in glossy hardwood. She browses the contents. Leather-bound antiques, hardbacks of contemporary novels. There are illustrated wildlife encyclopedias. An impressive row of first-edition poetry volumes: Auden, Eliot, Douglas. A large Audubon folio. It is a civil collection – with nothing particularly revealing. But what clues does she expect to find anyway? Tomes of the occult? Fairy tales? Has she imagined Thomas Pennington to be a Gothic fetishist? A Romanticist with a liking for exotic pets? Who is this man who has expensively summoned her across thousands of miles?

On the mantelpiece above the fire is a heavy bronze replica of the Capitoline wolf, the infants Romulus and Remus on their knees suckling beneath her. For all Rachel knows, it could be the original. The truth is she suspected – as soon as she knew whose name was attached to the project – that this landed British entrepreneur, known for causing trouble in the House, for sponsoring sea eagles and opposing badger culls, is deadly serious about his latest environmental venture. That's why she is here. Not for Binny, who is simply benefiting from a stranger's generosity. She shuts the library door. She goes back into the drawing room, sits in the chaise longue, leans against the plush upholstery, and closes her eyes.

After forty-five minutes Honor Clark wakes her, with a polite hand on the shoulder. She is wearing a brown raincoat, belted at the waist, and carrying an oxblood lady's briefcase. A paisley headscarf is knotted under her chin. Rachel wants to ask, Do the shops in the county still sell such items, without irony? Are these fashions still depicted in the country magazines?

We're going to have to scratch, Honor Clark says. Can you come back tomorrow?

The tone is faintly triumphant. Clearly, she knows her boss's habits; clerical intuition and rescheduling are a normal part of her job description, and it is certainly not within her remit to apologise for the errant Earl. The airline ticket from Spokane was business class; Rachel's hire car is a BMW. Any additional expenses are being covered during her stay; all she has to do is keep and submit receipts. If the man himself is chaotic, or even a lunatic, his sovereignty seems not to suffer. Rachel stands.

Sure. Tomorrow. What time?

Let's try eleven. He has t'ai chi from nine until ten.

Of course he does, Rachel thinks. As she crosses the room, the tag inside her trousers scratches her lower back. She reaches in and snaps it from the plastic frond, crumples it, and puts it into her back pocket. She has a week's leave from Chief Joseph, during which time her soliciting benefactor can put in an appearance or not, as he so chooses. It will make no difference either way; her obligation ends after their meeting. She knows she will not take the job, however appealing the proposal or curious she may be. Foolish and time-wasting though the courtship may result, it has at least given her a reason to come home.

*

Is that you, my girl?

You look smaller, Mum.

It's true. Since Rachel's last visit, Binny has shrunk considerably. She clutches the doorframe of her care-home apartment, a stoop-lump on her back under the quilted dressing gown. Her hair is almost gone, her scalp as cracked and dull as a shell. The hand holding the doorframe looks fossilised, like something extracted from a bog or petrified forest, out of proportion with her thin arm. On her face are brown flaky cancers. The descent since Rachel's last visit, when her mother was still able to lob a vase at the wall, has been steep.

You look like an American. You're not a bloody citizen, are you?

Not yet, no.

Good.

Binny releases the door and they embrace. She holds Rachel fiercely, a grip far exceeding her frail demeanour, a grip reminding her daughter just how long she has been gone. From under the quilted gown comes the reek of sweat and ammonia, and a masking perfume – not the Paestum Rose Binny once favoured, gifted by suitors and worn high in the wen of her thighs, but something sweeter, cheaper, a scent that will cover the body's sins. The yolky eyes of her mother look her over.

Lost a bit of weight, too. You're not living on hamburgers and chips, then.

Most of the time I am.

I did teach you to cook.

There's a slur when Binny speaks, a glistening collection in one corner of her mouth. The stroke, three years ago. Somehow Rachel has managed not to register the impediment fully during their phone calls. Binny is trying to look her daughter in the eye, but her vision is shot, and she's lost her height. *You taught me to cook*, Rachel thinks, *because you never lifted a pan, and Lawrence was always hungry.*

I hate cooking. You know that.

I suppose you just drive through those places in your car.

Sometimes. And I'm an expert with a can opener.

Oh, Lord.

Her mother appears to be stalled, as if she wants to turn round and re-enter the room but her body won't cooperate. Or perhaps she is not quite sure whether to invite her guest in. Rachel looks down at her. This can't really be Binny – the toxic, striking Londoner who charmed and upset the northern villagers with her brassy left-wing talk and fashionable looks. Binny – the woman who broke up several marriages, casting aside the borrowed men as soon as they were hers, or keeping them as lodgers. The woman who ran the little post office as if it were a social club, giving out cups of tea and sexual advice, stacking the tiny entrance hall with controversial items – frosted cornflakes, condoms, the *Guardian*. Who raised a young daughter alone. Or, rather, let that daughter raise herself. Communist in the Tory heartland. Self-declared red-blooded sensualist, whose second child, Rachel's half-brother Lawrence, left home at fourteen rather than argue with the men frequenting the house.

And now this – an impotent, leaking ruin. The reality is more shocking than anything Rachel had anticipated. And the feeling filling her is dire. Pity. Regret. The desire to return this sick-smelling woman to those years of virility and concomitant notoriety. Return her to the postal cottage, to the hoo-ha and scandal in the village, the old blue Jaguar always breaking down on the road to town, and the caravanner's wardrobe. Restore her, even though it would mean all the rest, too. The arguments. The name-calling in school. Other women banging on the door. Not bringing boyfriends home because they would stare, and stammer through Binny's flirtation, then be ardent upstairs in Rachel's bedroom and not understand why.

Finally her mother turns, without catastrophe, and shuffles inside.

Come in then. Hope you've eaten. Dinner will be an atrocity. They think we can't tell sirloin from slop. Most can't, mind you. You'll want to sit next to Dora – she's the only one with any noodle left.

The same wit. The same vim. The bad old personality locked in the mortal tomb, struggling to get out. But it sounds like a practised line.

Dora. Got it.

Rachel picks up her bag and follows her mother into a small sitting room, the temperature of which is subtropical. A green leather armchair – her mother's chair from the post office kitchen – is the only recognisable item from the past. Rachel has never been to Willowbrook before. It's nice, as such things go, converted from an old hospital. Lawrence moved Binny in and cleared out the cottage. Lawrence takes care of things financially and does not ask Rachel for a contribution, much to his wife's chagrin. She has not arranged to see her brother. She has not emailed him for a while, in fact, though Binny has probably kept him in the loop about her visit. Now her mother is struggling to get out of the quilted gown, inching it down over her shoulders, her hands more an incapacity than a useful tool. Rachel steps in to help.

No. Get off. I can manage. You have a seat. You look knackered.

Binny shuffles into the bedroom and comes back a few minutes later wearing a blue winged jacket, an astoundingly conservative garment. She has on a matt smear of burgundy lipstick and a string of beads. Is this the usual effort for dinner, Rachel wonders, or is it being made for the prodigal's return and introduction? Binny moves slowly towards the chair, leans over it, positions herself, and sits. She sighs with the effort.

You better get changed. They'll be serving in a minute. Then you can tell me what Lord Muck wanted. And who you're on with these days. Not that wet one who works with you, I hope. He sounds like a prevaricator. The other's far better – Carl, is it? You can put your stuff in there.

She gestures towards a door on the other side of the room.

Kyle. And he's just a friend. I'm wearing this.

Right. Well, do something with your hair. It's sticking up like a loo brush. Why did you cut it all off anyway? You look like a lesbian.

Rachel doesn't rise to it; she has made a pact with herself not to for the duration of her stay. In the small adjoining room, a narrow cot has been made up. Willowbrook allows guests to stay for seven days, free of charge. She puts her bag on the bed. When she goes into the bathroom the smell of urine is overwhelming. There's a grey wig with improbable nylon curls in a wicker basket on top of the toilet cistern. The towels on the rail are stained with talcum. The walk-in shower has a seat and a safety handle; an alarm bell is nearby. There are boxes of incontinence napkins. Flags of Rachel's future, perhaps, if it's all laid in the genes. Come on, she thinks, you can do this – one week. Back in the little spare room, she unzips the side pocket of her bag and takes out a mottled feather, which has survived the trip uncrushed. Her mother is hunched awkwardly on the edge of the armchair, waiting. Rachel holds out the feather.

Here you go, present from the Reservation. I think it belonged to a hawk owl.

At dinner, the cogent residents make a fuss over Rachel, asking about her work and her life. It is apparent they think she is some kind of veterinarian, though her mother is perfectly capable of explaining. They ask whether she is married or has any children. No and no, she says. Oh well, she's still young, someone comments. Binny snorts.

Nearly forty!

Rachel carefully lays her knife down and reaches for the salt.

Isn't that how old you were when you had Lawrence? Elderly primagravida?

Laughter from the other ladies at the repartee, the mother–daughter spat. Does she have a boyfriend?, they ask. Rachel shrugs. No. She thinks of the centre workers' jokes about relationships: 'Pissing in tandem', like the urinary markings of the breeding pairs. But she holds her tongue. Despite the residents' enjoyment of that which is mildly risqué, such an observation would not be appropriate at the dinner table. Among these leached, desiccated beings, she is already feeling too burlesque, too live. The woman to her right – Dora – a tiny wobbling creature, takes hold of her wrist and informs her that Binny is a very popular member of the Willowbrook community, one of the fun personalities, a good card player, a huge flirt. Dora maintains a lucid flow of conversation, pats Rachel's arm, and name-drops as if she will recognise the people being spoken about, as if Binny keeps her in the loop. While the ladies cluck and gossip, her mother remains silent, scowling, pushing apart a piece of fish, trying to lift the grey skin away. There's the soft clicking of dentures and the scrape of cutlery. The meal progresses interminably. The food is boiled and blanched, easy to digest, but the exercise of eating still seems too rigorous for most. Almost every resident has a box of pills next to their place setting. Statins, anticoagulants, pain-killers, steroids. Her mother's medication is for high blood pressure and the ruined bladder. She hasn't taken Herceptin for fifteen years; is deemed no longer at risk. Her left breast is whole; the right was never reconstructed. The surgery heralded the end of an era for her mother; either she lost interest in men, or they in her. Rachel notices very few men at the home, but then longevity is not their strong suit. Opposite her is a woman in a gaping blouse, her chest furrowed and crêped, her face vacant. She is helped from time to time by an orderly. There are a couple of empty chairs at the tables and the health of whomever is missing is openly discussed. Such-and-such has fallen, broken a hip, been hospitalised, has a bowel obstruction, infection, isn't expected to return.

Rachel is past hunger and so tired that cruelty begins to creep in. The knotty hands and flaccid jowls, the drooping and slippage of body parts, begins to look grotesque. The tablecloth is garish with sauce stains. They spill. They tremble. They are ghouls that have passed over the borders of worthwhile existence into demented limbo. Such life-support isn't natural, she thinks. They should be assisted. Last year she and Kyle performed an autopsy on Nab, the oldest male in the Chief Joseph pack, who was killed by a young adoptee, Tungsten. The collar was still signalling; they got to his body quickly, so he was fresh on the slab, slack, his hind legs gristle-edged, the penis retracted. On his forelegs were old battle scars. The bite marks in his neck were not survivable. But humanity's demise, she thinks, is dreadful. We eke it out, limp on, medicate, become expensively compromised. For humans there will be no final status fights, no usurping, no healthy death. Decay continues, on and on. Only merciful ends come quickly or during sleep.

After dinner, she and Binny get ready for bed and squabble about who will use the bathroom first. Though a shadow of herself, her mother will not relinquish authority.

You look like shit. Black circles under your eyes and everything. Just get to bed.

I'm fine. I have to spend days on end awake, when I'm in the field.

You're my guest and you'll go when I say, my girl.

My girl. Rachel is too tired to fight – why stymie what little control Binny still has? She showers and cleans her teeth. She can hear her mother bickering with Milka, the Polish orderly, in the living room.

The folding cot is hard and narrow, bowed in the middle, but after a moment or two the room stops kiltering, the static in her ears quietens, and she is unconscious. All night, she barely moves, waking only once in confusion, not knowing where she is. In the morning she is woken properly by light through the unclosed curtains, and Milka, getting her mother up.

Not much on the sheets today, Binny. That's better. Well done.

Get that leg out of the way, Milka. Must you poke me about?

Rachel lies on the cot, looking out the window at the flat grey sky. She checks her phone. There is no news from Kyle, which isn't a bad thing. The transmitters fail; sometimes they are pulled off; sometimes they give out. She imagines Left Paw climbing over boulders, bounding up off his powerful back legs, crossing the plains and forests, covering miles in search of a mate. Then she pictures him splayed in the undergrowth, muzzle open, eyes slit, blood around the entry wounds. Since the harvest quota was increased, the workers are never without worry, even on the Reservation where they are protected. The hunters still come for them in planes, or on foot, using electric calls and giving false coordinates when they turn in their tags.

The grey unobstructed sky seems unreal. England is unreal, a forgotten version, with only a few pieces of evidence to validate it – and Rachel's memories. Even her mother can't be identified. In an hour, the Earl will be taking t'ai chi, like a new-age prince, some kind of attempt to revolutionise a decrepit system. She can't help but feel she shouldn't have come back, even as a courtesy. She watches the sky and listens to her mother bossing the orderly. *Don't yank me, Milka! Do they do it this way in Krakow?* Rachel gets up, stumbles through to the living room. On the radio the news headlines are being broadcast – the search for a missing child in the Midlands, release of the much-anticipated Scottish national white paper, the wettest autumn on record. There is only instant coffee in the tiny kitchenette. She makes a strong cup, adds sugar, waits for the bathroom. Her mind drifts back to Chief Joseph and the pack. By now they might have covered a hundred miles. Tungsten will be leading the others after the migrating deer, through the high snowdrifts, each using the same efficient track. The further north they go, the safer they will be.

*

Thomas Pennington drives himself, but only around Annerdale, he tells Rachel as they tour the estate, not on public roads. What with all the functions, he can never be sure he isn't over the limit. Doesn't want to shunt anyone. Or take out a horse. Or roll the Landy. The Land Rover bumps across fields, alongside hawthorn hedges, over hummocks and ditches, at a fair speed. Rachel holds the strap above the passenger door, rocks in her seat, and listens as he regales her. Besides, he can get a lot of work done on the train – wifi – and the Pendolino from Oxenholme now gets in to London in a matter of a few hours – extraordinary, when he was a boy it took six or seven.

You probably remember, he says, everything went through Crewe.

She nods. Many of his questions are rhetorical. It is hard to know whether a reply is necessary. He is a tall man, as elegant as she expected despite his informal attire, corduroy breeches, plaid shirt, and jacket – his knees jut upward as he drives. She gauges his age; late fifties, sixty, perhaps, with slightly greying hair, though a full, gusting crown of it, envied among men of his generation, no doubt. His face is temperate, devoid of obvious stress, like the south side of a mountain. Hazel eyes, dark brows, a long, straight nose with wide nasal vaults – somehow French colouring, Rachel thinks. He is not unattractive, quite handsome in fact, but exhibits no trace of sexuality – the neutering of British private schooling, or he has been docked by high-level politics.

She clutches the hand-grip as they veer over the brow of a hill and tip forward on the descent towards the river. The lane they are driving along is narrow. Undergrowth thrashes against the wheels and doors. Ahead, fallow fields, young woods, and the broad rippling shallows of the ford. The Earl prefers a safari route rather than the tarred roads latticing his land. The vehicle is stripped down and lacks comforts, an ex-army model, Rachel guesses, something of a toy.

I read about you in *Geographic* a few years ago, he is saying. Thought, there's a good local lass; hasn't she gone far. But people from here do, don't they – they range out around the globe – into all sorts of bother sometimes. And success, equally. You're from Keld? Parents still there?

No. My mother moved out a few years ago.

Lovely little parish, Keld. Cromwell's Army holed up in the church, you know, on the way to sort out those troublesome Scots. Oh, dear. Seems like we're back to all that again, aren't we? Have you read the white paper?

No, I haven't. I thought it was only released today?

Don't bother. It contains quite a lot of fantasy and nothing of a business plan. Interesting thoughts on ecology, though I suspect Caleb Douglas hasn't the courage, nor will he have the cash, to follow through.

Rachel nods again and says nothing. British politics have been off her radar for a long time. But she is aware of the reform plans across the border – public acquisition of private land, recalibration of resources – a notion that must make the likes of Thomas

Pennington more than a little uncomfortable. The BBC is full of debate about independence and the forthcoming referendum; she's been surprised by how close the polls are, how *troublesome* the matter is proving for Westminster. Perhaps sensing her reticence, the Earl continues his historical rhapsody of her home village.

The font in Keld church is medieval – a splendid piece. And there's a Viking hogback in the graveyard in excellent condition. What a lovely place to be brought up; how lucky you were. So, give me the potted history of Rachel Caine. You went to the grammar school, no doubt, then read biology, at Cambridge?

Zoology. I studied at Aberystwyth.

She does not mention the postgraduate work at Oxford, or the honorary fellowship. Let him assume.

Ah, Cymru! Excellent! Well, our future king is one of your alumni.

Not by choice, I imagine.

Thomas Pennington laughs, though she intended no humour.

Quite! Did you enjoy it? Must be a jolly good course if it produced you.

The Land Rover chassis clangs against a boulder. The river is fast approaching.

It was fine. It's a good department. I've gone back and given lectures there. We've taken one or two volunteers at Chief Joseph – sort of an exchange programme.

Marvellous! Yes, we must make opportunities for the young.

For all her companion's levity and volubility, the conversation is not easy. His enthusiasm borders on tyrannical, is giddying. She feels artless, unpractised; there are social mores at which she has become deskilled, if ever she was adequate. She cannot forget who he is. Still, her required input seems minimal. Thomas Pennington is blithely able to cant and hold forth, despite the lack of reciprocity. She glances over at him. He is smiling broadly and seems very pleased.

And then it was off to America? Now, Rachel, have you noticed there are quite a few presidents with Reiver surnames? What do we make of that?

She does not reply. The Land Rover tips gamely over the riverbank. Rachel braces. Thomas Pennington pushes the accelerator hard and the engine roars. He leans over the steering wheel. She notices he is not wearing a safety belt. The vehicle dashes across the shingle bed, pebbles gouging up and growling in the wheel arches. River-water splatters the windscreen and streams away.

Geronimo!

On the far bank he brakes and throws the Land Rover into climbing gear. They grind up the steep thistle-covered slope, crushing the stalks underneath, the fronds rustling and squeaking. Rachel looks to the hills, and the dark creases between. Just talk, she thinks. Tell him what he wants to hear.

I worked in a rescue centre in Romania first. Then Belarus. There were problems with industrialisation and the packs coming into town. They ended up scavenging, getting bad press. Then I volunteered in Yellowstone, and then the Nez Perce job opened up. I didn't think I'd get it.

Of course you got it! Aberystwyth's premier zoologist!

Thomas Pennington slaps the dashboard with a palm, a flamboyant, almost fey action. She glances at him again. Is he mocking her? Or is it a campaign of flattery? He is, she supposes, likeable, or at least enthusiastic, a positivist. Perhaps rich as he is and influential, he has a social duty to be so. In profile, there's a boyish brilliance to him, a Pan-like yaw. He has probably played all his life, despite the expectations, the serious nature of privilege, and the obligations of sitting in the House.

I mean there are employment protocols on the Reservation.

Of course. And Idaho. Do you enjoy it there?

The first test as to her availability.

Yes. I do.

I've never been up that way. I've been to Seattle, of course – my father used to do business with Boeing. But that corner is rather a blind spot for me. I do know those casinos were a bad idea. No routed nation ever did well trying to win money back using alcohol and algorithm. I voted against the supercasinos here. The last thing this country needs in the middle of a recession is more gambling.

She does not disagree, though the revenue streams on the Reservation and in Britain follow very different courses. She watches the estate roll by. Oak trees, damson, and birch coppices, newly planted. Between them, the yellow swards of moorland, patched darkly by gorse, reefed by flowering gold, and purple heather. Thomas Pennington slows the Land Rover, then stops, and points.

Look over there, Rachel.

Standing thirty feet from a stretch of woodland is an area of construction – a long, deep trench, gently curving. The foundation of the enclosure barrier.

Not much more to do now, he says. We're on the final few miles.

Must have been tricky to negotiate. Isn't this inside the national park?

Oh, he says, evasively, we managed.

The disputes are ongoing, she knows, but the new legislation has allowed him scope. She does not push him; he would probably deny any negative aspects to the project anyway.

Above the moorland and trees, the Lakeland mountains castle. Above the crags, sky, occluded clouds. As a child, the territory seemed so wild that anything might be possible. The moors were endless, haunting; they hid everything and gave up secrets only intermittently – an orchid fluting in a bog, a flash of blue wing, some phantom, long-boned creature, caught for a moment against the horizon before disappearing. Only the ubiquitous sheep tamed the landscape. She did not know it then, but in reality it was a kempt place, cultivated, even the high grassland covering the fells was manmade. Though it formed her notions of beauty, true wilderness lay elsewhere. Strange to be sitting next to the man who owns all that she can see, almost to the summits, perhaps the summits. It is his, by some ancient decree, an accident of birth and entitlement – the new forestation, the unfarmed tracts and salt marshes towards the edge of the Irish Sea. She could applaud the project without reserve, were it not for the hegemony, the unsettling feeling of imbalance. Still, it is England; a country particularly owned.

She can see, between hills, the glint of grey water – the west coast, where once rum-runners came ashore and where nuclear cargo now ghosts along railway lines at night. The Earl is talking again, about reparation debates, the law-making powers of the Reservations – the cultural respect for the land, by which he is deeply inspired. Isn't she? he asks. He is better informed than most, but still romanticising. Yes, she thinks. If you'd been fighting for decades over broken treaties, and had, only within the last presidency, been invited into the White House, if you were overseeing class-action settlements worth billions, the buying back of territory and compensation for mismanaged trusts, you would respect the land, you would know its worth. But the track record of some of the First Nations is nothing exemplary.

The redistribution of power is always complicated, she says.

He unbuttons his jacket and leans back in his seat, and she notices the supporting brace underneath, waistcoat-like, perhaps a daily fixture since the microlight crash and subsequent spinal surgeries. He turns slightly towards her. She is aware her sceptical tone has been noted.

I can certainly take criticism, he says. This isn't the democratic republic of Annerdale. Our system is very antiquated – I've campaigned for reform along with my party. Meanwhile, I consider myself a custodian of sorts. The plans we have here are very sound. I don't need to tell you the benefits of reintroducing a level-five predator. The whole region will be affected. It'll be a much healthier place, right down to the rivers.

Rachel nods.

Yes, it will.

She looks towards a small, brown, unextraordinary hill with a winding path and a conical cairn at its summit. He follows her gaze.

That's Hinsey Knot. You can see the Isle of Man from the top on a clear day.

He turns the engine over and they drive back, towards the hall. On the way they pass a ruined cottage, almost a bothy, and an old fence wire strung with black-jacketed moles. Thomas Pennington slows the vehicle and peers at the bodies.

Oh, Michael, he murmurs. Is that really necessary?

Some old-school farmhand or estate worker, Rachel assumes. She remembers the tradition from her village. She and Lawrence would see rows of the creatures on the way home from school, splayed open, pinned like lab specimens. The wind seems to have gone a little from her host's sails. He points out the occasional landmark, but chats less. He must sense her resistance. Who will he approach next, she wonders. With the barrier fence almost complete, approaches must already have been made. She is glad of the quiet and takes in the landscape, which she has missed. The river is slate-rimmed, flashing, much clearer than the peat-steeped water of the eastern district. Near the lake, in a walled plot, is a church with a round tower, where the Earl's ancestors and relatives are probably buried, including his wife, Carolyn. Rachel's knowledge of her death extends no further than the tabloid reports. A freak air-disaster, the microlight stalling too low, half-gliding half-plummeting to Earth. The Earl was in traction for months. His wife was killed on impact. The church roof looks new, the graves well-tended.

The Land Rover clears another bracken-covered ridge. Thomas Pennington pulls over and croaks the handbrake on, kills the ignition. He rolls the window down. Wind stirs the yellow grass. Below is the lake, six intricate miles of it, pewtered at its head as clouds move over from the Atlantic.

So, Rachel. I appreciate your time and I'm very glad you've visited Annerdale. May I ask your thoughts?

She looks towards the central peaks. There are grand and celebrated elevations among them, but after the Pacific-Northwest, the Rockies, and the arboreal plains, they seem diminutive.

Well, she begins. Thank you for the opportunity to see the project.

She has planned what to say. All she needs to do is stick to the speech. She knows he will be convincing, and the money hinted at is unusually generous. Nevertheless.

I have a good team at Joseph, she says, and reliable funding. Our new visitor centre opened last year – we've got quite a few educational programmes. But with the amount of hunting now in the state, we have to be more vigilant. It's not a good time to be a wolf in Idaho. The scheme here – well, it's captivity, for all its merits. It would be a step backwards for me.

This is more than she has said all morning and the speech is delivered without pause. She looks at him, hoping to avoid awkwardness. There were no guarantees; he knew that. He returns her gaze, considers what she has said, nods.

Of course. England lags terribly in terms of ecology. We've barely got our 'toad crossing' signs up. But it's an exciting time, things are changing; we've already changed them.

We, she thinks. Who is this *we*? This is his dominion, his private Eden. She looks away. Greyer clouds are heading up the valley on a brisk wind. The ground darkens beneath them. She can smell the rain coming, like tonic in the air.

You must like being home again, he says. It's such a special place, isn't it? It's somehow gloriously in us.

What do you mean?

His question feels too intimate, inappropriate. Again she feels peculiar being so close to a man of such power – even the tribal councils, with their elders of utmost gravitas and authority, do not disarm her as much. She suddenly wishes she could get out of the Land Rover and walk back to Pennington Hall.

I mean it has a resonance, he says, and sighs. I used to dislike being away, even as a young man, and I was away a lot, boarding and London and whatnot. I still dislike being away, when the House is in session. This is a unique area. 'The form remains, the function never dies.' We are so very lucky, you and I, to belong here, Rachel.

She has no inclination to enter into a sentimental discussion. She tries to remain focused.

I'm not sure what that has to do with it.

Thomas Pennington smiles. His teeth are capped and polished. He is gearing up to make his case; she can see the signs, the poise, the mental garnering of argument. Let him say his piece, she thinks. He's paid you.

I know you're a woman of honesty – I admire that. So let's be honest. This is a real chance for environmental restoration in a country that desperately needs it. The whole process has been incredibly bureaucratic. All the things one has to prove about wolves: previous inhabitation, suitable territory. God forbid they should be able to hunt their own prey! Government has become extremely adept at legislating its urban squeamishness – my chaps too, I'm afraid to say. Anyway, we got there.

He makes a dismissive, swatting gesture, as if cutting through and casting aside the opposition.

If we were going to be anything less than a self-sustaining enclosure, I wouldn't have prevailed upon you. I wouldn't have wasted your time, Rachel. Or mine.

He turns his hands over, palms facing upward. Behavioural assay of state, she thinks: humility. He is appealing to her dominant position. He is not without guile, nor lacking sincerity – the consummate politician, perhaps.

I know getting you back would be a coup. America has everything you need. But, if I may say it, America isn't the real challenge. America has wolves walking back down from Canada of their own volition. Aren't you just overseeing what already exists? Here, even behind my ridiculous fence, they will be able to hunt and breed; they will be able to do what they do, and for the first time in centuries! Isn't that extraordinary? Imagine what it all might lead to. Perhaps even full reintroduction.

It is raining lightly now. The windscreen begins to speckle. The shadow of the clouds arrives, darkening the Land Rover's interior. The Earl's eyes are greenish-brown. There's Huguenot in him. His nails are manicured; his eyebrows shaped. The tweed in his coat is probably customised. Yes, she thinks, it is extraordinary. But there's something about him, something about his energy, that she does not trust. The waxing and waning – the peaks and troughs. Almost bipolar, and she is familiar with that condition. The mania. The terrible aftermath. They are a convincing breed, made charismatic by ideas and self-belief, with plans so persuasive that it's hard not to be swayed. Hard too when the life gust is vented and the black mask slides down. Oran. The day she and Kyle found him sitting by the Clearwater River in his pick-up, a loaded gun on his lap, the radio blaring. *Just watching the steelheads swimming*, he said.

Full reintroduction. In thirty years maybe, and not in England. She shakes her head. She has not come professionally unprepared.

The Highland studies are speculative – I know, I advised on one them. This country isn't ready for an apex predator yet, won't be for quite a while. The Caledonian Park took ten years to get off the ground, and then it was dismantled. The issue is just too divisive for Britain.

Eight years, the Earl says, quickly. But Campbell messed it up. He didn't spend the money. You have to spend the money.

She shakes her head again.

I don't want money. No one in my line of work does it for

money.

No. That's not what I meant.

Thomas Pennington's smile broadens, becomes enigmatic. Does he mean a bribe? Or perhaps he is alluding to the returns he might make if he offers wolf-watching tours in the enclosure. He is determined; she can see that. And he has excessive confidence.

People here don't care about the countryside in any deep way, she says. They just want nice walks, nice views, and a tearoom.

That may be, he says. But I have an exciting vision. Sometimes a country just needs to be presented with the fact of an animal, not the myth.

Now there is pathos in his argument; he knows he has failed to win her over. Still, he seems hopeful. The eleventh Earl of Annerdale. He could almost be another species. Specialist cologne. No wallet carried in his back pocket. Regardless of democracy, the greater schemes are led by those in the upper echelons, the moneyed, she knows that. Perhaps he will do it. For a moment she thinks about the possibilities. She looks ahead, through the misty smirr, towards the lake, which would, she thinks again, be a good territorial boundary, if this were wilderness. The rain lisps and taps on the Land Rover roof, old and sensual, an influence long before language. The smell of it – so familiar – iron and minerals, the basis of the world. But she is not ready to come back, and may never be.

She faces him, holds out her hand, and after a moment Thomas Pennington takes it. They shake.

I'm sorry, she says. But best of luck.

The Earl smiles.

I hope we can still count you as a friend of the project.

Of course, she says.

*

After their meeting she is offered lunch at the hall, which she declines. It seems unnecessary to linger. Her host is, in any case, leaving to go south – there's a helicopter standing on a hardpad near the back of the hall, its blades bowed, the helmeted pilot sitting in the cockpit. Leaving the estate, she tries to spot finished sections of the enclosure barrier, but the trees have yet to lose their leaves fully and it's cleverly hidden from view. The cost must have been astronomical: millions, perhaps. There are other estates in the country with small wildlife parks, housing bison, boar, and wildcats, but they are not free-ranging, they are fed, cared for – glorified zoos. Nothing as ambitious as Annerdale exists.

The gate opens to allow her exit and closes slowly behind her, and though it's her choice, she feels expelled. She picks up the western road, which is narrow, unwalled, and crosses the high moors. There are few properties on the way; no working farms remain, and the stretch is not popular for second homes. On the near horizon is Hinsey Knot. She decides to stop and take a walk. In a stony layby, she changes into jeans and boots, zips up her jacket. The grass underfoot is springy and dun coloured, the path wending up the fell made of shattered rock. She ascends, without haste but swiftly – it is not a taxing climb. She puts up her hood against a sudden squall, her thighs dampening. She passes no one. The mountain is more of a grassy mound, the path barely steepening past thirty degrees. The sun emerges, still with warmth in it. Two buzzards turn loops on the currents of air above. A rabbit darts across the slope and is granted amnesty. When she reaches the cairn she sits and looks at the view, land graduating towards the unspectacular brown sea, belts of cloud moving in from Ireland and strobing light on the ground between. A stiff breeze tugs at her sleeves and rattles her hood. She calls Kyle. It's still early in Idaho, but he answers.

Christ. You sound like you're in a wind tunnel.

Sorry. Hang on.

She turns her head, then moves into the sheltered lee behind the cairn.

Better.

They catch up, briefly. There is no news of Left Paw. There have been no sightings, alone, or with the pack, and none of the coordinated aircraft have picked up the signal. The radio collar appears to be dead. She cannot help but be suspicious.

I just don't like coincidences, she says.

Shit happens. Nothing we can do. This is expensive, go back to your mom and spend some time with her.

Yeah. Is it still snowing?

Yep.

Everything else OK?

We're good.

Alright, then.

She hangs up, pockets her phone and begins down the slope towards the hire car.

On the way back to Willowbrook she stops off at a pub – The Belted Will, a stacked-slate building with empty hanging baskets outside the front door. She orders supper. She will miss dinner at the home, but she can't quite face the experience again. The bar is pleasant enough. At the counter a few locals sit on stools; there are one or two passing travellers – late-season walkers, perhaps.

A vinegary smell piques the air, combined with hops and cleaning fluid. A coal fire glows orange at one end of the room; she sits at a table nearby. While she waits for the food she takes a stack of printed papers from her bag and reads through – the chapter of a book she is working on. It's slow-going – too slow; it seems like she is always rewriting as more study results come in. The pub conversation is sporadic, mostly between the landlady and the punters, occasional laughter from the end of the counter, where a young man is standing, watching Rachel on and off. The village in which the pub is located is relatively large, but for Friday evening the venue is too quiet; it will not last long if this is the extent of its patronage, will go the way of so many unfrequented Lakeland ale houses.

She looks up. The young man is staring at her again. He raises his pint glass and smiles, drinks the remaining beer, leaves a spit of white foam webbed in the bottom of the glass. He is fit under his shirt and jacket, bullish, very blue-eyed. He is wearing a wedding ring. A wife at home then, watching television, drinking wine with her girlfriends, or minding a baby, perhaps. A wife who knows nothing, or maybe chooses not to care. The rules are always the same.

In America it's easier: the codes, the expectations, what is and is not on offer. Oran is the easiest choice, and always available, but the hope and petulance afterwards are tiresome. She sees him most days in the office, must navigate tensions. He's too close, too keen. Sometimes she goes to the casino. The gambling is uninteresting, and she doesn't bother with it. But there are new faces, and a lone single woman such as her, not wearing a low-cut dress or heavy make-up, is no cause for concern, is not touting for business. The casino bar is busy. She steps through bodies to the counter and orders a drink, scans the room, as if searching for a friend who is late. Something about the cut of one of them – it is hard to know what exactly, the way he carries himself, his movement, or strength of bones – appeals. The way he acts can be interpreted: confidence, frustration, availability, a man on the border of a relationship, leaving or entering it, feeling entitled either way. She'll lean past to take a serviette from the dispenser, between him and his friend. *Sorry, hun – excuse me. That's OK.* A conversation starts up, designed to facilitate, nothing more. Her occupation is controversial, divisive – she avoids talking about it. Every man has an opinion. Often she will lie, limit the truth – *I work on the Reservation; I'm in conservation.*

The hunters are easily identified – close-shaven, militaristic, or long-haired and greasy, white marks from the sunglasses along their temples. Western liberals are preferable, the polo players, the pseudo-ranchers; their shirts neater, leather money-belts, a new truck. If her job is ever revealed, they are surprised. She is not a woman of hemp trousers and dry braids, neuter, husband-less, not an eco-freak. A woman like her someone will be fucking, or want to fuck. Her eyes are between colours – towards green, and in the daylight unquestionably green.

The rest is easy; everything plays out. *Can I freshen that drink for you? Thanks, but I was just leaving. Hey, you're Scottish?* He is tall, looking down, his hand resting along the counter where she stands, almost mantling her. His friend is ignored, so turns away. *No, just the other side of the border. Well, I've been to Edinboro – let's have a scotch for Scotland,* he suggests. *OK.* Three drinks is her limit. There will be a discreet place to test it – outside the restrooms, or in the parking lot. Proclivities can be detected, risks. A few will pull back, suddenly ashamed or guilty, but not many.

The drives are sometimes long to get to an apartment, or the house of a compliant friend. She does not take them to her cabin. There are cheap motels on the way out of town. She's crossed the Lolo Pass before, has gone into Washington State. She drives her own truck. He follows behind.

Or, more recklessly, she pulls off the road, down a dirt forestry lane, past seized-up logging equipment and stacked lumber. He parks behind her, gets out of the car, walks up slowly. *Wrong turn? Got a flat?* The darkness is not deep with the wattage of so many stars. She opens the truck door, steps out, leaves it standing open. In the cab light copper moths flicker; there are fireflies pulsing in the grass between pale trunks. *Pretty night.* She says nothing. She can't really see his face. He keeps talking, makes another joke. Then he figures it out. He steps in, kisses her, one of evolution's stranger necessities. It does not take much to accelerate him, the angle of her body, her tongue. He backs her against the truck, trying to judge the levels of permission: is this an interlude or the main event – his thoughts almost audible. He runs a hand over her shirt, over her breasts. She puts hers to his groin, the bulking jeans. Now he believes. Then it is like gentle fighting, both with each other and the impediment of clothing. They climb into the flatbed of the truck, and her shirt is taken off. She has a scar on her back, kidney to fifth thoracic, the line is buckled, stitched by a regional surgeon. A good story, but she doesn't often tell it. She is swollen with blood; he slips his fingers in. The flash of a wagon's headlights on the other side of the trees; a low rumble on the asphalt. Transporters, for whom the night is ephedrine and bluegrass.

The metal truck bed is damp, smells of oil and blood from the occasional deer carcass. She reaches into her pocket for her wallet, but he already has his open, is tearing the foil, fitting it over. She turns on all fours, not for his benefit, but the presentation is not lost on him. He murmurs agreement: *hell, yeah*. Another night he might go down on her, on any woman, make her swim, but this is different, sudden, abandoned. He kneels in place, pushes against her. He needs help to get inside, or he doesn't; the moment is invariably erotic.

She braces against the cab wall and he holds her hips. There is just movement and noise, flesh slapping. Outside the truck: pine resin, tar, moths. A dry storm above Kamiah, lightning flashes like late-night television. The country underneath seems raw and heavy as lead, as if never intended to be unearthed. She rears back. He puts an arm around her stomach, pulls her for more depth. He reaches round to stroke her, courteously. Then it is automatic, impossible to stop. A man's identity is revealed in the habit of climax; it is the real introduction. *Fuck. Jesus Christ*. He slumps against her. But the true psychology is in the withdrawal. Quick, perfunctory, or inched delicately out. Whatever was seen in the bar, in his face, his body, predicted correctly. *Can I freshen that drink for you? Thanks, but I was just leaving*. Sometimes she walks away.

She arrives back at Willowbrook a little after 1 a.m. She enters the apartment quietly, opens the windows, lets the dense, airless heat flood out into the night. There's a note on the coffee table in her mother's appalling handwriting. *Lawrence here for dinner. Where were you? Gone back to Leeds – he's your brother!* She sighs, crumples up the note. Typical of Binny to have planned this without telling her. And typical of Rachel not to have been there.

*

Binny will die soon; of this everyone seems certain. Willowbrook's manager speaks to Rachel softly when they meet, with excessive pronunciation and compassion, as if in fact death had already happened. The young visiting doctor, who Rachel has a quiet discussion with in the corridor outside Binny's apartment on his rounds, says they just need to keep her comfortable. And Milka, who attends to Binny's intimate needs most days, informs Rachel quite straightforwardly that her mother is ready. It's in the eyes. *Nie jasne* – no light. Even Lawrence's intermittent emails have talked of there *not being much time, if you want to reconnect.* But upon questioning, the various care-givers have no definite information, there seems to be no fatal disease. Binny will no doubt set her own schedule. She will go on for as long as she cares to. Though she is clearly fed up with the incapacitation, if the days still prove interesting enough her heart will jab on, her systems will sluice away. Now, in the sitting room of the apartment, while Rachel pours tea into standard-issue china cups and rattles biscuits from their plastic sleeve – something of an afternoon ritual, Binny holds forth.

It's all about choice, you see. Everything is, except birth – no one chooses to be born. Get off the bus when you know it's your stop I say. I cannot abide this poor-me attitude. Didn't get me out of Wandsworth. Didn't help me after your father left.

She strains to speak, is lazy over her vowels. Her head nods intermittently. She still has her faculties but there are fissures in her memory, and in her stories.

I thought you were the one who turfed him out, Rachel says.

Binny grunts, but lets the comment pass. The skin on her forearms looks so frail, the veins so knotted, she might bruise simply from the press of a finger. Rachel slides a cup of tea towards her mother.

Women always have a choice, Binny says. I taught you that, I hope, if nothing else.

You did. You were Socratic.

With surprising force, her mother bangs a hand on the top of the coffee table.

Don't get smart with me, my girl! Can't we just have a conversation? You are such a clever beggar sometimes.

Am I? Right.

Rachel sits, and holds her temper. One more day before she flies back to America. The tension has been mounting all week. She is annoyed with Binny for, among other things, simply growing old. They have worked in their own ruthless, autonomous way for decades, orbiting each other only if it suited them, not required to show love or compassion. She will be obedient for the next few hours, she will be civil. Tomorrow she will bid her mother goodbye, for who knows how long. Meanwhile, she will try to behave as a good daughter. She will sit through another interminable meal and shuffle around the flower garden listening to Binny stammer, being polite to the other residents. She will help her mother fit pink orthopaedic bandages around her arched, horned toes and fasten her thick-soled shoes, as if readying a toddler for the outdoors. They will attempt to discuss Lawrence's marital situation again, as any close female relations might: meaning Binny will complain and Rachel will listen and try to reason.

I can't bear that woman. He should never have proposed to her, she wasn't even pregnant!

He likes doing things properly, Mum – he's conservative.

Well, he didn't get it from me!

She will try to make a success of the visit, somehow. Each morning during her stay she has walked up the small hill next to Willowbrook and looked over the hills to the strip of silverish estuary beyond. She is not sorry she came, but she feels no closer to reunion of any kind, at least, not with her mother. Binny, too, is clearly not satisfied. Her daughter is beyond her understanding. Idaho seems to her a nest of right-wing extremists, which she cannot parse.

What do you mean no one pays tax? Are these Indians bloody Republicans, too? I blame Thatcher. You're all her children.

Rachel tries to explain, again. She goes where the work is, she goes where there are wolves. Her mother wants something from her, something she cannot ask, or does not understand. Binny keeps trying to speak, in her brusque way, to open up and get at the meat of things.

Now she spills tea into the saucer as she manoeuvres the cup onto her lap. She spills sugar from not one, but two heaped spoonfuls – Tate and Lyle, pure refined white, the real thing, Binny remains a Londoner to the bone. One stroke, one cancer, and dodgy waterworks, versus years of smoking and bacon fat, sugar and salt. Is that such a bad equation, Rachel wonders. It is not. Though damaged, Binny's tremendous body prevails; she still *enjoys*. The spoon clatters round the edges of the cup as she stirs. A good daughter, what is that, Rachel wonders. She might not be able to unearth any tenderness towards her mother, but she can at least be companionable.

Actually, I agree with you, she says. The female of the species usually chooses the male, and you could argue true power lies with the decision-maker.

Comments such as this have, in the past, resulted in exasperation. *You're always on about science. Why don't you talk about people more? Where's all your blood going, my girl? Upstairs is where.* Occasionally her mother takes credit for Rachel's intellect, for producing a smart, go-getting daughter. Today, rather surprisingly, she simply asks a question.

So. You're happy at that place, then, doing what you do? Well, you seem like you are.

I am.

I haven't ever been.

To America? Did you want to go?

No. Never fancied it. Africa, though, before all the nonsense, now I would have gone there. No wolves, eh? Just lions and elephants.

Binny caws. Rachel dips the stiff ginger biscuit into her cup, lets the fluid rise up and soften the crust. English biscuits, hard as relics, like something from another century.

Actually, there are, she says.

They are the most distributed predator on Earth, she could say, but she refrains from lecturing.

Well, you'll like getting back to it. Better than some kind of glorified estate-keeper here. I don't know why he'd want to spend so much money on that, anyway. And if you worked for him, you may as well join the Tories.

He's a Liberal Democrat.

Binny leans forward, painfully. There's a dribble of tea on her chin.

Same thing. No, it wouldn't be wild enough for you.

No.

She is still astute, knowing – she might mean something other than professional preferences.

I could have gone to Africa, Binny says. I had the opportunity. Don't know why I didn't. No point regretting it now. You always liked getting away though, so off you went. Didn't like taking

orders, even at school. Never did do as you were told. That job –
it's not your kind of thing.

Rachel glances at her mother, then away. Is this an exercise
in fond memory or chastisement? She can't be sure. They were
always contrary beings and never really knew each other as
adults. But Binny is under no illusions about the nature of the
visit or their family choreography. She is simply getting-down-
to-business while her daughter is at hand. One thing the woman
has always been good at is directness. *You've got your own money
from the milk round, so use it. We're going to have to put the dog
down – no, stop crying and look at it, Rachel; look, it can't even walk.
Ask for the combined pill, it's better. I've got to leave in five minutes,
how much does it hurt, Rachel?*

Rachel?

No, you're right, it's not my kind of thing. But it was worth
a look. I'll probably leave before breakfast to miss the traffic
tomorrow.

Rachel.

Binny reaches across the table and takes hold of her daughter's
wrist, firmly, as she used to when she wanted to stop her running
away after an argument, out of the house and onto the moors.

I hope there's something more than following those creatures
about all day. I hope there's something more for you. You aren't
to give up, my girl.

Rachel waits, uncomfortably, until her mother lets go.

What, like a husband? Didn't you teach me how to avoid them?

There is something unintentionally harsh in her tone. The joke
is wrong, if it even was one. Binny makes a startled, indignant
noise and alters position in her armchair. Leakage. Too much
tea. Rachel leans forward, as if to help, then stops. What can she

do? The body breaks when it breaks. The pads her mother wears are dense and absorbent, but there is probably no way of accepting such a loss of function, the warm wet shocks. Binny grunts impatiently.

It's no laugh, getting old. Let me tell you now. I hate it. You will, too. Get off the bus when it's time.

She could take her mother's hand, perhaps, and try to forge something in their last hours together. But what could she say? The good memories are not the usual ones, of demonstrative affection. *We used to walk for miles on the moors. I remember the backs of your legs, your strong muscles. I remember trying to keep up with you.* It is all too far back in the past, and inarticulable. She does not take her mother's hand. Instead she finds herself repeating a line she read once, in a poem, in a book on a shelf in a house where she spent no more than a few illicit hours.

Everything tends towards iron.

A nameless man, asleep in the slurry of sheets, his legs sprawled. A random piece of text found while she roamed wakefully, before dressing and leaving. She could remember more if she wanted to, about him, about all of them. But the line was beautiful, and felt meaningful.

What? What did you say?

Binny is leaning forward on the seat again, hunched, almost crouching, wanting something from her daughter, if not intimacy then a marker of some kind. It is within Rachel's power to deliver it.

Never mind, Mum. Listen, you know that bad knee I had as a child, whenever I was growing – that lump of cartilage that used to swell up. You remember? It used to keep me up all night and you'd spray it with that awful stinking hot stuff. And you'd bandage it up so tight, I couldn't even bend it! Anyway. It's come back.

Maybe I'm getting taller. What do you think?

She stands and straightens her back.

Taller? What?

Binny peers up at her daughter, her brow avalanching towards her eyes. She does not understand.

What, she says. What?

She does not understand, and then she gets it, her daughter is fooling around, kidding with her, and suddenly Binny is laughing, barking, like a crone, which soaks her gusset and leaves her wheezing.

You are a silly beggar, she says. You really are.

Rachel sits down and smiles and drinks her tea. The truth is, from time to time they did get on. They lived together in the post-office cottage for eighteen years. They burnt pans, left rings in the bathtub, argued like murder, and squabbled over who would mind Lawrence. But sometimes they got along. Sometimes they laughed.

It's amazing the levels of human kindness that suffice, Rachel thinks. This will be the moment she will take away and think of as success, of a kind. Looking down over the black coast and frozen wastes of Labrador, with a plastic wine glass in her hand and the in-flight film sounding tinny inside the headphones, she will remember this laughter and think, yes, that was her mother, revealed. The gamey woman smelling of urine and sweat, cackling in the chair, was Binny. Fuck the doctor and the orderly and all the other doom-mongers. There was still brightness in her eyes.

THE RESERVATION

The airport is a brown stone building, compact and utilitarian, with one desk serving Horizon Airways, a hire-car pick-up kiosk, gift shop, and a small coffee counter. The sign above the arrivals gate reads *Welcome to Nez Perce Idaho*. Kyle is waiting for her on the other side of the plastic cordon, one of a few dozen people standing in front of the squeaking conveyor belt waiting to greet travellers or collect luggage. Denim, snakeskin, expensive suits and briefcases, braided hair: the usual commuters and residents mill around, regional traders and ranchers, the exceptionally rich. Kyle is tall, taller than anyone else, his hair tied back above his neck, hatless. He waits, hands in his pockets, not especially watching out for her, nonchalant almost. His presence is alarming. She was expecting to get a connection to Kamiah, then call for a lift. Left Paw, she thinks, bad news. She walks over and drops her bag next to him.

What are you doing here?

His hands remain tucked inside his jeans.

Going to Bermuda. What do you think I'm doing, Rachel. Good flight?

At first all she can think to do is drill him with questions. Did they pick up a signal and do a focused follow? Did they find his body? Inside or outside the Reservation? Kyle raises his eyebrows, and regards her for a moment. Then he reaches down to take her bag.

That's a piss-poor greeting, crazy lady. Thought they were all about manners in England.

Yeah, well, what are you doing?

I'm giving you a ride. I was in town.

They shot him, didn't they?

Christ! I was just in town. I had some business.

Business?

Business. Whoa.

He places a hand on her shoulder for a moment, as if calming a frisking horse, then swings her bag over his shoulder. He turns and walks towards the exit. She follows.

We've had nothing on Paw, he says. But the others are good. Got an air report yesterday. They're about a hundred miles from the border. Doesn't look like they've gone back to any carcasses. They're in the western corridor. They might run into the Cascade pack but it should be OK.

She is still tense, primed for bad news, though it would have been delivered by now. Kyle is guileless; he does not hedge. If he says he had business in town, then he had business in town. She walks by his side. He is long-legged but slow-moving, a stroller, a saunterer, not prone to hurry. Without boots, she barely reaches his shoulder. Strange that after only a week away someone so familiar could look new to the eye. After the pale English northerners and the care-home residents, he seems gigantic, very American.

You shaved, she says.

I shaved.

Got a date?

Nope.

Wait up a minute.

They stop at the coffee counter. Rachel orders a tall black and a cinnamon twist. She searches through her pockets and her wallet for dollar bills.

Want one?

Nope. That stuff'll kill you. They didn't feed you on the plane?

Since when did you get all health-conscious?

He puts a hand to his belly.

Since I hit forty.

Oh shit. I missed your birthday.

I wasn't so present myself. Went to The Barn. Tequila.

Rachel smiles. She can picture the scene. For a big man Kyle is unable to hold much liquor – the end usually comes suddenly, they must carry him out, put him in the truck and take the keys out, lay him on his side. After negotiating Binny and Thomas Pennington, it's a relief to be around someone she knows and likes, someone relatively uncomplicated, and she can feel the knots slackening. But Kyle is not without occlusion. In the hothouse environment of the centre, with its poorly kept secrets, gossip, and cabin fever, he is a favourite topic. To the volunteers he is the real deal, half Lapwai Indian, of which he seems neither proud nor indifferent: he has limited interest in the tribal councils, though he is the centre's representative, and few opinions on other local affairs, petitions for removal of the Nazi camps, suits against polluters. In the summer he sails. In the winter he skiis. When kids visiting the centre ask him if he's related to Chief Joseph, he gets them to stand on a chair and recite the *No More, Forever* speech, then tells them it was invented by an army officer. There are occasional girlfriends. Rachel knows it often seems like he and she are a couple – they speak the familiar language of work, ethograms, predation rate, biomass; they co-host barbecues, alternate decks to drink beer on.

Oran frequently acts jealous. But they remain, simply, friends.

The terminal doors slide open. A gust of austere air breaches the fug of the airport. They walk out into the keen, glinting light, new snow. A Pacific winter sun, low on the horizon. The sky is luxuriously blue; it's the hour before dusk. The brown hills of the valley are white-capped and it's a good five degrees colder than when Rachel left for England.

Need to pick up anything in town? Kyle asks.

I don't think so. Is the road open?

Yep.

They cross the parking lot to Kyle's truck. Salt and grit crunch underfoot on the pathways and bolsters of ploughed snow lie along the sides of the runway. The propellers of the Dash that brought her from Seattle start up, gain pitch and volume. The aircraft jolts into action, buzzes away from the terminal building, turns down the runway, and rises after only a short distance. It will barely reach five thousand feet before landing in Pullman, then will head on to Sea-Tac. Kyle unlocks the truck.

I can drive if you like, she says. I'm not that tired.

Hell, no. You've been on the wrong damn side all week.

She opens the passenger door but lingers outside. The cold air nips her ears, refreshes her lungs after the stale air of the plane.

So, how was it? he asks over the roof of the truck.

You mean did I take the job?

I meant seeing your mom. Been a while.

Fine. The care home is nice. It's private.

That's good.

They get in and shut the doors. Kyle starts the engine and turns the heating on. She adjusts the passenger seat's setting – one of the long-legged male workers at the centre has been in before her. He glances over at her and reverses out of the bay.

Still wearing those nice pants, I see.

Funny.

What did you bring me?

Actually, I've got you an article on the Chernobyl Grays. It's pretty interesting.

Oh, nice. Lupus radio-activus – am I right?

I took Latin, you know.

Go on, then, impress me.

Inter canem et lupum crepusculum.

Fancy. What does it mean?

Between the dog and the wolf, twilight.

You are wasted on the colonials.

Kyle pulls out of the airport exit onto the highway and heads towards the bridge. Traffic is thin. The truck purrs over the arching concrete span. Below, the river is a deep wide cut of blue.

I never get used to it, she says.

What's that?

Seeing Rainier so close from the plane. There's nothing like it back home.

Yeah, she's not too ugly.

After ten minutes they leave the highway and follow a convoy of empty timber trucks north. Kyle indicates and overtakes. The lead truck flashes its lights as they pass. They stop at a roadside diner and order burgers. They talk about the volunteers, the forthcoming conference in Montana. The local news. A body has been found dumped near Lolo. A senator has been caught in bed with a rent boy; KTVB reporters have been sitting outside the wife's hotel.

You weren't even tempted to work for the prince, then? Kyle asks.

Earl. No. I don't know. Not really. He's a –

She picks up the sugar dispenser, fiddles with the lid.

He's what?

He's crazy, probably. But very ambitious. He's got a lot of clout.

Clout?

Yeah. Politically. It's a good scheme. But a mad hope-and-glory project – he wants to re-wild, eventually.

Sounds good.

Maybe. Britain has a history of wealthy eccentrics who love grand schemes, especially if they can be named after themselves. They think they can do whatever they want. Maybe they can – a few handshakes with old-school friends in Parliament and off they go. It's not like here.

Kyle jerks a thumb over his shoulder.

Ha. Who do you think is living out there? The democratic anti-corruptionists? The communist party? Gandhi?

She laughs, shakes her head.

Tax dodging is different. In Britain there's a set at the top. It'll never change, no matter who is in power or how many proletariat rock stars get knighted by Her Majesty.

Liam Gallagher is a Sir?

Probably.

Well now I feel confused. I'll have to get rid of my CDs.

She takes the remaining pound notes out of her wallet, folds them, and slips them into a side chamber. They eat their food quickly, split the bill, leave a good tip, and head for the door. Kyle takes a mint from the dish next to the cash register.

I'm going to Coeur d'Alene next weekend to fix the boat. Want to go?

Is Oran going?

Nope.

OK.

Kyle shakes his head.

I hope you keep quit. That guy is like a dog. He thinks if he trots along faithfully, one day you'll fall in love with him and everything. It's not going to take much to fuck him up again.

He doesn't think that. I've assured him.

If you say so.

Back on the road the day is almost gone, leaving an immense plain of grey sky. The dark, arboreal wings of the road flash past, vast trunks, interstices where the forest has been clear-cut. No lights are visible but in the trees there are compounds and saw-mills, factories, swimming pools, and hunting lodges.

You know Scotland really might vote for independence, she says.

Is that so?

It's looking that way. The No campaign is floundering.

Will it be a republic?

No. They'll keep the Queen.

Would you vote for it?

I don't know, she says.

She leans back in the seat, stretches her legs out. She is glad to be back. Tomorrow they will start analysing the month's data, video footage from the den, audio recordings from the pack's patrols along the buffer zone. She will email Lawrence and apologise for not managing to see him while over. While the visit is fresh in her mind she will look on Amazon for a Christmas present for Binny. She'll make the introduction between Stephan Dalakis in the Carpathian rescue centre and Thomas Pennington – she will be *a friend* to the Annerdale project; she'll help get him his wolves.

Night presses down on the road. The headlights of the truck shine into the distance. A deer blunders from the verge, across the road and into the trees opposite, the red disc at the back of its eye flashing. Kyle doesn't flinch or brake. She cracks the window open for a second, then presses the switch to close it again. They drive on in silence, then she says,

I remember Chernobyl.

When you were a kid?

I was ten. They told us not to go outside if it was raining. Where I come from, it's always raining. We had exercises in school for nuclear disasters afterwards. This bell would ring and you'd have to duck under the desk and count to one hundred.

Scary shit, Kyle says.

Yeah. They've only just stopped testing the lambs before sending them to the market.

When St Helens blew, he says, we got the ash. You could see the cloud coming, like this huge black column. Mom took me and my brother out of school and made us stay under the bed for three days. She fed us tuna sandwiches under there. There was black shit on everything. The windows, the grass, everything.

Do you think the hide-under-something strategy works?

Nope. It's like wiping God's ass with a Kleenex.

Kyle switches on the radio and tracks to a popular music station. He sings along, out of key. He turns off the road onto the timber route, towards the Reservation. They gain altitude. The road closes over with white. Flakes spiral out of the black void onto the windscreen and are swept away.

You want to stop and put the chains on?

Nah.

They pass a sign – *57 km to nearest gas*. The snow is falling faster now. In December the centre can be cut off for days. They have to ski into town until the grit truck arrives. The back-up generator stinks the place out with diesel fumes and smoke, and they play cards while the big weather subsumes them, and the buried landscape seems like a trick to desolate the mind.

So, what was this business in town then? she asks.

In the glow of the dashboard she can see Kyle's profile.

Brother was in court, he says. Dealing meth again.

*

Back to the routine. Her house in the woods, on the periphery of the centre complex, rough-hewn yellow pine, one of seven cabins. Loading the stove wearing gloves and pulling tarpaulin over the woodstack next to the porch to keep it dry. Unpacking cans into the cupboards. More blankets on the bed as winter comes on, and showers so hot in the morning, her skin is laced red. In the office she and Kyle mop muddy snow off the floor. Administration: entering data into the system, specimen samples, weight of prey, observed behaviour. Howl patterns, the length of their solos. The two new volunteers reorder the filing system and send out sponsor renewal packs. The girl, barely a college graduate, is approached very obviously by Oran one night when they are all out in a bar. Were it not for the blatancy, the show, Rachel would believe he has moved on. In the quiet December evenings she adds a few hundred words to her book chapter, somewhat speculative. She needs to understand more about serotonin levels before any conclusions can be reached. Thomas Pennington remains in touch, through Honor Clark. The barrier is nearing completion – the quarantine pens are ready. The introduction to Stephan Dalakis has proved to be very useful. The Romanian rescue centre will supply an initial pair, as Rachel suggested. The wolves must be unsocialised, their gene pool well mixed. A cheque arrives for her consultancy work; issued by a private London bank, the royal bank, the amount winds her, and it is complicated paying it into her American account.

The following week, Left Paw's radio collar arrives by courier, sent by a Mr R. E. Buke, postmarked Clarkston, Washington. Kyle opens the package and holds up the device to show her, then tosses it onto the office table. The collar has been cut, the transmitter is broken, its electrical chip pried out – probably smashed or doused in solvent. A sudden heaviness enters her, confirmation of the worst.

They got him, she says.

Kyle reads the note and relays its information. Mr Buke found the collar lying on the path near the Snake River Bridge. The centre's address and logo were printed on the inner tag. Perhaps it was tossed from a vehicle travelling on the overpass, he speculates – the spot being notorious for dumping.

Good of him to send it back, I suppose, she says.

Kyle looks at her.

Oh come on. R. E. Buke? Rebuke?

What. Really?

Yeah. Tossed from a vehicle, what an asshole.

He shakes his head, swivels the office chair back towards the computer and the loose stack of envelopes on his desk, and begins to sift through them for hand-addressed ones – possible donations.

Really? she asks again. That's a bit too clever, isn't it? And brazen.

If you want to try to find him in the Clarkston and Lewiston phone book and write a thank-you note, be my guest.

He continues sorting the mail. Rachel reaches over and picks up the collar. The strap has been sawn through, some kind of industrial cutter. She hopes to God he was shot, rather than trapped or run over or anything worse. She isn't angry. The game is stupid and sufferable; she and the other Chief Joseph workers are often agents for the losing side, but she must play the part. She puts the collar down. The Reservation is protected, but there are almost 800,000 acres, with few enough tribal members and settlers that witnesses will be unlikely. The authorities cannot help. Such crimes are seldom prosecuted. Meanwhile, the hunters are good at what they do: they know the movements of the packs, the trailways. And a dispersing male is, for some, the highest prize. She knows the refrain well. *Spreading their goddamn scourge. Let them get a foothold and they will be upon you, threatening your livestock, your home, your family.* Bullshit, semi-biblical paranoia. Left Paw will be a good trophy. Plenty of taxidermists would agree to the work, even the ones in town with award-winning mounts and sophisticated websites – no need to go to some unlicensed backwoods skinner. The pelt is probably already on display, in a den or hanging on a timber wall, arousing admiration. She picks up the phone, dials the number of the US Fish & Wildlife Service, asks what tags have been turned in. Kyle swivels in the chair, holds up a cheque.

I have a winner. Five-hundred and eighty-nine dollars and twenty-five cents from the Greer High School charity drive. Go Roosters!

So the game continues. Some days this is as good as it gets, transforming the prejudices of the next generation. Hearts and minds won by Kyle's high-school 'Paw-Talks', by the eager T-shirted volunteers who steward busloads of children round the visitors' centre and clear up after their picnics, and by her, the hours spent in the makeshift lab, considering serotonin and keeping the anger down, though it rises like indigestion.

She likes the routine. The stove burning through cords of wood and the walls of the cabin creaking and clicking as they warm. A young black bear – not hibernating – demolishes the communal bins. On nights when the road is clear they go to Sammy's, or The Red Barn, or Big Sky Shack, play pool and drink beer, listen to eighties music. The weekly special: venison burger, venison stew, Ma's Trapper Loaf. They receive Canadian footage of the pack and upload new photographs onto the website. There's a debate on the website forum about using numbers rather than names. A debate on the forum about the definition of animal intelligence. New portraits of the centre workers are taken, too: Kyle, laconic, his dark eyebrows shadowing his dark eyes. Rachel, actually smiling. Oran, grinning and woollen hatted, looking like a West Coast stoner, which he is. She continues to avoid Oran. It has not lasted with the volunteer, who is sniffling while she works and being comforted by her co-worker. Twice he knocks on her cabin door late at night. She ignores him.

   Late in the month the centre receives another report from the Canadians. Caribou numbers are down: the pack has split to become more effective. The radio signal shows them a hundred miles apart. Christmas arrives. She receives a luxurious card from Annerdale, the paper glossy and gold embossed, and an invitation to join the Earl for drinks at the hall on the morning of the 25th, if she is back in Cumbria for the holiday. On the day itself, while the others are preparing the communal meal, she phones Willowbrook. 10 p.m. GMT. Binny sounds tired, congested, and out of sorts. Lawrence has been there most of the day with Emily, who has no doubt rubbed their mother up the wrong way.

We could Skype, Binny says. Dora has it on her computer.

I don't have a camera on mine, Rachel says.

Can't you click it or whatever you do? You're not working today, are you?

No. Day off.

Though she has been rereading her chapter. Binny coughs, coughs again, the phlegm thick-sounding. Finally she clears her throat.

Have you rung Lawrence?

I was just about to.

Ring your brother.

I was just about to.

Ring him.

At the New Year's party they put tin lanterns up in the office and push the tables against the wall. Rock music hammers from the stereo. She dances with Kyle. She dances with Oran. The volunteers are a couple. There is nothing else for them to do, especially at night. A few friends from town and from the Reservation join the festivities. Kyle's brother, who came to the last two New Year's parties, has been sentenced to nine years. White brandy has been brought in from someone's still, a lethal demi-john. It is eye-wateringly strong, tastes of Vaseline and sour apples, and burns all the way down. Oran is smoking hydroponic weed, heating knives on the hot plate of the boiler. They party hard, one of dozens of groups lost in the woods, getting industrially fucked up. She dances with Kyle again. He does not usually dance. They dance slowly, their closeness unfamiliar, disarming; she thinks, *Shouldn't I know?* The brandy is cut with something else maybe, will crystallise her brain or send her blind; she doesn't care. It strips sense and inhibition. The back of his shirt is damp. She can feel the slow ride of his back. Midwinter's Law of Misrule. He says something into her hair. The question is unfathomable, or wasn't a question. Her hands, when she stares at them, are like dead birds on his shoulders. So what, she thinks. Soon everything will end, even the stars. *OK*, she says, *OK. OK.*

Midway through the act she loses concentration or realises the mistake. They begin to move out of unison. They change position – her on top. It does not work. It becomes ridiculous. Slap, slap. Nothing feels right. They stop. *Sorry.* The failure is humiliating. She kneels and goes down on him, but the sensation of her mouth is too light, or he is impartial, or alcohol has killed their nerves. He pulls her up and kisses her, but she leans away. He turns her round and on her side, takes hold of her hip, locks her neck inside his elbow, which is better. His movements are enormous, too strong, going on until she might break, the chaos of bedding, the bed trying to shift across the floor. Then it is over. Wetness like blood slopping inside. Fumes of liquor and sweat linger in the room.

When he is unconscious she leaves to go back to her own cabin, through the stiff iced branches. No sound, no wind, the year is too stunned to begin properly. The stars are nailed tight, holding up the enormous black sky. The air is immaculate, too difficult to breathe. She stops and kneels and vomits, acid washing up her throat, her nose and eyes stinging. She feels raw. Under her hands, the ground radiates cold. She lets it creep up through her bones, like an infection. Impossible to think of seasons now, of summer's spontaneous brush fires, grass so aspirated the reflection from a parked car's mirror could ignite it. Her hands begin to ache. After a while she stands and walks on through the white branches.

The following morning there is a phone call from England – the manager of Willowbrook. The line is faint; Rachel is not properly awake. Her head blooms with pain, terrible and frontal. Her mouth tastes evil. The conversation begins murkily – a message from Binny, or something about Binny. In the end the hangover acts as prophylactic for the shock, when everything finally becomes clear. Binny has taken an overdose of aspirin and Amlodipine. She was taken to hospital in Kendal as soon as she was found. She was listed as a DNR. They worked on her until the seizures became too much for her heart. He is sorry to break the bad news, he says. Perhaps he could call back later when she has had a chance to absorb the news? Rachel thanks him. She hangs up. She sits for a moment, in the quiet of the cabin, then looks up her brother's number and dials it. She does not expect him to answer but he does.

It's Rachel. They just rang me.

Lawrence is too distraught to speak coherently.

I can't believe it, he says. She isn't. Why would she do it?

Rachel does not say – but she could – because Binny wasn't a hysteric, because she was a dyed-in-the-wool, high-calibre, selfish bitch. Then again, was the action really so inappropriate, really so bad? *Get off the bus when it's your stop.*

I think maybe it was her plan.

I don't understand. She planned it?

Maybe.

[65]

How do you know?

Something she said when I was there.

What the fuck?

Her brother begins to cry, hard sobs, which he muffles. Rachel's heart begins to bark and her head swims; she feels as if she will be sick again.

Why didn't you warn me? he asks.

Lawrence, she says. Come on.

But he is lost in grief. She listens to him weeping, the sound both awful and remote. Emily takes the phone from him. No greeting. No consolation.

I think we better call you back later, she says. He needs to rest.

Is he alright?

Obviously not. His mother just died.

His mother. As if Rachel were not related, as if she were a stranger to the events. There is little point trying to liaise with Emily. Rachel hangs up. Whether they will call back, she does not know.

She sits by the ashy stove, a blanket cast around her shoulders, her feet bare and numb on the floorboards. She pictures a pure, clear glass of water, but it seems like a fantasy, out of her reach. The soft layers inside her skull throb. After a time, there is a knock at the door. She does not answer. She hears Kyle's boots breaking the crust of new snow as he walks away. She gets up and moves cautiously to the kitchen, runs the tap and puts her head underneath it, drinks as much as she can without vomiting. The brandy from the previous night seems to reanimate. The room hazes. She sits by the cold fire, feeling drunk again.

The manager of Willowbrook calls a second time – the hour late in the UK. He is sorry again for her loss, he says. Dreadfully sorry. Everything was done by the book, interviews have been conducted with staff, there were no signs, such a situation is unusual. Covering his ass, she thinks. Does she have any questions? he asks. She doesn't. Among the possessions there is an envelope addressed to Rachel from her mother, he says. The care home will post it immediately, of course.

No. Just open it, Rachel tells him.

It looks like private correspondence. It's no trouble to post. I wouldn't want to intrude.

She convinces him that it will be simpler this way. Another heavy snowfall is due in Idaho. Postal deliveries may not reach the centre; it could be weeks before anything gets through. There's a pause, silence. She imagines him sitting at his desk, in lamplight, the envelope being opened, probably with a paperknife, respectfully.

It's more of a note, really, he says. I wonder if it mightn't be better to send it on to you.

No. Please just read it.

I'm sure your mother would have wanted you to know how much she loved you, he says. She talked about you all the time. About how proud she was.

Rachel baulks. His words are excruciating to hear, ludicrous. The comment so blatantly twee and false, it is almost as bad as his breaking the news of the death. This man knew Binny; he knew her proclivities, her disposition. Rachel sits rigidly, waits for it all to be over. The manager clears his throat, then reads.

Dear Rachel. We all choose. You can come back home now. Binny.

*

A polar vortex over North America. The heaviest snow for fifty years, structures locked in ice. January is all drifts; the forest disappears under white cataracts. Bannisters of ice form along the stacked roadside timber. The sky is iron-grey and unforgiving. Idaho exists in a delirium of cold, the number of old people dying soars. The neighbouring states, too, report record snowfalls. The Snoqualmie and Lolo passes remain closed. Avalanches in the Cascades.

Rachel misses the funeral. She does not send a wreath. She does not supply words of remembrance for the service. Communication has ceased between her and Lawrence, that is to say, between her and Emily, who has assumed control of the proceedings, and after a huge argument on the phone about duty and emotional incapacity, excludes her. She is now fully a criminal in exile. Another hard layer forms around her heart against her brother's wife. The end ceremony is irrelevant, she tells herself. It is meaningless. What matters is the relationship through life. Would Binny care if she attended? She would not. She tells herself this, pours a drink, opens the cabin window, and leaves it wide until the cold is unbearable.

The centre winds along at its winter speed. In the evenings the workers play cards, watch DVDs, are sequestered in their cabins reading. Rachel tries to continue with her book chapter, but cannot concentrate. Her mind drifts back to her mother, and New Year's Eve. Bereavement has displaced any initial awkwardness with Kyle that might have occurred. He is kind to her, gives her space, does not raise the subject. She tries to write a letter to her brother, but she hasn't the skills, emotional or linguistic, and she is full of bile. Something massive and primary feels as if it has broken. Their connection always seemed pinioned by their mother. So what, she tells herself. Let it go.

The snow keeps coming, blanking everything. When she

walks out in it she can barely see. Days pass, weeks. Thoughts of her childhood: high-stakes weather in the Lowther valley, almost legendary in her imagination, helicopters flying over Lakeland carrying new electricity pylons after storms had brought the others down. She and Lawrence, clad in woollens and wet boots, watching them cut the cables and lay the poles down on the moors, like a game of matchsticks. In the mornings she feels sick and tired, viral; her body knows the wrongness of what has occurred even if her mind won't metabolise it.

When the thaw comes, she and Kyle venture out to reposition the cameras by the den site. They drive into the Reservation and then hike seven miles, sharing water, saying little. The ground is turgid, swamp-like. The hardwoods are scarred by black frost, their bark sodden, their deepest membranes still rigid with ice. They labour over the winter debris. There are small new lakes in the forest, melt-water runoff. In the brush a loon stumbles about, lost, directionless. It eyes them, panics, flaps and trips over twigs. Kyle steps away, quietly. Rachel watches the bird for a moment, then follows after him.

And still, they have not talked about what happened. She is grateful not to have to. It's her call, she knows; he will wait, perhaps indefinitely, he will not push, and she does not have to think about the meaning of what happened. She could tell herself it was a dream, an altered state, brought on by the moonshine brandy. Nor has Kyle criticised her for not attending the funeral. The only assistance he offered:

I can get you over to Spokane on the old silver road, if you want to go.

As if it were simply the snow preventing her. No doubt he would have found a way to the airport, but when she said no, he nodded and left the subject alone, intuiting, perhaps, the difficult navigation of families. His brother has written to him, asking for money to support his girlfriend and baby while he is incarcerated.

Will you give it? Rachel asks.

She's still dealing from the house, he says. Yeah, I'll give it.

The Clearwater River is in spate, hauling debris down from the Bitterroot Mountains, rolling dead branches up along the banks, and ferrying the carcasses of mammals, half-submersed and unrecognisable in the water. There are high reefs of silt. They walk uphill, away from the flood zone, and arrive at the abandoned den. One of the cameras is lurching from its mooring in the tree. There's no guarantee the dugout will be reused but it has been occupied for three consecutive years, so the chances are good. The root system is sturdy. It is in good repair, even after the hardest of seasons. Kyle reroofs the camera's shelter. The branches drip and twitch. It is still cold, but the world has softened and will soon bud.

Rachel sits and watches Kyle hammering the bolts.

You alright? he asks, without turning.

Yes.

But there is a strange heaviness in her, like the beginning of flu. Not sadness exactly. She is not sad about losing Binny. Nor regretful about the nature of their relationship – things couldn't have been different. Nothing would have changed the dynamic, no more than the elliptical orbit of planets can be altered by human hand. She had the only version of her mother she could have had; Binny had the only daughter. In some ways they were motherless, daughterless. It feels more like an existential malaise of some kind. Sorrow for time, for its auspices, its signification. She feels, for the first time in her life, weary, and old. But that isn't really it, either. She doesn't know what's wrong.

I think that'll hold, Kyle says.

Great.

Ready to head back?

Yes.

Sure you're OK?

I'm fine. Tired. Think I need some sun.

She stands, tries to shake it off. They begin back through the great, dank arboretum.

The following day Kyle makes an appointment to visit the executives of the tribal council – a courtesy call. The arrangement is not under threat. Hikers will be steered away where possible and the territorial section of land will remain undeveloped. The Nez Perce have sponsored the project since its inception, before hunting bans and their reversals. It is a relatively small affair for the elders to consider – the Reservation's campaigns and lawsuits are wide and more complicated than species, involving ideologies, citizens versus sovereign nations, and Supreme Court interpretation. The Chief Joseph pack is safe, if only on host land. Meanwhile, photographs have been posted on an Idaho hunting site, of a wolf in a steel foot trap. Not one of theirs, but disheartening nevertheless. The circumference of pink, limped-over snow is sickening. They study the shot. Kyle shakes his head.

Ah, buddy, he says.

Rachel cannot help feeling depressed. Just for a moment she wonders about putting her head against his shoulder. Would it be such a terrible thing? It would, she knows. She feels unusually low, vulnerable. She wishes the bug in her system would just materialise and lay her out fully. The memory of that night is like a fever; it is passing, but there are vivid flashes. His grip across her neck. The rawness. She attempts a joke, about whose turn it is to refill the office coffee pot – who is the wife? He does not respond to the banter as he ordinarily would, but fixes her with a look, patient, undefended. And it is this that convinces her there is something more, something very real underneath the silence. The unspeakable is always louder than declaration.

True panic comes only days later, while looking in the bathroom cupboard at the unused tampon box. How many weeks have passed? There was a little bit of blood maybe; she has sore breasts. She picks up her keys and walks out to the truck in her T-shirt, her trainers unlaced, impervious to the chill, zombie-like. She drives to town, to the all-night pharmacy, does not even wait to get home before opening the packet and doing the test, but squats at the side of the road like a destitute. Positive.

She drives back to the Reservation, pulls off the road, sits in the pick-up, and stares ahead.

Now every rule is broken. Her programming is that of the serialist, she knows it, and that's fine. Romance fails because it is never supposed to work, past the act itself, the momentum of lust. She was raised by an expert. Binny was practically Roman in her operations: arriving in the village, taking the spoils, then razing everything to the ground. Through the walls of the post office cottage Rachel could sometimes hear the sound of male weeping, a sound exotic and horrendous. And her mother's vexed responses. *Buck up, man, there was never anything to it. Go back home to her.* How desperately they tried to convince her of love.

The next day she calls her doctor's office, then calls her insurance company, but there is no additional rider to her policy; she is not covered, and there is no life endangerment. She'll have to find a doctor and pay for it herself, after state-directed counselling and a wait period. She is furious with herself. A baby! It seems impossible. It is the worst possible scenario, the worst of all failures. Not even a stranger, but her best friend, her colleague, whom she must face every day. In the storm of it all, she does not consider that for years they have been together, companions, lovers of sorts, mutually obsessed with the family under their care – with their feeding, their nurture, their scat, the routes along which they travel – as if parents already.

*

It is mid-February when she calls the estate office and asks to speak to Thomas Pennington. Honor Clark puts her through. The line is bad, the sound of an engine, he is in transit, on board a plane perhaps. If the position is still open, she will take it.

Yes, yes, he says. Wonderful, Rachel, I'm so glad you are joining us. Honor will get a press release together immediately.

As if she is some kind of celebrity. She does not ask about salary, or for any contractual details. She writes a formal letter of resignation, though to whom can it be sent? She is project manager; the Chief Joseph Trust is a cooperative entity. Kyle will run the project solo, until a replacement can be found at a later date. Almost ten years of her life; it is no small commitment. In the end it's more difficult to break the news to Kyle than she had expected, but he hears it almost as he would an expected weather forecast.

Yeah, fair enough. That's about right.

They are sitting on his deck, drinking beer and wearing heavy coats against the cool wet mist. Mist drifts between the trees, conveying the fetid, arable smell of the paper mill downriver. He laughs.

Off to live in a castle. Well, we can't compete with that.

Hardly. Anyway, I won't be living at the hall. Just somewhere on the estate, I think.

On the estate!

She does not apologise for leaving, or offer any explanation, and he does not ask her why. He goes to get another beer, uncaps it, holds it to his lips.

I'm going to grill some steak. Want some?

OK.

Over the food, they talk about the same old things. Perhaps he is a little quieter than usual. Later that evening she books a one-way flight. Two weeks, then she will be gone.

News from the northern partners is that the pack has reunited and is coming south. She hopes she'll see them before she goes. The workers track their progress towards the Reservation. They arrive a few days before Rachel's flight. The yearlings have all survived. There's the glinting of eyes on the night camera, the writhe and scramble of black bodies near the earth walls. The breeding pair, Tungsten and Moll, are sleeping close together. He is attentive, licking her muzzle. Good signs for a new litter. The centre prepares for spring visitors and Rachel packs up her cabin. There's not much to box. Meanwhile, some breathtaking aerial footage is sent down from Canada, which Oran uploads onto the website. The pack is on the frozen edge of a lake, waiting in for-mation for a cornered grizzly bear and its cub to come out of the water. Tungsten and Moll flank, their tails lowered, inching forward, the others are lined up like guards, like a firing squad. The bear cub flails around and its mother roars at the hunters, but they do not retreat. The pilot circles back over the scene, say-ing, *Holy shit, Andy, are you getting this*; and the co-pilot, filming, replies, *Yeah, is that even possible?* Within twenty-four hours it has 20,000 viewings.

Rachel watches the clip again and again in the office. Over the years she has learnt never to be complacent, that they are capable of extreme feats, but the manoeuvre is astonishing: their audac-ity, their strategy. The aircraft circles twice more, then pulls up and continues on its course. Whether the kill was made, she will never know. But, watching the footage, the decision to leave Chief Joseph suddenly feels easier. They are matchless predators; they exist supremely, she is irrelevant to them.

There's a small, low-key leaving party. Two of the tribal elders attend and some friends from the Reservation. They drink punch from plastic beakers, barbecue. It has been a warm day; it's a warm evening. There are no speeches. When pressed, Rachel stands up and thanks everyone. They give her a tourist sachet of wolf hair, with *Cat Repellent* written on it, and a Kwakwaka'wakw carving of a she-wolf by one of the local artists. The woodwork is beautiful, a fecund representation, the muzzle elongated and stylised. There are many teats beneath her belly and the shell eye glimmers. No one knows her condition, but she wonders for a moment – have they guessed? She is moved, uncomfortable in her skin, and excuses herself to fetch more beer.

On the day she is due to leave, Kyle takes her to the airport. She does not have much luggage. Her books are being sent via freight. Her employment documentation will be surrendered to the embassy at a later date, if she doesn't come back.

I might come back, she says. Who knows.

Well, we aren't going anywhere, Kyle says. Unless they come fracking for oil.

They drive in companionable quiet most of the way. From time to time she glances at him. When they speak it is about the pack. He pulls into the airport parking lot.

Thanks a million, she says.

She does not want him to come inside with her. There's no point, he'll just be hanging about, and, finally, there might need to be acknowledgement of their actions. The information she is living with is too sensitive – better to cut and run. He parks, turns off the engine, opens the door.

Come on, he says. Let's do this properly.

Do what?

Rachel. Don't be a hard-ass.

OK.

They print her ticket from the machine in the terminal. She checks her bags. Through the window they watch the plane landing from Pullman, steering down, nose pulling up at the last moment, a burst of smoke from the tyres as it touches down. She turns to him, looks at him properly – for the first time in weeks, it seems. His hair is very long again; he hates having it cut. Dark eyes. He is attractive.

You will keep me up to speed about them, won't you?

Yeah, of course.

The plane taxis up. The propellers are cut. The ground crew wheel the steps up; passengers dismount and filter into the terminal building. The stewardess begins to take and tear in half the boarding passes of the outbound.

Well, he says.

He takes hold of her waist gently, with both hands. She flinches, draws her stomach in, though it is too early to be rounded, blushes, is both annoyed and upset. *Please don't*, she thinks. He doesn't try to kiss her, just smiles.

Get on home now, crazy lady.

Let me know about them, she says.

Sure.

He releases her. He turns and walks through the terminal and out of the building. She steps up to the gate. The stewardess tears her boarding pass, tells her to have a good flight. She walks down the short corridor, past the sign that says, *Thank You for Visiting Nez Perce Idaho*, and out onto the tarmac.

EVERYTHING TENDS TOWARDS IRON

Seldom Seen Cottage feels suitably abandoned when she arrives. The taxi drops her off and reverses back down the unmade track. The key has been left in the front door, trustingly. She unlocks it and walks inside. The building seems not to have been inhabited for quite some time – the prevailing smell is of stone, a graphite emptiness, and recent cleaning products. Like the island folly, it is built in the same pink sandstone, and is oddly romantic-looking under the trees – whimsical almost. Pennington Hall is a mile and a half away – far enough. She drops her bags in the hallway, walks from room to room. The interior has been painted white throughout. There are new white goods in the kitchen with labels stuck to their sides. New wooden sash windows – double-glazed. Nothing on the estate, it seems, is allowed to moulder and rot. She opens the back door. Even the garden has been cut: grass clippings and boughs left in tidy piles by the back fence. There are dark patches on the slates around the chimney where moss has been scraped up, stubs in the wall cracks around the doorway where vine has been stripped. The logs in the lean-to by the porch are yellow and freshly cut, enough to last all spring, and beyond.

She goes back inside, opens cupboards and drawers. There are no souvenirs from previous tenants, trysting couples, or estate workers – no condom packets, lost shoes, or final bills. She walks into the sitting room. Something flutters up the chimney, dislodging a skitter of soot. A packet of paraffin firelighters and a stack of kindling have been left by the hearth. There's a flat-screen television. The furniture is plain but quality. Stiff new curtains smelling faintly of chemicals. But there are no cushions, no welcome flowers in a vase on the table.

The stairs are narrow, with a dog-leg halfway. Her bags scrape on the walls as she hefts them up. She dumps them in the larger of the two bedrooms, whose window overlooks a blossoming quince tree in the garden. Petrified globes of the previous year's fruit hang under the whitish blossoms. There are towels folded on the bed and a voluptuous, airy duvet. More linen and bedding in the airing cupboard. In the bathroom next door, a lemony tang and lurid blue bleach spanning the toilet bowl. She sits on the bed and looks out. The quince's leaves agitate in the wind. It seems too far north for such a tree, but the estate also has its forcing houses, an orangery, alongside the traditional meadows and the rose beds. A small grey bird is creeping up the trunk, pausing, creeping up again. An ersatz paradise, she thinks. The tree, the pink house, the dense, deciduous woods – she is the wrong woman for such a story. But it is too late. She will not stay long, she tells herself, just until she can find her own house. She will rent in one of the villages nearby, and commute. She has had enough of living and working in close proximity, in a closed community – there are no borders, no escapes. Meanwhile, she has the cottage, and use of a car, a newish Saab, parked at the side of the house, its key left on the kitchen table. A converted coach house in the estate's complex will be available as the project hub. There are funds for one full-time assistant, whom Rachel will interview and select, a hugely competitive position.

She stands, opens the catch on the bedroom window, slides the pane up, and sits back down. *Home.* The sheets are luxurious, hotel-like – a high thread count. It is undeniably an upgrade from Chief Joseph.

The woods beyond the garden rustle and flicker; the branches mesh and lift gently. On the other side of the trees is the fence. The taxi driver had asked her about it on the way in, seeming to think it was some kind of science experiment, animal testing or the like. There have been protests already, gatherings at the estate gates. *Individuals expressing concern*, as it was described, somewhat evasively, by Honor Clark, when Rachel asked to be filled in. Such matters are never insignificant. She must press for more details, names. Annerdale is less than a tenth the size of the Reservation; any achievement here will be small scale, microcosmic, any hype misfounded. There will be trouble, she knows, because they are never without enemies, they are too successful a creature, too good at what they do. It will be up to her to convert suspicion and fear into something positive.

The soft purring of a telephone downstairs – she had not even realised one was connected yet. She goes in search, finds it on the windowsill of the kitchen, and picks up hesitantly, as if she hasn't the right.

Hello?

Rachel?

It is Honor Clark, of course.

Yes.

Settled in alright, I hope? We've set you up.

Yes, fine, thanks.

Got everything you need?

I think so.

Excellent. Just to remind you, Thomas is hoping you'll be able to join him and a few other guests for dinner this evening. A small welcome affair, but it would be useful for you to attend. Will that be convenient?

It is less of a question than an expectation.

Yes.

Good.

She wonders whether she will be summoned regularly to the big house, now that she is in situ, and biddable. The thought is unsettling. But this is her first night, after all.

What sort of time?

Seven for seven-thirty.

I'll see you then.

There's a pause.

Thomas will look forward to it. *I'll* be in touch again in the morning about the advertisement – we thought the *Guardian*, *Times*, *National Geographic*, the usual.

She senses mild rebuke – a reminder of the separation of staff and employer, the strata of the estate. She will have to get to know the system. She will have to ascertain where she herself fits in, or doesn't.

OK, fine.

Pop over when you're up and about, let's say nine?

See you then.

Rachel hangs up. Too late she wonders about dress code, then thinks to herself, No, there must be some limits, preservation of the ordinary. She is as she was the day before: the same person, charged with similar duties. Even here. She opens the refrigerator door. Inside is a bottle of fresh milk. She opens a cupboard. Gold-label tea bags, Illy coffee, sugar cubes. Set up, yes, and welcomed, but she has a distinct feeling that something may be forfeit.

The thought of a formal dinner is not appealing. She would rather settle in, be by herself, and try the fireplace. And think. She has been not thinking, and has been making a point of not thinking. She isn't due at the Hall for a couple of hours – there's time for a short walk first. The light is good outside: pale spring light, citrine. The cottage is near the lake, she knows, there were glimmers through the trees from the taxi window. She takes a cagoule from her bag and changes into boots. She locks the front door, though it seems unlikely anyone will attempt to break in, unlikely anyone will even pass by along the lane. A stray walker, maybe. A horseback-rider on the bridleway. She starts out along the track, which is rutted on the outside with deep tyre marks from the transit of large construction vehicles, then she cuts into the trees, walks through a beautiful stretch of old woodland. Buds and blossom; there's a sweet, spermy fragrance in the air, a scent both exquisite and intolerable. The last few weeks she's noticed a strange sensitivity to such things, aversions, smells that are nausea-inducing. For all that the business of pregnancy is interruptive and alarming, she cannot deny it has its interesting frontiers.

All about her, the season is surprisingly lovely, unsettled and kinetic, then windless, held. The air is moist and downy. There are flashes of tropical colour on bare twigs. She does not remember Cumbria looking so exotic. The path disperses, broken up by surfacing roots. Moss and columbine. The boulders are occluded, starred with orange and yellow lichen. Ahead, through the low branches, she can see the lake water rustling with light. She breaks clear of the trees, walks along the shore, and sits on a flat rock at the edge of a shingle bay. The wooden island has no reflection today, but floats, like a mirage. She cannot see the folly from this angle. The river-mouth is nearby, rushing and spilling. She breathes in, exhales, tries to relax, to formulate a plan.

Tomorrow she will register with a GP and make an appointment, get the process moving. There will be, at worst, a day or two's inconvenience. She will buy groceries, stock the cupboards, then take one of the estate's quad bikes and go into the enclosure. Perhaps she will even call Lawrence, try to sort that mess out. She must, of course, sort it out, though part of her, a faulted, habitual part, would let the aggravation fester, let the gap grow until it is too wide to bridge. She gets up and walks slowly along the lakeshore to the river, where the water is very clear. Fish glimmer in the shallows, dark gold, blunt-headed – trout. The wolves might go for them, once released, straddling the rocks and snapping them out – she's seen them fish for salmon before. The rich protein in the brain is worth the wet paws, the patient vigil, and many misses. She wonders how things are at Chief Joseph. The same, no doubt, without her.

On her way back to the cottage she snaps a few sprigs of blossom from the trees. Yellow, star-shaped petals, and boughs of willow. She regains the lane a few hundred yards from the cottage. A man is standing further up the track, next to Seldom Seen. He has on dark trousers and a wax jacket. His back is to her. He is looking into the garden of the cottage, as if he has knocked and waited and is now searching the grounds. She calls out – *Hello, are you looking for me?* – but he is too far away to hear. Without turning, he walks up the lane, rounds a bend, and disappears. The quick confident gait of a local, she thinks. She goes into the porch. There is no note on the door, no sign of why he might have called. Perhaps he was simply passing, and the cottage is not as secluded as she assumed. Perhaps it was sensible to lock the door after all.

*

She arrives at the Hall early, having crossed the estate's grounds wearing her interview suit, the trousers tucked into her boots, and carrying a pair of passable shoes in her bag. She exchanges the footwear by the ornamental shrubbery under a ha-ha wall, stashing the cast-offs beneath a bush, feeling slightly ridiculous, like a peasant in a folk tale. Pennington Hall is magnificent in the glow of evening, lit up by the setting sun; suddenly the red stone, transported miles west from the Eamont quarries, makes sense. Rachel wonders if it will ever feel natural, approaching such a building as if she has the right.

A moon-faced woman answers the front door, tall and slender, blankly beautiful. She introduces herself, murmuringly, as Sylvia, and offers a hand to shake. The girlfriend of Thomas Pennington, perhaps, though she is very young. She has on a structured, mustard-yellow gown, knee-length, silken, and nude-coloured heels. At once Rachel feels under-dressed.

I've mistimed, she explains. The walk from the cottage – it's quicker than I thought.

Not at all, Sylvia says. It's a marvellous evening, isn't it? How clever of you to walk.

The young woman shows Rachel through to an unfamiliar drawing room, a family room, perhaps: pale botanical green, full of flowering plants, its ceiling reminiscent of a cathedral. The Earl is, for once, present, standing by a large, crackling fire.

Rachel feels she has intruded, interrupted their privacy. Thomas – it is clear now that she must call him by his first name – greets her as if they have known each other for decades.

Rachel! Wonderful to see you again! And here you are, our most worthy project leader.

He leans in and kisses her, then hands her a flute of champagne, which was sitting amid a galley of others, waiting for the guests. He is dressed with intermediate elegance: slacks, an open-collared shirt, cufflinks, a blazer. The lunar woman lingers by his side, smiling at Rachel.

Settling in OK, I hope, Thomas says. Is Seldom exactly as you need it to be?

I only arrived today. The cottage is very nice. You must let me pay rent while I'm there.

Thomas Pennington swats a hand through the air.

Not at all. Part and parcel of the job. The place hasn't been used since, oh, goodness knows how long. I really don't like the idea of unoccupied buildings; it's such a waste. You've met Sylvia, my youngest?

The daughter. Rachel feels immediate relief. They do not look overly similar, other than their stature.

I've got her for the holidays. What was Paris going to do with her anyway? Ruin her, Rachel, that's what. She'd have come back terribly angular and filled with ennui.

Sylvia protests playfully.

Oh, Daddy! You love France.

He shrugs, turns the corners of his mouth downward, and rolls his eyes.

La vie, c'est une chose pareille obscurité.

Stop being naughty, Sylvia insists.

She smiles at her father, fondly collaborative, and links her arm through his. He kisses her hair like an adoring, neuter lover. Under the expressionless, obscuring beauty, Rachel tries to discern her age – twenty, perhaps a shade older, though she could pass for sixteen.

I don't even like Paris, Sylvia says. Too much stone and no green anywhere. Our city parks are bliss, aren't they?

The question has been directed towards Rachel, who nods politely, though she would not go so far in praise for a few boating lakes and stretches of shorn grass.

That's because nature is in the British soul, Thomas says. We must recreate it wherever we can, or we'll go mad.

Their enthusiasm and positivity is like a miasma. It could be a scene from the back pages of a society magazine, Rachel thinks, or a parody. Father and daughter are clearly used to holding court together; they are mesmerising and faintly sickening to watch – polished, too enjoying of each other for the average family. She cannot imagine such a relationship with a parent. She and Binny could barely manage three sentences without barbs or sarcasm. Sylvia is obviously well schooled in elegance and courtesy, with only enough of the coquette remaining to seem unspoilt. When she raises her glass of champagne, she barely sips. Her colouring – the light English umber and lash-less, crescent-shaped blue eyes – is presumably the dead mother's.

How about some music, Soo-Bear, her father suggests.

Yes!

She crosses the room to a discreet piece of equipment in a cabinet. She moves with extreme, but sexless, grace. The dress drifts a few millimetres from her hips and chest, its creases flocking and darkening as she moves. A demure but flattering item, the kind of thing lesser royalty might wear. Thomas Pennington asks if Rachel has any requests. She does not – she could not name an album or a band if she tried.

Put on something to annoy you-know-who, he says to his daughter, mischievously.

He seems less restive than previously, as if the presence of the daughter has a calming effect. The kind of man who fares better in female or familial company, perhaps. The older son, Leo, is absent. There are dark rumours, passed on to Rachel by Binny during her stay. A drop-out, a hellion. Talk of dis-inheritance, though it is hard, given the current show of unity and wholesomeness, to imagine rifts in this family. Thomas raises his glass.

Cheers, Rachel. We couldn't be doing any of this without you.

Clearly this is not true, the scheme was well underway before her acceptance, but Rachel thanks him.

Now, this is a bit off the bat, he says, but Sylvia has a question for you. Don't you, darling? I'd fire away before we're marauded by the others. Catch Rachel while you can.

Sylvia shimmies back over and smiles.

I hope you won't mind, she says. I wonder what you might think of an idea I've had.

She gives a theatrical little pause, her eyes wide, almost dollish; she understands charm, enough to hold Rachel's gaze a fraction too long, an act of harmless flirtation. There's not a blemish on her face or neck to suggest hormonal disruption or regular par-tying. Up close she is copper-haired and lightly glossed; some subtle, translucent powder sparkles along her cheekbones. Her face seems enormous, a cosmic presence. Fletches of brown in the left eye. At whatever establishment she attends the men will no doubt be hounding her, while she tactically refuses. Rachel can see she is a powerful asset – deployed among the socialites, the local country; her appeal is immense.

Can you already guess? she asks.

She's going to ask me if she can name them, Rachel thinks. She braces.

Go on.

OK. I'm taking a year out before law school, to recalibrate, which I really think will be useful, and I was wondering – well, I was hoping – that I could be on the project with you. I can't imagine a more exciting thing than volunteering.

There's a pause, during which Rachel feels her impassivity slipping. This is the last thing she wants or needs.

I'm desperate to be involved, Sylvia says. And I'm a really hard worker, aren't I, Daddy?

Thomas concurs.

Oh, yes, she is. Terribly hard.

They wait for Rachel's reply. She has always been forgiven dead air in conversations, people assuming her to be ruminative rather than rude. Often her silence is followed by something curt or dismissive. But these are the Penningtons. Clearly the Earl has already sanctioned the idea or it would not have been mooted. Rachel tries to imagine the girl in shit-covered boots and overalls, hefting deer carcasses, gloving scat into a sample bag. It seems impossible. She is project manager, yes, but how far does her authority extend? Can this really be denied?

Well, she says, that's an interesting idea. I'm only just putting the team together, as you know. So let's come back to it once things are underway.

Rachel glances from Sylvia to Thomas Pennington. The stall

is diplomatic enough, probably. The girl is clearly doted upon, indulged. But both seem happy with her response and are smiling. The doorbell sounds. Thomas Pennington excuses himself and takes a turn as greeter. Sylvia touches Rachel's arm, her hand light as a nest, and takes up the conversational slack.

I do think it's marvellous what you're doing with Daddy. He's so excited. It'll be good for him to have another project. He hates it when there's nothing new. And it's going to be amazing for the region. It's about revitalising the modern British wilderness, isn't it?

Rachel nods politely. Depends on definition, she thinks. The girl is repeating her father's sentiments, his rhapsody, almost verbatim. She is accent-less, clearly out-schooled. Perhaps the work placement is his idea. Good publicity, having his progeny working on the scheme, not slumming exactly but certainly *getting down* with the causes. Or is it some kind of punishment? Is she being kept close to home, for screwing, taking coke, substandard grades? Does the veneer mask high decadence? Surely the girl wants to be in London or New York, with her aristocratic peers? Not stranded here in the boondocks.

Rachel watches her as she talks. But she talks without cunning, about biodiversity, the North Carolina Red Wolf programme, which she has read up about. The cynicism seems misplaced. Sylvia's appeal is natural, unforced; there's no venal whiff. She is, very probably, a country girl, for all the wealth and coiffure. She will have spent hours taking care of her horses or the estate dogs, taught to love this remote western Elysium and to champion it; attending gymkhanas and trials, garden parties and shows; maybe having a drink now and again with local friends in the aggrieved west coast towns – a reminder of reality. She clearly wants to be involved. But what does she expect? That they will be pets? That they'll be fed milk from a bottle, like orphaned lambs? She will have to explain to Sylvia, give her the facts. They will rarely be seen – defined as much by their absence as their iconography. If she really wants the job, Sylvia will have to learn to track; she will have to endure hours of monotonous surveillance, reading prints, weighing carrion, data entry. Unglamorous at best.

Thomas Pennington crosses the room with a new guest, first dignitary of the evening. Rachel recognises the man he's accompanying, a bright young politician, ex-military and a media darling, headhunted by the current government and installed in a safe seat. Described by Binny as *the baby Tory*.

Rachel, this is Vaughan Andrews, our local MP, Thomas says. Vaughan's been hard at work getting us faster broadband. A jolly good enterprise and very uncontroversial. We've been disagreeing in the hallway about Scotland, haven't we, Vaughan?

The young man laughs, good-naturedly.

Yes, but we agree on the basics. Hello, Miss Caine, pleasure to meet you.

Up close he looks older, in his forties, perhaps. His skin is pocked, sun-damaged; he is thin, and the suit, though well cut, looks roomy. He still carries the air of the whippish officer.

I'm a great admirer of yours, he says. I'm very glad Thomas has won you over. I gather you're a native to these parts.

That he knows anything about her comes as something of a surprise. But the estate has no doubt pronounced her worth, at least to the Lakeland set.

I don't know whether I still qualify. I've been away a while.

Oh, you do, he says, I assure you. They don't rescind that

particular passport. Me, on the other hand, well, I belong over the border. In theory.

If indeed there is a border, Thomas says.

Whatever point he is making, or dig, is not immediately clear. Vaughan Andrews turns and holds his arms open.

Sylvia! Wow! You look amazing!

Sylvia's smile is moderately warm. The two embrace, kissing twice, some kind of Continental etiquette that has arrived during Rachel's absence. The young woman attends to the champagne with a redoubling of poise, but Rachel can see there is no real attraction. Vaughan hums sombrely as he takes the glass.

One and one only. I've got clinic in the morning. Can't face my constituents with a thick head. I've got the new Chartists bearing down, brandishing some kind of manifesto.

Ah, yes, Thomas says. They delivered their paper to the House, quite flamboyantly, on horseback. Harmless loons. I quite like the idea of a car-free Cumbria, though.

The doorbell rings again.

My turn.

Sylvia flutters out of the drawing room. The young politician tries hard not to watch her leave. He turns back to his host and Rachel listens to their small talk.

How many are we this evening, Thomas?

Oh, not many. Just enough to give Rachel a good welcome, not enough to upset Henry. He has this arrangement with L'Enclume – it's really very elaborate. I don't ask.

Is Mell coming?

He is.

He's on the way up to Edinburgh, then?

Henry. Mell. Rachel doesn't know who they are talking about.

It's the correct thing, of course, Thomas is saying, taking part in the debates. One can't avoid it altogether without seeming cowardly, or dismissive.

I'm not so sure. He may not be the right candidate. He's going to sound –

Colonial, Thomas suggests.

She stands awkwardly at the side, waiting for the evening to get going, and to be over.

Well-dressed, grey-haired guests arrive. Retirees and the district's rich. Conversation is of the World Heritage status bid, new speed limits on the lakes, the Scottish polls, and, intermittently, the wolf project. Rachel is introduced to various people. She is asked the same basic questions, which she answers patiently, mustering as much positivity as she can – she is, after all, representing the estate. Ebullient noise and laughter fill the drawing room. A waiter appears and takes over the serving of the champagne, leaving the hosts free to circulate. Trays of hors d'oeuvres rotate through the crowd. She meets the local vet, Alexander Graham, who will be responsible for monitoring the pair over the quarantine period, before release, and will help her with the implantation surgery. They shake hands. He is broad, well over six feet; he has the cut of a country vet, fully capable of wrestling out breech calves and clipping the hooves of prize bulls. His upper lip is fuller than the lower, and scarred – a souvenir of the profession, perhaps, or an old rugby injury – he looks the type. He seems out of place, like her, in his inexpensive civilian jacket and tie, though less awk- ward, and wryly entertained by the proceedings.

Here we all are then, he says. Seems a bit previous when they haven't arrived yet. Still, dinner and a do, I'm not complaining.

He drains his champagne glass, sets it down on a nearby bureau, and scans the room for the rotating waiter. As the hors d'oeuvres pass, he takes several and lines them up on his palm. Gelatinous fish eggs, slivers of raw, blue-looking meat; nausea rises in Rachel and she waves the offered tray away.

All set for bringing them over? he asks.

Seems so. The flight's booked. And they're fit enough to travel now.

Why were they in the rescue centre?

The male had a leg injury. The female was poisoned. But her system seems fine. She should be able to breed.

He nods. They speak casually for a few minutes. Alexander has been researching his new charges and their possible ailments – cataracts and cancers, and depression, which is not unlikely during their time in quarantine. The smaller enclosure, in which they will be kept and monitored for the first few months, will be hard after the Romanian mountains. The highlight of his day today, Alexander confesses, was cutting up a stillborn calf inside a cow's uterus using cheese wire, saving the cow in the process.

Something of a personal method.

Ingenious, she says.

Thanks.

He folds together two of the delicate tidbits and eats them. He is likeable, and will be a good colleague, she decides. There's stubble under his ear. His collar is not ironed. But his nails are in good condition, square and clean – the hands of a medic. There's a pale mark on his ring finger. Out of the corner of her eye, she sees Sylvia hovering with another pearled, vanilla-haired guest, waiting to introduce her. Rachel tries to extricate herself politely, but Alexander is oblivious, or not keen to have her company replaced. He begins telling her about an imported hybrid dog he had to put down several weeks ago, which did not fall under the licensing laws.

I can't prove it, he says, but it was definitely crossbred with something wild. There's a European loophole people are exploiting. It's a show thing. They like the big, hard, wolfy-looking ones. They can be pretty dangerous if they're trained wrong.

What did it do?

Went for a kid. Passersby got it off but he still needed stitches.

Christ.

You'll have seen a lot, though, over where you were.

I did. They get sold out of the back of vans at powwows. You don't know what you're getting half the time. Part-wolf. Part-husky.

Hello, Baskervilles.

She laughs. Sylvia guides the hovering lady away. Another waiter appears and calls them through for dinner.

Great, I'm starving, Alexander says. Good luck with the seating plan.

The dining table is long and formal, but new, artisanal, with a glass window in its centre filled with amber resin – another of the modern touches in the Hall. They are positioned around the table in some kind of meaningful order, Alexander at the other end – he catches her eye, smiles. Rachel finds herself between the director of the Woodland Trust and mayoress of Egremont. The cuisine is exceptional – hare pâté, escargot, local freshwater char – though she hasn't much of an appetite. Moments of queasiness overtake her as the rich aromas drift up from the plate. She sips the wine, thinking, it doesn't really matter, but the taste holds no enjoyment, either. The mayoress talks about chaos across the border, an impoverished state of Scotland, indebted and in need of European bailout, the usual independence scare story. She will not watch the debate tomorrow, she announces, to do so would be to credit the proceedings with unwarranted seriousness. Her tone of English superiority is annoying. *Is it any wonder they want out?* Rachel almost says.

They are halfway through dessert – delicate baked pear in a luscious red sauce – when Rachel hears the sound of rotor blades moving up the valley. The craft sounds big. Mountain rescue, a Sea King, perhaps. Some climber has come off Pillar or Coniston Old Man. The thrumming intensifies, renders conversation difficult, then pointless. The craft puts down on the helipad behind the stables in a glory of noise, and through the window she sees a flash of red and black livery. The engine powers down. Thomas Pennington stands.

Ahoy! he calls. Late, but forgivably so.

He drops his napkin and excuses himself. Two minutes later a black-suited security guard enters the dining room. He stands by the doorway, fists bolted together in front of his groin. The Prime Minister enters, with Thomas Pennington by his shoulder. The two are in casual conversation. It takes a moment for surprise to register fully in Rachel. She remains seated while guests at the table begin to respectfully rise, then she too stands. Alexander catches her eye again. His expression is droll. After the day's trick with the cheese wire, elbow-deep in a cow, perhaps nothing can faze him. Sebastian Mellor does not match the image of the man elected four years ago. The usual degradation in office has occurred. His hair is thinner, greyer; the stress of the job has taken its toll. He holds a hand up, greets the room.

Don't let me interrupt your delicious dinner, he says.

As he passes by, Mellor shakes hands with Vaughan Andrews, though there seems to be no overflowing warmth between the party members. There's an extra setting at the table, ready. The Prime Minister sits, a waiter politely confers with him, and he is brought a glistening pear. Rachel overhears talk of schedules, cloud cover, and visibility, night flying regulations. Polite laughter bubbles around the man. There is no vast charisma, but his presence is certainly felt; she can see people fidgeting and glancing, or trying not to. Everyone except Sylvia, that is, who is captivating her neighbour, attending to the task without pause. Clever girl, Rachel thinks. Mellor eats the dessert quickly, spooning the sauce while holding back his tie. He makes a joke about getting to Scotland for last orders, apologises, stands. The visitation has taken no longer than twenty minutes.

Before departure, Thomas Pennington shepherds him towards Rachel and she is introduced. She stands again. She does not know what the correct protocol is, what term to use. The moment passes in a haze; she says very little. *Hello. Hello. Wonderful project – very in keeping with our countryside-pride initiative.* His manner is inoffensive, bland almost; he is one of several beige Etonians at the top of the league. But his privileges are wealth-related rather than dynastic, and he knows how to meet and greet. He excuses himself. *Charles will be getting annoyed with me.* The pilot, perhaps, or the security detail. He leaves.

Conversation resumes, in a slightly giddy way, but the party is somehow lesser. After a few moments the helicopter starts, attaining a frenzied pitch before lifting, a racket of impossible physics. A beam of light crosses the dining-room window, followed by two tail lights. The valley echoes noisily as the Prime Minister makes his way north, into the lion's den. In the aftermath, their host stands to lead a toast.

Ladies and gentlemen, if you would raise your glasses please. To the grey wolf. May she come home after long years away. May she find a good home. To the grey.

The room choruses.

The grey.

Rachel drinks with everyone, though the ceremonial rituals seem a little unnecessary – silly, even. Here is the operating room, she thinks, the old quarters where men of power do business and break bread together. If she ever doubted Thomas Pennington's credentials, his ability to get what he wants, she no longer does. The thought is not entirely reassuring. They adjourn to a plush sitting room with enormous settees. Coffee arrives, brandy, exquisite filigree chocolates, stamped with the Pennington coat of arms. She still feels a little sick, in need of air, and decides to leave – she has done her duty enough. After a brief interval she finds Alexander and bids him goodnight. He is also preparing to go, seems sober, though there is an empty brandy glass next to him and he was never without wine at dinner. He will be up at 5 a.m., he tells her, the usual time.

You've got my number, but come by the surgery, he suggests. You can get me up to speed on everything.

He seems entirely and commendably up to speed, but she agrees she will come. She is glad to have a good ally for the project already. She thanks Thomas Pennington and Sylvia for the evening, which was, in the end, enjoyable. Thomas is redder of face, gently listing and faintly victorious, but Sylvia is as kempt and composed as when the evening began. She stewards her father as a chancellor might, or the first lady. A woman who understands abstinence, how to retain control; Rachel is impressed.

I won't chase you or Daddy, Sylvia says, but I am so madly keen to help. Do bear me in mind.

Yes, I can tell. I'm sure it'll work out. Goodnight.

There's probably no harm in a month or two's work, if she really wants it, Rachel thinks. She is given her coat, shown to the door, and she sets off across the private grounds, trying to remember the entryway to the path through the woods, wondering whether she will trip an alarm system and suddenly be surrounded by police and dogs. A torch would have been sensible. The darkness is punctuated by constellations, gleaming less brightly than above Chief Joseph, but as graceful, as old and absolute, and there is light enough. She collects her boots from underneath the topiary and laces them up. The rich dinner is sitting uncomfortably in her. Bending over makes the sickness worse. Bending, brushing her teeth, even coffee is beginning to affect her in such a way. She finds a ginger sweet in her pocket, unwraps it. The sooner the matter is resolved, the better. Her appointment at the GP is in two days. The air is clear, silvery, and as she walks back to the cottage through the mantle of faint godless starlight, she starts to feel better.

*

The health centre is new, located behind a housing development on the edge of town. She arrives early, parks outside, and sits for a moment, listening to the news on the radio. Dyspeptic voices report on the debates and clips of the more heated exchanges are played. The First Minister is goaded, accused of being racist, an economic dunce, but he maintains optimism. Scotland was, is, and will be a beacon of social enlightenment. He quotes one of the country's premier writers: work *as if in the early days of a better nation*. Optimism is all well and good but will not keep the lights on, the Prime Minister retorts. Mellor's Home Counties accent does him no favours, Vaughan Andrews was right; he sounds patronising. Better to have put forward a pro-union Scot. It is strange to think that less than forty-eight hours ago the man was shaking her hand; that she was, momentarily, inside the circle. The lights in England might soon depend on Scotland's hydroelectric power and oil, First Minister Douglas counters, unless extortionate business with Russia and the Middle East is preferable. The bulletin ends. The weather forecast predicts rain, spreading from the west, heavy at times. She switches the radio off and goes into the surgery.

The receptionist is talking on the phone and waves Rachel towards the monitor. She checks herself in on the touch screen and sits in the waiting area. She selects a magazine, scans the pages, then closes it. Ten minutes pass. She is the first appointment of the day but already there seems to be some kind of delay – early-morning emergencies being fitted in, no doubt. Heart attacks, farming injuries. She looks at the posters, for cancers of all kinds, and sexual health; signs warning that appointments are twelve minutes only, multiple problems require double bookings. She begins drafting an email to Lawrence on her phone. *Perhaps we could meet and talk* . . . The coward's method of reconciliation. She deletes it.

A doctor appears in the waiting room and calls her through. She is middle-aged, tired-looking. She starts back down the corridor, at an extremely brisk pace, and Rachel follows. The doctor glances over her shoulder and introduces herself.

I'm Frances Dunning. How are you today?

OK, thanks.

Good.

An odd question, given the circumstances. Inside the office Rachel explains that she is pregnant. She knows the conception date. She has taken a test, knows how many weeks. It is the first time she has said this out loud and it does not seem quite real.

I have a urine sample. Do you need it?

No. That's OK, I trust you.

The doctor looks over her records.

I don't have any old notes for you.

I just moved back to the UK.

How are you feeling generally?

Alright. A bit sick. I'd like to talk about the options.

The doctor glances up at Rachel and then out of the surgery window at the playing fields beyond. A grey ceiling of cloud has begun to form: the promised rain. She asks Rachel the date of her last period and then calculates on the ob wheel.

Yes, you're right. Twelve weeks or thereabouts. So we need to think reasonably quickly about everything.

The pregnancy was unplanned. I meant to sort it all out sooner.

Is this your first?

Yes.

Frances Dunning turns in her seat and faces Rachel fully. She has shadows under her eyes. A weekend locum, perhaps.

Might I ask why you delayed a termination?

I just moved back from America. It's a bit complicated. The state where I was living brought in a new mandate – you have to have an ultrasound before having an abortion. The clinics are mostly pro-life.

Oh, yes, right – tricky. Are you decided?

Rachel moves uncomfortably in her chair. This is the question. The answer should be simple and easy, and yet.

I think so. I don't think I want to have it. I'm not . . . a hundred percent sure.

Not sure you want it, or not sure you don't want it?

Both. I don't know.

Doctor Dunning nods.

Well, there's a little time. A termination procedure is slightly more complicated after fifteen weeks – it's not a straightforward evacuation. You'd probably have to go down to Lancaster. Would you like to speak to someone about everything?

Rachel shrugs.

I'm speaking to you.

Would you like to speak to a counsellor?

No.

The doctor nods again. Her shirt is a bright, ugly green – distracting. Between the two prescriptive lenses of her bifocals it is hard to see her eyes properly. She is probably the same age as Rachel. There's a silver framed photograph on the doctor's desk, of a girl and a boy, perhaps eight and ten years old. Planned, no doubt, to fit with her life. Rachel moves in her chair again, begins to feel foolish. What are you doing? she thinks.

Doctor Dunning prompts gently.

Are you in a position where you might want a child?

Rachel does not reply. She doesn't want a baby. She has never wanted a baby. A baby would be ridiculous. But how can she describe the feeling? The strange interest in it all, now that the situation pertains to her specifically. The mercurial days: fatal mornings when she is sure she wants rid of it, nights when the certainty evaporates. It's as if some rhythm – circadian, immune, hormonal, she does not know which exactly – waxes and wanes and, with it, her rational mind. How can this be explained to the doctor?

I just didn't think it would happen, she blurts. I'm not young.

Frances Dunning shakes her head, smiles very subtly.

You seem very healthy. And the commonly used data on fertility rates is a little past its sell-by, I'm afraid.

It was one night, Rachel says. I don't have relationships. Just sex. I'm usually more careful when I – I wasn't expecting this—

Doctor Dunning leans forward slightly and tilts her head. The confession, this new information, is clearly worrisome.

How many partners have you had in the last year, would you say?

Five, maybe. Six.

Last sexual health check?

A couple of years ago.

OK. We can discuss the pregnancy options again when you've thought a little more, but shall we do a few tests now? Just to be on the safe side.

Yes, alright.

I'll buzz for the nurse.

She presses an intercom and they wait.

I know none of this is ideal, Rachel says, almost apologetically.

She feels annoyed with herself, and like an undergraduate. The doctor turns to face her again.

Well, it's true. Children are life-altering. You're right to think it all through.

Her hands are held close together, turned slightly outward and upward, as if holding something – an imaginary baby, perhaps.

If the pregnancy continues, she says, we'd need to think about booking you in with the midwife, and a first scan around now. And possible screening. But I'm not going to push you. You're on our system, which is good.

There's a knock on the door and a uniformed nurse enters the room, carrying sterile swabs. They move into the curtained section. Rachel strips below the waist and lies down on the paper-covered table. The lamp is repositioned. The speculum inserted, swabs taken. It is a brief, inoffensive examination. The nurse hands her tissues and leaves. She re-dresses. Doctor Dunning is typing up notes on the computer. Rachel sits and waits for her to finish.

I'll get those sent off, she says. The results will take about a week. But why don't I call you in a few days, if that's convenient? Where do you work – can I reach you there?

The Annerdale estate, and yes.

Lovely.

I'm managing the reintroduction project.

Oh, the wolves. I read something in the *Gazette* about that. It's all going ahead then?

It is.

Will it be open to the public? My kids would love to go.

Possibly, once they're settled. Though it'll be more a programme than a park.

Rachel feels slightly redeemed; she is not a complete mess, not without professional skills, she would like that known by the woman sitting opposite. The doctor glances discreetly at the clock on her desk. She would probably like to continue the conversation, the subject is unusual, but she is running behind. Twelve minutes have passed.

OK, Rachel. Have a think. Here are some leaflets, with advice lines, just in case.

She hands Rachel a sheaf of pamphlets.

We'll speak in a few days?

Yes. Thanks.

Rachel stands. If she had anticipated resolution, here and now, backed into a moral or medical corner, it has not occurred. If anything, the meeting has left her feeling more confused. Frances Dunning moves to the door and opens it courteously.

These decisions are not easy. Best of luck. By the way, where are the wolves coming from? The paper didn't say.

Eastern Europe. They arrive next month.

Goodness me! That's amazing. Probably no need to ask, but you are up to date with your rabies vaccinations?

Rachel smiles and nods.

Yes, the doctor says. Of course you are.

In the car she sits and tries to think it all through, logically, while rain drums on the roof of the Saab and patients limp in and out of the surgery, closing and opening the blades of umbrellas, clutching paper pharmacy bags. She cannot imagine a baby, certainly not in relation to herself as its mother. She has barely ever held one, let alone changed a nappy. But here she is, delaying, ruminating, caught between states. Shouldn't she know what she wants: what to do and how to do it?

She starts the car, puts it in reverse, and pulls out of the bay. She thinks of Moll and Tungsten, all the past animals she has worked with. They know. Or some part of their system knows and there is no thought. Year after year, she's witnessed the behaviour of the reproductive females, in their oestrus periods, the sequences and solicitation, prancing, rolling on their backs. Even the naïve ones understand how to act when the time comes. Instinct activates, makes them turn their tails to the side, help the males mount them. Parenting is intuited. The loss of belly hair. How to nibble away the thin membrane surrounding the newborn pups. They have no choice.

What use are higher faculties now, Rachel thinks, as she indicates and pulls out onto the road. Cognition and invention, the internal combustion engine, intermittent wipers, peace treaties and poetry, the Homo Sapiens' thumb and tongue? Is optionality really evolutionary ascent when it leads to paralysis? She switches the wiper blades to full, and steers through the hard rain, back to the estate.

*

At first her brother will not even consider meeting without his wife present, like some kind of despotic moderator. Rachel holds the phone to her ear, listening to the silence. At any moment she expects him to hang up or for the despot herself to come on the line and ring-fence Lawrence. Her main offence of the last few months, it seems, has been to offend Emily.

Emily thinks you're going to cause trouble, Lawrence finally says. She hasn't forgiven you for the funeral. It was incredibly difficult, Rachel, doing it all without you.

Be calm, she thinks. Be calm, be reasonable, stay neutral. Don't fail at the first move.

I wasn't invited, she says, keeping her voice even. And it was made very clear to me during our last conversation that I shouldn't come.

Lawrence becomes slightly petulant, his voice wavers.

It was a hard time for everyone. But you could have come anyway. She was our mother.

Yes, Lawrence, she was *our* mother.

Possession, inference, the terrible shared knowledge of Binny. There's another long pause in what is already a deeply punctured conversation.

Emily knows all about the past, Lawrence says, I've told her. She always made an effort with Mum.

She does not know everything, Rachel thinks. Whatever power imbalance or *folie à deux* exists between her brother and his wife, she is certain Emily has little more than the basic facts about life with Binny at her disposal. Her brother's naïvety is staggering. She wills herself not to point out the obvious: that it was an unpassable test to set, coming to the funeral against the wishes of her sister-in-law. That the death of their mother is, at the end of the day, none of Emily's business. But the call is intended as placatory. The truth is, she does not like the idea of losing her brother, much as she has been telling herself that she could live with it. And for her brother's sake, they should fix what needs fixing. He does not have the disposition for war; she can hear the upset in his voice. Better to subtly out-flank the wife.

Lawrence? Are you there?

She can hear murmuring in the background on the other end of the line, the occasional muffled outburst. Emily is monitoring Lawrence's side of the conversation. *Tell her to . . . If she wants to . . . Why doesn't she . . . over here.* Rachel can picture the scenario: her brother's hand covering the mouthpiece, him trying to find some private space to talk. The small blonde woman flapping her hands spastically beside him, furious at being left out. Nor can her brother see what is really going on — women fighting with each other through him. Though raised in a house of its mastery, he seems blind to female psychology: the competitive undercurrents, the desire for control. In his mind the problem is likely to be due to the stress of the tragedy, the old Binny-Rachel conflict, and Emily's *concern* — dynamics he understands or would like to imagine.

Just a minute, Rachel.

Lawrence says something to his wife. His tone is gentle, but firm. Caught between hard places. Emily has had months, years, to dig her trenches. But, influential though she may be, Rachel knows her own position is strong, perhaps the strongest. She has historic authority, simply from being the older sibling in a family where dysfunction reigned. She was neither soft-hearted nor patient as a sister, but she still held his hand all those times, opened tins of mince for dinner, got him to school and back. And there is rare status in being prodigal; it creates a void, a longing even. Lawrence wants a stable family. He needs Rachel, and always has.

Lawrence, she says. Are you there?

Yes, I'm here. Just one minute. Sorry.

There's another muted outburst: *Don't apologise to her . . .* She does not envy her brother's position. He's a decent man, and tries hard. He has always hated mutability and mess, ever since he was small. A boy does not flee from a bohemian household without the desperate ambition to be proper, and act properly. He does not go on to become a solicitor, to marry, to pay for IVF and care homes without some kind of moral drive. Rachel hears a door shut.

OK. Sorry. Two conversations at once. Go on.

Look, she says. Binny and I didn't get along, granted, but that has nothing to do with you and I and we shouldn't let it muddy the water. I just think we should meet and talk. Start from scratch.

Her tone is level, calm, exactly as if she were talking to volunteers, instructing them on sedation, how to inject or take a sample, inserting the syringe into the big muscles of the hindquarters. *Be confident, you are in charge.* First law of an argument: those who remain reasonable will make others seem unreasonable.

My feeling is no one else can fix things for us, she continues. You and I need to address the problem ourselves. You said as much last time we spoke. I've thought about that and I agree.

The tactics are manipulative. An agreeable-seeming sister repeating back to him his own idea. He sighs. He is thinking now, about what *he* thinks, what *he* wants. Emily is clever, Rachel knows, but she plays a negativist game, which is easy to undercut.

I'm glad you phoned, Rachel, he says. Because I do think we should try. I'd like to see you.

Great. How about the Saturday after next? We could go for a walk. We could meet halfway between here and there?

No, that's OK. I'll come up to you. I haven't been back since the funeral. We can get a proper walk – maybe Blencathra?

Sure, if you can get up here in time.

I'll leave early. I'll get breakfast on the way.

Which will not make Emily happy at all, Rachel thinks. For a moment she feels vindicated, a petty triumph. But it was easy and perhaps unfair. Her brother loves the Fells; he is a nostalgic Cumbrian exile, rank and file. It does not take much to lure him home. His voice has altered; he sounds pleased, excited even. He would probably not admit it, not even to himself, but the idea of being untethered from Emily for a day must be heady.

OK, shall we say the White Horse car park, at eight-thirty, nine?

OK. See you there. Hey. Email me your new address.

I will. Bye for now.

Bye, Rachel. Look forward to seeing you.

They hang up. She feels better. She might have invited him to the estate, but she is not ready to bring him in that close, not yet. Small steps. She makes coffee, takes it out into the garden, and sits on the wooden bench under the quince tree. Yes, she does feel better. Deep down, the thought of estrangement from her brother has been worrying her. And the idea of failing him has always bothered her. Lawrence. *Little man*, the house visitors all used to call him. How he hated not being big enough to take them on. He never understood Binny, why she favoured the ones she did; he could not get past the visceral dislike of their presence in the small cottage: the sudden forced intimacies, strangers coming shirtless from the bathroom, kissing his mother's neck, looking at her rump or chest, some kind of hunger in them like starved farm dogs. *What's up, little man?* Shoving past them to get out, his face aflame. *Don't get your trousers in a twist. If I were your father, I'd soon teach you some manners.* The agonies in his face. His whacking of sticks against the porch roof and the tyres of their cars. Always talking about his friends who did have fathers: fathers who liked them, fathers who lived in the same house, who stayed. Always looking at Rachel as if she could explain, as if she could get him out of a fatherless world.

She'd collect him from school and walk him home along the river. Every rabbit warren and culvert and pile of leaves delayed their return. *Will Jonno be gone when we get back? Will Derrick have finished mending the car?* She'd let him linger, prodding dead birds and dumped badgers; she'd watch him from a distance. *Will there be anyone home except Mum? I don't know, maybe.* He was pitiful, that's how she'd felt then. Stupid. Only when he was a teenager and some girl showed him, or some friend revealed the details, did everything become clear. The atrocity of what they'd all been doing to his mother. The fact that she was complicit. Two years later he left home.

Rachel sips the coffee. It tastes too acidic. She needs to call the surgery back – the doctor has rung twice and left messages. Instead, she sits and watches the sky. The day and the weather feel split, still and mild at ground level, but the clouds above are moving fast and dark on currents of strong air. Her phone pings. She opens a text from Stephan Dalakis. A picture of the male, as promised, running in the enclosure. Since being found in the illegal trap in North Moravia by the Hnuti Olomouc patrol and the subsequent leg surgery, he has made a full recovery. He is pale, with almost white fur, perhaps three years old. She texts back. *Magnificent.*

Her thoughts drift back to Lawrence. They'll walk; try to get along, build some bridges. Either something will take, or it won't: these things can't be forced. Emily will have to be dealt with later. Rachel and her brother have spent so little time together as adults, but maybe they'll have more in common than she thinks. With Binny mediating affairs, nothing was ever straightforward. With their mother gone, perhaps there's a chance. The only way forward is to try. After another bitter sip, her throat stinging, she tips the coffee out onto the grass.

*

All week, rain. Big splashing drops on every surface like a child's illustration of rain. Blue vanishing light and winds from nowhere, bringing slant, destructive showers, or fine drizzle. At night there is rain that exists only as sound on the cottage roof, leaving doused grass in the morning and pools in the rutted lane. The streams and rivers on the estate swell. Spawn clings to submerged rocks and reeds as the current tugs. The lake accepts the extra volume indifferently. And then, when it seems the rain will never end, there's an explosion of sunshine, the startling heat of it through the cool spring air. Within days a green wildness takes over Annerdale. Dandelions come up, early meadow flowers; the moorland ripens, sphagnum, cotton grass, the white filament heads turning in the breeze. Rachel settles in. The fire in the cottage draws well, the place is cosy. A delivery van comes to the estate every few days with food – all she needs to do is supply an order. She hangs the Kwakwaka'wakw wolf carving over the mantelpiece. Her practical life seems simple. She gets into the habit of leaving the front door unlocked – it is a safe corner of the estate, and there have been no more lurking visitors. There's less to secure than at Chief Joseph – no bear-proof lids on the bins, no summer mosquito plugs.

The surgery calls again. She arranges to have the scan and combined screening. It is not deferment exactly, not a decision. She does not know what it means. She tries to hold it all loosely in her mind, tells herself she can still go back, undo it. Things begin to come together on the project. The importation paperwork is completed, freight flights confirmed. She interviews candidates for the position of full-time assistant. Eleven in total, after a ruthless CV cull. The interviews are held in a room at Abbot Museum in Kendal – Thomas Pennington is chairman and sponsor there, naturally, and it is not far from Oxenholme station. The job goes to an earnest – and, she suspects, Buddhist – South African, who has cut his teeth in the game parks of KwaZulu-Natal, worked with jackals and other predators. A PhD in the UK, time in India. His credentials are excellent, an expansive mind, calm-natured. He arrives at the museum on a bicycle, which seems fitting. Twenty-four hours later he is invited to take up residency at the estate. She agrees to let Sylvia work on the project. The girl will have to muck in, get used to the order of things. She will have access to the quarantine pen, will be inoculated; she will be fully one of the team.

Rachel walks the estate, gets to know its broad rises, the woods, the lake circumference. The distance to the Horse and Farrier and the village Co-op is not far. She carries a stash of granola bars, and a plastic sick-bag when she drives, though she doesn't need to use the bag. She thinks about calling Kyle, but doesn't. It is better to give herself some distance, never mind the blossoming sense of guilt.

A few days later she is summoned again to Pennington Hall to be introduced to staff members. Among them is the gamekeeper, Michael Stott – the man, she is fairly sure, who was watching the cottage the day of her arrival. His frame and gait are familiar – the tipped shoulder, the rightful stride. He is lean, with carved cheeks and a sore mouth, hair so full and dark it seems false, given his age; he must be pushing seventy. His trousers look as if they've been made from tar. There is an immediate hostile crackle between them. He does not meet her eyes when she says hello, and the handshake is cursory, patronisingly soft. Within minutes, everything becomes clear, and she has the measure of him. *Louveterie.*

Much to our relief, Michael's decided to stay on, Thomas says, standing between the two of them. He's been here a very long time. His father worked with my father. He knows the country here like the back of his hand, don't you, Michael.

Worked with not *for*, she notices. The modern sensitivities of class. Michael Stott sniffs and nods and says nothing. Behind the Earl's statement is the question of whether and why he might have left. He does not look the type to retire – ever. A mutineer, then, who does not approve of the radical new project. And why would he, if he is the herdsman?

I'll leave you two to get acquainted, Thomas says. Michael will be able to assist you with anything you need, Rachel.

He closes the door behind him, leaving the two of them alone. She'll be damned if she'll make small talk. No doubt Michael will want to stake his claim, assert his authority. Sure enough, after a moment he clears his throat, and offers her some advice.

Now then, Mrs Caine. You might want to park the car round the back of Seldom Seen. It's hard getting anything through with it left so casual.

She doesn't bother to correct his mistake. But she won't have him think she's town-bred and insensible.

I intend to. Once the ground's dried out a little – don't want to get stuck, Mr Stott, and have to be towed. That would waste everyone's time.

Right. When is it your pups get here, then?

Pups. She holds his gaze.

Two weeks.

Michael takes a leather tobacco pouch from his inside pocket, removes but does not light a pre-rolled cigarette. He is house-broken, she can see, enough to shake her hand in front of the master and abide by the rules of the house. But it is clear that he is not happy. Not happy about being displaced in the chain of command, for she now holds a lateral position, perhaps even a higher position. Certainly not happy about the reconstitution of Annerdale, with its new apex predator. She, and they, represents dire competition, beyond his experience. The beloved deer, previously targets for the noble shotgun, are to become glorified dog food. Over the years her sensibilities have been honed. Michael is a king's soldier: good at tradition and old orders. If he'd lived twelve centuries earlier, he'd have made substantial money for their pelts from Charlemagne.

She looks at his hair – real, unnatural, something oddly lusty about it. Good genes. They will have to find a way to work together.

We should talk about the health of the herds, she suggests. Next week suit you, Mr Stott?

Fine.

They do not fix a specific time or date.

The next day she sets up the office in the carriage house and for the following two days she answers letters and emails from locals, tries to educate and placate. There is more livestock in the east and north of the region; the correspondence is mostly from paranoid west Lakeland smallholders foreseeing escape and slaughter on an almost gothic scale. Concerned mothers. Photographs taken by French shepherds of bloody-necked flocks are forwarded to her. *We do not want this type of thing in our country.* She sends back links to EU collaboration projects. There are queries about compensation – how much will the estate offer per head for a kill if they get out? Despite the campaign the estate has tried to run, there is much ignorance and fear, much education needed. To each reply she attaches the project's mission statement and an information sheet.

The opposition groups are more troubling. The Ramblers. The Farmers' Union. They are organised and have funds. Towards the end of the second day, she opens a garbled email from a person or entity simply called 'Nigh', accusing the estate of a variety of sins, cruelty and corruption, satanic tendencies, and playing God. There's a Virgil quote: *Here we care as little for the cold north wind, as the wolf cares for the number of sheep in the flock.* What does it mean? She smiles. If Kyle were here he would enjoy such a missive. *Batshit crazy*, he would say. *Delete.* For a moment she feels sad – not sad but wistful. Kyle. He was a good friend. She saves the email in a folder entitled 'Cranks'. There has been no correspondence from any animal rights activists. The silence is not comforting, and does not necessarily mean inactivity. The project is in every way humane, but it will be on the radar.

The following morning, perhaps in response to her send-outs, there's a small protest at the main gate of the estate, next to the CCTV camera. She receives a call from Honor Clark alerting her.

No need to come down. It's all under control.

You're sure? Rachel asks. I can come. I don't mind.

Absolutely. It's all under control.

She goes about her business, meets with Alexander at the local veterinary clinic. The waiting room has several people in it, but he invites her in, past the Gorgonian receptionist, makes them coffee, which she struggles to finish. He seems ill-suited to the environment of the clinic. He is wearing glasses rather than contact lenses, but the scholarly look seems imposed on his large head. They discuss keeping antibiotic prescriptions on site at Pennington Hall and the forthcoming implantation surgery. The telemetry equipment has been ordered from Arizona – a company she knows and trusts. Alexander is skilled, has performed a similar procedure a few times before, pit-tags, though not on a large canine.

Will it go in the abdomen? he asks.

Yes. A benign spot, but pretty deep. It can't just slip under the skin or they'll chew it out.

They bring up a picture of the device on his computer. The implant is state of the art – three inches long, including the transmitter and antenna, housed in a plastic sleeve and coated in physiological wax.

It'll wall off in the body, she says. The radio signals are very good. And we'll get other data – temperature, activity levels, heart rate, that kind of thing.

That's bloody cool, he says. And they just get on with it?

They do. I've seen great results. It doesn't impair hunting or effect breeding. We'll have to do it in the quarantine pen – are you OK with that?

Yeah, fine. Not sure Sally could cope with them in reception anyway.

Leaning close over the screen, he smells of deodorant and sweat. He reminds her of the boys in school years ago, blunt, funny, without deliberate romantic charm, but somehow possessing it.

Afterwards, she goes to the shops, then returns to the estate. As she passes the main gate, the gathering seems to have dispersed. But that evening her attention is caught by a piece on the regional news. . . . *The now-turned Willy Wonka of Wolves, who is no stranger to controversy* . . . She turns the television up. A local news crew has filmed the protest. There's a group of about twenty or so: a parked miscellany of walkers, agriculturalists, and upset housewives. A spokesperson lists their grievances to the reporter. The fence's impact on the landscape, newts, bird-life, the view. The reintroduction of a now unnatural species. The restriction of public access to the estate. As the spokesperson is interviewed, the estate gate opens and Thomas Pennington strides down the driveway, looking – as Rachel has not yet seen him look – every inch like landed gentry. The camera focuses in. Top to toe tweed, a flaneur's casual step. A cane! Oh Christ, she thinks, this cannot end well. He arrives and greets the crowd. The reporter's tone becomes slightly hysterical as he conducts the interview. The wilder charges are put to the Earl: that keeping live prey inside a closed unit with predators is cruel, that the game enclosure bill was passed due to bribery. All are refuted, gracefully. Wolves hunt deer, he says, it's simple evolution. And in this age of transparency and freedom of information, all bills are open to public scrutiny. A woman in the crowd calls out. *You're a danger to society. They kill people!* Thomas Pennington turns to her. *My dear lady, these creatures are no harm to you or I. You could leave a baby in a pram in the enclosure and it would be quite safe, quite safe.* Rachel groans. There's a swell of indignant noise from the protesters at such a suggestion. *A baby!* The scene looks like a pantomime. The publicity is terrible, and Thomas Pennington, she realises, is a liability. The reporter summarises to camera. Thomas bows his head slightly – *thank you for coming* – as if they had all been attending a tea party. He turns and walks back up the oak-lined driveway. The report cuts to his biography, sweeping aerial shots of the estate and old photographic footage of the microlight crash – the tangled frame, shorn of both its wings, a black patch on the ground where the contraption burnt. The insinuation – that the Earl's projects fail spectacularly. The next report begins.

Rachel switches off the television, goes to the phone, and dials the estate office, hoping to speak with Honor, hoping Honor might somehow be enlisted – as a blockade, if nothing else. The recorded message plays. She hangs up. She has Thomas' mobile number, but is hesitant to use it. She will have to address the matter, though. He is too recognisable, too rich, and there are too many scandalous associations where he is concerned.

*

They begin from the roadside, passing over a stile in the wall, and walk through a field of green lacy ferns, up the steep east-facing skirt of the mountain. In the car park of The White Horse, a discussion about whether to tackle Sharp Edge has taken place, which, after a consultation with Lawrence's weather app, they decide against. Rain will make the ridge more difficult. There are flocks of grey clouds along the horizon and the breeze is strong, even at ground level. Looking up, they can see snow still locked away in the dark crevasses.

She is feeling well, not too tired or sick, but soon there are twinges in her knees and ankles. Her breath thickens and her thighs ache. Even after hiking the rough cross-country terrain of the Pacific Northwest, the relentless gradient of Blencathra catches her out. She wonders if she will make it. The ferns give way to short, wiry tufts of grass and heather, a mile-long moorland slope that turns and steepens, turns and steepens. The body of the mountain falls steeply from the sky. She paces herself, fights for air. But Lawrence suffers more. He pauses with his hands on his hips, leans back, his face reddening and beading with sweat. He looks very unwell. His equipment is state of the art – breathable, waterproof shells, gloves, boots. She'd imagined not being able to keep up with her younger brother, but in the end it is she who leads. Perhaps he has a hangover, she thinks, or the life of a city solicitor has left him out of shape. They do not talk much – talking is impossible on the gradient. For a while they move in the shadow of a colossal leaden cloud, rain spitting against their foreheads, a smattering of hail, then there is brilliant sunlight. They remove their coats, squint up the path of the blazing Fell. Lawrence takes a pair of wraparound sunglasses out of his bag.

Four seasons in a day, he says.

Looks like it.

Their conversation is polite, careful. Rachel tactfully asks after Emily. She is well, says Lawrence, though she is having more IVF treatment, which is uncomfortable and stressful. Rachel nods – Binny had mentioned this during the visit, disparagingly, as if childlessness should be endured, as if it were a reprieve, even.

How many rounds will you try?

Her brother keeps his eyes on the path.

I don't know. We're having it done privately, so as many as we can afford, I suppose. The whole thing is quite fraught.

Sorry to hear that.

For a few moments they fall back into silence. Underfoot are fragments of broken stone, swollen moss, and the first fissures of black upland peat.

And you? All OK your end?

Yes, great, she says.

Rachel cannot now say she is pregnant, even if she had wanted to confide in her brother. It would be like one-upmanship. Day to day, she continues to ignore the fact of her condition, though the reminders are perverse: sudden nausea brought on by motion, types of food, even some words, *Syllabub*, *Gannet*, as if the sound, the very texture were too visceral. And deathly sleep. She sleeps as if drugged. What would Lawrence's reaction be, anyway? Not delight, surely, nor sympathy for her confusion. Her situation implies a careless imbalance to the universe. He and Emily have been trying for years. And Rachel – one reckless, drunken night. No. She doesn't know her brother well enough to confess.

She sets off up the track again. Behind her, she can hear Lawrence's heavy boots making regular contact with the rock. After a time he stops moving.

Hey, he calls, look at that.

She turns, faces back the way they have come. The world has opened. Immense sky. Grey, heraldic clouds over the hills, and repeated horizons. Directly below, the A66 is a silver thread with toy cars. The mountain does not sit in isolation from its range, but is independent; its heavy arms plunge down and away. The lofty feeling is dizzying, breathtaking; she could almost jump and fly.

Wow. We really made some height. About halfway, do you think?

I think so. Shall we take a break and eat something. All I've had is a terrible pasty at Scotch Corner.

Sure.

They find a good spot to rest, a pulpit-like buttress of rock overlooking a tarn. Lawrence unpacks sandwiches. Brie, with some kind of rustic, gourmet pickle. Apples. Chocolate. They eat quickly.

Thank goodness you didn't bring any Kendal Mint Cake, she jokes.

No way. That stuff makes my teeth hurt, he says. You didn't

pine for it while you were away, then?

God, no.

You don't sound totally American. Mum always said you did.

Yeah, she really hated it if I said cookies or candy.

There are many things Binny disapproved of that she could mention – probably Lawrence has similar experiences – but Rachel stops short of criticism. It is enough to be in her brother's company, without spoiling the mood. Lawrence seems sensible and placid away from his wife. She watches him, sitting slightly below on the crag, re-wrapping a large chocolate bar, zipping it into an outer pocket of his rucksack, careful, tidy. His hair ruffles in the wind, parts at a white seam of scalp. There are tones of red in it. Binny never admitted who his father was, though Rachel remembers the man, who ran a stable and already had a family. Her brother has come into his looks. The cachexic, baleful boy has gone. His face is less startled and dismayed, though he is still haunted-looking.

How's work? she asks.

He turns towards her, leans back on an elbow.

Fine. We're busy. It's all construction law, there's so much in limbo at the moment. Everyone's run out of money and no one's getting paid. I won't bore you.

She shakes her head.

Not boring at all.

What about you? How's it all going? Is Pennington a total nutter?

Yeah, a bit. But he's the boss.

I suppose he can't be all bad if he's got you working for him. What exactly are you doing? It's not like a zoo, is it? Mum was a bit vague.

She tells him about the wolves, when they are coming, how they will be reintroduced.

You should come and see them, she says.

Can I? I'd love to.

He grins. He is disproportionately pleased at the offer. It is almost as if they are on a first date and she has just stated her intention to enter a relationship. He asks a few more questions about the project, taken by the exoticism of her job. The air rushes past them, a continually buffeting lyric. Now that she is not moving, the sweat on her neck and back begins to chill. She shivers.

Should we get going?

OK. Do you want a hat, Rachel? I've got a spare one.

Oh, no, thanks. Well, OK then.

He takes a fleece hat out of the rucksack and she puts it on. They continue upward, into the cold, fast-moving currents. The effort is double with the wind hoving against them. The latter part of the route is incredibly difficult, almost beyond her limit. Rachel's legs shake; the undersides of her toes burn. The dense sedge grass vibrates all around and blurs her vision. There are no birds, just the occasional ravaged-looking sheep, bleating uselessly in the wind. They push on, up and over a false brow. She can hear Lawrence breathing hard. Is he asthmatic? She can't remember. She looks back. He is leaning over, his hands on his knees. He spits.

Sorry!

Almost there, she calls. You alright? Want to stop?

I'm alright!

She waits for him to catch up.

I'm not properly designed for this, he says.

No, nor am I, she says. You know, a wolf's breathing mechanism is superb. The way the structure of their nose has evolved. They have an incredible ability to oxygenate.

Lawrence frowns. His face is purplish and his eyes are streaming. The wind hammers. They adjust their feet and lean slightly together. He puts his hands on her shoulders. There was no hello kiss in the pub car park; they did not embrace. They have not touched each other for years, perhaps not since childhood. He shakes her gently.

Lucky bloody wolf, he shouts.

On the final stretch there are annals of peat, sinkholes and bogs, and the thin path to the summit. The uppermost expanse is broad, a shattered tabletop. They aim for the cairn, which is made of heavy, storm-resistant stones. Skiddaw hulks to the east, bronze-tinted, the heather not yet blooming. The Langdale Pikes needle up to the south; Scotland drags the lowlands north. They take shelter in a walled pen near the cairn and hunker down, but the wind still infiltrates. Lawrence has warm tea in a thermos, possibly the most welcome thing Rachel has ever drunk in her life. He is squatting and smiling as he pours the liquid into a cup, his jacket hood pulled tight, his face barely visible.

We made it, Rachel! I didn't think we would!

Suddenly she feels moved. All those moments together when they were young and she felt nothing, an emotional deficit. She even used to think, once she'd learnt enough biology, that her programming meant she wasn't supposed to care for him – they had different genes. *Roll the other egg out of the nest and watch it smash below.* Her throat constricts. She wants to correct the error. Stupid to feel such things now, she thinks. She is strangely not herself: the power of hormones.

They stay at the cairn until the exposure becomes uncomfortable. There's another hail shower, after which they begin down. Rachel's legs are weak on the descent, lactic, buckling every few paces. Walkers coming up in breathless agony look enviously at them, bid them hello, stand aside on the path to let them pass. The mood is victorious, at ease.

Do you remember that Christmas, she asks, when the pylons came down?

Is that the year Mum tried to cook a goose?

Did she? I don't remember that!

There was goose fat everywhere.

Then, endorphin-silly or simply salutatory, they belt out a carol. *O come all ye faithful, joyful and triumphant.* The sheep, stuck on the outcrops, turn their heads away and bleat into the void.

Would they come up this high? Lawrence asks.

Sure.

Sure, he says, mimicking her. That's 'yes, definitely, my girl'.

She laughs at his impression of Binny, and is pleased he isn't sanctifying their mother.

Et tu, Brute.

They can travel much higher, she tells him, and they do. In the Ethiopian Highlands, Canada, Alaska. They can cross deserts and ice sheets; they live comfortably in any climate, gelid or desiccated, arboreal, tundra. While she talks, he looks at her with admiration, as if it is she who is capable of such feats. I'm not what you think, she wants to say, but she likes his interest in the work.

In the car park of The White Horse they decide against a drink, though the pub is a good one, the chimney is smoking and the waft of pastry baking, hops, and vinegar is inviting.

Long drive back to Leeds, Lawrence says. Emily wants to go out for dinner with friends tonight. Sorry.

A curfew of sorts, Rachel assumes. Penalty for the day's freedom.

But it was a really great walk, he says quickly. Thanks for asking.

Yeah, no. Thanks for coming.

They bid each other goodbye, semi-formal again.

See you soon.

Yeah. Bye, Lawrence.

For a moment he looks forlorn, as if everything – the day, its efforts and successes – will vanish the moment Rachel disappears from sight. As if he is standing at the front door of the post office cottage again and she is walking away. She wants to reassure him, but what is there to say? Already he is climbing into his car, reversing round and waving through the window. He is pulling onto the main road and accelerating. His car clears the brow of the hill and disappears.

On the way home, Rachel makes a detour. At Binny's graveside in the little cemetery near Willowbrook she stands for a few minutes. There are good reasons to have a termination. There are good reasons to carry on as she is, solo up the face, the way she has moved for years. But here, by the small white stone and recently seeded mound, where she had expected those reasons to overwhelm and finally make a decision, she feels no relief, no surety, only the awkwardness of hope.

THE WOLVES

The fence is twelve feet high, the limit of their ability to jump, sloping inward at the top, a forty-five-degree angle. There are no barbs and it is not electric. As she walks along the structure, Rachel can see that care has been taken not to build it too close to any existing elevations, trees, walls, or hummocks. They would certainly exploit it. She's seen them perform a running climb before, almost vertical, going after small prey, marsupials. In Yellowstone, one of the ranchers told a story about having seen one use the back of a bull elk as a springboard to take down another elk. There have been many such stories over the years. She thinks of Setterah Keep, the escape, which she does not remember. That fence was old, rusted, or perhaps it had not been sunk deep enough, perhaps one of them dug out. Underneath the Annerdale fence are reinforced foundations extending four feet into the earth. The construction is wolf-proof.

And incredibly impressive as it rises before her, reels of heavy-duty steel, green coated to lower the environmental impact. Six feet away, on the exterior, is a secondary barrier, to keep people back. Signs are fixed along it every third of a mile – like forts along a Roman wall – hazard triangles around a stylised and distinctive silhouette. It is not altogether a good message, but part of the project's inevitable red tape. She walks a section, through the barrows, up above the lake. She had expected something more industrial-looking – penal, even. But the estate runs close to and then into the national park; such a thing would not be permissible. At each of the entry points around the enclosure – eight in all – there are digital coded locks. Access will be limited: those working on the project and special permissions. Pennington Hall, her cottage, and most of the other estate buildings lie outside the fence. No doubt Thomas would have preferred to be inside, among them.

She leaves the fence and walks down towards the river. It is warm. She strips off her jacket and jumper. Underneath, the waist of her jeans is feeling tight; she is beginning to round out, though not noticeably. The river runs at leisure over grey tumbled boulders. In a clearing on the bank, between thistles and wild rhubarb, the new assistant has pitched his tent. There's a dark, scorched patch where he has had a fire, with turf stacked next to it. Between two bushes a laundry wire is strung; a T-shirt, socks, and boxers jig in the breeze. A mountain bike is propped up on its stand. It is early in the morning, but the tent zip is open.

Hello, she calls. Huib? Anyone home?

Huib pops his head outside and puts his thumb up.

Rachel. I'm coming out.

He emerges. He has on a pair of shorts that seem entirely made of pockets, and a flannel shirt. The skin on his legs, arms, and face is burnt a deep, sub-Saharan brown. A high, balding forehead, jug ears, warm sorrel eyes.

You picked a lovely spot, she says.

I know. It's good of Thomas to let me pitch. He said I could go anywhere I liked until the apartment is ready.

Thomas. Huib seems to have no problem with the informality, but it still sounds wrong to her, and she avoids using his first name wherever possible. She has watched them chatting casually down at the hall, discussing politics and current affairs with no awkwardness. Post-colonial confidence meeting reconstituted aristocracy.

Do you need anything? she asks. It's quite spartan down here.

No, I'm fine. I'm going to swim later; there's a really great place just upstream, with a kind of diving rock.

He is smiling and pointing with a thumb. He is only thirty years old, but the African sun has already lined his skin. His remaining hair is closely shaved, the same nut-colour as his scalp. Huib was an easy choice, and if anything over-qualified. A stint in Mozambique on the leopard restoration programme – one of the most competitive and desirable in the world, a trump card. But it was his temperament that had appealed. Through the window of Abbot Museum she'd watched him cycle into the car park, swinging one leg over the frame and running a long, single-pedalled dismount, stunt-like, teenager-ish. There was an air of casual immunity about him, though he had on a helmet. Before he rolled his trouser leg down, she saw an oily tattoo of the bike chain on his calf. It is in such moments that decisions are made. Perhaps he had reminded her a little of Kyle.

I caught some signal crayfish last night, he says. They're delicious! You just have to lift up the rocks slowly, then pinch them out.

I used to spend hours doing that as a kid, Rachel says. They were mostly white-claws then – the native ones.

Ja, he says, nodding. Terrible decline. I'm going to apply for a trap from the environment agency, if Thomas doesn't mind.

He won't mind, she says.

I found a website. I'll show you.

Huib squats, reaches back into the tent, and brings out a laptop. He holds it on the splayed fingertips of one hand and opens the lid.

Here we are.

He tilts the computer round.

How are you connected?

I've got this gizmo. It's a bit slow. I've been trying to Skype my brother in Jo'berg but his face is all fuzzy; it's like talking to Mr Potato Man.

She looks at the web page. It's good to have another wonk with whom she can discuss such things.

I've been wondering if they'll fish, she says. The river's full of trout.

That's exciting to think about. Trout are super-fast, though.

True.

How are they doing over there?

Great, apparently. They're in the same pen, being chummy.

Not long now. Do you need me to come to the office today to work on the press release?

No, that's OK. Just enjoy your days. Enjoy this.

She gestures at the river. The water trickles by, beautifully sounding out the rocks and shingle bed. Huib deposits the computer back inside the tent. She looks around at his supplies. He's well equipped. On the ground is a folded fishing rod, cooler, gas lamp, and a water filter. There are bags of rice and cans of lentils in a raised storage box. He has collected a stack of sticks for kindling and there's a roll of tarpaulin. A typical, self-sufficient field researcher. She wonders if he looks at pornography on the laptop after dark. Or reads Dostoyevsky. He re-emerges.

When's your apartment ready? she asks.

Next week. There's some kind of bat infestation issue at the minute. I like to camp, though. I used to go to Drakensburg all the time with my brother.

Which probably means he pitched on the ledges of the highest escarpment. She is aware that he is not contracted to start work for another week, and that while he is the type to give up his spare time for the job, as she is too, she should not outstay her welcome.

Well, she says, glad you're OK down here. Enjoy the swim.

Ja. See you later, Rachel. Congratulations, by the way.

She stares at him quizzically for a moment. He returns her gaze.

When are you due? If you don't mind my asking.

She is startled, and for a moment thinks about lying.

Not for a while.

That's exciting, he says.

I haven't really told anyone yet.

OK, he says, no problem. See you later.

See you.

She walks up the slope towards the fence. She looks down at her midriff. The development is definitely not noticeable, not to anyone but her. Either she has given something away or Huib is unnaturally prescient. Soon, though, the powers of divination will not be necessary – she will be showing. And she will have to be ready with the news, know what to say to people, how to frame it. Halfway up the hill she looks back, but Huib is out of sight, either back inside the tent perusing crayfish traps, or perhaps upstream, standing on the diving rock, about to cast himself into the cold blue Lakeland water.

*

At the antenatal clinic she sips a bottle of water and waits for her name to be called. There are two other women also waiting, one young and bored-looking, with a spotty partner in tow, one alone with a toddler, slightly haggard. The child smashes a toy tractor against the wall, makes a rumbling sound, and drives it along the skirting board. A video screen plays on a loop, instructions on breastfeeding, latching, angles, and advertisements for push-chairs. The situation feels unreal – she does not belong among the expecting and the mothers of the world – yet here she is. She has been given a thick maternity pack from the midwife at the GP's surgery, and has leafed through. Forms, codes, labels. The whole thing seems very bureaucratic. Her bladder is full; she needs the toilet but is not allowed to relieve herself. Nothing about the situation is comfortable. After a few minutes she is called into the ultrasound room. The sonographer checks her name and date of birth and asks her to lie down on the paper-covered table.

First time?

Yes.

Anyone with you?

No.

OK, the woman says. No need to get undressed. If you want to just lower everything, that's fine.

Rachel undoes her jeans, pushes them down, lifts her shirt.

You're the first today so the gel will be a little cold – sorry.

The woman applies fluid to her lower abdomen. She swirls the transducer across the surface, spreading it out. Rachel looks at the ceiling, tries to relax, tries not to think about anything.

Sometimes it's a little slow to get a good look, the woman says. If I'm quiet, don't worry. We'll get our angle. If we don't, I might try an internal scan. OK?

Rachel nods. The woman talks as she works, her voice soft, without drama but not without enthusiasm. Her accent is French African. She alters the position of the device by fractions, expertly.

Here we go. Ovaries OK. And a baby.

There is a pause.

Everything in the right place. Good.

Rachel is not worried, but neither is she naïve. As Binny gleefully declared at the nursing home, she's almost forty. She knows the risks. There are things she wants to hear, about nuchal measurement and the nose bone. There will be a combined test – she is giving a blood sample down the hall after the scan and they will issue her with a percentage chance of abnormality. The device moves through the gel, conducts its revelatory business. She looks at the ceiling, at the walls, anywhere but the screen.

You're nice and calm, the sonographer says.

Am I?

Not a fretter.

No.

Rachel watches the woman while she works. Her face is calm. Day in, day out, these expositions. She jiggles the transducer, to get the baby to move position, a practical action, like shaking out laundry before hanging it. Her manner is of one so used to reading signals that she might be on a ship's bridge or analysing meteorological data. Has the mystery of human reproduction become mundane, Rachel wonders, or is it that technology moves past all miracles eventually? In Alexander's veterinary clinic too there is a small hand-held ultrasound device that he uses for diagnosis and guided surgery. Rachel thinks of her own mother, who, in the seventies, proudly did not avail herself of any such information and took her chances, like millions of other women before her. Her bladder protests as the device moves lower, presses down harder.

Everything is good. Normal range. Baby is waving at us.

The sonographer changes angles subtly again, and takes measurements: crown of the head to the end of the spine. Limbs. Organs. The date of conception. She narrates the anatomical view – upper and lower jaw, hands, feet. Rachel is still not looking.

Do you want to see? the woman asks, reaching over and moving the screen slightly.

Rachel takes a deep breath, turns her head. At first it is like looking into deep space, or a snowstorm. There are indistinct contours, static cavities of darkness and light. The sonographer points everything out. Head, chest. Bones. The heart, flashing rapidly. And a face. A face.

She finds herself looking away again, feeling oddly shy, and amazed that she, at this moment, is creating something recognisably human. What would Binny say? She cannot imagine her mother here, now, though she remembers the vast expanse of stomach under her mother's coat before Lawrence was born and the long screaming ambulance ride. She can hear Binny's voice, haughty, patronising. *I knew what you both were; I didn't need to be told.* The sonographer lifts the device off Rachel's belly.

OK. I'm happy with that. I'll print pictures and leave them at reception. You can get tokens from the machine.

She rehouses the transducer and hands a wad of paper towels over. Rachel sits up, wipes the gel from her belly, and buttons her jeans.

Are you going for bloods?

Yes.

Down the hall, left and left again. Follow signs for Phlebotomy. The toilet is right outside.

She thanks the woman and goes into the bathroom next door. Then she navigates the hospital corridors to the blood station, takes a numbered ticket from a dispenser, and sits in another waiting area. Beside her are men and women of all ages, being tested, she assumes, for everything. Cancer. Anaemia. Diabetes. She looks down at the vein on the inside of her right arm, which is bluish-green and rises easily. She puts a hand on her stomach. A baby. With bones. And a face. The sonographer made it move, almost dance. She is called through, sits in a plump chair, and the vial is taken.

You look happy, the phlebotomist says.

Do I?

Yeah. Nice to have a smiler.

She makes her way back to the antenatal clinic with a pad of cotton wool taped in the crook of her elbow and collects her maternity notes.

There's minor confusion on the way out of the department. The receptionist comes towards her holding a small envelope containing a printed copy of the scan.

Miss Caine? You forgot this. There's a cash machine one level down if you don't have pound coins for the tokens. We can't take actual money.

I don't need a copy, Rachel says. Thanks anyway.

The woman scowls.

Are you sure? There's a cash machine downstairs.

Her tone borders on suspicious, as if Rachel is simply trying to get out of paying, or is somehow not understanding the system. Perhaps there is even some dereliction of motherhood going on. Not everything meaningful happens on camera, Rachel wants to say. Very little does.

That's OK. Really. I don't need a picture.

You'll want one, the receptionist tells her.

No, thanks.

In the end, irritated and sure that it is simply a ploy, the woman capitulates, thrusting the envelope into Rachel's hand, turning and stalking back towards her desk. Rachel looks at the picture, framed in a white paper mount. The skull is lit like a strange moon, eye sockets, nose, a chubby chest. She puts the picture in her bag.

Outside the hospital, the city of Lancaster glints in the rainy light. Slate roofs and windows refract, like a hundred lenses. There are dense, anvil-shaped clouds banking to the north. Another batch of rain is coming. She gets in the car, puts her bag on the passenger seat, and starts the engine, but she leaves it idling in neutral for a moment. She takes the envelope out of her bag and looks at the picture again – at the little being, mindless, its cells forming rapidly – which in some places would be used as evidence. She still does not know what she thinks about it all, though she feels herself smiling again.

*

By the end of the month they are fit to travel and everything is ready for their arrival. Rachel drives to the airport to meet the cargo flight. She breaks the journey overnight, stays in an industrial Travelodge. She cannot sleep. She checks the weather app on her phone. Sunny. 15 degrees. She is restless, not tired. A mania has arrived, a combined excitement. In her belly, when she lies flat, there is faint movement, or the boding of movement. Flutters. At 4 a.m. she turns the light on and tries to read but can't concentrate on her book. She looks at the list of contacts in her phone, thinks about calling Kyle; he will still be up. Should she now tell him? Shouldn't he know? For courtesy's sake, if nothing else? She switches the phone off and turns out the light.

In the morning the sky is mackerel-dappled and serene. She checks the airport website – there are no delays. She receives a text message from the transport company – Vargis – the driver has been dispatched and is on his way to the airport. She showers, dresses. She leaves the top button of her jeans undone.

The coffee in the breakfast room gives her heartburn as usual. At the buffet she selects oily eggs from a metal tin, and larvic tomatoes, which scald the inside of her mouth. She eats as much toast and jam as she can. The wonders of a returning appetite. She checks out, puts her bag in the back of the Saab. In the boot is a kit with extra sedative darts, though only a delay or extreme stress will warrant using them, and the transport company is also equipped. At 7.30 she calls Stephan in Romania. He shouts into the hands-free.

Bună ziua? Bună ziua?

She can hear the engine of his truck, and the radio blaring; he is already driving back to the centre, through the alpine meadows.

I wonder if you can help me, she says, I'm looking for two missing wolves.

Rachel, he shouts. I have sent them to you with my greatest love!

Are they OK?

Yes, yes, he says. Being rocked in arms of Morpheus. Let me tell you – next time I'm flying wolf-class too. They've got it the best. Like celebrities. They're going to be a great pair.

I know. I can't wait to see them.

You have to come visit us soon, he says. You won't recognise the place – we're getting very high-tech now! It was a generous donation your employer made to us.

Good – he can afford to be generous. And you must come and see them here.

Of course!

They finish speaking and hang up. She texts Huib with an update, sets the GPS, and drives the rest of the way to the airport. Rush-hour traffic eases. She follows signs for British Airways World Cargo. She is early, but the flight is also scheduled to arrive early. On the link road an Airbus roars overhead, tilting and straightening, its wheels locked, its undercarriage close enough to see scratches in the paint. If everything goes to plan they will be back in Annerdale by the early afternoon. The sedation is strong enough that they will not have been disturbed by the flight and the transit north, but she does not want them under for too long.

It does not seem long ago she was arriving at the same airport: her inglorious return home. She parks at the side of the cargo terminal. There are various haulers and transport companies. The Vargis men are waiting in reception, dressed formally in company jackets, carrying cases in which are plastic suits and masks. She too is equipped with a quarantine suit. She greets them and they exchange a few words. They are polite, professional – ex-military, she suspects. She spends twenty minutes with the airport officials. The paperwork is all in order – waybill, licences, CITES, and veterinary documentation. Payment is made. The crates, IATA standard, have been inspected in Romania, but will be inspected again by UK staff, for correct ventilation, bedding; the wolves are not harnessed inside: if they woke under restraint, they would damage themselves trying to get free. While the flight's cargo is being cleared, she waits in a small lounge. Other consignees are waiting too, for what freight, it is impossible to guess. Mammals, plants, alien matter. Or the prosaic family pet.

Soon she is called through. She changes into the suit and goes into the disinfected unloading zone. The crates are brought in, the two Vargis men wheeling them slowly, unfazed by the contents of the covered structures. In bold print the labels read: *LIVE ANIMALS – DO NOT TIP*. The blue transport van is being reversed into the secondary loading bay, the back doors opened. Rachel gently lifts the overlay on the first crate and opens the small viewing hatch. She shines a torch. The female. Darkness, portions of a hind leg, long, crescent-shaped claws. Her breath sounds are even. Thomas has suggested not naming them until they arrive, almost superstitiously, like a father with newborns. *Let's see what their personalities are.* But Rachel has already christened her, after seeing the photographs sent by Stephan and noticing an uncanny resemblance to a particular starlet. The thin nose, tilted eyes, and lupine brows; a face from Hollywood past – Merle Oberon. Merle. She pulls the cover back down. She moves to the second crate and checks the male. He is big – bigger than she anticipated – pale fur, with long black guard hairs. He was lucky to make it out of the trap alive, lucky there was no infection in the bone. She listens, then briefly shines the torch inside. The glimmer of a slit eye, atypical blue. The Rayleigh effect. Somehow it is harder, even than with humans, to remember there is no real colour. He is not alert. There's enough meat and water. She takes the docket out of the waterproof shield, scans and signs it.

They are brought out to the truck and loaded carefully. The Vargis men keep the crates level, moving swiftly but carefully.

The transport company is top of the range. Bullet-proof glass, armoured siding. She would not be surprised if they were equipped to carry nuclear arms, presidents. The crates are secured to the bed of the van and the doors shut.

On the way out of the airport she follows at a safe distance. The van keeps to sixty-five miles per hour. She checks her mirrors with tense regularity, for idiotic drivers, problems, the police. The journey could not be more regulated, but it still feels like a bank robbery, a crime – like the van is filled with explosives. As they drive, her mind flashes through worst-case scenarios. She imagines a crash: the van tipping, its doors swinging open, and the crates smashing on the verge; the wolves limping into the road, horns blaring as they shake their heads, cut through the wreckage, and lope off. They could be halfway up the country in forty-eight hours, disappearing like ghosts.

The van brakes moderately, keeps its distance from the traffic in front. In some part of their brain, even drowsing, they will comprehend motion. Through the seals in the van doors they will detect traces of passing substances: clays, flints, grasslands, under diesel and bitumen, exhaust fumes. And humans nearby – perspiration, hormones. They are intelligent analysts. In those in captivity, she's witnessed incredible responses to human conditions: aggression towards drunks, defence of pregnant staff if a threat is perceived. If they are starting to rouse, they will be communicating with each other, low-toned, almost whistling. But the sedation has been finely administered and should last.

Warning signs flash overhead. Roadworks around Birmingham – long delays. She follows the Vargis van onto the M6 toll road, which is glossy and empty. They pass through the Midlands. Black Country residue. Towns bleeding together along the river basin. It would have been easy to have taken them from visitor centres in Norfolk or Reading, but they must be unhabituated. They must understand range, be able to hunt, or the project will not work.

She sips water from a bottle, not much – she does not want to have to stop at a service station. Neither does the driver of the van pull over for a break – probably they have helpful devices to relieve themselves. The country rolls by. She indulges in a dark daydream, imagines the Vargis men stopping in a layby, stepping into the nearby bushes to urinate. When they return the vehicle is gone, opportunistically stolen. Miles away in a lock-up its doors are pried open. She imagines the shock of these particular spoils – the thieves recoiling. *What the hell? Is that a . . .* Then incremental bravado, goading the animals with a stick or a piece of pipe through the crate hatches – bragging and phone calls. Either they'd be kept by some thug on a chain in an outbuilding, or dumped in the fly-tipped hinterlands of England amid old washing machines and corrosives. Worse: they'd be pitted against some trained brute of a dog in a gore-smeared ring. A mastiff. A cross-hound. Such things do occur. She's seen appalling Spanish footage of a wolf matched against a Presa Canario, the most hellish of breeds, 160 pounds of thick-packed muscle, its ears illegally cropped. The fight was brief. A torrent of snarling, spittle flying, eyes filling with red – both of them up on their hindlegs, heaving against each other like boxers, their heads shaking. Within seconds the dog's brindle was muddied with blood, its jowls torn, and the wolf's side rent open. The onlookers cheering and exchanging bets, chanting the name of the dog, *Rafa, Rafa, Rafa*, which would, given the extent of its injuries, still have had to be shot. People look at her with surprise when she says that hunting is at least an honest sport.

The thought passes. The blue van makes steady progress. By Manchester she begins to relax. The roads are relatively clear. She turns the radio on, then off again. The tarmac hums under the wheels. Her phone rings – the number unlisted. She does not answer. Probably Thomas, who was hoping to be present for their arrival, but is sitting in the House. Traffic slows over the ship canal. The road rises and falls, then everything speeds up again. There are multiple lanes around Preston, a cavalcade of undertaking and overtaking. She grips the wheel tightly, flashing her lights and cursing as a car veers between her and the transport van, across three lanes, onto the slip road. The northern cross motorways draw much of the traffic off. After Lancaster the way is clear. They exit the motorway and take the dual carriageway along the county's southern edge. Oyster-coloured skies above Cumbria. The estuary glimmers in the sunlight. Shallow waves traverse its surface, moving both directions at once – a Janus tide.

She concentrates. It will take another hour to get to Annerdale. She signals to the van, overtakes, and leads the convoy – it is unlikely they will get lost but she doesn't want to take the chance. They continue on, into the mountains, sedately, like some kind of royal procession, the diplomatic arrival of a crowned couple. And it is historic, she thinks. It's five hundred years since their extermination on the island. They are a distant memory, a mythical thing. Britain has altered radically, as has her iconography of wilderness, her totems.

Once in situ, she knows they will divide the country, just as they will quarter the imagination again. Always the same polar arguments. Last year, during documentary filming at Chief Joseph, two hunters had shouted in her face. *They devour their victims alive, while their hearts are still beating! They revel in death!*

As if the animals were some kind of biblical plague – many do believe it. She had calmly explained on camera the hierarchy and tactics of the hunt, the fact that eighty per cent of hunts fail; the fact that herds, after the culling of the weak by predators, are always healthier. Facts versus fear, hatred, and irrationality. As for glee during a kill, such a thing cannot be ascertained, though females seem to express great excitement the first time they hunt after a new litter has been weaned.

Ahead, the mountains seem to smoke, white clouds pluming above as if they were not dead volcanoes, but live. The new bracken is electric green in the lower valleys. She leaves Alexander a message, so that he will know to set off. She slows for a hump-back bridge and sounds the horn to warn oncoming traffic, checks her rear-view mirror. The van is close behind, carefully navigating the narrow structure, its wing mirrors only inches from the stone walls. The screen is tinted; she cannot see the drivers. Its hold might be carrying anything: gold bullion, masterpieces, the body of Jesus Christ. There has not been a public announcement about the arrival – she does not want to risk any controversy. The Annerdale wolves are being brought in, to all intents and purposes, secretly, under the radar, like contraband.

In the quarantine enclosure, Rachel and Huib stand next to the crates, boiler-suited and disinfected, their hands placed on the sliding-door mechanisms. Outside the fence, Sylvia is filming. Alexander is with her, observing – he will do so every day for the next week and then weekly. Michael is not in attendance. A new deer carcass lies at the far end of the pen, wet, aromatic, freshly cut. After six months they will be freed into the main enclosure with the herds, as close to a hard release as possible.

The crates are silent, but the sedation will be lifting. Huib looks over at Rachel. He holds up a thumb – ready. Rachel signals back. They open the doors and step quickly behind the crates. In no more than a second or two the pair has bolted, the male a fraction faster, startlingly pale, with Merle hard at his heels. Huib punches the air.

Boom!

The wolves divide round a stack of logs, make for the end of the pen, and are lost from sight behind a cluster of bushes.

Let's leave them to it, Rachel says.

She and Huib wheel the crates backward towards the gate, where they are stowed. They step into the disinfectant zone and change shoes, strip out of the boiler suits. Rachel shuts and locks the inner gate, which is screened. Although they can no longer be seen, they are well within the auditory and olfactory field, and will always be detected when this close to the pair. They wash down, strip out of the suits, exit the outer gate, and join Alexander and Sylvia in the viewing area. The pair have gone to ground and remain hidden from sight. The group speak in low tones, almost whispering, congratulating each other. Sylvia keeps the camera still and trained through the hide's panel. Alexander nods to Rachel.

Looking good, very alert.

Let's see if they eat anything, she says.

They take up their field glasses and wait. After five minutes, pointed ears come up out of the grass, then heads emerge. The wolves step out from behind the bushes, cautiously, sniffing, a forepaw held aloft. There's a cold austerity to the male's blue-fired gaze, a rarity. Merle is quietly confident in the new sur-roundings; she beings to lope towards the carcass, investigates it, but does not eat. She returns to the male and he licks her muzzle. They make short forays, close together, in the bottom half of the pen, criss-crossing scent trails to the fence and back, keeping their noses to the ground, lifting them and reading the air. The enclosure is big, several hectares, though as quarantine progresses it will seem limited, Rachel knows, and will induce lazy behaviour, habituation. She has prepared a series of preventative tactics. In the centre of the pen is a pile of dead wood where it is likely they will den. They move closer, towards the hide. For a long while the male stands looking in the direction of the screen where the humans are hidden. The strong April sunlight renders his fur brilliant, pale gold and silver-white, like the blaze of a matchhead. He could almost set fire to the trees. He's going to vanish, Rachel thinks, against the snow and the limestone pavements on the moors, against the blonde sward of the grassland.

I think he knows we're still here, Sylvia says.

Ja. I feel like he knows what I had for breakfast, Huib says.

Alexander laughs quietly.

Muesli, and he's not impressed.

He is going through a health checklist, ticking boxes, the first of many formal documents. They are inquisitive, their tails are up; there is no lethargy. A good score. Sylvia keeps recording.

I wish Mummy could have seen this, she says after a time. She was the one who first suggested the idea to Daddy. She'd be so, so happy.

Rachel glances over. This is the first mention of the project's conception she has heard, and was not aware of the memorial aspect. Sylvia is dressed as a standard volunteer: T-shirt and jeans, a fleece jacket, work boots. Her face is not made up; her hair is tied back, though there is still a quality of refinement to her, a strange Martian beauty. She has spent her first full day on the project, preparing the carcass with Huib, answering the phone. There has been no cause to doubt her commitment, and now Rachel understands why. She is doing it for her dead mother, the most banal and powerful of all motivations.

The pair lope softly to the bottom of the enclosure again and disappear. Sylvia lowers and switches off the camera.

I'll upload this when I get back to the office, she says. I'll send it to Border News and the BBC. Daddy left us some champagne, by the way, if anyone feels like it.

This day gets better and better, Alexander says. Merle is a great name, by the way, Rachel. I saw *The Dark Angel* when I was a kid. I think I would have sent my best friend off to his death for Kitty Vane.

Ja, me too! Huib agrees. Good job you didn't call her Kitty, Rachel.

Alexander snorts.

Kitty the wolf.

I didn't have you two down as film nerds, Rachel says. But we should think about a name for our boy. Anyone?

Sylvia holds her hand up, eager as a schoolgirl.

May I suggest something?

Rachel thinks back to the welcome party, her assumptions about Sylvia's mettle and her tastes. They can always vote on it if needs be. But the mood is high, it is a celebratory day, and she does not want to dampen the spirit by penalising a member of the team. She will have to learn to trust the Earl's daughter.

OK. Go on.

Well, he's just so very bright and brilliant. What about Ra?

As in the sun god? I like that, says Huib. I like that a lot. Our creator!

Sylvia's smile broadens; she is lit up with keenness, and looks a tiny bit smug. Rachel nods.

Actually, I like it too.

Alexander is bent forward, peering through the viewing panel again.

Hey up, he says. Action stations.

They take up their field glasses. There is movement in the enclosure. Cautiously, Merle is approaching the carcass for a second time. She stands over the downy body, sniffs, assessing the state of decay. Scavenging is not the preferred mode, or perhaps she is still suspicious after the recent poisoning. As Stephan Dalakis pointed out, she was extremely lucky the incident did not permanently affect her stomach and bowel. Whatever the meat was laced with left her desperately sick. Another way of killing them. Over the years Rachel has seen several cases along Idaho's sheep superhighway where the hunters use Xylitol, which is easy to buy and toxic to their livers.

Merle looks towards Ra. Her ears rotate forward, black-tufted. Her eyes are tear-shaped, dark-ringed, her expression quizzical. The eye might be drawn to her big, pale mate, but she is more than beautiful, Rachel thinks. Ra arrives and they begin to tug at the flesh. The legs of the deer jerk as they pull it about. Another tick in Alexander's boxes. After feeding, they retreat towards the dead wood, and lie down in the grass. Merle inches over and they lie close together. Ra yawns. He is not yet fully interested in the advances; she is simply practising until he is. She yawns too, puts her head on her paws. She may not have a godly name, Rachel thinks, but she is the vital one, everything rests on her ability to breed. She is the true grey, true to the name; she is tawny as the landscape, and utterly congruent.

*

Once news of their arrival has broken, protesters flock back to the estate. They set up camp at the gate again, and settle in for the duration. The previous motley band has grown some-what, Rachel notices, as she and Huib drive up. Numbers have swelled. Now there are placards, banners, even costumes. She parks the Saab in the row of cars along the verge, by the estate's high wall, and they get out. The crowd mills about. Someone is videoing on a mobile phone and the local newspaper has sent a photographer, who looks a little desultory. There are children, including a girl dressed in white party frills and a red cape, some kind of fairytale motif, or perhaps she is simply on the way to a party. Lurking at the side of the group is a man wearing a pinstripe suit and papier-mâché wolf's head. The head is lewdly made, though not unskilfully, with giant teeth and a red tongue. He is carrying a briefcase. The photographer singles him out and he poses. This is perhaps some kind of comment on Lord Pennington himself, Rachel assumes, rather than the wolves. The apex class; the financial raiders in charge. It all seems a peculiarly British display, Shakespearean almost: absurdity combined with intellect, adults engaged in mummering. They approach the group.

Nice day for it at least, Huib says.

He seems unfazed, amused even. But then, he has faced down illegal poachers in Africa, armed, ambitious, and far more dangerous.

Watch that guy, will you, she says, gesturing to the wolf-headed man. He seems quite full on.

Probably nothing, she thinks, but he has gone to a lot of effort with his costume. She wonders for a moment if this man is the mysterious 'Nigh', whom they have had several more rabid emails from. Something in the exhibitionism of the disguise and the lack of inhibition fits. But the presentation is too articulate, not in keeping with the chaotic communications pinging into her inbox. As they approach, she steels herself; such confrontations are never easy, even if harmless. She feels embarrassed for those who have misunderstood, the irrationals of the world. When the crowd realises she and Huib are not joining the group, but are here to defend the project, the protesters take formation, hoisting their painted placards. *Right to Roam. Protect Our Children.* The wolf-headed man begins his pantomime. He drops the briefcase and holds his hands up as if they were claws. The fingertips are painted red. He begins to stalk forward, growling. There are murmurs in the crowd, and nervous laughter.

Great stuff, someone says – the photographer.

He crouches down and snaps off a few shots.

Bit slower, can you? Look over to me, Mr Wolf.

The man continues forward, towards Rachel and Huib. The growling intensifies. The courage of the masked – clearly he has rehearsed and wants to perform. Rachel feels a blush begin to creep up her neck. How to tackle the silliness of it? But she does not have to. Huib applauds and steps into his path.

Bravo, mate, bravo. Minor criticism – the sound's not quite right. It's a little low-pitched for an attack. You've got to get more of a moan sound in there.

His voice is non-confrontational, but deliberately loud, loud enough for the lecture to be heard by the crowd. He begins to make a snarling noise himself. The impression is honed, and surprisingly accurate. He is physically blocking the pantomime's progress. The wolf-headed man stops.

And for a happy greeting, you've got to whimper or whine. A bit like this.

He delivers another wolfish impression. The crowd is watching him now – he is stealing the show. Genius, Rachel thinks. She sidesteps them and addresses the rest of the group.

My name's Rachel. I'm project manager here. I can answer any questions you have and address any concerns.

The group rallies, begins a song – a ditty whose lyrics have been written to the tune of Jerusalem. She musters patience. She will let them have a verse or two – it's what they came for. She puts her hands in her pockets and waits. The little girl in the white frock and cape breaks from the group, prances forward, and smiles up at her. There's grime on the hem of the dress where it's been trailing on the ground, which is quite pleasing. Rachel smiles back. The girl seems too young to know what's going on. She skips off. The song concludes. A woman in the crowd – the self-selected spokesperson, perhaps – pipes up, complains about the danger to children that the Annerdale wolves pose. She places her hands on the shoulders of two of the other children present, boys of about six or seven, smartly dressed in breeches and velvet Victorian-style jackets. Brothers to the little capering princess, no doubt. The boys step forward and present themselves, to illustrate a point, certainly the point of their being children, if not in mortal danger. They look past Rachel to the wolf-man, who Huib is still corralling – a far more interesting scene.

We want to speak to Lord Pennington, the woman declares.

Her tone is rightful, entitled, as if she is requesting an audience with her bank manager after the erroneous bouncing of a cheque.

I'm in charge of the project, Rachel repeats. How can I help?

The woman glares at her, sizes her up, and then looks around, as if Thomas Pennington might materialise, simply from her summons, not unlike the devil. She does not want a representative, no matter how expert, but the real thing, a tall poppy with a worthwhile head to scythe. Rachel decides to follow Huib's lead – to explode rather than defuse the situation.

I take it you're worried about your children getting into the enclosure by accident, perhaps? Or being curious and trying to break in?

From the corner of her eye she sees the photographer angling the lens, catching her in profile. She turns her head away.

No, the woman says. No! They wouldn't do that. They're good kids.

Yes, Rachel says. And they couldn't get in, anyway. They'd need industrial cutting gear.

Behind her she can hear more wolf vocalisations; a large part of the crowd is also listening and watching with interest. But there's only so long Huib will be able to manage things, she knows.

I mean if they get out, the spokeswoman continues. If they get out, what's to stop them running riot and plundering!

Plundering?

Rachel tries not to laugh, though the rhetoric is in fact ridiculous. She talks the woman through the specifications of the fence: height, depth, impenetrability, inescapability. The woman's scowl deepens. Construction measurements are not what she came for. Reality is not what she came for. Rachel knows exactly what she wants – to twitter on about her nightmarish fantasy: wolves that pass like fog through the wire and head unerringly and specifically to her house, nosing open the door, and creeping upstairs, howling at the moon before tearing apart her starched and overdressed children. She should try to be more understanding, but the hysteria, the desire for a bogeyman, is tiresome.

They really can't get out.

But if they get out, the woman repeats. I can't have my kids walking to school in the village. There isn't even a siren to warn people. You're a mother? Aren't you anxious?

The woman gestures towards Rachel's swelling belly. Rachel feels her modicum of patience ebbing. Don't tar me with the same brush, she thinks.

Let's think this through, she says. A siren might cause panic and would make no difference at all, because they wouldn't want to interact with humans anyway. But I assure you, they really won't get out.

The woman shakes her head in denial. She is desperate for tabloid disaster, desperate to mainline all the fear she can. She is thrusting her children out like sacrifices before her. They are slickly combed and ironed. No doubt the poor kids are stewarded hither and thither, to school, to clubs, to the houses of sanctioned friends – every precaution taken to keep them safe from paedophiles, the internet, fires, and floods. There is no reasonable argument Rachel can make.

The little girl comes over and stands in front of her again. Her cape is askew, her hair wildly tattered. She peers up intensely. She is disarmingly attractive, more so for the dishevelment, the corruption of all attempts to groom her. Let me have one like you, Rachel thinks. The girl holds out her meaty little hand, fist clenched, containing a gift.

Is that for me? Rachel asks.

Nancy, come away, please, her mother instructs.

The girl does not move.

Nancy. Come here, please. Nancy!

The fairytale dress hangs off one shoulder, a size too big, and soon to be ruined. Nancy holds her hand out towards Rachel, traitorously.

Nancy! I won't tell you again! Must I count to ten? One –

A voice that suddenly means business. The hand snaps down. The girl turns and marches back to the region of her family. The mother gathers her in, recovering her form in response to being obeyed.

Tell us then. If they get out, what are we to do? Hide in our homes? Go and get a gun? Or is there going to be some kind of government helpline?

Behind Rachel, the wolf-headed man has begun a howl, saving her from fielding the question, or from calling the woman idiotic. She glances over at Huib. He shrugs apologetically. He has held the actor off valiantly but it was never going to last. The crowd refocuses its attention; even the spokeswoman shuts up. The costumed man gets down on his knees and tips his head back in baying parody. The howl sounds hollow and muffled inside the head. Crawling on all fours, he moves to the spot where he dropped his briefcase. The photographer is snapping away again, glad of some proper action. Nancy breaks free of her mother, roams forward, and watches the performance at close quarters. With deliberate theatricality, the man snaps open the briefcase clasps. He lifts the lid of the case and takes out a gun. There are murmurs in the crowd, then mild laughter – it is fake, a toy. The man puts the gun to his large, leering head and pulls the trigger. The cap pops loudly and the gun emits a wisp of smoke. Nancy jerks with shock at the noise but remains in the same position, watching the man tip over to the ground, twitch horribly, and then lie still. Rachel looks over at her mother, who is shouldering her way forward. One of the boys has started crying. The woman fetches Nancy away from the scene, roughly by the hand. The show is in poor taste with children present; the crowd knows it. A slow sarcastic handclap begins and then dies away – Huib.

Show's over, he says. No encore.

He's not with us, someone in the crowd says.

Huib moves to intercede, but the man suddenly stands. He swiftly gathers the gun and the briefcase and starts away. The role is over, but he does not unmask. He walks past Huib, towards Rachel. As he passes, she tries to see inside the cut-out eye holes. Blue eyes, maybe, impossible to distinguish. He says something as he passes – a threat, perhaps – but the head obscures the words. Then he is gone, down the road, past the parked vehicles and into the trees.

A feeling of unease is left behind. The amateur dramatics of the day have gone wrong. No harm has been done, but the incident has derailed everything. The crowd is dispersing; people are lowering placards and heading to their cars. The little velvet-suited boy is still wailing, louder now, committed to the act, while his mother checks Nancy over and Nancy strains to get away. The photographer is packing up his gear.

Let's go, Rachel says to Huib.

She tells the remaining protesters that she can be reached by email or phone. They walk back to the Saab.

Who do you think he was? Huib asks. Some kind of activist?

No, she says. Well, maybe. I don't know. He let that toddler get a bit close for comfort.

That made me uncomfortable, too. And he didn't have a car, did you notice?

She starts the engine and pulls away.

Right. No way of tracing him by number plates.

As she drives down the road, she glances in the rear-view mirror, half expecting to see the man materialise from the trees again, suited and waving at them, the red tongue of the wolf's head lolling out.

It's interesting, though, Huib says.

What is?

You can just pull a gun out here and nobody goes crazy. Back home, that guy would have been taken out.

In America, too, she says.

I don't know whether it's a good thing.

No. I'm not sure it's worth coming down here any more, she says. These people's minds are made up.

She decides she will not come back to meet the protesters again, not even for a show of diplomacy. The fearful will always be afraid; the ideological will believe until the last shred of evidence is offered. Only time will prove them wrong. The unrest will peak and end, she gauges. There will be the inevitable entropy of energy, and the swing of anxiety towards a new inflammatory source will put paid to the gatherings. Or the Lakeland weather will.

*

Why didn't you tell me earlier? Lawrence asks.

Why?

I don't know. I would have helped or something.

Rachel shrugs.

Helped with what?

Her brother is vexed, and a little upset, but not angry. He frowns gently, looking down at her.

I don't know.

Rachel shuts the front door of the cottage and they stand in the lane outside, facing each other. It is a hot May day. She still feels a little awkward being in his company, but she's glad he came, and glad to have finally broken the news. She has undone the belt of her cardigan so that her small bump is visible, pushing against her T-shirt. Lawrence starts to say something, stops. Then he says,

I could have helped you with the move or something. Carrying stuff. And we didn't have to go up a bloody mountain!

She smiles at the sentiment, his charming and misguided chivalry.

I'm fine. Really. I feel fine. And we did go up a mountain.

He sighs and the frown line above his nose deepens.

Oh, Rachel.

He is clearly concerned and won't be brushed off. It's difficult to navigate the new relationship. They have spoken a few times on the phone – she's even exchanged coolly polite words with Emily. In not telling him, maybe she has been too defensive, too excluding again. She is simply not used to having a brother, let alone one now trying to take care of her. All around them, in the woods, is the racket of birdcalls and squawks, like a playground.

Listen, I'm fine, she says. I just wasn't ready to tell people. OK? Come on, let's go this way.

She leads him down the lane. They walk past his car – a new silver Audi – towards the lake and the wolf enclosure. The ground is lush underfoot, the grass is young and has been softened by a recent shower. It's humid, notes of thunder in the air, though the sunshine prevails. She takes off her cardigan and knots it around her hips. Lawrence has on a long-sleeved shirt, rolled to the mid-forearm. He has patches of bad skin below the cuffs, picked and sore-looking, like when he was a boy. They make their way through the woods.

It's gorgeous here, he says, seeming to let the subject of her pregnancy go.

It is.

I can't imagine owning so much land.

No. But we need it. They need it.

Still, it doesn't seem – well – fair, I suppose. Not in this day and age.

Maybe we should follow the Scottish model. Re-nationalise the big estates.

She is half joking, but Lawrence nods.

Maybe. It might not be a bad thing.

I wonder if it would be harder or easier to set up a project like this.

Depends who's in power, he says.

Probably none of them would risk it.

She is aware she sounds like a cynic, but since returning home, none of the political parties have convinced her they are anything other than urban-centric and ecologically conservative. The pockets of English countryside are broken apart and seem to be regarded as gardens for the city; Annerdale is unusually large and unusually governed. Her brother is an optimist; she has begun to admire his spirit, though at times it seems forced, something of a mental straightjacket. *I don't think it'll rain. Emily will come round.* As they walk, she catches Lawrence occasionally glancing over, with possessive tenderness, as if she needs guarding, as if she might stumble. The attentiveness feels odd, noticeable, like a new shoe, but is not unpleasant.

You were worried about how I'd take it, weren't you? he says softly. Because we're trying for a baby.

Yes, I suppose I was a bit.

Are you pleased? he asks.

I'm nervous.

And you're really fine?

Yes!

Well, I'm happy for you. We should celebrate.

Rachel snorts.

Celebrate?

What? Weren't you trying to get pregnant?

Of course not.

Oh.

She shakes her head. He becomes quiet again, attempting to understand the situation. Rachel is aware of how it all must seem. Aware too that she has not, during any of the time they have spent together, mentioned a partner, a boyfriend, anyone meaningful in her life. Perhaps Lawrence was imagining a clinic scenario, her leafing through catalogues of donors' attributes and genetic profiles. Most uncomfortable is the awareness that she is to some degree following in Binny's footsteps: unmarried, independent, not at all leavened by maternity.

It is what it is, she says.

Through the trees, the lake water flashes. They cut down towards the shore, Lawrence leading. He holds tree branches out of the way for her rather than letting them lash back. A self-taught gentleman: there's little of their mother in him, if there is in her. They walk along the lake edge, the shingle clattering underfoot. Tiny waves lap the stones, wind-manufactured seiches. There are black-faced gulls bobbing on the surface. Summer is coming on fast. The district is very green, shaggy with foliage; flowers are beginning everywhere, bluebells carpeting the older woods. The brutality of Chief Joseph's winter feels a long time ago. Her brother seems pensive and sad. She wonders if he is disappointed in her, or whether he is imagining breaking the news to Emily. It will surely not go down well.

Hey, Uncle Lawrence, she says, to cheer him.

He turns and smiles.

Yeah, he says. I need to learn some uncle skills, don't I?

He pauses and picks up a flat, roundish pebble, squats, and skims it across the surface of the lake. Five hops and the stone sinks, flickering down through the water and disappearing. The rings disperse.

Good start, she says. Hope you'll teach that if it's a boy *or* a girl.

Is it unkind to ask or not to ask about their own attempts to conceive, she wonders. She settles for frankness.

Any news your end on that front?

Lawrence roots around in the shore debris for another good skimmer.

No joy. Miscarriage. We'll probably do another round, then see. We might have to call it a day.

Rachel says nothing. What can she say? Not sorry. Not good luck. There are no platitudes or reassurances. Emily may now be speaking to her on the phone, but she has not come to visit with Lawrence this time, even though there was no embargo. She is grateful, on some level, to avoid Emily's company – the tension, the loaded comments. *That's an interesting philosophy, Rachel. Lawrence doesn't really eat artichoke; he never has. We may need a second mortgage, if the care-home costs increase again.*

Actually, it's been pretty stressful, Lawrence says, and depressing. I'm not sure I've responded in the right way – I'm not in great shape. She's pretty pissed off at me.

He looks pained, now that Rachel is studying him, a little pale, with dark circles beneath his eyes. He was always prone to somatisation; had childhood aches and pains of no origin when upset, and was dismissed as a nervous kid by the doctor. She feels sorry for him, but he will not want to hear that.

Hey, I'm sure you're doing great, she says. Just hang in there.

It seems a trite thing to say, next to useless, but Lawrence nods. They keep to silence for a while as they make their way along the shore. The water is gunmetal grey under the trees, where the sunlight cannot reach, hostile-looking, though when she tests the temperature of the shallows with a hand, it is only moderately cold.

Shall we go see the wolves? she asks.

Yeah, great. Lead the way.

They head away from the lake, towards the enclosure.

How are they getting on? Lawrence asks.

Fine, she says. Actually, they're a bit bored. Merle is being a flirt.

A flirt? How can you tell?

She keeps coming up to Ra like this.

Rachel mimics the sidestepping movement, the sidle. Her brother smiles.

That's flirting?

Oh, yes.

Does he like it?

He's not convinced. He's too busy trying to figure a way out of the pen. Last week he dug up a buried tractor wheel trying to get under the fence.

Whenever she speaks about the job, her brother seems enthralled. It is as if she practises some kind of lost craft: augury, or alchemy. They make their way up towards the enclosure. When they reach the fence and the barrier, Lawrence stands for a moment, not in appreciation exactly, but impressed.

Wow, double surety. No messing around. Can people not access the lake now?

Not on this side.

He shakes his head.

It was quite a feat, getting that bill passed in Parliament.

Yes, it was.

Though she is now the project's advocate, she still has mixed feelings about the fence herself, the restrictions, the very nature of it.

Come on. Let's go to the wolfery, she says.

The wolfery?

Quarantine. It was originally a joke someone made. But it's sort of stuck.

They follow the fence towards the pen. She is walking slower than usual, not winded exactly, but the humidity and the extra weight of the bump are having an effect, on her gait, her heart. She can feel the extra blood. Lawrence slows, obligingly.

Why does there have to be a fence on this side of the lake, anyway?

If it was open both ends, they'd swim across, she explains. We'd lose them.

They could swim across? All the way?

Yes.

Her brother turns and gazes back over the water. The rim of the lake is darkly tinted. There are patches of yellow and white light drifting like aurorae across the surface.

It wasn't like this when we were growing up, was it? he says. It felt less – owned.

It was probably just more affordable then, less fashionable.

True. We looked into getting a house up here a few years ago, but there's no way.

He looks over at her.

Sorry I never came to the States to see you, Rachel.

It doesn't matter.

It does matter. Stupid to have gone years without being friends at least.

There's upset in the margins of his voice again. She should tell him not to worry about what can't be changed. The past damages, the old wounds. The trick is not to limp; one has to forget one was ever limping, like Ra, whose leg has healed. One day he could simply run again, without affliction. She puts a hand on Lawrence's arm.

Quid pro quo. I've never been to Leeds.

He grins. They continue along the fence. Either side of the wire is an abundance of tall grass, insects ferrying between the stalks, and butterflies. The landscape is beginning to thicken and become fragrant; the heather blossoming, and the gorse bushes exploding with heady yellow petals.

You must have missed all this while you were away, he says. I know I do.

Yeah. It was a good place to be a kid. You end up wanting to be outdoors all the time, wherever you are. I sometimes slept out in John Stacy's barn. And in the lime kiln. If I'd had a row with Binny.

Her moorland solitude. She still cannot really imagine herself as a mother, and does not regard her own upbringing as idyllic – far from it – but there is something reassuring or important about knowing the baby will grow up in the territory where she grew up. And then she thinks of Kyle, and the Reservation, and she feels the inching of guilt.

Well, I'm glad you're back, Lawrence says. Gives me a good excuse to come up here.

She nods but does not answer. The fence rolls on across the shallow gables of grassland, through stone pavements and cleared woods, to the near horizon. Seen at this angle, it looks as if it runs indefinitely, the illusion of holding, like the Viking stone walls up the steep mountains of Cumbria.

Hey, her brother says, and stops walking. I just figured out why you do what you do, Rachel. All that sleeping outside. You were exposed.

In the screened hide, she scans the pen, locates them, and hands Lawrence a pair of binoculars.

Behind the big tree trunk. Just left of it.

He takes the glasses and adjusts the focus, moves them away from his face, and then brings them back to the bridge of his nose. He is unaccustomed, she can tell.

Can't see anything except ferns and bushes, he says.

It might help to scan quadrants, she suggests. Think of a grid.

Right.

He continues to search. She wonders if this is the first time he will have seen one. Even with all the zoos and parks of the modern age, most people do not come into contact. Setterah Keep had closed by the time Lawrence was old enough to be taken, the animals donated to other centres or destroyed. She suddenly hopes it is the case – she would like to be the one to show him. He adjusts the focus again. They are well camouflaged, but he'll find one, if he's patient. Or they'll move and make it easier. She remembers again the mystic at the 500 Nations powwow, asking her for some kind of spiritual response to her first sighting, her blunt dismissal. After, Kyle had told her he'd gone through the weyekin ritual at the age of twelve – about the fasting and fireless nights, the alteration of mind, and the idea that attributes of the gained spirit would be lent to a person for life. It was unclear whether he subscribed or not. If Lawrence enjoys seeing them, if he is moved or simply appreciative, that will be enough for her.

He peers through the glasses. He tells her he can see an ear, twitching in the thistles and fronds; he thinks it's an ear. They are lying down, almost hidden in the tangle of undergrowth.

Bingo.

Rachel holds her own binoculars steady. They are in the shade, close to each other, keeping cool. A cloud of gnats hovers above them, and their ears flick now and then. After a few minutes, Ra stands and shakes off, expelling the dirt and flies, his ears flapping. He gazes at the hide.

Wow! Incredible! He's looking right at me. Am I talking too loud?

No. You could say nothing, he'd still know where you are. They're getting too used to us, which is a bit of a problem.

Ra sniffs the air, his long nose tipped up, the black, leathered nostrils flaring. He yawns and drops back down to the warm dusty earth, in plain view, as if doing them a favour by exposing his great lean body. He has given up scouting for exits and digging. The hot weather is making him doggish, as are the fresh carcasses being dumped at various places in the enclosure each week. Now he slumps to the side, rolling in the grass and exposing his underbelly. They will have to start implementing some scare tactics, prevent the pair from becoming too used to hotel life and human stewards.

They spend half an hour at the wolfery, watching. Lawrence is fascinated, asks when they might mate. The following winter, after release, she tells him. On the way out, they bump into Huib and Sylvia. It feels odd, introducing a member of her family to colleagues; she has never done so before. She stumbles and says *half-brother*, which is an unnecessary distinction, but no one seems to notice. They chat pleasantly for a moment on the wooded path, in dappled sunlight. It amazes her, the ease with which everyone can get along, as if it is the most natural thing in the world; perhaps it is. Sylvia mentions law school, and Lawrence wishes her luck.

I'm not sure about it any more, she confesses. I'm enjoying working here with Rachel too much.

Lawrence glances admiringly at his sister. The feeling of companionability is nice, she admits, though the compliment is unwarranted. Sylvia has been undertaking the menial work of any volunteer, albeit enthusiastically.

We're going to the pub for lunch, if you want to come along, she says to the others.

It is the weekend. The project requires daily work, but there is room for play, and the staff members have yet to socialise together without Thomas Pennington being present, hosting like a king.

Maybe we'll join you for a drink later, Huib says.

OK. Has Alexander been down today?

First thing. He charted and then had to go. He said to say hi.

They seem nice, Lawrence says as they walk on to the pub. That was the Earl's daughter, was it?

Yes.

She seems normal. No pearls and frills.

I wouldn't quite go that far. But she is doing well.

Outside the Horse and Farrier, they pass Michael Stott's utility vehicle – the small world of Annerdale. The gamekeeper greets them through the open window of the truck.

How do, Mrs Caine.

He seems less sullen than usual, perhaps because Rachel is with a man, perhaps because she is pregnant – the news is known on the estate now – and he assumes she might leave the project. A sleek, brindled lurcher pants on the passenger seat next to him, its pink tongue spooning out, brown bandit patches over each eye. She has yet to discuss the deer population with him, and a possible cull, but she does not want the mood of the day spoilt with a terse exchange. She nods hello, and follows Lawrence into the bar. He turns to her with a smirk.

Orange juice?

She points at the Guinness pump.

No, I'll have a half.

Of stout?

Binny had stout every day when she was pregnant with you, she tells her brother. She said the doctor told her to – something about iron deficiency. It might just have been an excuse.

Well, I turned out OK, he says.

Anyway, I've been reading the studies. The latest evidence is alcohol in moderation is fine. Caffeine and alcohol, yes, smoking and class A drugs, no.

Right-o, he says, grinning. This is a nice pub. I'm going to try something local.

He orders a pint of Helvellyn Gold. They sit at a table by the window with menus and their drinks. Now she has stopped walking, Rachel can feel the baby moving – a sensation somewhere between tender thumping and flapping, a sudden burst under the skin. Nothing is as she anticipated. There are moments she feels genuinely joyful, irrationally so, and other times the decision to go ahead seems ludicrous, a madness. But the screening results came back good. The second scan was clear – no anomalies, the baby is developing well, heart chambers, brain, spine. She glances at her brother, who is looking out of the pub window at the kempt village green, sipping his pint. He is decent and kind, though under the surface he often seems conflicted, true parts of himself hidden away. But then, is she not also reticent, giving herself over only gradually, if at all? It would be good to have him as a friend.

I have thought about it, she says. I have thought maybe I'll be a hopeless mum. Like her.

Lawrence turns back, barely missing a beat.

No, he says, firmly. No, Rachel. You'll be brilliant. I know you will.

He looks her squarely in the eye.

You'll be a brilliant mum, he repeats.

It is an irrefutable assertion. He does not know her, any more than she knows him. Life divided them early, made them strangers. How can he know anything so certain from the handful of times they have met? But it is not hysterical optimism or crazed fantasy. He means to believe and so he believes. Perhaps it is survivalism, she thinks, the method he used to get away from the intolerable reign of Binny, still a teenager, vulnerable, only half made. He could so easily have fucked it all up – school, a profession, his love life. But he didn't. He left, and he prospered. If he were the elder, if she had been less autonomous, less isolationist, he probably would have tried to take her with him. Whatever demons he carries, he also succeeds, she thinks. For a moment she feels almost ashamed, and humbled by his generosity. It is she who should express admiration.

Thank you, Lawrence. That means a lot.

He holds up his pint glass.

Right-o, he says. Cheers. Here's to the baby.

*

High summer. The district bakes in a rare spell of unbroken heat, week after week of open blue sky, elegantly cut through by swallows and martins. The upland grass parches, and in the valleys and the corners of fields, the smell of hay beginning, an elative smell – reassuring to the agricultural memory, perhaps. Heat shimmers on the roads as the horizons soften, and the tar melts. The wolves become nocturnal, moving about the enclosure at night, keeping to the shade in the day.

The morning that she and Alexander perform the surgery is beautifully warm. He arrives with sterile equipment and sheeting on which to work. His sleeves are rolled. Rachel moves quietly round the enclosure until she can get a clear shot with the gas-projector. The first barbiturate dart hits Ra in the hindquarters. He whimpers, turns to bite at the spot, takes a few paces. His back end sinks, and he drops. Merle tucks her tail, step-crouches away from him, pauses, looks back. Rachel reloads quickly and darts her.

Nice shot, Alexander comments. Remind me not to get on the wrong side of you.

They enter the pen, dressed in plastic suits and gloves, carrying the implants. It is hot inside the suit – the internal zip only just closes over Rachel's stomach. She blindfolds the wolves, to protect their eyes from the sun. They set up a makeshift outdoor theatre and move the two limp bodies onto the sheeting. She is careful of bending and lifting, her ligaments have started to soften and her back aches a little, but the work is not too difficult. Alexander does not ask if she would rather, in her condition, assist or sit the procedure out, and she is grateful for the assumption of capability.

While unconscious, the pair are weighed, checked over, blood samples are taken. A section of their abdomens is shaved and cleaned. They are laid out on their backs, their hind legs splayed. Both are moulting, leaving hair on the sheeting and the suits. Their heartbeats are monitored on a Doppler. Alexander works calmly, opening a clean wound in Ra, parting the sides of flesh, inserting the transmitter. The devices will be kept away from vital organs and muscles, Merle's uterus.

Deep enough? he asks.

Yes, great. Just so long as it doesn't travel to the skin and irritate.

He tucks the implant inside, secures it, stitching the inner lining tidily, then closing the outer with a subterranean line that will be harder to chew out. He repeats the operation on Merle. Though the technique is new, it is clear he is used to performing such procedures on site; he is efficient but unhurried, his gloves barely stained red. Sweat gathers on his brow, rolling down his temples. She feels beads slide down her back under the plastic material. The surgery is brief, twenty minutes in all.

You must have taken Home Ec in school, she jokes. Embroidery?

Oh, yes. And I can make a mean stuffed pepper, too.

Stuffed with what? she asks.

With pepper.

He cuts the last thread. He gives each animal a shot of precautionary antibiotics. They turn them on their sides, pack away the equipment and remove the blindfolds, then leave the enclosure, disinfecting on the way out. Within a minute or so the wolves come round, stand woozily, shake, and move about. Ra sits and licks his belly. Merle sniffs his underside; he hers. Iodophor. Something has passed while they were asleep, but what? They investigate their small territory but find no intruders. They drink from the well stream, lope back to the bushes, and lie down. There seems to be no inhibition of movement or negative effect.

Come and have a coffee and we can check the signals are right on the receiver, she suggests.

I never say no to coffee or good signals, Alexander says.

He might be flirting with her, she can't tell. They make their way from the wolfery to the office. The pair are checked regularly over the next week for altered behaviour, infection, inflammation; they lick at the wounds for a day or two, but seem as normal. Their blood work comes back clean.

Later in the week, Rachel swims in the river with Huib and Sylvia. The heat has become massive, almost solid, the fan in the office stirring turgid air, and there seems no better way to cool down. Her bump is properly declaring itself: taut, shiny, the belly button beginning to malform and nub outward, the linea nigra appearing. The pool is not cold, but cool, exquisite. The valley's rocks over which the water has travelled have been warmed;

patches of the river are warm, too. The slate bottom electrifies the water, renders it exotically blue, like something from a rainforest or a lagoon. Further up are waterfalls, in deep, shadowed gulleys, the miasma of their spray jewelled by sunlight. Everything smells of minerals: green and reedy. Sylvia and her brother Leo bathed here as children, she tells them. Huib, too, has discovered the spot, a short hike from the stone bridge near the wolfery, and has been using it regularly. Still, the place has a feeling of gorgeous secrecy.

They have become a team lately, the three of them, now splashing about, laughing, floating on their backs like lidoists. Rachel watches the other two jumping from the buttress of a rock into a frothing ghyll, fearless of anything beneath the surface. Sylvia is slender, pale-limbed, nothing too womanly protrudes; her collarbones are like vestigial fins, her hair slicks down her back as she surfaces, aesthetic, Piscean. Huib, whatever his proclivities or restraints, seems not to be appreciative of such a body, at least not beyond having an enthusiastic swim mate. They have become unlikely friends.

Huib, there used to be an eel, Sylvia says, sitting on a flat rock next to the pool. An ancient one, six hundred years old. I could always make it come out. It's down here.

She points into the water below. She slips back in, submerses, skims along the bottom of the pool, and takes hold of his ankle. Huib kicks away and she chases after. They lark about and Rachel enjoys their silliness. The camaraderie reminds her of Chief Joseph.

She lies back against a rock, lets her feet float up. Her T-shirt sticks to her bump. The water feels terrifically supportive, soothing. The baby kicks softly, then seems to sleep. Is this how it feels to be floating in amniotic? she wonders. Her body relaxes; her mind drifts. Who would not be glad of coming here? She has not left Annerdale in weeks. Skimming over the river, less than a wingspan from the pool's surface, are giant dragonflies, striped yellow and black, or vein-thin and green. One lands for a moment on the rock next to her, bonded, forewing and hind wing flickering, such delicate mesh it seems evolution can go no further.

She suddenly wishes Alexander were with them, imagines him arriving and stripping off down to nothing, his pale bull flesh, cock draped between his legs, leaping in and a tremendous splash washing through the pool. The erotic invitations of summer. Or perhaps Lawrence, though he was never a great swimmer; he and Emily are in Spain for two weeks, unnecessarily – England is almost as hot. She is glad to have these new companions in her life. She gets out and dries off. The sun burns her shoulders. Her skin smells of the river, a fragrance that is intimate somehow, reminds her of sex.

Back at the cottage she sits out in the garden with an enormous salad. She cannot stop eating avocados, radishes. House martins spurt into the mud nests under the eaves, folding their crescent wings only at the last moment. In the evening, forest bees bump against windowpanes, get into the house, and have to be put out under tumblers. She applies cream to her sore shoulders and thinks of Binny, almost fondly: summers in her damp cheesecloth blouses, and the big blue pot of Nivea cream that she and Lawrence were savagely coated with when sunburnt.

The heat continues and builds. The protesters at the gate of Pennington Hall wilt, put up makeshift screens and parasols, bring handheld, battery-operated fans. Their numbers dwindle. It is not the season to campaign: the children are off school, holidays have been booked – who wants to indulge in antagonism? Honor Clark has water delivered to the remaining few, a kind of humanitarian intervention on the part of the regime, which they leave in the box, then open, and drink. Rachel and Huib watch the CCTV footage. There is nothing alarming. The wolf-headed man does not return. It is as she predicted: things are beginning to gutter out. Another garbled email arrives from Nigh. She wonders again who he is – a tame maniac, or someone who poses a more serious threat? The latter seems improbable. Perhaps it is a woman – though she doubts it. Occasionally the wolves howl at night; she hears faint, exploratory calls, which are and will remain unanswered. Good, she thinks, at least they haven't forgotten everything.

Alexander drops by to see the pair twice a week, more often than is strictly necessary now. Afterwards he accompanies the group to the pub. He stays late, drinks a pint or two more than the driving limit, to no ill effect. Sylvia remains polite and careful, though always marginally guarded, and occasionally must join her father for a regional dinner party, a wedding in London. Once or twice Rachel has seen her getting out of the helicopter with Thomas – her other life. There seems to be no boyfriend, or she is very discreet. They are all celibate, as far as Rachel can tell, like a band of secular monks. A strange group, too, almost the beginning of a joke: the vet, the Earl's daughter, the Buddhist South African, and the pregnant wolf-keeper. As for Rachel, she is enjoying the second trimester, the energy, people telling her she is looking well – radiant, even. The extra blood and the weather act like aphrodisiacs. Her libido is high. At night, in the soft-boiled heat of the cottage bedroom, lying on top of the sheet, she imagines all manner of scenarios. The man in the pub in the village near Willowbrook, or Huib's tent, conveniently located. Idle thoughts, nothing serious in them. It is Alexander who watches her across the table in the pub. It is he who, if she is honest with herself, she fantasises about most often. Her desirable type. Broad, swinging. His reading glasses unnatural on his large face when he signs the quarantine paperwork, a Mallen streak in his hair behind his right ear. He unearths memories of her first times – the unabashed northern lovers of her teenage years. What are the rules now? She is single, though clearly her status is not so simple.

And what of him, his life? He is unsentimental. His wife has been dead three years, of ovarian cancer; he speaks of it intermittently: a two-year decline, the drives to get chemotherapy a county over. Awful, but endured; he is still here, and life rolls on. There is a daughter, who lives with him part-time, and also with a relative nearby – the maternal grandmother. He watches Rachel, sees the obvious, but sees the rest too. His work and war stories are directed at her.

It's all specialist cattle now on the farms. Belted Galloways. They look very chic in the pasture, but they topple over in the heat like Victorian ladies.

Everyone laughs.

How do you treat them? Sylvia asks gamely.

A tincture of lavender and a nosegay, he says.

More laughter. Rachel returns his gaze. He drains his pint glass and stands.

Right, that's me. The Westmorland Show starts tomorrow. Ribbons and hats and enormous bollocks. Anyone want a lift home?

You alright to drive? Huib asks.

I surely am.

He is six foot four, substantial, built for it: an agricultural drinker, as they used to say. Rachel stands, too.

I'll call it a night as well.

Shall I drop you?

I'll walk.

You sure?

It's a nice night.

OK. Night, all.

Not disappointment in his tone, nothing so obvious. The opportunity passes.

But the next week, having parked near the enclosure for a legitimate quarantine visit and opting to walk with them to The Horse and Farrier, he is at liberty to accompany Rachel back. Another warm, rusk-scented night. Bats careen in and out of the trees as they walk the wood-lined mile, missing them by inches. The leaves are sibilant in the breeze, and the head of the moon looms on the horizon like an alien silo. It is luxurious walking without coats, without jumpers, as if in another country. At the pub there is a debate about Scottish independence. The polls have tipped – for the first time the majority lies with the yes camp. Austerity measures and healthcare mismanagement have left Mellor, and his government, weak. Surprisingly, Sylvia defends the nationalists; Rachel had assumed her conservative, or at least part of the old order, not a devolutionist.

I'd like to see a shift to more regional power, too, she says. A lot of Cumbria's needs are not London's, or Cornwall's. My concern is what happens in England if they go. Daddy's party is really struggling as it is.

There'll definitely be a Tory apocalypse, Alexander says.

Huib, who has been unusually quiet during the conversation, finally comments.

Freedom is exciting – the idea of it. It becomes a force in itself. In South Africa we were really excited about the election in '94. It's what happens next that counts. I'm not sure the born-free generation understands what the original plan was when they vote.

The windows of the pub are open; warm night air circulates in. Rachel has never seen Huib look so serious. But neither has she met a South African who is blasé about politics.

Since Mandela's death, aren't people reassessing, Alexander asks, about whether or not the vision has been accomplished? What to do to get things back on track?

Well, that's easily answered: it hasn't. We have some pretty terrifying youth leaders. Terrifying and popular. It's a different mindset completely; it's not pedigree politics.

The mood becomes sombre. They finish their drinks and troop back to the Hall. Huib bids them goodnight and walks towards his river campsite, Sylvia to the big house. Rachel and Alexander head towards her cottage and his car. As they get closer a feeling of disinhibition descends; she offers him some tea.

I'd have a cup of tea, he says.

His tone is not convincing: polite and reserved – perhaps she has misread the signs. He follows her inside and she puts the kettle on, fiddles with cups and teabags. He leans on the counter, looks about. He seems very tall in the low-ceilinged room. She is aware of her plain decorating tastes. The walls are not elaborately adorned: a calendar, on which there are midwife appointments marked, the Chief Joseph carving, an embroidered cloth from Spain – thoughtful souvenir from Lawrence. On the kitchen table is a laptop and a few printed sheets – the eternally unfinished book chapter.

Nice place, he says.

Yes. I was going to look for something else, but I've settled in, and there doesn't seem to be any pressure to leave. I think it probably suits Thomas to have me on site.

Too right, stay put, he says. You won't want to move when the baby comes, anyway.

His shirt is partially unbuttoned, dark hair beneath. There's the faint discolouration of sweat in the blue cotton under the arms, a brownish smudge on one of the rolled-back sleeves – something the plastic veterinary apron has failed to deflect, perhaps. She mashes the teabags against the sides of the cups with a spoon, drops them into the sink, bends, and gets the milk out of the fridge. She catches his look as she stands – the bump is sitting entirely to the front and she has not gained weight elsewhere yet; her backside is still as it was. She feels surer.

Not a miffy then, he says.

What?

Milk in first. The Keighley method, as my mother would have said.

No.

I don't mind. I'm not a true Yorkshireman, just a halfie. It's been scientifically proven, though – the tea stays hotter if the milk goes in first. So, you're, what, six months now? Must be an interesting phase. Lots of weird stuff happening?

Yes, some.

She wonders if he is acknowledging her current state of arousal; he has a daughter, he may know the stages. She may be less subtle than she thinks. He sips loudly from the cup.

Had all your scans?

Yes.

Do you have a picture – can I see?

She is a little taken aback at the request. She had not imagined this would be part of the evening's choreography. Could it be a way of closing the proceedings down – talking about the baby, as if to undo any rogue fantasy, any denial? Perhaps he is simply acknowledging the situation, a courteous bow before their taking up the positions. She goes to the drawer and finds the latest ultrasound copy. The bones are brightly lit, luminous, like a sea creature, except that the creature looks remarkably human. She hands it to him.

Amazing, he says. Look at that head.

His voice drops to a tone of sensitivity she has not previously heard.

Dad's not around then?

No.

Alexander nods. She begins to feel awkward, and on the verge of trying to explain, or of stopping everything before it starts. He puts his hand to the side of her face.

OK. Just checking. I'm not a bastard, by the way.

He smiles.

Unless leaving the loo seat up counts as bastardly.

She looks at his mouth, the fuller upper lip with the white scar. She says nothing. He moves round in front of her and stands with his legs splayed. He kisses her, lifts her slightly. A slow, plush mouth, not quite what she expected. The mound of her stomach feels hard pressing against his groin. He draws back.

Are we drinking this tea? he asks.

No, probably not.

He kisses her again, less gentle, a kind of deliberate gambit. They do not take their time – whatever has been set up has been done so with licence. He untucks her shirt and touches the skin of her back. He unfastens her bra, pulls it and the shirt off together. Then he pulls off his own shirt and drops it on the floor. His skin is incredibly warm, a shallow depression between his chest muscles, dark hair. He lifts her onto the counter and begins to kiss her breasts, which are hard and full, the nipples incredibly sensitive. It is too much; she has to stop him. She unbuckles his belt and undoes the trousers, moves his boxers down. There's a heavy erection, the exterior seems too fine and silken for the amount of blood held, almost artisan, like medieval machinery. She pushes herself off the counter, bends, begins to move her mouth over it; under the soft bundle of skin is fluid, polished flesh, membrane and musk. He grips her hair, lets her, then asks,

Where should we go?

He follows her upstairs, his hands on her shoulders, as if blind and being led. Now it has started and they are touching, he does not seem to want any kind of separation. On the bed he is careful, but confident. He strips her out of the remaining clothing, goes down on her. Then he moves up the bed, leans in, not heavily, but without anxiety, and fits himself. A murmur of appreciation. He begins to move. She senses restraint, concentration – a man for whom it has been a while. He is sweating, breathing hard. His chest is hot and damp and immense, the heel of her hand fits into the hollow. He lets her dictate. Her orgasm is expansive, the contractions in her uterus mildly painful. A grating sound in his throat, as he comes he pulls out. He lifts up, aware he might be crushing her; underneath, her body is slicked wet, and small curls of his black hair are sticking to her breasts.

He props himself on his elbows and they lie for a while. Everything shrinks back, wetly. An owl is calling hollowly into the darkness. He rolls over, taking her with him, so that she is lying on top. She sits up. He is smiling.

That was great.

His chest rises and falls. She puts her fist in the cavity, which is deep, but not deep enough to mean heart problems.

Pectus excavatum.

Come here, Miss, he says.

He pulls her down by the shoulders and kisses her – her stomach only just allows it. Then he traces the dark line running up her lower abdomen, to her belly button. Her legs are folded beneath, the muscle of the left begins to twitch and cramp.

Ouch. I think I have to move, she says. Ouch.

He tips her gently to the side, one hand holding her back, then squeezes her calf muscle. They sit up against the headboard. She stretches her legs out, flexes her feet. The mood is light, permissive, strangely comfortable.

Are you one of those guys with a pregnancy fetish? she asks.

He laughs and touches her stomach.

Maybe I am. I hadn't thought about it. What a pervert. Are you one of those women with a James Herriot fantasy? You want the old vet to fuck you in the stables?

Of course.

She feels giddy, wary of standing. There's a chemical brilliance in her body. On and off, a breath of cooler air drifts through the window, not enough to refresh. She wants ice. The owl continues its empty lamentation, or the mate is replying. Alexander looks in no way as if he is considering getting up and going home. She begins to imagine the awkward conversation around departure, then puts the thought aside.

Better drink some water. Do you want some?

Yes, no more tea. I wouldn't say no to a beer.

I might have some. I'll look.

She gets up slowly from the bed and crosses the room. He watches her. She does not feel self-conscious, though she is still getting used to the new form, the stiff waist, having to kneel to pick things up, trouble lacing shoes. She is larval, half-staged, swollen at the central interval. She looks for something to put on, but it seems silly to cover up.

It suits you, Rachel, he says. You look like a fertility goddess. Listen, go and have a wee.

Excuse me?

She pauses by the door. His legs are sprawled, giant rimed feet sticking up at the bottom of the bed, his arms resting along the headboard. The sheets are spun about, twisted and half draped on the floor.

Helen got a few urine infections when she was pregnant with Chloe. You're more vulnerable. And after *that* –

He gestures expansively over the bed, palm open, as if to suggest an area where an extreme event or ruin had taken place. He is grinning, pleased with himself.

What? she says.

You thought I really was being a pervert. With the weeing thing. Doctor's orders.

You're not out of the woods yet, she says.

She pads down to the kitchen, the loam of semen slipping between her thighs. She opens the refrigerator door. No beer. Upstairs she can hear creaking as Alexander moves in the bed and stands up. The shunt of the window being opened wider. She drinks a glass of water at the kitchen sink. She fills another glass of water for him. Overhead, the footsteps of a hefty man walking to the bathroom, the drill of urine into the toilet bowl, and, midstream, a casual fart. He flushes. He returns to the bedroom, gets back into bed. This is new, she thinks. She can't remember the last time she spent a full night with a man. She heads back up with the water.

Later, she lies with him behind her, his arm cantilevered over her hip. He breathes deeply, sound asleep. She lies awake, her leg aching from lying in the same position. The baby is still, has been still for the last few hours. Finally, she moves his arm and turns over. She places a pillow between her legs, and after a few moments drifts off. At some point in the night she has an anxiety dream, in which she is carrying the baby downstairs, knowing she will drop it, and then she does drop it. Panic as she rifles through the blankets and finds that the baby has shrunk, is tiny and red and vascular; she cannot tell what damage has been done by the fall. She wakes, turns over, rests her forehead against Alexander's back, and sleeps again.

An hour later his phone alarm sounds – the Doctor Zhivago theme tune – confusing and slightly ridiculous. She is half awake, watching the greenish, alchemic dawn filter into the room. He rolls and groans softly as the alarm sounds again. Then he gets up in one swift determined move, as if from his own bed, searches for his boxers on the floor and puts them on, a man on automatic, used to forcing himself into action in the early hours. Rachel lies still, wondering how to tackle the situation. Is it better to feign sleep? He goes downstairs, not silently by any means, but considerately. She can hear him dressing, the clink of his belt, a tired cough. After a few moments of quiet she is sure he will leave, or has already left, but then she hears cupboard doors opening and shutting, the clink of crockery and the throaty purr of the kettle.

He comes back upstairs. She lifts her head from the pillow.

Tea, he says. Keighley style. It's the perfect temperature in case you're wondering.

Thanks. What time is it?

Five-thirty.

She groans. He takes a sip of tea and deposits the cup on the table, sits on the bed. She puts her face back into the soft swale of bedding. She feels him reach a hand under the sheet and fondle her bottom. Then he pulls the sheet down to her midriff, sighs, and stands.

You make it difficult to leave.

I'm not doing anything. I'm just lying here.

Exactly. So, shall I take you to dinner then?

She looks up at him.

Tonight?

Tonight.

I've got a meeting this afternoon. Can I ring you when I'm done?

Great. See you later.

He has taken this as agreement: a date. She wonders if she should clarify. But it's too early to think about what might be set in motion, and what might not. He bends down and kisses her on the cheek.

Bye. I had a very nice time, goddess.

Bye.

She tries to summon sleep but cannot. The racket of birds in the garden, the insistent light, her own restlessness. There are thumps against the walls of her stomach, a pedalling sensation low down – the little being inside her, causing her to have strange wild dreams and capable now, according to the literature, of dreaming itself. Though what dreams could it possibly have? she wonders. Textures and sounds, a man and a woman's voices like weather outside, the surrounding meat contracting and turning golden. She sits up and drinks the tea, which has become tepid. Outside the sky is primary-coloured, the red bladder of the sun coming up between the trees. Another thump, stronger, so that her abdomen jumps visibly. A reflex action, but it feels like intent. At the midwife appointment next week she will have to mention the clash of events in the diary – her due date, and the pair being released from quarantine into the main enclosure. She puts her hand on her belly, over the jerking spot. Don't you dare, she thinks, don't you dare be the first one out.

WE ARE ALL RED ON THE INSIDE

That afternoon she meets with Michael Stott and a representative from the county's deer management group, Neville Wilson, in a snug sitting room in the Hall – a rather old-fashioned venue, with leather chairs and a low table, a stag's head mounted on the wall, pictures of athletic black dogs. Rachel senses a certain pastiche irony in the décor. The two men are old friends, it seems, and are bantering when she arrives. A do at the rugby club, someone too drunk to get home, *bugger would not give up his key, so the Crusaders tipped his car onto its side.* Michael has on a tie and blazer, is dressed with respect for the venue, as is the rep, a raw blond man in a green twill suit. Coffee has been left for them, as usual, on the sideboard, and a stack of elegant shortbreads. They each help themselves; no one is willing to play mother. The room is hot, though the windows are open; the men remove their jackets, white shirts pressed by their wives underneath.

'Stotty', the rep keeps calling Michael. He – Nev – outlines the situation for Rachel. Aerial and foot counts of the Annerdale herds have shown that numbers are too high. A cull will begin the following month. They do not want to wait until the wolves are released. They do not want to risk disease. One final shooting season on the estate is what you mean, she thinks, a last hurrah. But she does not argue; she is not in disagreement with the plan. Michael is keen to walk her through the logistics, and speaks as if to a novice. He places the leather wallet of rolling tobacco and a box of matches in front of him, and taps the table to emphasise certain points. His fingernails are thick and clubbed, encasing the tips of his fingers.

It'll be the sickest first, those that won't survive the winter. Then we'll take a mix from the rest of the herd. Stags first, hinds and associated calves. We'll be done by close of September on the stags. They tend to get skinny after the rut.

The rep chips in.

I do assure you, it's humane, Mrs Caine. We use soft-lead expanders this side of the border. There's no chance of them limping off half fettled.

The patronising tone is annoying and offensive – perhaps deliberately so. They are communicating as if with a tourist from the city, someone for whom the untimely death of any animal is an atrocity. No doubt they have discussed her before her arrival, formulated a strategy even.

Glad to hear it, Mr Wilson, she says. Where I've been living, there's a trend for semi-automatics. Very messy. They like cross-bows, too – no permits are needed. The amount of deer I've seen walking along with arrows sticking out of their backsides, you wouldn't believe.

Neville Wilson laughs – the joke is on his level. Buried in the comment, were he clever enough to interpret it, is the accusation that he is the undergraduate, trumped by the bigger business of American sport. The polite rituals of British deer hunting, the stalk, the language, the weaponry, would seem laughable to the average Idahoan – something out of another age. Michael Stott remains silent, damned if he'll be entertained by Rachel's comments. She turns to him.

And no doubt you'll be after a six-point antler, Mr Stott.

He leans back in the chair, reaches for the leather wallet. He unpops the stud, takes out the paper dispenser and a clod of tobacco.

I dare say. This going to bother you – or the babe?

He gestures to her swelling midriff.

People are awful fussy these days.

No. Go right ahead.

It is a power play. There are ashtrays on the table, there's a faint aroma of cigar; they are in the gentlemen's smoking room – probably requested by Michael. She has not tried to cover up her belly, apologetically – why should she? She won't now issue a ban. The baby will be fine. Binny smoked during both her pregnancies. Michael rolls and lights the cigarette, cupping it inside his closed hand as if against a high wind. Black cherry tobacco drifts over – a man of sweeter vices, then. He offers the wallet to Neville Wilson, who declines, but looks longingly at the makings as if having recently quit. The man looks puffy and red, a candidate for heart disease. She watches Michael, who is weathered but healthy, thinks again that his hair is too dark and glossy for a man his age. It seems like an indicator of something corrupt, an unsavoury raw diet, some kind of deviancy. She has not yet seen his wife. She imagines her pressing napkins and boiling chutney, cowed and bird-like, in some dark village cottage.

Thing is, your pups probably won't get the job done in time, he says. When are they let out?

End of September.

September. Yep.

He knows this very well. At least he understands there are limitations to the number of prey they can and will take – she would rather a knowledgeable enemy than an ignorant ally. Oblivious to the tension, or simply part of the charade, Neville Wilson issues a surprising invitation.

You'd be welcome on the stalk, Mrs Caine. We're not fully signed up on numbers yet, are we, Stotty?

The gamekeeper's eyes quickly curtsy down to Rachel's bump and back up again.

That might be inconvenient for her, Nev. Lot of crawling about.

Thanks, Rachel says. But I'll pass. Will Thomas be joining you?

She's interested to know where her employer's right-on sensibilities end.

He will, Michael says. The Earl always hunts. Leo, too, if he's about. And Leo's grandfather never missed a season. It's in the blood. Shame it'll all end.

She nods. She does understand the disgruntlement. The traditions of Annerdale go back hundreds of years; Michael is the last custodian, a hard position to be in. In his mind, wolves are no doubt faddish, indicative of Thomas Pennington's contradictions, his liberalism and modernity, or worse, he is inadvertently sponsoring a return to the dark ages, to the primacy of the feral. The systems are cracking up. She understands, but holds no sympathy. And now it is her turn to lead the hand.

Can I ask, gentlemen, were you planning to use moderators?

Come again?

Moderators. Silencers. I'm wondering what the level of noise will be during the cull.

Got sensitive hearing, have they? Michael asks, sneering. Shall we fit them with ear mufflers?

Neville Wilson laughs again; anyone's joke and any joke, it

seems, amuses him. If he understood how much money the estate will save via predation he might soon sober, reassess his job, she thinks. Michael's upper lip is hitched, revealing the pleated arch of gum above his front teeth.

Incredibly sensitive, she says. But you misunderstand me. I'd like there to be noise – as much as possible.

He stares at her. He does not know what she means.

It keeps them alert, she explains, prevents them from becoming habituated – you understand what I mean by habituated, Mr Stott. I don't want them to get used to humans. So, can we agree you'll be as noisy as you can be for me?

She is throwing her weight around a little, being cocky, but he deserves it. Walk into the pen with ear mufflers, she thinks, and they would take your fucking arm off. Neville Wilson stands and gathers his jacket.

OK, that all sounds good. If we're up to speed, I better be off, Stotty. Be in touch. Give my best to Lena and Barnaby.

They shake hands. Neville Wilson offers his hand to Rachel.

Nice to meet you, Mrs Caine. It's been fairly educational.

He takes another piece of shortbread on his way out. Michael snips the smouldering end of the cigarette with his first and middle fingers to extinguish it, and puts the leather tobacco wallet in his coat pocket.

Are we all done? Rachel asks.

Reckon so.

Fine. See you at the next meeting.

She stands, gathers her things. Michael remains seated for a moment. He looks faintly smug, has one more card up his sleeve.

Good to have a vet on hand, he says. In case anything goes wrong.

He is looking down at the table, where one hand is resting over the box of matches, its fingers horned and crab-like, nicotine-stained. When he looks up, it is without direct accusation, a trace of lewd amusement, perhaps. He has been spying, or he is speculating, testing the waters. Alexander's Land Rover was parked near the quarantine pen overnight; they are often seen together, maybe the attraction has been on display. Or he is making a dig at the wolves again – their high maintenance during quarantine. But Michael is too clever for the comment to be innocent. Rachel says nothing; her face remains neutral, unreadable. If he cannot undermine her professionally, there is of course the traditional realm of sexual disparagement. Michael is a misogynist, for all his sitting at the negotiating table with her. Her neck feels hot, as if colouring with annoyance. She bites her lip, says nothing. Binny comes careening into her thoughts. Her mother would have risen to a comment like this, given up information. *Think of us like dogs, Mr Stott, like bitches that come into heat.* But she is not her mother – there are more artful ways to fight. If she is not careful, the running conflict with Michael will make her careless and weak. Binny never learnt how not to fan the flames with her anger and indignation. She always admitted to her indiscretions when accused. Rachel moves to the door, opens it.

I very much doubt anything will go wrong at this stage, she says. Goodbye, Michael. Good luck with the cull.

Driving away from the Hall, her annoyance builds. She grips the steering wheel, imagines all the things she might have said, satisfyingly cutting. Even at Chief Joseph, with its seclusion and hothouse gossip, and the Reservation's wider system of finding things out, she could maintain a degree of privacy. There is nothing Michael Stott can do, other than try to shame her with his knowledge. But she was not taught to feel ashamed, far from it; Binny was adamant on that front. Any time she got wind of an attempt, she would go into battle – marching down to the junior school to extract Rachel from bible studies, horrifying the vicar and baffling the other kids. *You're not filling her head with that rubbish, you tight old git. Original sin, my backside. Pick up your coat, my girl, we're leaving.* Heat prickling Rachel's face as she followed her mother outside, to the school gate, where she was made to wait until the lesson was over and the vicar had fled past. The feeling that came after such exposure wasn't shame, either – more like the flinting of aggravation, red filling the brain. Not unlike the feeling now.

She takes the long way home, over the moors. The baby kicks. She slows down a little and breathes, tries to let the anger disperse. The road is vividly blue against the yellow, friable grassland, the parched landscape. Haze vectors the distance. The heat is approaching American standards; it is being worried about on the radio, a brutal new climate. In the west the sky is darkening. A storm on the way. Meanwhile, the air conditioning in the Saab does little. She rolls the front windows down and aromatic moorland air buffets in. The heat feels land-made, furnace-like, as if some great portion of the island is burning, tracts of coppice and forest, a final solution.

When she pulls up at the cottage, Lawrence's silver Audi is sitting outside, in the middle of the lane rather than parked in the garth. It is midweek; they have not arranged a visit, unless she has forgotten. She gets out of the car. The cottage is rarely locked, as her brother knows, but the gate to the garden is standing open. She goes in. Lawrence's wife is sitting at the table under the quince tree. Rachel hasn't seen her for several years, but the face is distinctive, wide, cattish, a plain kind of attractiveness.

Emily?

Emily turns and stands. Her hair is shorter than it was, cut along the line of her jaw and thatched with expensive highlights: middle-age, chic. She is wearing a cream linen trouser suit, out of place and yet somehow fitting here in the garden, a modern Edwardian look, were she to be holding a wooden tennis racquet or a china teacup. Emily greets her quietly, blinks, and looks away; her eyes are very bright against the black mascara.

Is Lawrence inside? Rachel asks. I can't remember him saying anything about visiting today.

He isn't here, Emily says. He didn't come.

Oh?

It's just me.

Oh.

What's going on? Rachel wonders. Retribution time? Please let's not have it all out today, she thinks, not after Michael. Emily remains standing, shifting her position on the lawn slightly, touching the back of her neck. Something is stirring beneath the surface of her face.

You look well, she says. Pregnancy suits you.

Rachel frowns, geared now for argument. The last thing she expects is a compliment – the same one Alexander made not twenty-four hours ago. Alexander, she thinks, dinner; I haven't called him. Emily looks at her again and then away, struggling to start saying what she wants to say. Rachel notices the mascara has been smudged and reapplied around her eyes, the lashes are clotted together. Pinkness to the rims, which is why the irises look so green. Emily has been crying. She looks to the side, sighs, and seems to take hold of herself. Something is definitely not right.

I should have called you, I know, Emily says. It's just that Lawrence and I had an argument, a bad one. I got in the car and started driving and I ended up here. I don't know why. I wanted to see you.

Her voice breaks a little. Rachel doesn't know what to say. She cannot quite believe her sister-in-law is here, by herself, for any reason.

Is Lawrence OK? she asks.

No, not really. He's – got some problems. I accused him of terrible things, of not really wanting a baby. He left. He took his keys and wallet and walked out.

She makes a noise, a partial choke, as if about to weep, and puts her hand to her forehead, knuckling between the brows. Rachel stares at her. Six months ago you accused me of emotional retardation, she thinks. You cut me off from my brother. Now, this. What am I supposed to do?

I thought he'd maybe have called you, Emily says. I know you're closer now. You haven't heard from him?

No.

Please tell me if you have.

I haven't.

Then Emily does begin to cry. She lets herself go, her body shaking, leaning forward, her sobs loose and repetitive, as if the appeal for help was some kind of emotional emetic. Rachel looks at her, mortified. After their years of antagonism and contraspective dislike, the bitterness, to see an adversary so reduced, submissive even, is unnerving. There is no pleasure in it whatsoever. Emily fights to speak.

Then he'll be – he'll be. I'm sorry, I'm sorry. I don't know where he is.

Her shoulders hunch. Tears drip to the ground from beneath her hands. Moments of paralysed excruciation pass before something kicks in and Rachel steps forward.

Hey. Come on, she says, gently. Let's sit down. Over here.

She puts a hand on Emily's elbow, turns, and steers her towards the bench. They sit. She waits while the woman gets it out of her system. The weeping begins to taper off. Emily wipes her face, runs her fingertips along the soils of black make-up under her lashes.

I haven't heard from him, Rachel says again. Is he with a friend in Leeds, maybe?

It seems an obvious suggestion – stupid, in fact. She wants to know more about the extent of the argument, which has come as a surprise, but there's no way to ask. Simultaneously, the thought of knowing their intimate business is off-putting. Emily shakes her head.

He might be with Sara. I used to think there couldn't be anything worse than that, but there is.

Rachel doesn't recognise the name, or really understand the comment – is Emily alluding to an affair? she wonders. There's still so much about her brother's life she does not know. Emily looks up at Rachel, as if wanting confirmation, or admission, perhaps thinking she is withholding information about Lawrence. But Rachel is at a loss. She shrugs. It's odd. In her suffering, his wife seems far more attractive than Rachel realised – beautiful, even.

I said awful things about you, and your mother, Emily says, looking Rachel directly in the eye. I said he was brought up in a household where bad behaviour was normal. I told him he was too fucked up to be a father and we should stop trying.

What did you mean, he has problems? Is he seeing someone?

Emily does not answer, but continues to look at Rachel, reading, assessing. Then, as if making a conscious decision, she recoils from the details of confession.

It's nothing. Just that he goes through these bad times. He comes a bit unwound.

It's a vague thing to say, but the tone is too factual to be simple deflection or a lie about her husband. What does coming unwound mean? Rachel cannot imagine her brother fucking around or otherwise acting up. But then, she has seen little of him as a grown man. And all men are capable of straying. Most women, too. Lawrence was brought up a certain way; if not instructed in the school, then *let to see* the possibilities, the methods, as was Rachel. What is laid down in childhood is difficult to reverse; one might spend a lifetime trying. Suddenly Rachel does want to know more, never mind the awkwardness.

Who is Sara?

Just someone he works with. A friend in the office.

What did you mean, being with her isn't the worst thing?

It was just a stupid argument. We've been very stressed.

Emily wipes her face again, composes herself. It's too late. The guard is going back up.

Whatever it is your family's got, she says, I don't have it.

What do you mean?

You're so autonomous. So defended.

Is that a good thing?

Emily shrugs. Criticism or not, Rachel is out of her depth. She feels incapable of psychologising a brother she knows so little, or consoling a woman with whom she has frequently warred. Whatever window of insight into their troubles his wife might have provided has closed. Emily holds her hands tightly together on her lap.

Wait here a second, Rachel says.

She walks to the back door of the cottage and goes inside. In the kitchen she stands for a moment and tries to gather her wits. It seems bizarre that Emily has come all this way – on a whim, and to a former foe – asking for help. It makes no sense. And yet Rachel does want to help, or at least to understand. The idea of a marital rift, of her brother cracking at the seams, is unsettling. There's certainly more to it than Emily is letting on; that much is clear. Once, she might not have cared; now, she cannot turn a blind eye. She goes into the downstairs bathroom, gathers a wad of toilet roll, collects a glass of water from the kitchen, and goes back into the garden. She hands them to Emily. After blowing her nose and taking a sip, Emily rallies a little, sits straighter. She combs her hair behind her ears.

I apologise. This really isn't on.

There's no need.

No, there is. And I'm sorry for everything this last year.

In fact, the last thing Rachel wants is an apology – the hollow, unendurable victory of that. This declawed version of her sister-in-law still seems wrong. Shadows have begun to spool into the garden and the light is suddenly murky. To the portentous west, the sound of thunder, a long, deep tear, and there's a distinctive smell: wet herbs, cordite, the precursor of rain. Something big is about to unleash. She cannot, in all good conscience, send Emily away.

We should go inside, she says. I'm going to make some pasta.

It's about all I want to eat these days. You can have some with me.

She stands. Emily nods and stands also.

You look really well, she says again.

In the kitchen Rachel pours Emily a glass of wine, and quickly throws together a meal. The two do not speak much but there is a tenuous accord – enough to get through the evening. The rain begins, not with torrid, dehumidifying power, but a slow, intermittent shower, dysuric. Then the battering downpour comes, drenching everything. Emily catches Rachel looking at the clock.

I've ruined your evening, she says.

No, you haven't, Rachel assures her, but I do have to phone someone. And I think you should stay – you don't want to drive back in this.

After a quiet, reflective dinner, with limited conversation, they retire to bed. Emily does not expand on Lawrence's problems and Rachel does not push, nor are they keen to stray into the mined territory of the past. Emily borrows a T-shirt to sleep in, bids Rachel goodnight, and heads into the spare room. She seems less distraught, more resolved, though her frame of mind is hard to gauge. Although tired from the night before, Rachel cannot sleep. The house seems to ring with the presence of her brother's wife, but when Rachel goes to the bathroom, the spare room is silent and no lamp light filters under the doorway into the hallway. It occurs to her that her brother might be far less together than she'd always assumed, his proclivities far darker. Sara. Can it be true he has a mistress? The word, the idea, seems ridiculous. And what is the *worse* scenario Emily alluded to? Her mind shifts though fantastic, disturbing images: sex workers in the backstreets of Leeds, STD clinics.

She fidgets under the sheets. They smell of Alexander: oniony, a man's sweat and fluids. It was past eight when she called him – the phone went straight to voicemail and she left a brief, poorly explained message. She did not mention Emily. He has not called back. It is likely that he thinks her uninterested – God knows, she has perfected the impression over the years. After an hour or two's restlessness, she gets up, dresses, lets herself out of the cottage quietly, and walks to the wolfery. The rain is easing off. Between the clouds is a giant, tallow lobe of moon. The woods are still, giving nothing up, not a whisper. She walks carefully, so as not to trip, though the path is easy to see in the whitish moonlight.

When she arrives at the quarantine pen, she goes into the hide and looks through one of the night-vision cameras. They are at the bottom, by the fence, nosing through the grass and chewing. They are likely searching for large insects, mice, a toad, any living thing to kill, such is the boredom of being fed. Or perhaps they have found early mushrooms. After a while, they move up towards the hide, into plain view, their coats strangely highlighted, eyes eerie bulbs of light. Darkness is liberty for them, but what comes in darkness to challenge their dominance is the worst thing they face. Another pack, ambushing. Humans. Juggernauts on the highway. Tonight they are playful. Ra trots alongside and then passes Merle, falls back, passes her again. He rises on his hind legs, circles his head, like a boxer. He tugs at her ruff. The day's languid canine is gone. He is a night hunter, like the legend. Though he is big, he is agile, and will be good at taking rabbits, she thinks, if he can learn to chicane through the heather. Their feed is being carefully weighed and given just once a week, but they are still well bulked. There is fat under their skin, around their hearts, kidneys, and in the marrow of their leg bones.

Once they are released and have to go to work, the stores will be reabsorbed. Ra rolls on his back, rubbing the top of his head backward and forward on the ground, his legs kicking, dopey, submissive. Merle stands over him. Rachel smiles. It is at night that they give up their secrets, that they seem most sacred to her: ghost-like, elegant, and frivolous.

She leans back against the hide wall and watches them until she begins to feels better, less anxious. They pad soundlessly, even when they are within thirty metres of her. They do not howl. The nightly border tests of the first few weeks have lapsed into occasional bouts, their heads tilted back, throats perfectly straight to a funnelled point. Kyle had a trick for setting them off, if they were close by on the Reservation – he would howl mournfully until they howled back. Acceptable human interference, he called it. She is thinking of him less now. Their communication has been polite, but infrequent. The moral question still hangs over her, but time and distance are making it easier.

She arrives home a little after 5 a.m. It is already light. The Audi is gone. Inside there is a note on the kitchen table. *Thank you and sorry again.* She screws the paper up and puts it in the bin. She is tired now, even though the day is brightening and the birds are singing. Upstairs, the spare bed is made, as if never slept in, the T-shirt left folded neatly on top. She thinks about calling Lawrence, but the hour is too early and the fight – whatever it was really about – is not her business. What would she say? *Don't upset your wife.* No. She goes to her bedroom and lies down on her side, puts a pillow under her belly. An hour's rest, and then she will get up and go to work.

*

The midwife is a woman in her mid-sixties, with ash-grey curls and a stiff hip, past retirement age but not, it seems, retiring any-time soon. Her name is Jan. She is from Workington and sounds fractionally Irish, like many of the older residents along the west coast. She sits at her desk, one leg held straight out in front of her to relieve the pinch in the joint. On the desk is a lumpen, hardwood sculpture, a souvenir from her time working in the Botswanan clinics. Her uniform is deeply unflattering: brown, waist-less, almost a military tunic. But her manner is that of a jovial, life-worn aunt, someone who has seen and countenanced much, and has managed, through sheer will or remarkable fortitude, not to become jaded. She laughs frequently, chides the baby for hiding behind the placenta when she is trying to listen to the heartbeat.

Come out, you little beggar.

She moves the device.

No, now that's coming through the cord.

Finally she finds a clear sound and is pleased. Rachel's growth is measured. More blood is taken. They discuss a birth plan – birth wish list, as Jan prefers to call it, since plans often have to be altered. She expresses mild concern about a home birth – Annerdale is a fair distance from the hospital, it is a first birth – but is not unconfident about Rachel's choice, her health. She is used to rural deliveries. She is nurse-trained, able to catheter-ise and perform episiotomies. Twenty-eight weeks: the baby is viable.

You've got the main centre number and delivery suite num-ber, Jan says, but I'm going to give you my mobile. I've got NHS enhanced reception, so you can get me anytime. Anything at all, you just pick up the phone to me, luvvie. Now, tell me how you're getting on generally.

Rachel lists the discomforts, the pelvic pains, the heartburn, all standard. Walking to the enclosure takes an extra ten minutes, and often she feels winded. She can hear her own heart banging away when her right ear is on the pillow. Jan is sympathetic.

Let's see about getting you a support belt. Not the swishest fashion item, I'm afraid, but they do help.

The session overruns; all Jan's sessions overrun. Most interesting to Rachel during their time together is hearing about the strange phenomena of the job. The anecdotes, the decades of observed behaviour.

Don't be surprised if you find yourself wanting to be in the smallest room in the house when you're in labour. Box room. Downstairs lav. I've had women do the coal shed.

They have a conversation about the risks of the quarantine pen, but it seems belated. In any case, Jan is not the cotton wool and antibacterial type. Her area covers the west coast farmers. There is the issue of lambing; she has had one or two cases of Q fever, but if every pregnant lady in the county stopped associating with her husband's livestock, farms would shut every week up and down the district, she says.

She flexes her sore leg in and out.

I might draw the line at coming in with those wolves, luvvie.

Her smile is all uppercase: a row of tiny, identical teeth sitting on her bottom lip. She will be a good person to have at the delivery, Rachel thinks. Her patients, bellowing and begging for pain relief, punching their partners in the face during the ring of fire, the associated fluids – what else is there to do but see the funny side? She reminds Rachel a little of Binny, a benign version of Binny. Or is it just that she has begun seeing her mother in strange and unexpected places, in women of a certain age, straight-talkers, grand dames. She has started seeing Binny in restless dreams, too, in a capacity not wholly unwelcome or unhelpful. Swimming in the river, gloriously naked, her missing breast restored. Showing Rachel how to squeeze and palpitate to make the milk come. Making jam! The madness of gestation, strange chemicals and hormones, the other side of the brain's looking glass.

You're a sensible lass, Jan is saying, so I know you won't get all flearty when I say this. But I'm also going to show you how to programme in a set of emergency numbers, in case anyone else needs that information pronto. Better to be prepared.

Rachel nods and hands over her phone. Jan unlocks the screen and fiddles with the buttons – master of modern technology as well as midwifery.

Doesn't mean people can get into your nudey photos and private stuff, she assures, but they can access names of loved ones, the hospital, me.

I didn't even know phones did that.

Oh, yes. Air ambulance are always complaining when people don't bother. No one thinks how hard it might be to trace families in an emergency.

She hands the phone back.

Pop your other numbers in now.

Not like Binny after all, Rachel thinks. Binny couldn't even master ring-back or last number dialled on her landline. At the end of the meeting, Jan walks her to the surgery door, past a couple of other women in the waiting room at various stages of pregnancy. She points to a car in the staff row outside the health centre – a small, vulpine-looking vehicle, sporty, bright orange.

That's me, she says. The Renault. She goes like the clappers when she has to.

Jan bids Rachel goodbye and good luck, as if she is about to undertake a race, and heads back inside. Will it help to like her when it comes to the birth? Rachel wonders. Or will she not care whether the devil himself is in the room, telling her to pant and push, holding her knees, getting the scissors out? It will help, she decides. It must.

*

By the second half of quarantine, the wolves have become much less nervous, smelling the meat being brought to them and anticipating the spot where it will be dumped. They come close in the wolfery, and do not strike back into the enclosure if a sudden move is made, or the gate clangs. Rachel and Huib rotate feed personnel and times when the carcasses are delivered. But the pair still slope towards them through the grass, heads slung low, cunning eyes. It is impossible to decoy, or approach in secret. They are too clever, hardwired; they *know*. Sometimes it is difficult not to believe they have additional senses, abilities not biomechanical – a kind of clairvoyance. Sometimes they are waiting in the right spot for the food the moment she has chosen its location and begun to approach. She has seen them turn to look and sniff before the wrapped deer in the Land Rover has even arrived, when it is en route, as if there is preternatural knowledge of the blood travelling to them, rather than the iron waft leaking from the wound, through hide and fur.

They discuss the matter with Thomas at the monthly review meeting in the Hall. The problem is presented and extra scare tactics proposed, so the carcasses can be placed more quickly, staff members won't be as intrusive, and the wolves will reassociate their human keepers. Thomas listens attentively and seems regretful about the plan.

Yes, I suppose they're not pets and shouldn't act like it.

They're not pets, Rachel says. It would be wrong to let them become any friendlier. They're seeing too much of us. By which I mean, we're seeing too much of them.

Shame, he says. It's wonderful to observe them down there – they're so magnificent.

She wants to remind him of the seriousness of the undertaking, the experiment he has committed to; he seems less focused. She wonders whether he has been visiting the wolfery out of hours, though he knows the schedule is restricted. Sylvia explains again the need for distance. Her tone is patient, and slightly confiscating – clearly she understands her father's tendencies.

Daddy, the trouble is, if they get used to being around people, even if they aren't completely tame, they might learn to scavenge, and we don't want that. They have to remain as wild as possible, for their own good.

He smiles with tenderness and pride.

Yes, darling Soo-Bear. I do understand. How clever you are. No, you're right, Rachel. Whatever you think best. These scare tactics – what do you suggest? Play Bach very loud?

Puccini, Sylvia says.

The Earl and his daughter laugh, a quiet conspiratorial laugh – a private joke about musical tastes, possibly. There are occasional tells between them during such meetings, but mostly Sylvia remains professional, and does not play princess. She works hard, reads up on the subject. But at times like this, Rachel is reminded that she is guesting on the project, that it is a year out rather than a year in for her.

There are a few reliable methods we can use, Rachel says. Including loud noises. My feeling is it won't take much to restore a bit of caution.

Very good, Thomas nods. Is there anything else on the agenda?

Rachel considers updating him on the levels of protest, the regular occult letters from Nigh, and the more organised legal correspondence from The Ramblers, though his lawyers will surely be keeping him in the loop on the latter. She decides against it. He has been successfully distanced from the public face of the project, and she wishes to keep it that way.

No. We're in good shape, overall.

Excellent.

He claps his hands together.

And have they fallen in love yet?

He raises an eyebrow, begins to hum a tune. *Love is in the air.* Rachel smiles tolerantly, but does not find him funny. The spontaneous foolery of her employer, his hop-skip-and-jump attitude, still leaves her feeling awkward. She wonders if this is his persona in the House of Lords, too, whether he gets away with flamboyance and buffoonery, whether he prospers because of it in a climate of old schoolboys, all of whom aspire to or claim eccentricity in some degree. She thinks back to their original meeting, his studied attempt to win her over to the project. Since then, it seems his knowledge on the subject has gone into serious decline. But now that he has Rachel running things, perhaps he can afford to be less invested. It is perhaps his habit, to surround himself with experts, then dislocate.

They're bonding, she says. I'm hopeful they'll mate in the winter.

In fact, all the signs in the run-up to the release are good. The health reports are reassuring. The implants have proved negligible. They have been vaccinated. They are acclimated to the terrain, its hard carapaces and grasslands, via the microcosm of their acre. All that remains is for their human aversion to prevail.

And how are you, Rachel? Thomas asks. Not long to go now. We're all very excited about our other new addition to Annerdale.

She has no wish to discuss the details of the pregnancy with him, especially in front of the group. But the tenor of estate membership is such that almost familial interest is taken in the workers' lives, like a factory town, or Ford's empire. The baby is being regarded as part of the fabric, part of the community – she knows, an idea both securing and suffocating.

I'm fine, thanks. Everything's fine.

Wonderful. Anything you need, please just ask. Right, I better go. I've a tedious meeting across the border.

The Scottish referendum is in a few weeks and the Earl is part of the monetary committee. Rachel has heard him on the radio a few times; his position on independence withheld, talking about the cost of setting up new nations. Everything has overheated, politically; most days the news features fresh accusations and tactics, business leaders switching sides, spokespeople from the military, the judiciary, European representatives speculating on continued EU membership. Thomas leans down to kiss his daughter.

See you in Edinburgh, darling.

In the days that follow, the heat of summer lifts, and the sun becomes less concentrated. September. Rachel walks in the cool early mornings. Sometimes there is a text from Alexander first thing – he seems oblivious to any withholding on her part. They have spent a few more nights together – the arrangement practical, but affectionate and enjoyable. The trees fluoresce, as if in a final bid to stay green. There is already a tint of autumn about the roads, leaves beginning to gather and flutter along the verges, field-stumps rotting in the drizzle after haying. In the sky, a more complicated portfolio of colours: lilacs, yellows, like a warning – bad weather brewing in the Atlantic. In the hedges hang early sloes, unripened black drupes pinned to the spiny trees. She remembers Binny making gin with them; her mother could turn any berry into lethal poteen. The parties in the post office cottage were torrid, involved villagers with only the strongest constitutions, the pub diehards, the dancers. Binny would have gone down well at the Reservation parties, she had entirely the right constitution.

In Seldom Seen's garden, the quince fruit is also immature, grey-white; the birds check on it regularly, covetously. Rachel begins to feel more like staying home, holing up, *nesting*, though she is unwilling to admit that's what it is. She can feel little jointed limbs flailing under the skin of her belly, elbows, feet, the odd somersault as the baby spins. It's extraordinary – the feeling of a life force breeching, trying to break the surface.

A different kind of weariness arrives, broken sleep, she has to sit up fully to turn over, and her pelvic bone aches, her hips go numb if she lies on either one too long. She manages two or three hours at most, a deathly unconsciousness when it finally arrives. Her dreams are incredibly vivid. Of Lawrence, lost on the moors: searchers looking for him on horseback, and she is one of them. She rides between the gorse bushes, calling his name. She has talked to Lawrence a few times since Emily's visit, but the true nature of the incident is no clearer. The background static of anxiety remains; she is unused to worrying about her brother and does not know what to do. She dreams of her son, sometimes her daughter, in jeopardy, falling from branches, afloat on the lake like a burr of weed, or simply there, naked and kicking, in need of care. In one dream she gives the baby to a madman to mind while she goes to work, some cannibal from a ludicrous horror film. Then the madman becomes Nigh, who wears a wolf head and is in a wheelchair, IV tubing on a rack next to him. It will be OK, she tells herself, nothing terrible will befall the baby. She wakes breathless and furious with herself. The absurdity of it. But the good dreams of Binny persist, too, of a younger, helpful mother who never really existed. Is it forgiveness, or reconciliation of some kind? The dreams, so full of people. Perhaps the cottage is too lonely, she thinks. She has not made friends with any of the other expectant mothers in the district, has in fact only attended one antenatal class and missed the following two. She thinks about getting a dog, decides against it.

She likes it when Alexander stays. The sex is good, becomes gentler as she grows bigger; they find comfortable ways, her on all fours, or sitting at the edge of the bed. She is afraid to climax, the sensation is huge, her whole abdomen seizes. He is not offended by her, she realises, he has an autistic's practicality about their relationship, or is intuitively straightforward. If she does not call and he wants to talk to her, he calls; if she cancels a date, he rearranges. He arrives after work and cooks for her, hot meals with chilli and garlic and ginger – a man's understanding of flavour. He asks very little of her, and yet, by virtue of his presence, he is involved in her life, and the baby's. Among the groceries he brings antacid, laxative, Marmite – she cannot seem to get enough salt. He tries to get her to take vitamins. She is occasionally moody, takes the discomfort out on him, but he is thick-skinned. She apologises one night, for accidentally kicking him in bed, hard, on the shin. Another lurid thrashing dream.

I've bruised you, she says.

I've been hoofed by bigger and worse, he replies.

He shows her a crescent-shaped scar on his leg, from a shod horse rearing and landing on him, the flesh ravelled down to the bone. He admires the scar on her back, its puckered stitching. She tries not to think about where it is all heading, what it all means, even when he puts his hand on her belly to feel the gristly little heels pushing out, the rhythmic hiccups like firework pops inside, as a father might. She is more worried, she supposes, about the prospect of motherhood. She's never changed a nappy in her life. The plastic doll in the antenatal class she attended was so ludicrously false she set it down, made an excuse to go to the bathroom. Her mother used to tell a story about how Rachel had floated her only childhood doll off down the river. So she could go exploring, Amazon-style.

She confesses the antenatal incident to Jan.

Doesn't matter, Jan says. That's just entry-level stuff. You won't know anything until you actually have to do it. No one does.

What if I'm not cut out?

Oh, hell, who is? But I think you might be surprised, luvvie. When I hand the little one to you, something'll kick in.

As for the rest, what else is there to do but continue on as before? She carries wood in from the garden, lesser loads. She manages the project. Her wage is very generous – for the first time in her life she has decent savings – and will not stop during maternity leave, though she does not really intend to take official maternity leave. She orders newborn supplies online: nappies, a supply of clothes and various pieces of sterilising apparatus. A Moses basket. A book about animals. She gratefully accepts the Marmite jars Alexander brings, eats it spread thickly on toast, or heaped on a spoon like some kind of gory Victorian medicine.

Depraved, Alexander says, shaking his head. You're as bad as Chloe.

He sticks his finger in the jar, licks it, grimaces. He makes her laugh, talking unromantically about peridurals and prolapses. He suggests ridiculous names for the child – Algernon, Ignatius, Veronica. The whole thing seems uncomplicated, workable, though often she feels surely she must end it. She thinks of Kyle – they have not spoken since early summer, though she receives the weekly newsletter from Chief Joseph. The baby will no doubt be dark, a quarter Indian, Nimíipuu. What of that stolen heritage, the disqualification? There are formal tribal regulations for classification, she knows, proportions of blood measured. She remembers the solitude of her own childhood, mountain-bred, a condition aggravated by decades of remote locations in the northern hemisphere. Seldom Seen is lost in the woods – is she recreating such a world for the baby? She does not feel solitary now, but that is not Alexander's doing. She feels joined with something, viviparously, even if the physical tethers are temporary. Sometimes she speaks to whoever is inside her, after a series of insistent kicks. *Hello, baby. What are you doing?* They will have each other, she supposes.

After a couple more weeks playing phone-tag, Lawrence comes up to the estate to visit. He has been avoiding her, she suspects, so she pins him down. There might not be much time before the baby is born, she tells him. She makes sure he knows Emily is welcome, too, but Lawrence seems not to want to ask her. He makes an excuse as soon as the offer is made – she is busy, has a hair appointment, then yoga. Rachel suspects the invitation will not be passed along; he wants to come solo, perhaps to explain, or because relations are still fraught.

The following week – the day of the referendum – he arrives looking tired and pallid, but bearing gifts: a set of organic baby sheets and an attractive bird mobile to hang over the cot, which she had not thought about.

Wow, he says, when she opens the door. You're big.

Thanks!

No, I mean, nicely big. You look big because you're so small. Proportionally.

OK, point made. Anyway, it's good to see you.

You, too – that's what I meant to say. Not the big thing.

She doesn't mind the comment. It's true – her belly seems vast, a high, front-sitting dome, the skin stretched taut and scribbled with blue veins, still expanding. She is pleased to see him, relieved. They attempt a short walk up Hinsey Knot, a manageable altitude, and with the support belt not too painful. Even so, Rachel pauses regularly. She remembers walking with a backpack full of equipment on the Reservation. Her heart coped with the weight and bulk. Now it feels boomy, labouring away. Lawrence feeds her chocolate, a banana. Halfway up the hill, there's the sound of a rifle shot, barely more than a soft crack in the valley below. The deer cull has begun.

She waits for her brother to raise the subject of Emily, but he doesn't. He is withdrawn, quiet, though not unfriendly, and he is still attentive.

You doing OK? he asks. Want to stop again? We can head down.

No. I'm determined to get up there.

We can stop again, though.

I'm fine. Just slow.

Slow, and vulnerable-feeling, though she will not give in to it.

You seem fine, he says. Still stubborn. But you seem different.

Different?

I don't know. Less angular. Sorry, that sounds rude.

I can bite your head off for old time's sake, if you like.

He does not laugh. Nor does he read the note of encouragement in her voice, the invitation she keeps subtly issuing, to confide in her. She steps carefully up the tiers of rock and over the turf gulleys on the path. Near the summit of the hill, webbed lungs of cloud begin to obscure the view. They glimpse fields and forest, but no sea, no Isle of Man. The breeze is fresh, suggestive of cold currents streaming in from the gulf. They sit and rest, eat more fruit. Rachel unlaces her boots, leaning forward awkwardly, pulling the tongues forward to relieve her swollen feet.

Don't take those off, Lawrence warns. They won't go back on.

I know. Good grief! I didn't think this through! It's bloody hard!

You're doing really well.

Am I? I feel like a whale.

She turns to face her brother. It seems stupid to hedge.

How are you? You can talk to me, Lawrence.

He nods and stares straight ahead, pinning the horizon. The look of a man afraid to deviate from his course, she thinks. He has lost weight, around his face, his chest and stomach.

I don't know what to say.

What happened?

He shakes his head. He has not shaved — there are dark red whiskers on his chin — the prerogative of a day off work, perhaps, or an indication of continuing domestic dishevelment.

You don't want to know.

Listen, she says, I'm sure I still hold the trophy for biggest family fuck-up.

Again, he does not laugh. The success she has had in the past with humour, entertaining her brother, breaking the ice and the tension, is not working. He seems flat, pervasively melancholy.

Is Emily OK?

We're trying to work it out.

OK, she says. I'm glad to hear that.

Lawrence glances at her.

Really?

Really. You know she stayed with me that night. She's not the absolute monster I thought she was.

Yeah. She said that about you, too.

There you go. Pretty soon we'll all be sitting around the fire singing Kumbaya.

He does not seem cheered by the prospect of a new era of family harmony either. He points to her boots.

Come on. Do those back up.

OK.

She groans and leans forward, reaching round the mound of herself and fumbling with the laces. The last hook is impossible to find. Lawrence takes over the job — she watches him tying a double knot. He stands and offers an outstretched hand, and she lets him help her up.

I really do hope you work it out, she says.

It seems a wan thing to say. But her sincerity and concern

must be apparent. Lawrence sighs. Penitence and frankness vie with each other in his face. After a moment, he speaks.

It was a stupid thing, he says. With this woman who worked with me. It wasn't really a proper relationship. She doesn't work there any more.

This is Sara?

He nods.

Is it finished?

Yes, I think so. Yes, it is.

Were you in love with her?

The question is in a way meaningless, she knows, but one must ask. Love in such situations is rarely real. Sex is the engine, exalting and ruining people, sex and frustration. Love is what people believe is worth the path of devastation.

No. I was just . . . off the rails. And she –

She what?

We were just into the same thing for a while. We were bad for each other.

Rachel doesn't ask what this means, does not want the details. She can imagine, or sense, a seam of darkness, familiar to her, though she would not like to acknowledge it. Though he is finally being forthcoming, there is more to the situation than her brother is letting on. She wonders how Emily is coping. The world of women is split, she knows, between those who do and those who do not forgive. Even the willing sometimes can't. Men, too, though adept female duplicity often saves their finding themselves in either category. As they begin down the slope, she thinks of the rancher with whom she had a one-night stand, confessing to his wife and then driving to the centre, knocking on her door. She wonders if Sara told Emily, in a moment of heat or spite, or whether Lawrence confessed.

I was an idiot, Lawrence says, his voice full of self-reproach. I'm not proud. Even your wolves do better. Didn't you say they're monogamous?

Rachel shrugs. Such analogies are not helpful, though she, too, has in the past made comparisons.

It's a bit more complicated than that. There's sexual rivalry, plural breeding – never mind. The point is, these things happen, Lawrence.

I can't really use that as a defence.

I just mean, in the modern age, it's not all about mutually raising offspring. It's amazing people are as faithful as they are, given the opportunities, the appetites. As far as I know, you've been a good husband for years.

You're just one of a thousand possible selves, she wants to tell him. Genetics, nurture, choice – he is nowhere near the worst version. Lawrence stops walking. He shakes his head and holds a hand up, as if defending himself from the compliment. He turns away. He does not want absolution.

Don't.

She casts around for better advice.

I know I sound like a wonk. Sorry, that's just my language. I'm not very good at this. I just mean, we all make mistakes, but for a lot of the time we do OK.

When he faces her again, his eyes are bright with a sheen of tears, he is struggling to keep himself together.

I know. I just feel like shit. That's all. I've been feeling like shit for weeks. I don't feel well.

His voice is soft and rough. It is surprisingly moving to see him so upset. She feels her own eyes pricking. She puts a hand on his shoulder, squeezes. He tries to smile.

Thanks, Rachel.

The stories I could tell you about philandering, she says, lightly.

No, please don't. I always worried about you.

His face becomes pained again – this is not the moment to assert their similarities, or tell war stories. He looks out over the fells, at the pluming cloud. She can't be wholly satisfied with her efforts to help him, but at least she has tried. Inch by inch they are getting closer, undoing the past, or mitigating it. They are in the world as themselves, she knows; flawed, capable of better, and Binny cannot be blamed. They continue down the hill. Her back begins to ache and she stops to adjust and refasten the support belt. Lawrence waits patiently. Around them, the bracken is already turning reddish-brown, corroding. The wind is fresh. Autumn is her favourite time of year here – the county is at its most vibrant, flaring ruddy and golden, like a furnace. A year ago, she was saying no to this. A year ago, she could not have imagined such progression – but it does feel like progress, on the whole. As they walk slowly back to the car, she wonders about the baby. How much will she influence it, teach it, damage it? If she does damage it, will it end up hating her, blaming her? Will it go on to create a better self? No one is without choice, she thinks. No one is condemned to be changeless.

*

The next morning, while she's running a bath and listening to the victory speech of Scotland's First Minister on the radio, the land-line rings. It is Honor Clark; Rachel knows before she even lifts the receiver. Honor is the only person who phones her at home and at this hour. Overnight there has been an attack on the enclosure – the main fence, not the wolfery. The police are on their way, and Michael, who discovered the the sabotage, is waiting down at the Hall.

I'll be there as soon as I can.

Good. And of course, if you could treat the information as confidential, Thomas would appreciate it.

He knows already?

He does.

She turns the taps off. She is due at the hospital for an appointment at 11.30, which cannot be missed. She dresses, gets into the car, and drives down the lane. The morning sun is gilded, with mist above the lake and the river, white reefs over the fields. Frost tips the grass and the north-facing walls, and patches of yellow smoulder in the hardwoods, as if something is burning through from the other side. She takes a granola bar from the glovebox, one of the stash left over from her weeks of sickness, unwraps and eats it. Michael. She is annoyed that he is involved; any act against the project will please him. She's seen little of him since the stalking season began – he is busy leading groups of shooters around the estate, friends of the Penningtons and other visitors who have paid extraordinary amounts of money to crawl through the heather and sedge of Annerdale.

She turns the car radio on. There is no deviation from the subject on this day of high drama and history. A slim margin of votes has cut the north of the island free. Live on the BBC, Caleb Douglas assures sceptics and unionists that he will work to include them all in the decisions and the future of a new Scotland. The morning programme host, also a Scot, conducts a typically aggressive interview, reveals nothing of his own leanings. From tabloid editors there's idiotic talk of cars streaming south down the M74, queues outside estate agents, an exodus of second-home owners, English residents, and 'realists'. The American president and the leaders of other nations have sent messages of congratulations, ranging from guarded to ecstatic. No one knows what the political protocol is – an expert is brought on to explain the possible stages. The excitement is terrible and contagious. Great Britain no longer exists.

Pennington Hall rises redly from a white sea of frost. Rachel drives faster than she usually would up the driveway, the tyres of the Saab spitting gravel. Michael is standing outside the main entrance, smoking. He eyes her as she pulls up. She gets out of the car, pushing herself off the doorframe as she must these days, tries and fails to button up her coat, and makes her way over. Michael has on matching jacket and trousers in dark green hunting plaid.

What happened? she asks.

He breathes the sweet cherry smoke into the air, shakes his head.

No idea. Just saw it as I was passing.

When?

This morning.

What's the damage?

Well, they haven't got through, but they've had a good go.

Who?

She is aware her tone sounds accusatory. He sniffs, pinches out the cigarette, and pockets the stub.

It's probably kids larking about with a pair of clippers.

Clippers, she says. It would need to be something a little more industrial, don't you think?

As I said, they've not got through.

He meets her eye. He does not look furtive or gloating. Still, she doesn't trust him entirely. She wouldn't put it past him to be involved, by proxy. But that would be stupid. He has already outed himself as a naysayer, marked his own card. And what would be the point of sabotaging the main enclosure before the wolves were in it? She would like to ask more questions, but Huib is making his way towards them from his quarters above the carriage house, still wearing cargo shorts, despite the early-morning chill.

Are we going down to see it when the police arrive? he asks.

I would reckon so, Michael says.

Where exactly is the hole?

Back of Ulver Scar, near the woods.

That's a long way from the main road, Rachel says.

Michael nods.

It is.

Kids, she says.

I reckon so.

Good job you saw it, Huib chips in. We might have missed it in that location.

Vexed by the conversation, Rachel leaves them for a minute and heads into the Hall. Honor Clark is in her office, on the phone. She holds up a finger, signs for her to wait. Rachel lingers in the office doorway. Honor swivels in her chair as she speaks. She's lost a few pounds, though still remains curved, a country weight. Blue blazer with a neck-bow blouse, a very good complexion – she could not appear more suited to her situation.

It's at Rannoch Mhor, she is saying, the flight leaves at six. No, press aren't invited. Of course, of course. Douglas and a few others.

On the desk, next to the photographs of her grandchildren, is a white orchid in a pot of curling moss. On the laptop screen, an elaborate grid of appointments – Thomas' diary, extremely full as always; today's column is marked with a red background – an important day, clearly. Honor hangs up.

That was Thomas, she says. He won't be back until the end of the week. But it doesn't sound too serious, by Michael's account.

No, luckily not.

Can I leave it in your hands, then, liaising with the police?

Honor taps her pen. Her expression is expectant, marginally harassed, that of an overburdened chatelaine. She does not seem especially surprised by the attack – it is simply another event on the estate that must be dealt with. Her personal opinion of the project has never been expressed, at least not to Rachel. Beneath the solicitous exterior, she might be of Michael's ilk – a right-wing rustic. Most likely she is paid not to have an opinion, to be dutiful, to facilitate on behalf of the Earl, and, when necessary, handle fallout. Or perhaps, it would not surprise Rachel, she is a member of his unpopular party, a loyal follower, a genuine believer. They must exist.

That's fine, Rachel says. But could you arrange a meeting with Thomas when he gets back? I'd like to get on top of this, compile a proper list of those who have officially come out against the project. I feel there may be gaps – from before my time.

Do you need him for that? Honor asks.

Yes. I do.

The secretary swivels in her chair, faces the screen. Rachel does not say so, but she feels Thomas must be tackled on certain other issues as well. Michael, perhaps.

I can do Saturday morning, at eight-thirty?

Fine.

What shall I reference?

I don't know. Security?

Honor types. Rachel pauses for a moment before leaving.

We'll need to get the fence repaired as soon as possible.

Yes. I've spoken with the company. They're sending someone out this afternoon.

Of course you have, Rachel thinks. Everything put back in order straight away; the estate must keep up its face. She heads to the main door. Access to Thomas has become more difficult lately, she's noticed. Despite his initial enthusiasm, he has been extremely disengaged in the last few weeks, not replying to emails or messages. She thinks of Sylvia's comment the night she arrived in Annerdale, the night Prime Minister Mellor set down in the grounds on his way to the debates – doomed, though he did not know it then, to be the premier on whose watch the nation dissolved. *It'll be good for Daddy to have another project; he hates it when there's nothing new.* The Earl has got what he wanted, near enough – wolves roaming the estate. Has he simply moved on?

Outside, Michael is holding forth about the referendum results. They'll be bankrupt in a year. They take more money than they're taxed anyway. It'll be cap in hand to Europe.

She is hungry, and suddenly very annoyed by the events of the morning – its players, the cynical old systems. The English, bred to feel superior for generations but lacking any real desire for improvement or vision, seem intolerable.

Isn't that what we used to say about America, too? That the country would be bankrupt and fall into obscurity?

Michael turns to face her, scowling at the interruption.

What?

The Second Continental Congress disagreed. They've done OK, don't you think?

I forgot you were a Yankee for a bit.

I think the expression is a damn Yankee, Huib says, trying to joke. Michael turns back to him, to take up the lecture where he left off.

It's not enough of a majority to be causing havoc with the union. It's economic suicide. Brown says so, and he's a Scot. They can't just depend on North Sea oil, which isn't even theirs by rights.

Natural resources, Huib says quietly, are a contentious issue, especially when exploited by a foreign country.

Michael does not reply, knowing perhaps that he is straying into very dangerous territory: African politics. The conversation is interrupted by the appearance of a police Land Rover, making its way up the long drive, lights unlit, sirens off. The vehicle pulls up and two officers climb out, wearing high-visibility jackets over black. The younger looks about at the opulent surroundings, manicured grounds with sculpted hedges, the impressive red facade of the Hall, and is clearly awed. The sergeant introduces himself and his colleague. There's a brief discussion about the events; Michael's account is given again. He was passing; he happened upon the damage. Rachel listens closely for any deviation.

But they're not yet in that section of the enclosure? the sergeant asks.

No, they won't be for a couple more weeks, Rachel says. They're still in quarantine.

And that cage hasn't been tampered with?

No. It's not a cage.

OK, let's go and take a look.

They set off in convoy to the site of the damage, Michael leading in his utility vehicle, Rachel and Huib in the Saab, then the police. They follow the moorland inside the estate walls and turn off down a narrow service road, disused, overgrown, its slabs of concrete breaking up. It is not a part of the estate she is familiar with. The briar scrapes the sides of the Saab and the mudguards grate as the suspension dips over potholes.

Doesn't look like anyone's been down here for a while, Huib says.

No, it doesn't. But obviously Michael has.

After a quarter of a mile, they reach a wooden gate, which is padlocked; the sign on it reads, *Private Access Only*. Michael gets out and unfastens it with a key; the three vehicles pass through and continue on. After another mile or so, he pulls over in a clearing by a row of goldening woods. The others follow suit. There is raucous cawing from the trees nearby as they get out and shut the car doors. The ground is still white but the sun is dissolving away the frost. The younger officer looks at the fence and outer barrier spanning the near horizon.

Very Jurassic Park, he says. Is it just going to be wolves inside?

At level five, yes, says Huib.

What's level five?

Briefly, Huib explains the food chain and ranking system.

So where are we? the policeman asks. At the top? They start up the hill towards the barrier. Rachel glances back towards the road. The spot is very secluded, difficult to access, but also cleverly chosen for its remoteness, she suspects.

How often is the enclosure checked? the sergeant asks.

About once a week I go full round it on the quad, Michael says.

Rachel looks over at him, surprised by the declaration, unaware he was patrolling the barrier so regularly, and so thoroughly. This is not something he has mentioned before.

Any security cameras?

On the gates, she says. But they're not running yet.

Michael leads them over to the site of the sabotage. The barrier is undamaged. It is clearly mountable, and has not been designed as a blockade, just a method of keeping people back from the main fence. The officers pause to look at the triangular warning sign. On the other side of the barrier, the wire has been hacked. The damage is minimal, almost certainly not enough to have allowed an escape, even if the wolves were inside. The gash is ragged, about a foot long, waist-height, and gaping slightly – the work probably abandoned once the tensile strength of the material became apparent. The links that have been cut curl outward like surgical staples partially removed. The police spend a moment inspecting the handiwork.

Bolt cutters?

Pliers, maybe.

The section is photographed for the records. The sergeant takes out a notebook and pen.

Any ideas who might have done it?

Michael steps to one side, as if dissociating, takes out his tobacco wallet.

Miss Caine?

We've had a few threats in the last few months, Rachel says. The usual organisations and a crank or two. It's typical for projects like this. I can forward the correspondence, but there wasn't anything worrying. It's been much quieter lately.

She can feel Michael looking at her.

Any names you can give us? Greenpeace?

No, she says. Environmental groups are not our problem. We've had letters from The Ramblers. The Farming Alliance.

Michael cuts in.

Ramblers wouldn't have the gumption. Bunch of Manchester middle-class tea-drinkers. As for the farmers – they're all good fellows round here and too busy to bother.

The sergeant glances at Michael, then looks back at Rachel. She does not disagree with the assessment, much as Michael's tone annoys her.

Anyone else?

She exchanges a look with Huib. The wolf-headed man with the toy gun would be a candidate. But he is untraceable; the CCTV footage gave nothing of his identity away. And there is Nigh, in his, or her, religious delinquency.

No one I could name, she says. Anonymous emails. We have a website letting the public know about the project. It's probably someone who hasn't been following that closely or they'd know we haven't released them yet.

Nothing from any extreme animal rights groups? The Cambridge lot?

She shakes her head. She knows the group – there has been a spate of laboratory attacks in the last year, which they have claimed responsibility for. But the small, botched attempt on the Annerdale enclosure is not the work of such terrorists, she knows. They do not fire shots across the bow; they plan and execute intelligently; they succeed in creating havoc and publicity, even if it means subsequent arrest. The hole in the fence is messy, not professional or well timed. The sergeant closes his notebook. He opens another pouch in his jacket and takes out a card.

If you think of anything else, ring me at the station. It might be an idea to check things more regularly, once they're inside. Set up more cameras.

A paternal note has entered his voice – faint, anticipatory caution. The call-out now may have been a waste of time, but he can foresee trouble, and does not want to have to chase down escaped predators.

Kids, Michael says again, shaking his head. It's silly season. They're bored stiff before they get back to school and looking for stuff to bugger around with.

The young constable chips in.

We have had a lot of tombstoning this year. They just pulled a lad out of Thirlmere last week. He got caught in the dam mechanism.

Bloody idiot, Michael says. And it's not just themselves they get killed. It's the fellas going in after them.

They make their way to the cars in the clearing. Rachel checks the clock on her phone. Almost ten. The morning feels like a waste. She will barely have time to go back home before the appointment – but she must, the bag she has been instructed to bring in case she is admitted to the ward is sitting in the cottage hallway. She is hungry and her bladder is uncomfortably full. From the copse comes the earthen, muddy aroma of decay – roots, rot. A few bright leaves drift downward from the canopy. The policemen get into the Land Rover and head back towards the main road. No doubt they will have much to discuss on the long ride back to the station: the enclosure, Lord Pennington's extraordinary wealth. The young officer was right, Rachel thinks, it is Jurassic. The Earl is a behemoth among ordinary men; he resides at the apex, above all trophic levels. She checks the time again.

Michael, do you mind dropping Huib off? she asks. I'm not going back that way.

She needs to urinate and does not want an audience. Michael shrugs.

Fine.

I'll hopefully see you later, she says to Huib.

Yes. Good luck.

Huib opens the passenger door and Michael's brindled lurcher jumps out, begins to sniff the ground and scout about, its tail held rigidly behind it. The dog steers along scent trails, past Rachel, and towards the woods.

Tess! Michael calls sharply. Tess. Git.

The dog looks up expectantly, her big, soft ears folding forward like wings. Topaz eyes, a long, slender, upturned nose – one of their ancestor's closer-looking cousins, though Michael would not want to hear that. She is high-haunched and handsome, leaning slightly forward, in readiness.

Git, Michael says.

The dog scrambles up inside the utility van.

I'll follow on after you, she tells them.

It's a D lock on the gate, Michael says over his shoulder as he gets into the van. Just fasten it shut behind you.

She watches them drive down the narrow lane, then finds a nearby dell in the woods. The sound of the van dies away. All is quiet. The ground underfoot is plump and springy, upholstered with moss – rising up, the musty smell of wet bark and fungus. There are frilled orange brackets growing around the trunks, berries, dusty blue and blood red. She squats and relieves herself, the weight of the baby making it awkward to hold her position – she leans back against a tree. The branches rustle behind her, the lipping wind or birds flitting between trunks, something stepping back under cover. There's no one there, but she suddenly feels self-conscious, watched. She stands and looks into the trees, their dark old republic. The perfect environment for ambushing lynx, or bear. She would like to believe Thomas, to think that the country as a whole will one day re-wild, whatever its new man-made divisions created at the ballot box. She would like to believe there will be a place, again, where the streetlights end and wilderness begins. The wolf border. And if this is where it has to begin in England, she thinks, this rich, disqualifying plot, with its private sponsorship and antiquated hierarchy, so be it. The ends justify the means.

She walks back to the car, looks up towards the barrier. She doesn't really believe the attack was random. Whoever went for the fence must have known the topography of the estate; they knew this section was off the beaten track and there would be no witnesses, no one to raise the alarm. Little else about the attack makes sense. It is too early in the project to have been a genuine threat. Perhaps Michael is right, perhaps there was nothing more to it than opportunism and boredom, a lark. But in less than a month the wolves will be out. It was a near-miss.

*

Thirty-seven weeks. The baby is breech. They have decided to try an external cephalic version. The obstetrician, a small Indian woman, walks Rachel through what will happen, the risks – abruption of placenta, reduction of blood in the umbilical cord – though these are low. Chances of success are about fifty-fifty. If the procedure is too uncomfortable or if the baby cannot be turned, they may try again with an epidural, they tell her. She signs the consenting paperwork.

In the procedure room, she is cannulated and given terbutaline to relax her uterus. Jan pops in to see her as the preliminary ultrasound is underway.

You're probably going to feel like a piece of dough, getting kneaded, she says. But you'll be fine – Dr Nirmal is very good. She has magic hands.

Jan wiggles her fingers. Her hair has been dyed an unnatural shade, something between redwood and plum; her scalp glows with the colour, in need of a few shampoos to calm it down. One of her ladies is giving birth in the midwife unit, not in any particular haste, it seems.

I'll come back in a bit, she says.

Rachel tries to make herself comfortable. The placenta and levels of amniotic fluid are checked, and the obstetrician begins. The magic hands are small and strong. She puts on pressure-sensing gloves, feels for the baby's head and buttocks, pushes upward away from her pelvis. Rachel tries to breathe slowly and not tense. The discomfort is bearable. She breathes deeper, in through the nose, out through the mouth. A medical student is in the room, observing and making notes, a horribly young-looking man, not altogether interested, possibly just rotating through gynaecology. He asks her to score her pain, on a scale of one to ten.

Three. Four, maybe.

He ticks a box – some kind of survey or study project. Then he offers to sit next to her, like a substitute partner. She shakes her head. Alexander had offered to come that morning, too, but she'd declined.

Either he turns or he doesn't, she'd said.

He, is it? Reckon I could do it, and save you the trip.

She'd smiled at that, thinking he probably could. All the cows' cervixes he'd manipulated, reaching in to find the struggling hooves and ankles, then deeper, to the sloppy, upside-down head. The brute force of calving.

What at first feels like a deep massage becomes more like a rearrangement of abdominal wall and organs. Dr Nirmal pushes and rolls, pushes and rolls, inch by inch, concentrating, checking the position with the ultrasound. Rachel tries to relinquish control. She thinks of Binny, swearing as she tried to locate, by touch and stretch, the recoiled elastic in the waist of Rachel's school trousers. *Bloody thing! It's gone all the way. Here, madam, you try! You're the one who snapped it!* It is frustrating and bewildering, that at these times she can't stop thinking of her mother, who would have been a grandmother, and no doubt amazed by the prospect.

You're doing really well, the doctor says. Almost there.

Rachel breathes. In through the nose, out through the mouth. The baby's heart rate increases as the procedure continues, healthily, perhaps even indignantly. It is moved, to the transverse position. Then at an upright angle. Finally, after twenty-five minutes, the head is down. Dr Nirmal finishes and removes the expensive gloves.

Feeling alright? she asks.

Yes. I think so. A bit –

Like a loaf of bread?

Yes, actually.

Rachel is helped to sit up slowly. The obstetrician writes in the maternity notes and then leaves. The medical student asks a few more questions, then leaves too. The cannula begins to itch in the back of her hand. She and the baby will be monitored for an hour or so then allowed to go home. After a while, Jan knocks and comes halfway into the room, leaning round the door.

Success?

Seems so, Rachel says.

Jan jabs her thumb up, like a teenage boy.

Good one. Now, just stay that way, little one. No cartwheels, please.

How about you? Rachel asks. Success?

Yes, I better get back in; she's nearly on the go now. See you next week, luvvie. We'll talk about our options then.

The door closes. The building radiates quiet, though is discreetly busy, departments bustling in other wings. Her mother's final hours were spent here, in the AMU of the same hospital, while the medics did everything but resuscitate. Binny was not cogent, Rachel was told by the care home manager; she probably saw nothing beyond the thick walls of her unconsciousness. She wonders if Lawrence feels easier about their mother's decision to end her life – they have not talked about it. She imagines Binny lying on a trolley, the tubes, the report of machines, the final call made. An old woman in her eighties, no one knowing anything about the life she has lived. Lawrence arrived an hour after she was declared dead; she struck out alone, which would not have scared her. Now, Rachel will probably give birth in the same hospital, and a little piece of Binny will continue on. The prosaic event of birth, being replicated millions of times the world over, every minute of the day, except that it is happening to her, and it feels extraordinary, rare, nearly impossible, now that it is so close.

*

A week of suffering gigantism and soreness. Her abdomen aches. Her lower vertebrae feel displaced, and there's a grinding feeling against her ligaments. Her bladder goes into overdrive. The sensible portion of her brain kicks in and she stays home, does not go to the wolfery or the office, or even try to get into the car. She reads, lies on the bed surrounded by a mountain of stacked pillows, or wallows in the bath. The delivery van brings groceries. She cannot stop eating apples, four or five a day, until her stomach gripes. She cancels the breakfast appointment with Thomas – now is not the time to tackle him – the fence has been mended, and she wants to concentrate on the release, be as fit and rested as possible. It feels almost like training for a marathon: the endurance, the daily limits, the stairs almost defeating her. She tells Alexander – kindly, she hopes – not to come. She is terrible company, she says. He still comes, after work; he brings fish and chips from town, cool and vinegary in the wrapper, delicious. They sit by the fire for an hour, not speaking much, watching the flames flickering in the grate, greenish from copper deposits in the wood. He fetches more logs in for her, hulking a great quantity in one go. She can't say she isn't grateful.

I don't know why human gestation evolved like this, she says. If I were out there in the wild I'd get picked off in a minute.

You'd just have stayed in the cave, he says. On a pile of furs.

Two days later, Sylvia arrives with a basket of exotic fruit and best wishes from everyone on the project. There are pineapples and mangoes, dragon fruit – no apples. The arrangement looks like something out of a still-life painting.

I'm not ill, Rachel says.

I know. But Huib says you're probably living on baked beans and toast. I've got to make sure you eat something good. I've got to report back. No arguments.

Rachel stands aside, and Sylvia carries the enormous basket into the cottage kitchen. They sit drinking tea outside in the garden, Sylvia in her expensive Karrimor jacket with the Annerdale project logo stitched on, Rachel wrapped in a tartan blanket, though she is if anything too warm these days, overheated by the extra weight and blood. It is the first insistently cold day of autumn, a true October day. Already there's talk of a bad winter coming.

I do love this little cottage, Sylvia says, looking around. I'm so glad you stayed on.

Rachel is, too. She feels settled. There's a brilliance to the woods around the cottage, as they fire up, deep reds and golds; the treetops frisk in the breeze. In the upper quadrant of sky are long wobbling Vs of migrating geese. They drink the pot of tea and talk about the release. Sylvia has been working hard with the press and liaising with the BBC, which is making a documentary on the wolves; one of the most respected cameramen in the country will be arriving the following week – a coup for the project. Overall the affair will remain low-key. Sylvia has displayed an impressive sensitivity towards the animals and their privacy, turning down requests to attend the event while maintaining goodwill with all the charm, grace, and wiles of one schooled in the art of diplomacy. A benign version of her father. The subject of law school raises itself again.

Honestly, I'm not sure I want to go. I don't want to disappoint Daddy, but this year has been wonderful. It's felt, I don't know, worthwhile. I'd like to stay on.

Rachel nods, feeling a little wrong-footed by the confession, though it is not unexpected: Sylvia has been hinting as much for months. What can she say? Do as you feel, do as you like. This is the Earl's daughter – is she really at liberty to choose her life's path? The girl doesn't have the look of a lawyer to her; she would surely have to activate some grade of occupational distain and cynicism that would ruin her best qualities.

I can't really advise you, Rachel says. This is what I do, and I love it – everything I say will be biased.

It's your calling, I know I'm just not sure what mine is. I suppose one day it'll be this.

This being the estate, Rachel assumes. Sylvia's enormous dollish eyes become wistful. There are tiny suggestions of lines at their corners, though she is no doubt protecting her complexion from the outdoor work with top-of-the-range products. She's easy to like, easy to be around – even for Rachel, who has eschewed close female friends for most of her life. At worst she is an innocent, a naïf, unaware of the vast gap between her and the rest of the country; at best a romantic, good in the marrow, one might forgive her the privileges. But then, what presents, even genuinely, may not be truly authentic, as Rachel knows. She remains uncommitted to the friendship.

Mummy would have said don't let the idea of what you should do get in the way of what you want to do, Sylvia is saying. She didn't like the idea of sacrificial duty.

How old were you when she died?

Twelve.

That's tough.

Sylvia blinks, but there are no tears. Enough time, and perhaps counselling over the years, to have quashed – or at least checked – the grief. She tilts her head, rubs her ear on the shoulder of her jacket, keeps her hands wrapped around the warm mug of tea.

Leo had it much worse. He was a teenager. He was having a really bad time already – at school, and here. He saw the crash, poor thing.

Rachel is startled by the abrupt revelation.

You mean he saw the microlight go down?

Sylvia nods.

That must have been traumatic.

There is so little talk about Leo Pennington. He is the great unspoken subject of Annerdale – as if some pact has been made within the family. Only the staff gossip, speculating about whether he has been written out of the will. Rachel can't say she isn't curious. The tenor of the discussion now seems permissive – confidential, even. She risks a gentle line of enquiry.

He doesn't come home much, does he?

No, Sylvia says. Not right now. He and Daddy quarrel a lot. And Leo isn't very reasonable sometimes. He's rather volatile.

Isn't very reasonable. Rather volatile. It all sounds euphemistic to Rachel. The Pennington family is enlightened; from the old order, they have evolved into a new breed of aristocracy – integrated, liberal, positive investors in a floundering nation, but aren't lunatic sons always stashed away? Personality disorders, gamblers, syphilitics, and cripples, stuck in expensive institutions, oubliettes? She wonders how aggrieved he is, whether he blames his father for the death.

So, where is he now? she asks.

South of France, I think. He moves about a lot. He crews a boat in the Mediterranean, so it's hard to know exactly.

Sylvia flinches then, almost imperceptibly, but Rachel catches it, the tiny electrical pulse travelling up her body. She has said too much, stepped outside the bounds of loyalty and discretion.

But you still hear from him – or maybe see him?

Not much, Sylvia says briskly. Which is a great shame, really. He is my silly brother, after all.

Rachel searches Sylvia's face for more information. It is a strange face – so beautiful that the beauty is almost moot, more concealing for its faultless surface. If she has been taught not to lie, then she has also been taught a set of different qualifiers to justify untruth. She has certainly been taught to remain level and polite, to protect her family from the damages of a problem son, or perhaps to protect her brother. The Pennington code. There are times when Rachel suspects the Earl's daughter is the perfect weapon.

Mummy used to come and work here, Sylvia says. It was sort of a bolt-hole. She liked being in the woods.

Yes, I think I knew that.

She was a very good painter. She has a landscape in the Royal Academy. Have you seen the ones at home?

Yes, Rachel says.

The paintings are small, furiously detailed landscape pieces, almost pre-Raphaelite in their hyper-focus, not Rachel's kind of thing. They are hung discreetly around the Hall, mostly in the personal living spaces. Apropos of nothing, Sylvia points to the gable of the cottage.

There used to be a tawny owl up there. A juvenile. He'd come out in the daytime. He was always looking about as if he'd forgotten what the night was.

It sounds like the last line in a play. Sylvia smiles, a little sadly, and stands.

I'm going to fetch you that piece of fruit or Huib will be cross.

Could you make it an apple? Rachel asks. They're in the fridge.

She watches Sylvia walk across the garden, sleek as a pike in her jeans. She has become used to her poetic, emotive language, her lack of inhibition, not unlike her father's. On the surface she seems open and giving. But any intimacy soon dead-ends. The change of subject away from her family was graceful and deft. Maybe she would be a good lawyer after all, Rachel thinks.

*

The next ultrasound scan shows the baby back in the breech position, cross-legged, cramped, and Buddha-like. Rachel stares at the screen. There is no meaning to it, she knows; if there is meaning, it is anatomical, structural. Still, she cannot help wondering. An inherited stubbornness, perhaps: doing it *my way*. She discusses the situation with the doctor and Jan. A vaginal delivery is improbable; the hospital policy recommends a C-section. Jan, straight as ever, steers her in that direction.

Lord knows, she says, I like a good home video, but there's really no point in risking it. They're queuing up for a section these days.

Are they?

They are. Out through the sunroof. So long as you and baby are healthy, that's all I care about.

Rachel can't fathom it. Why anyone would want to have their abdomen voluntarily sliced open is beyond her. She had thought herself exempt, fitter, luckier. The date is scheduled for the surgery – three days after the release from the wolfery. Far too close for comfort. She will be given steroids, to bolster the baby's lungs. Jan sends her away with an information sheet and a DVD to help her prepare, which she watches at home that night with a glass of wine. The video is short – thirty minutes, five of which it takes to get the baby out. In the theatre, the mood of the medical personnel and the mother is light. The woman talks to her partner; she is given a spinal block, screened at her lower half; she is calm, smiling, joking with the anaesthetist. The surgeon begins the procedure. The initial cut is vast, layers of yellows and pinks are latticed apart, an astonishing gulley made in the body. Less blood than one might have thought. The smeared gloves reach inside. An assisting surgeon pushes down on the top of the woman's abdomen. *Feels a bit odd*, the patient says. A helmeted red mass is pulled out of the hole, not without force. The trailing creature is taken to one side, respirated and cleaned very quickly, then it is brought to the mother, whose face is all tenderness and joy, and tucked nakedly against her breast. The crying father supports it. The woman is emptied of placenta, suctioned, folded up, and stitched. There's something macabre about the combination of the wound and the alertness of the patient. Something amazing, too. Afterwards, Rachel feels queasy and cannot drink the wine. She rings Alexander, but his phone goes through to messages. Come on, she thinks, get it together. Binny would never let you get away with such nerves.

The following day she rallies. Though she is not due in work, she gets up and goes down to the Hall, where the team is meeting with the BBC cameraman, Gregor Carr. They are all in the office, drinking tea when she arrives; she apologises for being late.

No bother, Gregor says to her. It's a busy job you've got on there.

He gestures to her now magnificent bump, stands, and the two shake hands.

We're delighted to have you here, she tells him.

Delighted to be here. I love this part of the Lakes.

He seems humble, though has every right not to be – the many awards he has won for his patient filming, and his remarkable location work. He is one of the most sought-after men in his profession. She is a fan. Even Huib, usually unruffled by fame and prestige, seems in awe. But the man in their midst emanates grace, is deferential, inclusive; he chats easily, asks questions about the wolves and the staff. Of late, he has been in the Himalayas, working with snow leopards – Rachel has seen the now famous clip of the fat-horned mountain goat being pursued along a near-vertical fissure, the big paws of the cat swatting its back legs from under it, the goat skittering downward in a hail of debris, being lunged upon, then dragged up and across the rockface to the leopard's cave. All at a staggeringly high altitude; three months' vigil, camping in a dizzying, sickness-inducing zone, a world above clouds. The Invisible Scot, as he is known among his associates. Animals behave as if he were not there, rutting, fighting, exhibiting moments of extreme gentleness. Gregor is smiling serenely at Rachel. He has not let go of her hand. He keeps glancing at her belly. Her condition seems to be giving her special status. There have been several men, over the course of the pregnancy, whom she has met and in whom she has noted a wildly enthusiastic streak for reproduction, a very attractive masculine feature it turns out – Gregor is clearly another. He is small and compact, in his mid-thirties, though his hair is completely white, as if exposure to the elements has taken its toll. His eyes are near to black, striking in contrast. He is both frail and hardy-looking, like the son of a vicar, or a free climber. The Annerdale wolves are a tame commission for him, almost a busman's holiday, but he has taken the assignment and over the course of the coming year he will make visits to the valley to film the pair, and hopefully, in spring, their litter.

Rachel asks about the Himalayas. He answers politely, but would rather talk about her pregnancy. Is she feeling well? She must be due soon? Does she know what she is having? She tells him her due date; it's odd now knowing it. His wife had twins last year, he says – Bonnie and Clyde, traditional Scottish names – Rachel assumes he is joking – also by Caesarean; she was up and about and nursing the very same evening. He speaks of his wife reverently; also a very attractive feature. It'll be great, he says. It is the greatest thing, in fact, having children, certainly the best thing he has ever done. This surprises Rachel, given his CV, and she feels suddenly reassured, or endorsed, or as if – perhaps it is the white hair, curiously celestial – she has received a blessing of some kind.

Would you like to see the enclosure? she asks.

Perfect. But I'll make you a cup of tea first, then we can go and take a look.

Gregor Carr, three times recipient of the Calder Lee prize, moves to the office kettle, puts a teabag into a cup. He asks if she wants sugar, tells her sugar is a great energiser, she must have sugar, or better still, honey, and proceeds to carefully make the brew, while she sits, spoiled and embarrassed, at the table with her colleagues.

Later, when she looks at the film footage of herself from this time, she will barely recognise the woman she has become. A strange, lumbering version, whose belly is enormous and shelf-like, defies gravity. Her hair has grown around her ears and neck, almost down to her shoulders, her face is full, soft. She walks leaning backward, her arms swinging at her sides. She is almost mythical, a creature hostage to maternity. She crosses the moorland grass in the main enclosure with Sylvia, towards the gate of the wolfery. Gregor has set up his rig fifty feet or so away from the gate, and has disappeared under a drape of camouflage netting and twigs.

Beautiful day for it, he'd said earlier that morning when they'd convened, somebody approves of our plan.

Sure enough, there is a high blueness to the sky, rich colours on the heath, and long, slanting light. A resurgence of warmth during the last few days has seen a late flurry of insects; they flit about the dying grasses. It is beatific weather, unhoped for.

Higher up on the moorland, behind a raft of yellow gorse, Thomas, Huib, and Alexander wait in the Land Rover with binoculars and the handheld receiver. The Earl is allowing his daughter the royal privilege of setting his wolves loose. She's earned it, as far as Rachel is concerned, and the project has come to mean a great deal to her. No doubt the honour would have been Carolyn's, had she lived. The paperwork is signed: quarantine is finished, and their formal immigration is complete. All that remains is to let them out.

In the wolfery, they remain hidden from view. The scare tactics of the last few weeks, the blaring horns and firework bangs, have worked well – they are far less willing to interact and be seen by humans. But they will be close by, sensing something, smelling the adrenalin, intuiting a change or event of some kind. Prescient experts of biological codes. Their movements will be monitored for the first few weeks – the explorations, the preferred routes, rendezvous points, and hunting strategy, how they begin to dominate the territory. Huib will conduct a focused follow, using the tracking system, while Rachel is in hospital; Gregor will spend a few more days filming; and Sylvia will gather samples and data from the abandoned wolfery.

Sylvia types the code into the digital lock. Perthshire, 1680: the date of the last reported wolf killed in the old kingdom. It registers, beeps, and the gate slides open. She and Rachel move slowly away, back up the hill towards the others. Rachel breathes hard on the incline, stops several times and turns to look back – there's extraordinary pressure on her spine, her ribs, her heel bones. At any moment she feels she will rupture.

Are you alright? Sylvia asks.

Yes. Just about.

She struggles on, and they make their way to the Land Rover.

Below, the wolves are assessing the opportunity, she knows, looking beyond the wolfery at the new horizons, the heather still burning with flower, burrows, the citadels of rock, smelling the stag musk, rowan and mountain streams. It will not take them long to be restored, she thinks. Their unbelonging, reversed. Nothing of history will matter to them; land is land, articulate, informative; soon they will dominate Annerdale. Wherever they are released, the world over, their geomorphic evolution is remarkably swift.

Rachel does not join the others, but stands to the side – old habits, the desire for privacy during moments of significance. The mood is reverent, contained. No one speaks. Thomas has a hamper of champagne on the back seat, of course. There are no extra guests, though there were many requests, from the Mammal Society, the British Wolf Society, even politicians like Vaughan Andrews. Rachel takes up binoculars, looks towards the open enclosure gate, and waits.

This time it is Merle who leads the pair out of confinement. She slips through the gate, lifts her nose high to scent the surroundings, lopes a few feet along the fence, and then she runs. Soon she is at full tilt, flooding across the moorland. Within moments there is a large white wolf alongside her. The pair veer away from the gorse-covered hillside, divide, and make for the nearest cover – a gathering of thorn woods on the hill, spindled and bent by the wind. Rachel watches them go. They cover the open moor in less than a minute. One dark, one light, stellar and obverse, their hind muscles working sumptuously under their coats. The months of docile quarantine are shaken off in seconds; power always lay just underneath. She watches the unmistakable motion of their running – the hard, short bowing of their heads, like swimmers ducking under the surface. They climb the gradient of the hill opposite without slowing, then disappear from sight in the broken terrain.

From nearby, there is laughter, applause, and cheering, voices small in the landscape. *Hurray!* Rachel sits down heavily on the grass, leans back, tired and exhilarated. They've made it. She has made it. She hears the pop of the cork and the wet crackle of the champagne being poured. A glass is passed down to her by Alexander. His big hand rests for a moment on the back of her neck, squeezes gently. They are all saying, *Well done, Rachel, well done, here's to Rachel.* She takes a sip. Something very fine and very old from the Annerdale cellars that is lost on her.

She looks towards the hide. Under the netting, Gregor will still be filming, focusing the high-powered lens, perhaps following their progress between the thorn trees, along the ridge to the summit, where they will contemplate the broad expanses of Annerdale, and decide which route to take. Rachel looks over the estate. Russet ferns and the knitted furze. The signature fells beyond. Long silhouettes drool from bushes and trees; all the land's contours are exposed, every curve, every corrie and glacier cut, everything looks shadow-cast, so beautifully sheer.

*

She leaves her bag in the room where she and the baby will spend the next two days. She signs more consent forms, goes to the bathroom again. A nurse preps her, gives her a gown, checks her identity bracelet for the dozenth time. She is not wearing rings – she owns no rings, no jewellery, in fact – and has no lacquer on her nails. She has fasted in case they need to perform a general anaesthetic, taken antacid. She is walked down to the anaesthetics room next to the theatre. Her blood pressure and the baby's heartbeat are checked again. The anaesthetist and ODP are introduced and chat about baby names, to distract her from the sensation of the spinal block, the cold trickling sting. She leans forward on the gurney, tries to remain still, tries to relax, but it is impossible. The medics sense her tension. The ODP, Sam, is mannish, short, and has exceptionally blue eyes. She kneels in front of Rachel, grinning.

So you breed wolves then, Rachel. Are you having a wolf today?

I wouldn't be surprised.

Good luck with that.

After they are done, she is helped to lie back down. Her legs begin to numb. They apply ice – she cannot feel the cold, just wetness. They attach heart-rate monitors to her chest, take her blood pressure again, insert the catheter.

All alright so far? the anaesthetist asks her.

Alright, she says.

Off we go then. We'll be done in a flash.

The trolley is wheeled forward, through the theatre doors. It is going ahead, there is no choice. A different midwife is in the room – one she has never met – Jan must be on call. She is suddenly afraid. She is not as tough as she thought she was, or wants to be. When Alexander dropped her off at 6 a.m., her heart was barking madly; he had hugged her, told her it would be easy, said he would see her afterwards, and she had calmed a little. Lawrence, too, is driving up from Leeds and will visit her this evening, by which point she might be up and about. In the end, she does need them.

There are lights in the theatre, great bright discs. Staff in scrubs and hats – the consultant is smiling. She has met her before, cannot remember her name.

Hello, Rachel, she says. Doing OK?

Yes, OK.

Good. Everything's looking very good. Ready to meet the little one?

I think so.

What else can she say amid the banal, undramatic language of the medical world? *How will I be a mother? Will I feel love?* Her identity is checked again. The sheets go up, partitioning her.

Don't worry, the midwife says. Soon be done.

The painkillers seem to have a mild sedative effect too. People are talking to her. She does not know if they have started the operation. There is someone beside her head, trying to get her attention – the ODP, Sam. Sam, with her lively blue eyes and boy's face. Talk of holidays and a recently read book. They are still positioning her, she thinks, there is the sensation of pressure, things moving, pulling, but no real feeling. Then she realises, because of what the consultant is saying, that they have opened her up. She puts her head back, and her breaths begin to come unevenly.

I'm sorry, she says, though she does not know to whom she is apologising. Kyle? Binny? The baby?

Alright? Sam asks.

No. I don't know, she whispers.

You know, I remember seeing some wolves when I was a kid, Sam says. In a park. There were a load of other animals too. Do you know the one I mean?

Where was it?

Near Penrith, I think.

Setterah Keep, Rachel says.

Yeah, Setterah, that was the name. Did you ever go?

I lived near there when I was a kid. We must be about the same age.

What, twenty-one – good for us, hey.

No. I don't know –

The ODP takes and squeezes her hand, the gesture unequivocal.

Sometimes helps to close your eyes, Rachel. Some people even go off to sleep for a bit.

Do they?

They do. May as well get a nap before the bawling at 4 a.m. starts.

Rachel closes her eyes. How many minutes have passed? She forces herself to breathe deeper, slower.

Good stuff, Sam says. I think I tried to feed them a hotdog once through the bars. I got a right bollocking.

Rachel breathes and tries to imagine a still place inside, the well of the self, where a person is unreachable. There was talk of it at Chief Joseph, in the sweat lodges, the mind was let go there.

You're doing great, Mum.

[252]

Rachel breathes. There is darkness, perhaps a drug. And then she thinks, *Where are you, Mum?* She feels something hot slide from her eye. She feels Binny letting go of her hand. *Be brave, my girl.* And she is walking. Through a gate, into the woods, where there are green pathways between trunks and the quiet of the trees all around. The ground underfoot is soft, tides of needles spilled from the pines. She walks into the forest. It is there, where she knew it would be. It is standing on the path in front of her, head turned and lowered, yellow eyes. A creature long and grey. It is standing in the shadows of the branches, earth on its back and on the bridge of its nose, where it has been digging underneath the wire. Small, clever, yellow eyes. It blinks and turns its head and lopes into the trees.

There is the sound of crying, a pitch from a liminal realm, though she is sure she's heard it before somewhere. She opens her eyes and lifts her head. There are surgeons at her waist, draped in blue, busy. The midwife is coming towards her holding a sheet in her arms; two tiny red fists are rising from the folds.

Here he is, the midwife says. He's got a very good shout. He's not sure about being in this world at all, are you?

She lowers the bundle towards Rachel, and Rachel lifts her hand and reaches out and touches the flailing arm. Blood warm. There is still blood on him, and the white vernix. His skin. His dark hair. His mouth is open – soft, asking tissue, like the gape of a bird. His eyes are tight shut as he wails, and there is a tremendous crease in his forehead.

You've got a little hero.

Rachel nods. She cannot stop looking, as if seeing him will confirm it.

Can I have him?

Just a few more bits to do, the midwife says, then I'll bring him back to you for some skin to skin and we can really get going.

She moves away and Rachel rests her head back down. Don't take him, she thinks. Give him to me, he's mine. She watches as he is administered to. Is he alright? He must be alright. They are placing him on the scales, checking reflexes. She wants to get up and go over there, pick him up. The surgeons are at her waist, taking too long. She doesn't care. There seems no need for anything else now. There is no wound. The only wound is life, recklessly creating it, knowing that it will never be safe, it will never last; it will only ever be real.

FOLLIES

December. She has become the servant of winter. The early darkness keeps her home, wrapped up warm by the fire, the lights blazing. She nurses the baby. There are colossal yellow clouds above Annerdale, loops of sleet, and serious snow on the fells. She does not go out. The last few months the world has come to her: deliveries of food and equipment, the midwife and healthcare worker, the men in her life, work. She nurses the baby; he takes an hour to feed, falling asleep halfway through, waking, continuing. She reads while he suckles. The cottage keens in the wind, the woods outside creak and rub. If it weren't for the double-glazing, the wifi, and mobile signal, she might be in another century. Outside, too, there are wolves, no longer medieval – she can hear them calling occasionally from the enclosure, or imagines she can.

By 3.30 p.m., the sun has almost gone, its pale sump sinking on the horizon. Black wind at night, howling back, demonic almost. And rain, beginning to solidify. She worries about snow as she never worried before, worries about becoming trapped. She is unused to the long darkness – this first winter back in England is shocking, brutal, how could she have forgotten. Daylight feels incredibly valuable, if only she could access it. She leaves lamps on downstairs overnight. The baby sleeps in the Moses basket by her bed, within arm's reach. At 4 a.m. she nurses him, while the darkness rolls past. It feels like the end of the world. Needles in her breasts and great pressure as the milk lets down. To have chosen love-enslavement to this little being means forfeiting everything.

He is Charles Caine, a family name, though no one knows it. To give a title to another human being is to acknowledge history, or to refute it – to say, we err, but forward we go, improving, hopeful. A full, dark head of hair. Long legs. One of his ears is folded over inside, like a shell, in some cultures lucky, in others, a bad omen. He is exceptional company; that is to say, he demands everything of her and is given it. She nurses him. She changes him. She nurses him again. He likes the firelight, turns his head towards the flames. He is beginning to differentiate colours now, beginning to smile, though many of his expressions remain less happy as he tries to absorb the world's visceral information. He dreams, grimaces. She nurses him, at one hot breast, then the other. He is at his most immaculate afterwards: composed, bow-mouthed, his chest rising and falling, fists clenched as he sleeps. One in three hours given over to active care, she was told: a low estimate. She has buried the bellybutton stump next to the quince tree.

She can carry him for longer periods in the sling now, without the ache in her abdomen and back. He lies against her side like a warm, external organ. Below, the scar itches. A majestic scratch, still red, but unbelievably small given its yield; one buckled section where the suture alignment was off, or hurried, closed by a junior – it doesn't matter. Now and then there are sharp electric jolts as something knits back together, or nerves resurrect. The memories of those first days are hazy. The limping, stooping walk, with a nurse on her arm, to the cot to change his nappy, down the ward corridor. Sitting on the toilet, terrified to shit. Cramps as she first tried to nurse him. Small bodily triumphs she could not have imagined to be so meaningful. In the kitchen drawer is the thin subcutaneous cord with its blue beads – a surgical trophy, removed by Jan, that she has not thrown out. Her flesh sags over the wound, but is retreating daily.

She nurses the baby by the fire and reads reports sent to her by Huib and Sylvia. Ra and Merle have found their range and are tracking the herds. They have denned; a good indicator for mating come February, the coordinates almost exactly central in the enclosure. She makes a note – the pups would then be due late April, perhaps early May at Britain's latitude, a sixty-day gestation. The abandoned deer carcasses in the enclosure weigh less than a third of their original body weight; they are being stripped, efficiently. She reads but it is hard to concentrate. Charlie is mesmeric. He draws the eye, for no reason, like a newly unwrapped gift. Everything else retreats – there are no other stories. The story is the child. She puts her mouth on the soft fusing crown of his head. She wishes he would sleep so she could sleep. She wishes he would wake, prove that he is alive and animate, see how his eyes find and recognise her face.

Just enjoy it, Huib tells her when she phones. Our guys are doing fine.

Not that she doubted it. Annerdale is a utopia for Ra and Merle: plentiful biomass, no other packs to compete with or species of similar prowess. The temperature, though low and dropping weekly, is mild compared to the bitter Romanian winter. She checks the project website, reads the messages – there has been a flush of positive responses to the release, the scales seem to have tipped. Much of the criticism has evaporated – the wolves are a success for not being a catastrophe, like the Olympics, or a piece of public art. Only the faithfuls continue to complain. The security reports from Michael have been similarly good. There's been no more trouble around the fence periphery, and it is too inclement to protest by the main gate. Thomas passes on personal congratulations from the Prime Minister. She takes this with a pinch of salt. After the Scottish vote, Sebastian Mellor is desperate for good press, progressive policies – especially in the regions where there is growing agitation for devolved powers – and the project qualifies.

Lawrence visits almost every weekend, a couple of times with Emily. There seems to be an accord between the two of them. They bring gifts, clothes, food. Her brother is wildly in love with the baby. Bup, he calls him, inexplicably – some private pet name.

Hello, Bup. How's Bup? Come here, Bup.

He picks him up, holds him out, dangling and kicking in the fleece bag, examining him, then drawing him close into his chest. Emily is practical around the house – cooking, offering to clean, minding the baby while Rachel takes a bath. The sad truth is she's a natural, a childless natural; Charlie sleeps contentedly on her shoulder, against the cashmere jumper, her silk scarves dampening with his drool and possetting. Rachel passes her a muslin cloth, but she doesn't seem to care. If it is painful, holding in her arms something so longed for, she doesn't show it. Rachel admires her for that, begins even to like her. She has passed the test of her son, which is now the main test. She thoughtfully brings Rachel a breast pump, in order to freeze and save milk.

Rachel watches her and Lawrence. They appear stable, if slightly too polite with each other, their eyes occasionally locked in silent communication. They do not squabble in front of her or give anything away. It seems fine, but Rachel is aware that the true state of their relationship cannot be known by an outsider. Still, they are together, and she finds she is relieved.

Alexander, too, has been a regular visitor. He comes in without knocking, bringing enormous shanks of meat wrapped in plastic layers, given to him by farmers by way of thanks for difficult surgeries or merciful euthanasia. In the freezer are vacuum bags of yellow-tinted breast milk alongside primitively home-cut steaks, lamb legs – a bizarre mammalian cache.

You need 500 more calories a day, he tells her.

I never stop eating, she says. I feel like a prize pig.

Intermittently, she roasts pork and beef joints, becomes distracted, forgets to take them out of the oven, then eats them well-done, dry to desiccated. One evening, Alexander arrives with a guest. She hears the stomping of boots in the hallway, female chatter. She is nursing the baby, bra-less, her T-shirt pulled up.

Here in the kitchen, she calls.

He puts his head round the door.

I've got someone with me.

Right, she says. 'Fraid I can't move.

There is not much she can do; the baby is midway, being slow as usual. She reaches for a tea-towel and drapes it modestly over her left side. Alexander walks in with his daughter, Chloe. The girl is clearly related – even pre-puberty, she is big, and tall, with her father's forehead and mouth. She has on an unfashionable anorak, purple, unzipped, a jumper with crocheted dogs on it, wellies. Every inch the daughter of a country vet.

Hi, Rachel, Chloe says.

Hi, Chloe. Nice to meet you. Come in.

The girl takes a step inside.

Wait! Boots off, madam, her father instructs. Hope you don't mind us dropping in.

Rachel shakes her head. Chloe heels her wellies off and stands them tidily by the door. She comes into the room and looks at the baby, what can be seen of him under the towel. He is slipping off the nipple and falling asleep. Rachel shifts him in her arms, moves her T-shirt back down, and tosses the tea-towel onto the counter. This is Charlie.

Can I hold him? Chloe asks.

Whoa there, Alexander says. 'Hi, Rachel, can I hold him.' That was a bit quick.

Chloe shrugs. Rachel smiles at her.

Yes, of course you can. Do you want to sit over there and I'll pass him to you?

The girl moves to the neighbouring chair, sits, repositions her bottom several times in quick succession, forward, backward, side to side, and readies herself for the load.

Coat off, her father instructs.

She shrugs out of the anorak and hangs it on the back of the chair. Lanky arms to go with her legs, but not graceless or malcoordinated. She'll be good at sport, Rachel thinks, probably the star shooter on the netball team. Chloe puts her feet on the crossbar of the table so that her thighs are flat – no doubt the correct position for holding orphaned lambs. There's a high degree of confidence to her – the confidence of a ten-year-old. She lifts her arms in a receiving position and Rachel passes over the baby.

He might be a bit burpy.

Charlie stirs as she releases him, but doesn't wake. Chloe takes him, not entirely supporting the head, and with a slightly loose grip – the baby sprawls either end. She tightens her arms so that he is bunched in her lap. Good enough, Rachel thinks. Chloe looks up at her father, smiling, missing her front teeth. I'm holding a baby, the look says. This is her boyfriend's daughter. If only every introduction were as easy, Rachel thinks.

Have you eaten? Alexander asks. We thought we might take you to the pub with us. I promised this one some chips.

And Cumberland sausages, Chloe says.

Obviously.

Rachel is about to turn him down, leaving to go anywhere with the baby seems laborious, then changes her mind. The cottage and the winter darkness have begun to close in. She must keep sounding ahead, get used to travelling with Charlie.

Chips sound pretty good, she says.

The baby's things are packed and he is fitted into the carrier and into the car, the seat belt secured – an elaborate ritual for a five-minute drive. Rachel sits on the back seat with him, her hand over the blanket. Chloe sits up front with her father, her legs crossed on the seat. She jabbers freely on the ride, tells Rachel about her school – she is one of the oldest children in the village; there are only twenty-nine pupils. The school is in danger of shutting and the district is constantly campaigning to keep it open. She herself has written to the local MP.

There are too many old people instead of young couples with kids, Chloe explains, leaning round the seat. I'm good at maths and library.

This one is a brainbox, Alexander says.

Sounds like it, Rachel says.

Dad and I have good conversations because we only see each other half the week.

Alexander reaches over and musses her hair.

Hey!

Chloe takes her hairband out, smooths her locks back into a ponytail, and refastens it.

I might be a brainbox but I still smashed my teeth out, she says. They weren't even baby teeth! I've got to wait till the dentist makes me new ones.

Well, it won't be long, her father says. Meanwhile, no more galloping Sorrel down the fell, you maniac.

I wasn't galloping, I was barely cantering. Sorrel is my horse, Chloe explains. It wasn't his fault I fell off.

I should hope not, Rachel says.

She listens to the father–daughter chatter. It is interesting to see Alexander parenting – all of a sudden there is a new side on display. He seems adept, suited. He's no walkover, but neither is he untrusting – if his daughter is allowed out riding alone.

The Horse and Farrier is festooned with lights when they arrive, like a cheerful galleon, very inviting in the gloom. The bar is busy. They find a quiet table in the back dining room by the fire and Rachel keeps the carrier next to her chair. Charlie wakes up, shouts; she lifts him and holds him against her, and he settles but remains awake. Chloe dangles a multicoloured scarf in front of him and he concentrates hard on it. Their meals arrive.

Want me to take him so you can get stuck in? Alexander offers.

That's OK, thanks.

She picks up her fork and begins. She is getting good at one-handed cutlery use. They eat a vast meal, slabs of battered fish looming off the edges of the plates, a wheel of sausage, huge cut chips, extra vegetables. Dozens of sachets of ketchup are squeezed empty by Chloe and strewn over the table, red dashes everywhere like a battlefield. It is good to be out. The meal takes on the air of celebration, a feast. Chloe has a few sips of Alexander's beer, as does Rachel. He watches her across the table, clearly pleased with the way the meeting is going. They have not slept together properly since the birth, trying a few times and abandoning the act. Yet he still comes, exhibiting connubial patience; she doesn't know why. The answer is not complicated, were she to consider the question properly.

Dad says maybe I can ask you to see the wolves sometime please, Chloe says between mouthfuls.

It's the *please* that charms Rachel most.

Yes. Definitely. Next time I go into the enclosure, I'll take you along. We can either use the radio transmitters to find them, or if you fancy a challenge we'll track them ourselves – old school.

Chloe's face lights up.

I've got my own binoculars, she says. I can bring them.

Excellent.

Excellent.

The toothless grin again. The room is very warm. Chloe takes off her jumper. The first hint of breasts under her vest, but no bra. The flesh on her arms glows under a pattern of freckles. Her hair is utterly curl-less, sand-coloured, needs washing. The girl seems very happy with herself. Long may it last, Rachel thinks. When she's older, a teenager, she might be teased for her size, her generous frame and height; they will be difficult, halting years, until she's in her twenties perhaps, and men with proclivities for statuesque women begin to assert themselves – then she will ascend once more. Or she will sail through regardless; her intelligence and grounding will keep her safe. For now she is well liked, it seems, ethical, a champion of underdogs

– defender of girls being picked on at school – *Lucy and Illona, particularly, because they aren't very popular* – and as strong as boys when throwing a ball. Junior measures of success.

After huge steaming puddings with toffee sauce and ice cream, they drive back to the cottage. Chloe puts her favourite album on the stereo and sings along. Her father sings, too, and the two of them jive about in the car seats – the age of parental mortification has not yet arrived. Outside Seldom Seen, Chloe gives Rachel her mobile number – their friendship made official.

You can WhatsApp me, too, she says. By the way, my binoculars are Swarovski. They're incredibly strong. Dad bought them for my birthday.

Great, says Rachel. Perfect. See you soon.

Alexander gets out, sees her to the door, and gives her a quick kiss. It is still early – 8.30 p.m. The baby needs changing. She bathes him in the sink. His belly is tight under his soft skin, glabrous, like stone wrapped in chamois leather. He kicks in the tepid water, looks both panicked and joyful. His eyes are changing colour, from slate to brown. In the end they will probably be as dark as Kyle's, or maybe hazel, if the green fights through. She feeds him, goes to bed and lies listening to his breathing. Some nights he breathes like an old labouring sheepdog, keeps her awake. She sleeps deeply for four hours, until he wakes for a feed. She no longer dreams of Binny. She still does not know what to make of that strange season of appearances, so false in its compassionate instruction, a kind of golden nocturnal *folie*. The baby is real now, and she must learn and cope, perhaps that's why.

*

True to her word, she arranges for Chloe to accompany her and Huib on a run through the enclosure. Alexander drops the girl off, a packed lunch in her rucksack, walking boots laced, and the famed binoculars strung round her neck. She looks every inch the zoologist's assistant.

Good luck, he says. See you this afternoon.

Rachel leaves the baby in the care of Sylvia – not strictly part of her job description. He has been fed, changed – there's extra breast milk, though success with the bottle has been intermittent so far. It is the first time she has left him with a sitter. She tries not to feel anxious. Another hurdle, she tells herself.

The day is dark, with fast grey cloud obscuring the hills, but rainless so far. Giant billowing shadows move across the fells and valleys. There's the smell of loose, black earth, and minerals in the air, incendiary, like cordite. Big weather is coming; they will have only a few hours at best. In any case, she dare not leave the baby too long. Already her left breast feels full and aching. Motherhood: there seems to be a new minor ailment every other day. They collect the handheld receivers from the office, tune to the signals. She does not want the girl to be disappointed, though disappointment comes with the territory – the first lesson of spotting. Nor can she afford to spend hours tracking. Chloe sits quietly on the back seat of the estate's Land Rover while Huib drives. Her excitement is well contained, but obvious. She'll have been instructed by her father to do as she is told at all times, not get too giddy. This is a special privilege. She is practically breathless.

It's great you could come along, Huib says to her.

He has already given her one of the receivers to hold, tuned to Ra's transmitter, with an explanation of how it works – the basic operating procedure; Chloe is not intimidated. She is of the generation that intuitively understands technology. She leans forward towards the driver's seat.

Thanks for having me. Dad says it was his favourite thing, looking after them.

So, are you going to be a vet, like your dad?

She shakes her head.

No, I'm not quite exactly sure yet. I think I'm going to be a geneticist.

Oh, really?

Rachel smiles. She is very glad Huib is coming along; his ability to make conversation with anyone will be an asset if she herself stalls with the girl. The idea that she might be expected to bond makes her slightly nervous, much as she likes Alexander's daughter.

I saw a programme on the telly about crops, Chloe says. It's all very well having people and animals, but they have to eat and soon there won't be enough food.

That's very true, Huib agrees. We do need more disease-resistant strains. I read an article in *New Scientist* last month about it.

The TV programme said lots of money has been spent on making tobacco better. But we don't actually need that.

But it's big business, right? Smokers spend a fortune.

Yes, Chloe says, a little sadly, and leans back. If only they'd stop.

Moral, kindred spirits, Rachel thinks. It is heartening to imagine the girl could go on to such achievements, and that Charlie could too.

Do you want a mint, Chloe? Huib asks, taking a packet off the dashboard. He holds the tube over his shoulder.

Thanks. I've got some rhubarb and custards in my bag. We can have those later.

Good one, Huib says. But wait a minute. Is it rhubarb and custards, or rhubarbs and custards?

Chloe sucks her mint and thinks for a moment.

Rhubarbs and custards?

Rachel laughs.

You are a pair of pedants.

What's a pedant? Chloe asks.

They drive cross-country alongside the fence for a few hundred yards and pull up at the western gate of the enclosure. Rachel gets out, keys the code into the lock, and the gate opens. They pass through, the gate closes, and the lock reactivates. As little estate traffic as possible has been inside the domain since the release; the codes are held by a handful of workers only. Rachel asks Chloe which way she thinks they should go. Chloe checks the signal and they head south, following an old drove track. Light strobes across the grass and bracken, over blackened bushes. Somewhere on the reddish, sleet-dampened moors Gregor is using a shepherd's bothy as a base, and has been filming their progress. There are several dun hides set up across the estate, covered in besoms of heather and bracken, camouflage netting. She sent him a text message that morning saying they were heading in.

They drive to one of the known rendezvous points, where the wolves have been returning frequently, park, and head towards the coordinates. They walk downwind. They do not hurry but Rachel feels unfit, the breast is heavy and sore inside her coat, burning – the start of an infection, perhaps. Chloe doesn't speak – she is now in silent mode. She walks alongside Rachel, hands cupping the rims of the binoculars, ready. The signals are strong, but Rachel feels obliged to issue another gentle disclaimer.

If we don't see them we'll try again another day. They might be in the forest, in which case probably they'll stay hidden.

The girl nods.

OK.

They walk on. There's a pause, then Chloe says,

But they'll see us, won't they?

Yes, they will, Rachel says.

Chloe grins and is pleased. The logic: being seen by a wolf is nearly as good as seeing a wolf. Rachel is relieved. The girl is clearly very sensible, but one never knows when disappointment might lead to tears or sulking. The cold, streaming wind has made Chloe's cheeks very red, and her nose glistens. She holds her sleeve up to blot it, strides on beside them.

Rachel checks her phone for messages. There's nothing from Sylvia. Her plan was to be an incautious, trusting mother, able to come and go without obsessive monitoring. In practice, it seems harder. They walk over the rough, gingery moorland, between granite slabs and patches of bog. Chloe has fallen back in a state of hyper-awareness, not speaking, scanning the terrain. Rachel leans towards her and speaks softly.

What we'd like at this stage is for them to want to have a litter. To be nuzzling up to each other and sleeping really close, that kind of thing.

Chloe turns and nods. *Yes*, she mouths.

They walk for an hour or so, looping round towards the lower bields. The signals are strong; they are close, but remain out of sight.

We might do better staying put and seeing if they make an appearance, Huib suggests. Let's go over there. We don't want to go too high, Chloe – they don't like you being higher up than them.

Because it's an advantage for watching things? Chloe suggests.

Exactly. And ambushing.

On a shallow rise, near a brisk upland stream, they sit and eat sandwiches. Huib and Chloe swap halves – ham for hummus – like bosom friends. For her age, the girl has an impressively high degree of patience. She does not fiddle with her phone and seem bored. Every once in a while she lifts her binoculars and scans the terrain, replaces them against her chest. They wait – forty-five minutes, an hour. The wind flushes past them, freezing, hinting at more snow. Chloe's sleeves are dark with wet patches where she has wiped her nose. Her sniffs are regular and adenoidal. The light is fading. Rachel is about to suggest they leave – the ache in her breast is intense now, and it is not feeling like a lucky day. Then, a text from Gregor arrives. *Wolf coming over Caston Bield.* He must be close to where they are sitting, stowed like a sniper in the moorland grass. They raise their binoculars. Chloe tugs Rachel's arm. She points.

Is that one? I think that's one.

On the horizon, bracketed between two trees, Ra is standing looking towards them.

Bingo, Huib says. You have good eyes.

Chloe rests her elbows on her bent knees to hold the glasses steady. Merle walks up behind Ra. Her coat ripples in the wind. The pair take stock of the intruders, then begin along the hill, laterally, cutting down towards the river, picking their way past boulders and trees. They move mostly in plain view, disappearing for a time behind roods of stone, Merle smoking through the brown bracken. Ra's pale coat glows in the winter gloom like halogen. They disappear into a grove of trees beside the river. The group keeps watching for a time, but they do not reappear. Rachel hopes it was worth it for Chloe – less than a minute's payoff for half a day's investment. But when she looks at the girl, she can see the excitement and delight. She is the first child in England to see wild wolves at large – surely there will be kudos for it at school. Huib holds up a hand and they high-five.

Let's have those rhubarbs and custards, he says.

Chloe rustles around in her bag and brings out a handful of old-fashioned yellow and red sweets. Rachel hasn't seen them in years, not since Binny sold them in the post office in big, dusty plastic jars. The thought makes her anxious to see Charlie. They walk back to the Land Rover. Huib and Chloe chat casually on the ride back to the office – it becomes clear the child is excessively bright, interacts well with adults who are essentially strangers. Rachel tries to ignore the burning discomfort in the glands of her chest, the wet feeling against her T-shirt and creeping unwellness. Mastitis. When they arrive back at the Hall, the baby is crying, an acute pitch of great distress. Sylvia is walking him in her arms backward and forward across the office.

He wouldn't take the bottle, she says. I'm so sorry.

Rachel sits with him and nurses him. He latches, tugs hungrily – a savage pain passes through the swollen nipple, like broken glass crackling through ducts. She winces and adjusts position; all she can do is let him draw the milk. Chloe calmly tells Sylvia about the sighting. They avoided us mostly, she says, but when Alexander arrives, his daughter leaps all around him like a salmon up a weir, her chest skimming off him, completely shedding the afternoon's guise of adulthood.

I saw them, Dad! I saw them!

Her brother and his wife arrive on Christmas Eve, bringing with them heavy bags from an expensive supermarket, masses of gifts for the baby. There is still a strain between them – perhaps it will never be fully corrected – but they are together, and it is Christmas, and Rachel can't help feeling a minor miracle has occurred, simply because they are all together. Emily sets about baking, dusting the kitchen counters white; the savoury smell of mincemeat drifting from the oven. She seems to want to keep busy, task after task, wiping, washing up, making a clove orange for the mantelpiece. Rachel does not pity her. She has chosen to remain Lawrence's wife, chosen to stick it out, and there is something honourable in that. She'd hesitated before inviting them up, but in the end there was the feeling that, with the baby, they should be together.

While Emily bathes Charlie, Rachel and Lawrence go hollying, taking with them a hemp sack, like old-timers. It is cold, cold enough to snow – the eaves of soil between the tree roots are whitening. The trees ring glassily with birdcalls. In the bare upper branches, the black rooks look almost like spawn. Down by the lake there are three very productive holly trees, haemorrhaging berries. A few of the lower branches have freshly clipped stumps; someone has beaten them to it. But there is plenty to go round. Rachel snips off reachable sprigs, while Lawrence shins up the trunks boyishly. Boughs come rustling down, stick halfway; he shakes them free with a foot.

Watch out below.

This being perhaps the most private, and possibly the only, moment they will have, Rachel asks how things are going with Emily.

Better, he says. It's slow going. She says she trusts me.

Is she right to?

The words are out, bluntly, before Rachel has a chance to formulate a subtler enquiry. But this is the tenor of her life now, dealing with base and needful messages. Howls. Excrement. Vomit. Every problem must present itself honestly, if it is to be solved.

I haven't seen Sara, if that's what you mean. Not since she left the office. She sent me a card, but that's about the extent of it.

What did it say?

Happy Christmas.

He drops another sizeable sheering of holly. Rachel picks it up and puts it in the sack. The foliage is lustrous, ancient; its spikes dig into her wrists through the gloves.

Was there something else? she asks.

He looks down at her from the branch above, his face as pale and unreadable against the sky as the underside of a hawk's wing.

What do you mean?

It's just that I got the impression something else was wrong. That there was more to everything.

Nothing's wrong. I'm doing penance on a daily basis. I'm going to a counsellor – she asked me to and I am.

Right. OK. I didn't mean to pry. Come down, I think we've got enough.

The bag weighs almost nothing on the walk back through the woods. She senses a skittishness in Lawrence, he talks rapidly, about nothing much – avoidance talk. He walks quickly against the gloom, worrying they should get back soon, as if to be out in the dark would be an undesirable, dangerous thing. She has hit a nerve, perhaps, reminded him of his crimes, when all he wants is to forget and move on. When they arrive back at the cottage, he heads up to the bathroom, emerging twenty minutes later, composed, calm, ready to be festive. They eat Emily's mince pies and then strew the windowsills with the holly. They decorate the Christmas tree. Everything smells of green sap and spice. Sitting in the armchair, holding the baby, Emily looks Madonna-like. The Madonna of surrogacy, or of yearning.

The baby steals attention from everyone in the room, captivates; he is the focal point. They watch him on the rug. His head is heavy but controlled. Lying on his front he can lift it and look about; he issues noises of frustration and triumph. His expressions still seem mostly accidental, but he can smile, he does smile, and then the world is illuminated, the heart is enslaved. Vulnerability and emotional lure; a creature perfectly evolved to elicit the protection of adults. His skin is gorgeous but for two patches of dryness behind his ears.

On Christmas morning, they are invited for drinks at Pennington Hall, a traditional reception for the workers on the estate.

We don't have to go, Rachel tells them.

She would, in fact, rather not. She has no wish to navigate the Penningtons and the other staff today.

Shouldn't it be on Boxing Day? Lawrence asks. Alms for the poor and all that.

I'd like to go, Emily says. I haven't been down there yet. I'd be curious to see the place and meet your crusading earl, Rachel.

OK, Lawrence says. Let's go.

Towards much of what his wife says or suggests, Rachel has noticed that her brother is agreeable. This must be part of his repentance. It's understandable, the hangdog act, wanting to make amends, but is also slightly alarming. Bend too far backward and one breaks. Two against one – she cannot retract the invitation.

Maybe just for an hour, then.

The morning is bright and clear; they decide to walk. They gather their coats, dress the baby in his new arctic hooded suit. Lawrence puts on the baby papoose. Charlie has started enjoying facing outward while being carried; so long as he can feel a warm body and hear her voice, he is content enough. The sensory experience must be vast, Rachel thinks – so much to see and absorb. He swings his legs, puts his tongue out in the frigid air as if tasting a new substance. They walk through the woods, then along the stream and the gentle ramps leading to the back of the Hall. The lanes are frostbitten, the grass crisp. Pristine winter – the estate looks immaculate, untouched. In the newly planted copses, the birches have a mauve hue. A fine rind of moon is cut out of the sky, and only a few reaches away above the horizon is the pale, near-derelict sun. It's as if they are walking on another planet, with contiguous constellations. She would not be surprised to see another set of moons studding the heavens. Three adults and a baby, traversing a holy, alien land; they have entered mythology, or a memory of religion. They have survived great disaster and found paradise.

At the Hall, Emily and Lawrence hold their own, converse politely, try not to marvel at the interior, the gilt frames, furniture which at auction would be the price of a new car or more. The baby gives Rachel an excuse not to exert herself socially – people flock over, croon, admire. The Penningtons are welcoming, delighted Rachel's family is also in attendance. Sylvia serves Christmas punch from a silver cauldron into goblets. She has transmogrified back into a debutante: gone are the jeans, boots, and fleece; she has on a mallow-coloured dress, a white fur tippet, her hair is pinned up. Neither incarnation seems quite real to Rachel now. Sylvia and her father have been at the early-morning service, conducted by the bishop.

Michael and his wife Lena are present, as well as their son Barnaby, a thirty-something version of Michael, though stockier, bullock-like, perhaps more herd-able than his father. There are other old friends, and staff, including Honor. Huib has gone back to South Africa for the holidays. Michael shakes hands with Lawrence, greets Rachel civilly enough, and gently squeezes the baby's foot, a grandparently gesture. He is wearing a tweed sports coat and a burgundy, crested tie, a relic from school perhaps or the emblem of some local Conservative club. His wife is small, svelte, but not the diminutive partner Rachel had imagined. In fact, she is very attractive, has astonishingly well-preserved cheekbones, no doubt appearing as a model in their wedding photographs. Her figure suggests she has never borne children. She is confident, stands slightly in front of Michael, leads the conversation, and speaks presumptuously to Thomas as if she were his old nanny. She and her husband have served the house for decades; it is in some ways theirs to claim.

Thomas is expansive, as usual. He greets Rachel with the encomium of an agent, extolling her marvellous talents to those guests she has not yet met, embarrassing her in front of Lawrence and Emily. Midway through the reception, he insists on an impromptu carol.

Let's have a round of 'God Rest Ye Merry, Gentlemen'.

He begins to sing. Sylvia instantly accompanies. One by one the crowd gets going. Rachel joins in uncomfortably, unused to such jolly, outward displays, then, not knowing the words, she focuses on the baby, who looks unsettled by the noise and may or may not be about to cry. Afterwards, applause. The timbre of Thomas' laughter is that of a moral hedonist, chief of workers. It is Sylvia's soft exclamation that announces Leo Pennington's arrival. The young man who enters the drawing room is not shabby exactly, but he does not appear in any way like heir to one of the wealthiest estates in England. The look of someone associated with yachts and motorbikes, rough port-town night-clubs in France, Albania, and Israel. An expensive, worn leather jacket. Dishevelment to his clothing, messy unwashed hair, and a smoker's complexion. A partying rich kid. Sylvia glances briefly towards her father, goes to her brother, hugs him. Thomas, who has been regaling a group that includes Emily, holds face. Then, loud enough for the room to hear, issues his greeting.

Leo! Wonderful! You made it!

As if he'd been expecting him all along.

Daddy, come and say hello to Leo, Sylvia calls.

Yes! Yes! Please excuse me; I must go to my son.

He was not expected, Rachel is sure. It is clear that they are pedaling to get hold of the situation. Leo shakes hands with his father, but does not smile. Though his colouring is similar to Sylvia's, he has neither his sister's fineness nor her symmetry. A weaker face, small chin, and strange, sandy eyelashes. His sister's arm is threaded through his, but he does not look comfortable, as if the house and all its contents make him edgy, as if there's a deep intolerance of his old life. Michael and Lena make their way over to greet him, too. Lena kisses him, takes him by the elbows, and Rachel overhears her gentle chastisement. *Must come home more often. We all miss you.*

The carousel of Christmas begins again, drinks topped up, conspicuous merriment. Thomas works the room. At one point he takes Charlie from Lawrence, and Rachel winces. There is no way that he will be dropped, but she doesn't feel confident – the baby looks wrong in Thomas' arms as he tries to chat to his guests, his face is startled, and begins to crumple. She is relieved when Lawrence takes him back and shows him the paintings on the walls. Some grey-haired, kilt-wearing uncle is talking boorishly to her, about plans to drive on the right-hand side of the road in Scotland, ludicrous, a colossal waste of money, he says, and a ploy to please Europe, but Rachel looks past him towards Leo. The young man helps himself to the Christmas punch, drinks swiftly, refills the goblet. He barely circulates, but stands near the serving table and engages minimally with whomever approaches. There's a crackle around him: un-wellness, an ill mood, or his poor fit in the setting. Sylvia returns to his side often, which, on the surface, appears doting, but their talk becomes inward, and Leo agitated. *Always a bloody circus*, Rachel hears him say, his voice rising. A few heads turn but the guests continue to socialise. Thomas is at the other end of the room. Leo sways a little, blinks slowly, and looks disparagingly at his sister. He is well on the way to getting drunk, or the alcohol is combining with something already in his system. *Just a fucking show, a great big sham.* Sylvia puts her hand on his arm, says something quietly to him. *Because it's all so false and we're all liars.* Nearby, Michael hears the commotion and makes his way over. Someone steps in front of Rachel and she loses sight of them for a moment. When the person moves, she sees Sylvia, Michael, and Lena gathered round Leo, corralling him. Leo's voice reaches an insistent pitch. *Makes me sick.* Thomas looks over towards the group through the sea of guests. For the first time Rachel witnesses him in a state of discomposure – the man looks nervous, as if staring at a fire gaining height and power, unsure what to do; he does not approach, does not try to intervene. It is Michael who stewards, Michael who leans in very close and speaks to Leo in warning tones, as if to a dog that has pulled something down off a table onto the floor, but not yet wrecked it. Rachel can hear one phrase repeated: *your mother, your mother*. Rachel's conversation partner has asked her a question about a wildlife conference in Aberdeen; she looks back to him and tries to concentrate. From the corner of her eye she sees Michael, Lena, and Leo making their way to the door and leaving. Sylvia has soon re-entered the fray, wearing a broad smile, as if nothing untoward has occurred, as if there is no drama bubbling away elsewhere.

By one o'clock, the gathering dissolves. The baby is hungry. Rachel, Lawrence, and Emily begin a round of goodbyes. They are given a gift box on the way out by Sylvia, which turns out to have excessively expensive items inside – champagne, a silver fountain pen, an electronic reader, fine commissioned chocolates – nowhere near the alms Lawrence had joked of. They walk back across the estate grounds. The sun is already low, energy-less, unblinding to the naked eye. Mist is forming over the river and the fells are a deep, dying blue.

Nothing like a bit of family drama at Christmas, Emily comments. Good to know they're maintaining the traditions like the rest of us.

You noticed, Rachel says.

Oh, I missed it, Lawrence says. What was going on?

There's some bad history between Thomas and his son, Rachel explains.

The daughter seems nice, though, Emily says. She's working with you?

Yes. I had my doubts about her but she's proving me wrong.

She was very enthusiastic. She's extremely beautiful, isn't she? Sort of off the chart.

Then to Lawrence –

You must have noticed that?

Emily's tone is not jealous, neither is it aggressive, but there is an undercurrent. Beautiful women are always on another woman's radar, but perhaps Emily is more sensitive now, reading their allure like radiation. They walk on in silence for a while, crossing the stone bridge into the woodland. The air is colder inside the trees, frost climbing the trunks. Rachel adjusts Charlie's fur hood. He is fast asleep, oblivious. Lawrence's curiosity gets the better of him.

How much do you think it costs to run a house like that? I mean, how does he manage it – so many of these places are going under and being taken over by the National Trust.

I don't know, Rachel says. He seems to have a lot of business interests. He's the lead donor of his party.

Christ – that's a waste of money, Emily says.

I'm sure there are tax breaks, Lawrence says. There always are. He's probably got registered companies overseas.

The political echo of Binny in her brother. Rachel begins to feel a little uncomfortable, part of the machinery of segregation, which always enables the elite. It cannot be completely divorced from her role on the project. After the Reservation's system of land ownership, its allocated plots and council management, Annerdale is essentially feudal, a realm so antiquated it seems impossible that it has survived the reformist centuries. An English estate still owned by an English earl; Lawrence is right: it is rare. Across the border, great swathes of foreign-owned land is being recovered, taxes levied on the distilleries, the salmon farms. She doubts such radicalism will be imported here.

The afternoon is glorious. Charlie is still asleep, and they are not eating until later that evening. She suggests they visit a Neolithic site nearby, only a small detour. There is a way of aligning the winter solstice sun with the central stone, she tells them.

We're only a few days late.

Shouldn't we get back? Lawrence says. We've been gone a while. I could do with getting back.

Her brother's lack of desire to be outside, away from the cottage, seems uncustomary. But again, Emily expresses a preference to visit the stone circle, and Lawrence concedes. They walk half a mile, onto an open rise. The mountains appear built like a stadium, encircling them, the summits recognisable – a geological alphabet. Round the base of the stones, the grass is long and ragged. There are sixty or so monoliths, slanted in all directions, some tipped over completely and impacted in the earth. A single sandstone pillar stands twenty metres off, exiled from the ring, a vast exotic geode hauled west across a nameless country, like the red stone of the Hall, millennia later. They tread around it. Emily examines the spirals carved into its body, unknowable symbols. There is a deep groove sculpted on top. She and Rachel speculate about the type of machinery required to get it there and upright: wooden rollers, piers and joists, excavation. Lawrence is quiet and a little agitated; his patience seems forced. They stand between two portal stones in the circle – the setting sun is close to the pillar's groove, but off-centre. Thousands of years of astronomical bustle. If ever the planetary cogs were accurate, they have now slipped.

It reminds me of Skara Brae, Emily says.

Lawrence looks at her, and then at Rachel.

In Orkney, he says. I proposed there.

There were huge hailstones, Emily says. Like golf balls.

He puts his hand against his wife's back. The moment might be tender, but there seems no tenderness in the gesture. His hand lingers and then drops. It is not Emily punishing Lawrence, Rachel realises. Emily is pushing ahead, gamely, trying to be positive, trying to reconnect and fix. The husband routine is automatic, and Lawrence knows he must kneel for forgiveness before the one he has hurt, but something in her brother seems to have switched off. Rachel turns away and begins down the slope towards Seldom Seen. It is painful to see the withdrawal, like having a mirror held up before her, or her former life, revealing her incapacity.

Later, in the cottage, Lawrence seems more content and at ease. The Christmas dinner is a success, and they exchange gifts, turn the tree lights on. He gives the baby a fluffy toy lion. He stalks it along the carpet, growling, much to Charlie's delight. They christen the lion Roary. For the moment, all seems well.

*

A few weeks later, in the office, Rachel watches an early preview of Gregor's film footage with Charlie on her knee. The camera closes in on each wolf, on the wolves together, their candid moments. They work in unison to bring down a young deer, closing in from either side, trapping it in a narrow granite gulley. It tries to cut back, spins about as they attach themselves to its neck, and drops. They open it up, work at the red flesh, and afterwards lick each other. Sleet drives across the moor, catches on their longer fur, lines their backs. Blood, snow, their immunity; they are in their element. She has missed seeing them.

There's footage of Ra emerging from the den, which has been dug in the broad root system of an oak tree, on a mound not too far from the stream where the sighting with Chloe was made. Gregor has managed to stow himself in a position close enough not to unsettle them. Above the dugout, the oak trunk is immensely solid, spreading widely and guarding against collapse. The loose soil underneath has been moved. There are two entrances. The hollow openings are large, distinctive. Freshwater, a vantage point, a stronghold. The herds range on all sides. There's a wonderful stretch of film of Ra clearing the site – flares of earth from his back paws as he digs the den run.

Look, she says to Charlie. Look at clever Mr Wolf. What's he doing? Is he tidying up?

The baby lunges forward and then presses the back of his head against her chest. He kicks. He wants to be down, able to move, but his muscles aren't yet coordinating. She holds him in a standing position, his tipping feet on her thighs, bounces him up and down. He looks at the screen, and she thinks, it is a nursery story of sorts – the wolf and his bride.

What's Mr Wolf doing? She asks.

What indeed. Biological theories of behaviour: much is guesswork, or extrapolation. The rising prolactin levels in his mate are motivating him, perhaps. There is still insufficient data to be sure and the implants are not yet subtle enough, cannot measure protein and hormone levels. Ra sniffs the air, continues working. The camera focuses in. He scrapes the ground. The fur along his throat and round his ears is tinted beige. Smuts of grey and even black around his face. The glacial eyes seem colourless, then, in the tilting light, like shale flame. He lopes off.

Later, in the snowy rain, Merle stands next to him with her

muzzle resting on his back – a beautiful moment of ritual bonding, all the more intimate for the unedited nature of the film, the lack of narration. Though they are a naïve pair, Rachel has confidence. It is a natal den. Merle will encourage him, and Ra will work out how to mount her. This is her marker for the project's success. Not that they should be accepted by the land, as if ascending to a throne; Thomas' goal was never in doubt. She wants them to be unexceptional, common. They should exist here as anywhere, and in so doing recreate their common selves.

Charlie helps or tries to help the bouncing movement, and chirps with delight.

Look at Mr Wolf, she says. What's he doing?

The same phrases, repeated a hundred times a day. *Where's Charlie? Say Mama.* She sometimes feels like an automaton. But he is learning, and fast.

Gregor comes into the office with a battered duffel bag and a reinforced laptop case.

Hi, Rachel. And if it isn't bonny prince Charlie, he says, laying a hand on the baby's head. What a handsome fellow you are.

Charlie cranes back. Rachel pauses the film.

This is amazing. Thank you.

No bother. It's a bit rough but I thought you'd like it. Just popped in to say toodle-oo. This fellow's getting big!

Are you flying out this evening?

Wednesday. I'm away up to Dundee first to see my beloveds.

Though he has been camping in the bothy for weeks during the winter, Gregor has gained weight. His full, curly beard is trimmed short, as is the white hair; he does not look as if he has suffered privation. The Annerdale gig has been soft compared to Nepal. A stove to heat food and water, a local pub. He is taking two months off to return to the leopards, and will come back in spring for the final stage of Merle's pregnancy, should it occur, the early phases of pup development.

Thanks again, she says. Have a good trip. And best of luck.

Gregor nods, tickles Charlie's belly, and Charlie squeals again.

I'll bring you back a parasite. Keep watching that – there's a good bit coming up.

He hoists his bag over his shoulder and heads out the door. She presses play and continues to watch.

*

After Lawrence and Emily's visit, Rachel becomes determined not to mess things up with Alexander. Seeing their helpless atrophy was depressing. She does not want that part of herself to be vestigial: a withered stump of a heart. She will try to be open and giving. Almost as soon as the resolution is made, she finds herself mired in a series of misunderstandings, as if sabotaging herself. Randomly, he sends her flowers. They did not exchange Christmas gifts – neither one of them felt the necessity – and she becomes immediately suspicious. The note reads, *Dear Rachel, looking forward to later. A x* They are due to have dinner, then Alexander will probably spend the night. But why send flowers? Is it not a raising of the romantic stakes, a declaration? Does he want something more from her? She broods all day, panics on and off about the meaning of it. The flowers are beautiful, all winter reds and whites, luxurious, expensive; she leaves them under the cellophane wrapper, only taking them out and arranging them in a vase an hour before he arrives.

He makes a casserole, which smells delicious as it bubbles

away. She puts Charlie to bed and they open a bottle of wine and eat. She is quiet, toying with the food, not drinking the wine, kicking herself all the while for not relishing what is extremely enjoyable. Halfway through the meal Alexander puts his cutlery down.

OK. What is it? Too much salt? Not enough salt?

No. It's lovely.

Why are you sulking?

I'm not sulking.

Have I done something to upset you?

No.

Rachel.

No, really.

She tries to smile. The truth is she has been braced all evening. For words she does not want to hear, the slipping of a ring box out of his top pocket, perhaps – wild fantasies based on very little evidence. He is acting the same as ever – chatting casually, telling funny stories. There are flirtatious looks, but he is certainly not mooning. He is not nervous or looking for a right moment.

Sorry, she says. Just an odd day.

How come?

Oh, I don't know. We had another email from our friendly nutter.

Nigh?

Yes.

Saying what?

Very little that made sense, as usual. But he's persistent, which generally means there's something to it – in my experience, anyway. Over Christmas it did cross my mind that it's Leo.

Leo Pennington?

Alexander's tone is sceptical.

I know, she says. I thought maybe it was a way of getting at his family. Silly.

From what I hear he's a good kid, just a bit of a black sheep. I doubt he'd be against the project.

She nods. She does not mention the flowers, other than to thank him, briefly, for them. He tells her she is welcome. The transaction is low-key. It was a gesture with no ulterior motive, she decides; he simply felt like sending them, or perhaps he had vouchers, or there was an offer on. A romantic blip in the practical run of things.

Later, upstairs, he watches her from the bed as she undresses. She strips unprovocatively. In the mirror she glances at herself: stomach, slack, with silky creeping at the sides where the skin was stretched. The telltale line between her hips is less vivid, a few inches wide, still slightly overhung. The scar sits just below the hairline and contains tiny gristled knots. It is not offensive. Her breasts are full, white and veined, the nipples hard as cartilage – in a month or so she will stop breastfeeding, meanwhile they must contend with spillage during any sexual act. Her hair has reached her shoulders for the first time in a decade. She must get it cut.

Come here, Alexander says.

She turns back to the bed. He is waiting, naked and smiling, half erect. His gaze is soft, blind to any imperfection, a body altered by utility, if not blind then unaffected. He is enjoying the view overall, and its prospect. He will have seen far worse, she knows, during his wife's illness. There is no noise from the cot in the neighbouring room. She moves to the bed and sits. He puts a hand on her thigh, but otherwise waits for permission. Her body feels far less fragile than during the previous attempts, not the hive of strong muscles it once was, but functional, desiring. Now he is hard. A faint dark line runs the length of his cock, a scribble of vein. He reaches round her back, to the old scar, which, though she hardly ever sees it, is much worse, and puts his other hand on her lower abdomen.

Front and back, he says. You match. I like it.

The erotic nature of damage. She kisses him. He will be passive, a considerate lover, she knows, as he has been since the surgery, lying back, gently pulling her over him – a kind of sexual supplicant. There are men who make the world seem populated by good men, those who are intuitive, or have been taught. She straddles him, sits proud, moves his hands from her hips to her breasts. Their size and weight are enormously pleasurable, a weapon almost. There's a thrilling power to seeing him so aroused. She slides down his body, cups the end of him in her mouth, moves her tongue confidently trying to dispel the mood of caution. It is in part a test, of course, to see what he can withstand. He holds her head. Then curses. *Fuck*. He hefts her up, rolls her onto her side, facing away, puts his hand between her legs. Then he pulls her closer, angles her leg up, takes hold of himself and pushes in. He butts firmly against her, the flesh of her bottom slapping, and does not last long.

How small is their window for breeding? he asks.

Small enough.

Not like dogs, then. At it all year round.

He bites her collarbone playfully. They are lying facing each other, wetly stained, happy, a slight sting to her broken tissues.

A shorter period of fertility means males have less incentive to abandon a pregnant mate and find another.

Ah, clever.

He knows enough about wolves, does not need the education, but he enjoys having her teach. He rubs a finger over the tooth marks in her skin. The wind is beginning to get up, playing the trees like instruments. Above, the sound of aerial tectonics, as if great portions of the sky are moving apart or grinding together. The windowpane reveals absolute blackout, the occasional volley of white. A true winter's evening. The idiocy of the flowers is forgotten. The mood is warm, suggestive, with the possibility of more exchanges. Then, out of nowhere, she says,

I've been thinking about telling Charlie's father.

There's a brief pause.

Right. About?

Alexander leans over her and takes a sip of water from the glass next to the bed – old water, several glasses have been left uncleared.

About Charlie.

Right. So he doesn't know?

No.

Now the words are out, she's not sure what she expects him to say in response, or even why she mentioned it. Something subconscious, unearthed by the talk of mates and disappearances, perhaps. He has, other than their first night together, never asked about the situation. Perhaps it has not mattered to him. Perhaps he has not wanted to know details, or has constructed a phantom rival in his mind.

He lives in America.

I assumed that was the case.

I didn't want to involve him.

And now you do?

The question is level-toned, and yet it cannot be that simple, so much depends on her answer. She shakes her head, sits up, and leans forward, away from the heat of his body.

I don't know. Not really. I just don't know if it's OK for him not to know he even exists.

Are you sure he doesn't? In this day and age –

He doesn't. He would have said something.

So you're still in touch?

Sometimes.

He places his large hand on her shoulder, pulls gently. She leans back against his chest and he puts an arm round her. For a while he is quiet.

Is he a prick? Is that why you didn't involve him?

It sounds foolish either way, she thinks. To have been involved with someone unappealing, or to have excluded a good man from a child's life.

No, he's not a prick. He's pretty great, actually. I worked with him at Chief Joseph. He was a friend.

Oh.

I just mean, that wasn't the reason. I was the reason. I'm not very good at any of this.

He puts his mouth to the side of her head, his words muffle in her hair.

You're very good at it.

He means the sex, or he is being overly kind about her level of effort. They do not ring each other regularly with news or for no reason at all, just to say hi, as lovers in the fast spiral do. It is Alexander who comes to her. She knows better than to assume, as she did for years, that men enjoy her casualness, her coolness, that it suits them better, or that they are less invested. It doesn't take them long to sense that such an attitude stems from something else – a fear, a flaw, stuntedness. Finally, with Alexander, with the baby, or simply with her coordinates in life, the game seems up. She is exposed. Silence. She feels tension creeping in. The mood is still light, but something is slipping, spoiling. She tries to explain.

There was nothing really between us. There wasn't a relationship or even the possibility of one.

There was something, Alexander says.

No, she says.

But why should he believe her? There is, after all, a baby: irrefutable evidence.

It's alright, he says. Everyone has a past. I'd prefer Charlie's dad to be someone you liked, someone decent.

You'd prefer it, she says.

A small flare of anger. It is not really a question, or a reiteration of his point. She is about to say more, that he doesn't get to have a preference, that he is not in a position to choose, even theoretically, what kind of man he would like her baby to have been sired by, but she stops herself. He sighs.

Look, I think if you want to tell him, then you should tell him.

I haven't made up my mind.

OK.

His arm is now stiff about her shoulders, uncomfortable; it should not be there but is stranded. The baby begins to cry, a faint inquisitive wail, quickly escalating. She moves away and gets up.

Do you want me to go to him? Alexander offers.

Not unless you can express.

She sounds like a bitch; she knows. How easily the attitude comes, once the mood is active, even in the face of amelioration, attempts to restore good terms. She looks down at him. He says nothing. His face has firmed, become slab-like. She goes next door, shuts the nursery door, leans over the crib, and picks up Charlie. Her heart is flurrying, the baby feels her unsettlement and struggles in her arms. It seemed unlikely she would ever argue with Alexander. No, not that: she has never really made it past a first argument with a man; argument always signifies her extraction. She has been happy these past months, and to imagine cross words and nastiness would have meant imagining the end.

She comforts the baby. She sits and tries to nurse him, but he screams louder. The wrong smell to her, perhaps – the residue of sex. Or Charles Caine is expanding his repertoire of mysterious complaints. He feels hot, tussles against her chest, spits out the milk. This is what happens, she thinks, when the embargoes are down. Things are said, stupid intimate dissembling things that do more harm than good. Perhaps Alexander will leave, she thinks. Of course he will leave; he is dressing right now, gathering up his phone and watch and wallet. Any moment she will hear the front door slam. Soon she becomes sure she has already heard it.

It's a long time before the baby will settle. She takes his temperature, changes him, strokes his hair, adjusts the blankets. By the time she's finished and returns to the bedroom, the desertion fantasy is complete and she is miserable. But Alexander is asleep in the bed. The lamp is still on. His glasses are on the bedside table, his legs splayed. She climbs in next to him. He stirs, turns, and puts an arm around her, the subconscious automatic of affection. She lies rigidly by his side, her hand barely daring to touch him, wanting to. I'm sorry, she thinks. I really am no good at this.

In the morning, Alexander brings her tea, as usual. She lies quiet and unmoving, as if asleep, still troubled, unable to fully embrace the reversal of disaster. Alexander goes to the bathroom to shower. She hears him coughing, blowing his nose clear under the stream of water, singing a few lines of a song – one of Chloe's favourites, maybe. The baby sleeps on, exhausted by the night's huge fit. She examines herself. You're programmed to backstep, she thinks, to make them come forward, then to break fully away. She understands the dance – it has served her well, as it served her mother. But she cannot keep blaming Binny, not for the habits of a lifetime, not when she knows exactly what she is doing.

Alexander comes into the room, dripping wet, towelling his hair. He drops the towel on the floor and begins to dress. His body is familiar now, the vast chest with its dark central cavern, the long legs, and small buttocks. She does not love him. That is, she does not feel love as described by others, the high and low arts, not in relation to the person here in her room. But all that is misnomer, poetry, an unproved chemical; he has survived her tendencies; he releases something in her, if only a feeling of wanting another day, a feeling that the day with him is better than ordinary. She sits up, reaches for the mug of tea, and takes a sip.

Are you coming back later? she asks. After work?

He pauses in the lacing of his shoes and looks at her quizzically.

*

The weather deteriorates. There are days and days of snow, unlike anything the district has seen for decades. The condition feels eternal; in reality it is just three weeks of chaos. There's a fast fall at the end of January – sticky, dense, a substance perfectly manufactured to mask the fields and fells, to stack against walls, blocking roads, and upholstering buildings. On the roof of the cottage hang precarious cornices that collapse with little warning. The garden is arctic, a lost world. On the estate, tractors cut through the drifts, leaving deep chasms in their wake, still impassable by car. The Penningtons' helicopter is grounded, flights across the entire nation are grounded, and the Pendolinos south run at half speed, then are cancelled. More snow follows. Thomas misses the second vote on currency union. Supermarkets begin to run out of food. Then, the clouds disperse, the sky is as clear and dangerous as burning oxygen. Plummeting temperatures. The thermometer reaches minus thirteen at night. In the Highlands: minus nineteen. Petrol freezes in tanks. The death rate of pensioners soars; there's talk of a flu pandemic, a deadly new variety.

In Annerdale, it is too cold even for river fog; the rivers freeze over, the lake begins to solidify – even the Irish Sea crisps at the edges. Pipes in the converted outbuildings of the Hall burst, and the staff, including Huib, decamp to the main building, like evacuees brought into the big house during a war. But they are guests, and are made to feel like guests. Every morning they are served eggs in the giant kitchen, from copper pans. Poached haddock. Fresh bread. Chopped herbs. The larders of Pennington Hall are well stocked. Huib texts Rachel – *On holiday, come and join us.* But the tyre ruts in the road are now glaciers, the snow is too deep and hard to walk across. She cannot get out of the woods, even for Charlie's next immunisation appointment.

She takes the baby outside to look at the world. They stand wrapped in coats and scarves. Cumbria is a whiteout, as far as the eye can see. The mountains are brightly coated and seem bigger, amplified. At night, the stars are exceptional, with the lustre of old cracked diamonds. Charlie will remember nothing of it, she knows. She wonders, though, if it is laying something down in him, forming some sensibility? Will he always seek colder places, the beauty of frozen massifs, blue locked into white, the immaculate?

She keeps the heating high – she is not paying the bills and she does not want to risk a plumbing catastrophe. 1847, the date stone of Seldom Seen reads. The place has been upgraded, and well insulated, but gelid air still makes its way around the windows and under the doors, radiates through the walls. Rachel sleeps with the baby in her bed, against the advice, but she does not want to leave him in the bassinet. She tries to get the Saab out again, but the undercarriage scrapes and grinds; the back end swings out. Finally, it beaches itself at an angle and the wheels spin uselessly. The engine protests. She abandons the car in the lane, takes the baby out of the travel seat, and carries him back to the house. That night, another snowfall: lesser, but substantial enough to cover the treacherous layer of ice. Michael arrives on a quad bike, clad in woollens, Gore-Tex, and agricultural boots. The lurcher is balanced on the seat behind him, tongue out, its breath steaming in the air. He knocks on the door, says nothing about her car blocking the lane, and asks if she needs anything. A lone woman and a baby cannot be abandoned in such conditions, never mind who they are.

Think I'm OK, she tells him. I stocked up.

Anything for the little one?

No. Thanks, though. Incredible weather.

Expect another good week of it, he says.

Small talk, about that most English of subjects: weather. It feels like a temporary ceasefire between them. He climbs back on the quad, and she watches him drive away – the dog riding pillion, adjusting its paws as the bike tips and wallows over the polar rifts, at one point springing off into the new snow, then mounting itself up front between Michael's legs. She doesn't need anything, not yet. Her cupboards are full. There is ample baby formula, nappies, medicine. There's still meat in the freezer, unlabelled purple and red packages now mysterious with permafrost, bags of summer berries and green beans. If she was in danger of forgetting the practicalities of a rural Cumbrian childhood, the Pacific Northwest continued her education – and seriously. There is dry wood for the fire. She has cans and jars stacked deep. They will sit it out.

She keeps the radio on for updates, a lifeline. All over the country airports have closed, schools, hospitals are running skeleton crews; the economy is haemorrhaging. Every day there's a debate about why England can't cope with extreme weather conditions, while in Berlin and Kiev and Japan flights leave on time, the workforce remains productive. The government has ordered salt from abroad, which will arrive by tanker ship in May. Not so across the border. Calling in to the morning programme, the new transport minister says Scotland is equipped and faring well. The ploughs are out; the roads are gritted. Glasgow airport is open for business, flights to Heathrow are being redirected there.

Charlie burbles over the sound of the radio. He wants her attention. She learns to become verbose, to blether. He likes her voice, understands something about it, if not language. She reads to him, all kinds of books when repeating the same baby prose begins to send her crazy, a gory thriller – she stops when the serial killer begins to dismember a victim. His eyes are huge and preverbal. He makes long, purring, grating sounds, trying to talk back. She reads her own book chapter to him, edits it a little as she does so. She even sings, her voice flat, tuneless, but does she not owe him disinhibition, rhymes, the silliness of the nursery? *One two, buckle my shoe, three four, open the door* . . . If she stops, he protests. She is desperately in need of sensible conversation. She calls Lawrence, but there is no answer. She calls Alexander. Chloe answers.

Carrick 205, hello, Chloe Graham speaking.

As if she is answering the phone in the 1950s. The vintage chic of landlines.

Hi, Chloe; it's Rachel.

Hi, Rachel.

Are you off school?

There is no school.

They speak in a friendly fashion for a minute and then Alexander takes the receiver.

Do you need rescuing?

No, I'm alright. How's it there?

One catastrophe after another. Some idiot crashed through the bridge into the river, had the first responders out with the defibrillator paddles. The pub's run out of ale. There'll be a civil war any moment. How's Charlie?

He's fine. He's driving me nuts. He wants me to talk all the time. I could read the phone book to him and he wouldn't care.

There's laughter down the line.

Yeah, I remember that stage.

Shit. He's awake. I have to go.

Alright. Call me back if you need rescuing. Or if you want to talk dirty.

The snow begins to melt and the ice beneath reveals itself like broken glass, the weapons in a Saxon hoard, instruments of havoc. The country begins to move slowly, to right itself again. Then, more snow. Huge white floes, like a nineteenth-century dreamscape. Everything stops.

In the middle of it, away from the malady of humans, the wolves sit watching the red deer moving across the moor, high-stepping daintily, testing each foothold. They assess the prospects of the hunt, judge the expenditure of energy, the resistance, the lack of traction. The herds keep to the best routes, ground where the snow is thinnest, where they will not have to flounder to escape. Since autumn, their behaviour has changed rapidly. A new nervousness has arrived; the running past has caught up with them. Ra and Merle watch from a high vantage point, ready to accelerate down the slopes and across the valley bottom, muscling through the drifts, bipartisan hunters of the mountains and the plains. But there is a refractory quality to their watching. Below, the deer pass by, single file, ears twitching, eyes glimmering black. They move safely on. A carcass lies close to the entrance of the den; another hunt is not yet necessary. Several times during the month they've been locked in a tie, rear to rear: their season of cold union.

When the weather lifts, it feels as if a dire, convulsive event has passed: miscarriage or seizure. There is a sudden upswing in temperature, ten degrees and more, alarming in its own right. Meltwater flows over the measled remnant snow. The earth is left slack and raw, streams trickle in the road, downhill, into culverts and under cattle grids. Pools of water all over the landscape flicker like poured metal. Rachel brings the baby outside again, a woollen blanket hanging around him like a holy robe. She turns slowly, holding him against her chest, a ritual figurine, showing him all the angles of the sacrificial world. He is the prize of all agonies. A strange little god, incapable and testing, who has taken over her life. She kisses the back of his neck softly, and he squirms and barks. How unlike herself he has made her. That night, reading in bed, she turns to look out the window. The skull of the moon glows, internally, as if tallow-lit, its surface cracked and pitted. A symbolic relic, reminding those beneath that not everything survives. Her mother has been dead for more than a year. She gets up and goes into the baby's room, watches him sleep for a few minutes, something she has not done since he was newborn. One morning soon after the thaw, a giant toad presents itself on the doorstep like a muddy gift, a messenger. Spring is arriving.

She drives to the office, most days, weekends also, trying to recover something of her role. She brings Charlie, sets him on a blanket on the floor with a contraption of mirrors and swinging toys above him. He kicks, tries to grab things. She works in efficient bursts. She goes into the enclosure with Huib again, but the wolves are much more reclusive, a good sign, and the decision is made not to disturb them again until later in the year. She studies their transmitter signal patterns. They have been staying near the den site, returning to carcasses more frequently, picking them clean. Biding. Merle's movements especially are becoming conservative. When Gregor returns from Nepal, he will leave a discreet, motion-triggered rig by the den, and they will know for sure.

Work is difficult. Charlie demands time; he demands love and energy. Keeping him is fascinating and acutely boring. There are slow, torturous hours in the middle of the night when he screams dementedly, his face hot and wet, the ridges between his eyes and ears lined with salt, his body taut as a drum. Extreme tiredness begins to wear her down. She wishes she were still breastfeeding; there was comfort in it for both of them. She wishes he would shut up. *Shut up*, she thinks, and then says it to him, almost shouting, actually shouting. Immediately, she feels wracked with guilt. He cries so much, he vomits. His shit is green. She calls NHS Direct, Jan, Alexander. She takes him to Frances Dunning. He is not sick. It is a stage, then: growth, or an experiment in anguish. He throws his bottle away, knocks things out of her hand, so furious, so inconsolable, his tongue beaking out of his mouth. *What*, she says, *what's wrong!* A malevolent changeling has been exchanged for Charlie, like the gurning, earthen toad on the doorstep. In his face, hatred, scorn, or is she imagining it? She is being punished, of course, for everything she has done wrong, every sin. She takes hold of herself – such thoughts are pure, fatigued irrationality. She walks with him in her arms, backward and forward across the floor, shushing, cooing. He exhausts himself finally, and she collapses back into bed. He wakes in the morning, contented and smooth, smiling, giggling, as if nothing was ever wrong. The following night, the same bawling demon possesses him.

And then he does get sick. Every week it seems he has a new virus, a cold, or gastric upset, some germ picked up from nowhere, from spores arriving in his cot. An oozing eye infection, yellow crust around the lid. Diarrhoea, evil-coloured and noxious, which brushes through her too, leaving her green-feeling, her insides churning. Then a cough that sounds lethal, *hack, hack, choke*. She has had the whooping cough vaccination, and Charlie has, too, but she panics. She goes to the doctor again, collects more medicine, antibiotics, which she knows will give him thrush. Frances Dunning administers to him expertly, and Rachel feels like a failure. The doctor is sage.

Try not to worry; it's just the way it is. He has to create

antibodies. Childhood is about illness, that's what they don't tell you.

Dr Dunning looks at her.

How are you, Rachel? Are you getting enough support?

She says she is. But she is exhausted and fuddled, and it shows. When she gets home, she calls Sylvia, asks her to babysit. She goes to bed and sleeps for a few hours, a fatal, unmoving sleep. When she wakes, the room is in focus. The house is beautifully quiet. There's a note on the table downstairs saying Charlie has been taken out for a walk. She sits at the kitchen table, drinks coffee, thinks of nothing, not even the wolves.

The baby gets better. The pus dries up, the cough slackens. She begins to relax. She resumes work at the office, recreates the little corner crèche for Charlie, claws her way back through correspondence and administration. She even writes more of her book chapter. Green shoots appear on the trees outside; light expands the day's length. Everything seems on the up, until Michael's wife contracts influenza, the dangerous variant sweeping through the country, for which there is no trialled vaccine. When he comes into the office to report on the enclosure, Michael also seems unwell, is pale-looking, sweaty, and breathing hard. Like a condemning harbinger, he breathes over them, stands near the baby. Rachel wants to shove him forcibly out of the office. The following week Lena is hospitalised and Michael recuses himself. Rachel watches the baby, filled with dread. She takes his temperature daily, checks him again and again. She watches over him with the intensity of prayer. It is excruciating. To be so out of control emotionally, to have so much and so little control over another living thing. Had she known it, had she even suspected the debilitation, the decision at Binny's graveside might have been different. But no. No. There is no retrospective history where children are concerned, no what-ifs. He is here, he is here, he is here. His arms open and reach out, wanting to be picked up. *Mammmmum.* He is close to saying it, some version of it, and confirming her new identity. She lifts him. He fits against her side. Rightfully made. Unquestionable.

*

In April, Lawrence and Emily separate. He calls Rachel to tell her – it is a terrible phone call out of the blue, halting and awkward. She sits at the table. Outside Seldom Seen, a ragged spring evening, with sunlight crashing through the windowpane, then, moments later, rain, soft-knuckling the glass.

I just thought you should know, he says, flatly. Keep in touch with her if you want – she wants you to stay in touch.

Lawrence, I'm really sorry.

Yeah. Thanks. But it was going to happen. She's had enough. And I have, too.

There's a hollow ring to his tone. He is past embarrassment, regret, and apology, is deep into the inevitability of it all – an emotional dead zone.

For now just use my mobile number. I'm not in the house any more.

Where are you staying?

With a friend.

He gives no more details, no address. She wonders if this friend is the woman with whom he had the affair, whether there has been a rekindling. But now is not the time for reproach.

Are you alright, Lawrence?

Yeah, fine, he says. Anyway, there it is.

She can hear nothing of his usual self in his voice. In the background there's the sound of cars, many cars, moving fast, a motorway or main road. It's unnerving to think of him extracted from his home environment, calling from some transient place. He sniffs on the other end of the line. He says nothing more, has no desire to talk it all over, it seems.

You sure you're OK?

Yeah. Just thought I should tell you. OK then, I'll go now.

Lawrence, wait a minute.

He mustn't hang up. Everything seems precipitous; she's sure that he is on the verge of some disastrous course, or has already embarked.

Why not come here? she suggests. Come and stay with me and Charlie for a while. Lawrence?

Silence from her brother. The lowing of traffic. A passing siren.

Lawrence?

I can't, he says. It's bad enough at work already. Can't just disappear.

Take some personal leave. These things happen. Surely they can manage without you, under the circumstances?

No, I can't, he says. There are things I need to do here anyway.

What things?

Christ! Just things. Why are you bullying me?

I'm not bullying you.

Yes, you are. You always do.

What?

Yes, Rachel.

It's the first time he's lost his temper and snapped at her since their reconciliation. She is shocked at the sudden strength of his feelings, the dismantlement of their pact. Cut him some slack, she thinks, he just lost his wife, he doesn't mean it. But he sounds like a man to whom nothing matters – the way he is saying her name, without warmth, as if tolerating her.

Have you been drinking? she asks.

No, Rachel. And even if I had, so what? What's the problem with that?

Rain tip-tapping the windowpane of the cottage like fragments of bone.

Nothing. You just sound strange. I don't want you to –

I have to go now. I'm going to go.

She has heard him speak like this before – a long time ago. The petulance. The perfunctory despair. *I'm going to smash John in the head with my stick. Then Mum can come with us to swim in the river.* A lost boy, making all the wrong decisions, before he learnt how to make the right ones. Lawrence would never let his marriage dissolve; he would fight harder. Nor would he alienate his sister. Rachel scrambles to keep him on the line.

Wait, please, she says. Charlie would love to see you – he misses his uncle. Come and see him for a bit.

It's a bald, cheap play, using the baby as leverage, but she doesn't care; it's vital that he isn't swept along in any undertow.

Lawrence?

No. I've said I can't.

OK. We'll come down there then.

No, he says.

I'd be happy to.

No.

Her frustration begins to mount. It occurs to her that she

should let him go, that her pride is simply being knocked – her authority and influence are not working. He is an adult; he can take care of himself. But deep down, she doesn't believe that. Her instincts have branched; they have had to as a mother. Whether he wants it or not, Lawrence needs help – and some part of him must know it, he called her, after all. He tries to hang up again. He is late for something, he says, needs to meet a friend. She stops him, asks again – Will you come to stay? Charlie's favourite uncle . . . – begging almost, but she does not care. His tone softens a fraction.

I know you're trying to be nice, Rachel, but don't. I don't deserve it. You don't want me there. I'm a mess. It would be really bad for the baby.

She ignores the comment. She begins to talk at him. She talks steadily, fluidly – she can do this now, thanks to Charlie, who has broken the seal. He doesn't want sympathy or absolution, that much is very clear, so she makes the case selfishly, appeals to his old sense of duty: the weak spot. *I want you here. Come and help me. I'm really tired. You're so good with him, and I don't feel I'm coping.* Twice more he tries to extricate himself. His desperation to get away is painful; she droops at the table, feels physically vulnerable. There's a wound in her now it seems; all the people she cares for can hurt her. She keeps talking, asking her brother to come, for her sake, almost incanting it. He interrupts and his voice cracks.

Please don't, Rachel. Don't. I'll be no good around a baby. I don't want to fuck that up, too. Please don't make me.

She does not understand. Only later will she understand.

What? Lawrence, no. You are a fantastic uncle. Charlie loves you. I –

He is weeping now, muffled, and she feels her eyes sting. Someone passes him on the road, makes some comment that she cannot hear, asking him if he is alright perhaps, or calling him a name.

Lawrence, she says, as firmly as she can. I'll see you tomorrow.

He arrives the following night, by taxi, with one small bag. Emily must have kept the Audi, she thinks, as well as the house. Any relief she had anticipated in seeing him quickly ebbs. He looks extremely run down, thin, ten years older. His face is greyish and furtive. There's a small black scab near his upper lip. He follows her into the kitchen, puts down his bag.

Sorry it's late. The trains were fucked up.

That's OK.

The baby has already been put to bed. He shakes his head when she offers to get him up. She gives him a beer and starts to make supper. Her plan was to gently investigate the situation, enquire about the possibilities of patching things up with Emily. But he is in no fit state. Terrible, lasting damage seems to have occurred. Lawrence cuts onions listlessly, standing next to her at the counter. He finishes the beer and opens another. There's an odd smell to him, not unwashed, not unsanitary, but slightly sick, metallic – bad breath, or the tinge of blood.

Small enough? he asks.

Great. Could you do the garlic?

She passes him a bulb. She tries not to watch him. The skin on his arms looks dull, and there are more picked sores. The unspoken weighs heavily, and she begins to feel out of her depth, his depression seems much more serious than she anticipated. Lawrence dices a couple of cloves, puts the knife down on the board. He sits and drinks the beer while she finishes the meal. At the table the conversation never gets going. Lawrence makes little effort, and she does not push him. He eats mechanically, looking at his plate, taking no enjoyment in the food. He is very pale. He drinks two more beers – too many for the tempo of the evening. At one point she catches his eye, not confrontationally, but with intent. *You can tell me.* He looks away. He stands and clears the plates.

Don't worry; just leave them on the counter. I'll load them up later.

He sets them down. The knives and forks skitter off and clatter on the countertop. She sees him wince.

Do you want some coffee?

She is tired but willing to stay up, if it means helping him, or just being companionable.

No, that's OK.

They move to the lounge, sit by the fire. Her brother sits uncomfortably in the armchair, leaning awkwardly to the side and staring hard into the flames, as if he would, if he knew how, consume their lustre. The evening wastes away without television, talk, or progress. Soon, Lawrence excuses himself and goes to bed, and Rachel follows his lead.

In the early hours she hears him get up, move around the room, and use the bathroom. He goes downstairs. The front door opens and shuts. She listens for a car engine, in case he has called a taxi and is leaving surreptitiously, but it is quiet. She checks on the baby, goes downstairs, and opens the front door. A black wall of night – beyond which she cannot see him. Cool, after-rain dampness. The trees rustle invisibly. Even this far inland, she can smell traces of the sea: briney, ionic. She peers down the lane, waits for her eyes to adjust. The trees begin to loom, shouldering out of the darkness. There is no sign of him. He must simply be restless – why should he not be? – and needs some air. She closes the door, leaves it unlocked, and goes back to bed. She is dozing when she hears the stairs creak.

In the morning Charlie starts up, loud enough to wake their guest, but Lawrence stays in his room, and half an hour later, after the baby is fed, she cracks open the spare-bedroom door. He is asleep, still has his shirt on and the covers are knotted about his waist. The penalty of insomnia – mornings surrendered to late-arriving rest. Downstairs she calls Huib and says she is going to work from home today.

If there's anything urgent, call me.

Sure, he says. Gregor is due back today.

Oh shit. I completely forgot.

Hey, listen, that's OK. I'll meet him and take him inside.

Thanks. Is there anything else?

Not really, he says. But you should know – Lena is not doing so well. She's in hospital again, having tests.

I'm sorry to hear that.

I'll pass it on.

They hang up. She moves from room to room, listens for movement upstairs. The baby senses her anxiety and acts up, squalling and shouting, tossing his toys away. His wail is loud and penetrative. She keeps expecting Lawrence to emerge and brighten at the sight of his nephew. She is sure the baby will act as a tonic, if not a cure. She answers emails, speaks briefly with Huib again, checks that Gregor is safely in the enclosure. She eats lunch. In the early afternoon she hears Lawrence stir and go to the bathroom; he spends a long time in there. She stands at the bottom of the stairs

eavesdropping, feeling like a spy. She hears coughing. A flush.
The lock on the door opening. She waits for him to come down,
but he crosses the landing and returns to the spare room.

She puts the baby down for a nap, thinks about taking her
brother up some tea, but does not want to disturb him – he clearly
needs to recover his strength. On a spur, she decides to call Emily,
find out her side. Emily is curt, not rude, but neither is she glad to
hear from Rachel as Lawrence proposed she would be.

I haven't spoken to him in days, she says. Look, I've got to go
into a meeting in a few minutes. I really don't want to talk about it.

It's just that I'm worried, Rachel says. He doesn't seem himself
at all. He seems depressed. I mean, properly depressed.

No. He's not depressed.

No?

No.

So, what is it? What's going on?

There's a pause. Emily sighs.

Look, it's great he's up there with you. I'm glad, and maybe it'll
help him. But I'm done with it all. I don't care any more. You'll
have to talk to him. It's not my place.

What do you mean?

Rachel, please. I'm so tired of it all. It's been years. I can't do it
any more.

Rachel does not understand the sudden void of care. Only a
few months ago Emily was standing by him, loyally trying to fix
the relationship. She must still love him. The coldness, the blockade of feelings must be to protect herself.

Is he having an affair again? she asks. If so, he's an idiot.

Another sigh, deeper. She can feel Emily's exasperation
mounting.

No. You know what the problem is? He admires you. He doesn't want you to think badly of him. But it's not up to me to tell you. I have to go. I hope it works out.

The line goes dead. Rachel sits for a moment, thinking, scenarios flashing through her mind. Other men. Schoolgirls. Sex workers. Nothing makes sense. What is this unspeakable thing her brother is keeping from her? She checks on the baby. He's asleep in his victory pose, arms flung up, fists resting either side of his head. She crosses the landing and goes into the bathroom. There's the smell of digestive upset; the toilet bowl is cloudy with unflushed matter. She opens the door of the spare room. The curtains are drawn, but the window is open and it's very cold. The sour, ironish smell is there again, like rusting metal and dirt, somehow agricultural, like the aroma around the decrepit farms in her old village. Lawrence is in the same position, but his breathing is quicker, shallower. She steps into the room. His shirt is patched with sweat, and he is shivering.

Lawrence? Are you awake?

He turns a fraction towards her, then rolls back and faces the wall.

Don't come in.

Are you sick?

He makes a noise, either in agreement or convulsively.

Is it the flu?

I'll be alright. Just leave me be.

Do you need anything? Some water? I've got painkillers.

No.

I can bring you some soup.

No!

His declination is emphatic. She is aware she is playing the part of nurse; she feels it, foolishly, knowing there is falseness to the whole situation, some unexplained charade. She cannot maintain the act.

I think we need to talk.

He folds tighter, draws his legs in. The blankets and sheet slip from the bed, and his shirt rides up a little. He is naked from the waist down, his leg muscles clenched, a dark gulley running between his buttocks. He reaches a hand back, gropes for the covers, but they are gone. At the base of his spine is a pronounced, risen notch of bone.

Lawrence? Did you hear what I said? Can we talk?

Silence. Her patience begins to dwindle. Rather, the desire to know the truth, to confront him, rises, flu or no flu. He says nothing. His feet are rubbing together, paddling, working against each other, a child-like motion of discomfort or anxiety. She moves to the window, draws back the curtains. He puts his arm over his face, shielding it from the light. She stands at the foot of the bed and looks down at her brother.

I just called Emily. We talked about you.

He moans softly, almost whimpering. She bends and picks up the blanket and is about to lay it over him, when he turns abruptly, sits up, and puts his head in his hands. He moans again, as if fighting the impulse to vomit. Between his legs, from a dark nest of hair, his genitals hang, limp and small, hooded. The skin around them is rashed, and on the left side of his groin there's an angry red swelling – some kind of abscess. Nearby, on the floor, a bandage stained yellow and pink.

Christ! Lawrence! What have you done?

He does not try to shield himself. He scratches his scalp.

I'm sorry, he says. I'm sorry. I'm sorry.

He breaks, and starts to weep, his shoulders lifting and falling, with gathering power and sound. She looks down at him, at the raw thing on his upper leg, next to his crotch. The smell of rot is strong. Horror begins to fill her brain, disbelief. A site infection. Rigors. He is in withdrawal. He is not sick, though he is suffering badly. His distress gathers force, becomes unbearable. His body convulses as he cries, and he retches, saliva spooling from his mouth in a glistening stream. She cannot speak, she tries to say something but stops. He shakes his head and holds himself tightly.

I'm sorry, I'm sorry.

It's OK. It's OK, Lawrence.

What else can she say? He looks up. His pupils are massive, collapsing through the pale blue irises, strangely, wrongly beautiful. She sits down on the bed, and puts her hand on his leg, which is hot and clammy. The smell is very bad. The patch in his groin is glistening and clearly needs medical attention, though he must have been doctoring it himself. How long? she wonders. How long has her brother's life been like this? How long has Emily known? It seems an impossible secret to have kept. She thinks of him at Christmas, marching the toy lion across the floor. Anxious to get home. Disappearing into the bathroom. Lawrence shakes and cries and apologises, and his saliva drools onto the sheet. He turns again, lies down, faces the wall. She puts her hand on his quaking back, and he winces. She picks up the sheet and the blanket and gently covers him, as she would the baby.

It's going to be OK, she says.

She sits with him, tries to think about what to do. Call an ambulance? Let him go through what he must? She is not equipped for any of this, even though she's seen it – the margins, at least. She thinks of Kyle's brother – the awful descriptions he

[313]

gave her, the lack of medical insurance, the forced detoxes, locked doors. A kind of loving brutality. She thinks of the addicts on the Reservation, kids five generations down and old unemployed men, milling at the relief road bars, desperate for money, standing in the dock at the tribal courts where the punishments meted out were often harsher than American ones. She knows enough about the consuming power of it, the slyness, the requirements. It is perfectly possible to lie to your wife. To not tell your sister. To function outwardly and at the same time be hidden. How could you be so stupid? she thinks. How did you let this happen? But then, he is here. Even against his will, and in this anticipated state, he came; he must have known it would be a confession. And is that not a positive decision of sorts?

It's going to be OK, she says again, firmer, surer, though this too is a partial act.

He is still weeping, tremors running through his body. He clutches his stomach as it cramps, gets up, pushes past her, and goes to the bathroom, his walk crabbed and fast. The bathroom door shuts. She hears his bowels empty violently. After a while the toilet flushes. He comes back into the room, looking waxy and weak. He gets into bed, and she puts the covers back over him.

Across the hall, the baby wakes and starts crying. She stands and crosses the room, then stops at the door. She turns and walks back to the bed, sits, and puts her arms round her brother as best she can, while he shivers and Charlie shouts louder and louder.

Alexander arrives later that afternoon, carrying a small tarpaulin satchel, his workbag. He has cut short his appointments. He hugs her, keeps her held for a moment. She feels like crying in his arms.

I'm sorry to drag you here. I didn't know what to do.

Don't worry. How is he?

I don't know. Can you just have a look at him? I think maybe he should be in hospital, but he doesn't want to go.

OK.

She shows him upstairs, into Lawrence's room, and shuts the door behind him. She lingers outside for a moment, hears Alexander's voice, friendly, confident, as he greets and approaches her brother. Then she goes downstairs and gives them privacy. She plays with Charlie, building a tower out of blocks, which he topples and she builds again. He can sit unsupported, though he often topples himself. She tries to give her son her full attention – after leaving him to cry for so long, she feels guilty – but she's too distracted. After twenty minutes she hears the bedroom door open and Alexander comes downstairs.

He's getting dressed, he says. Can you take him to A&E?

Is his leg really bad?

It's not great. I've dressed it but I can't drain it properly. I wouldn't want to try. I explained the risks if it's not treated. He's not stupid – he knows.

Did he say anything to you about it all?

A little. He's been using clean needles. He thinks the dose was contaminated – an unlucky batch.

Unlucky?

He went somewhere different for it, apparently.

She shakes her head.

When did it all start?

I don't know. Seems like a while, though.

I feel terrible. I had no idea – none.

He puts his hand on her shoulder.

Come on. It's not something you tell your folks. He will have worked very hard keeping it quiet. I know people who've gone decades before it came out.

Really?

Really.

She nods, but there's little consolation in his assurances or such tales. That anyone could wall themselves away from loved ones and be privately, hellishly bound is tragic. She picks Charlie up from the play mat on the floor.

Do you want me to go to the hospital with you? Alexander asks. I can cancel clinic tonight.

No, no, you've already given up enough time.

What about Charlie?

I'll have to take him along. It'll be alright.

Lawrence comes downstairs, gingerly, his jeans unzipped and gaping, revealing a bulky patch of white gauze. His T-shirt hangs off him. Now that she knows, it seems abundantly obvious. The look of him; echoes over the past year. Charlie makes a sound of recognition. Lawrence glances at his nephew, his eyes watery and blown, and tries to smile, but is clearly struggling. Rachel gets a blanket from the back of the sofa, puts it over his shoulders. He walks barefoot to the car, refusing his boots, and she and Alexander install him in the passenger seat. She finds a couple of old plastic bags in the kitchen and hands them to him. Alexander waits by the car while she gets Charlie's bag and secures him in the back. She promises to call later.

Go straight to Lancaster if you can, he says quietly across the roof of the car. They'll just transfer you anyway at Kendal. He might need the ICU.

Thank you, she mouths.

On the drive Lawrence is sick in one of the bags. He apologises and opens the window. He keeps his eyes closed most of the way, lets the cold air blast against his face. Charlie bawls until she hands him a dummy, and then settles and is soon asleep.

The wait in A&E is relatively short – her brother is quickly assessed and taken through. She sits with Charlie in the kids' toy corner while the examination is conducted. Lawrence is transferred to plastics. She moves to a different part of the hospital and sits in another waiting room. She reads to Charlie. He is getting bored and hungry and unruly. An hour later a junior doctor tells her they are keeping her brother overnight. The procedure will be done the following morning. There is no emergency; his leg is not at risk. She asks to visit him on the ward, but the baby is not allowed. Instead, she sends a message via the house officer. She'll be back, first thing in the morning. She'll call him later.

Give him my love, she says.

Leaving the hospital feels like a betrayal, as if she has abandoned him, but there's nothing more she can do.

Lawrence is discharged and brought back to the cottage. The abscess has been drained and he is given the all-clear. A referral is made to a specialist treatment centre in Workington, where he will meet for counselling, but he has chosen not to sign up for replacement therapy. He will not use methadone as a crutch, he says, he knows it doesn't work. On the drive back to Annerdale he looks shocked and tender, like someone who has passed through a wall of fire. They decide that he will stay on with Rachel for a few weeks, maybe longer. There are too many triggers in Leeds, too much history. Recuperation and isolation in the countryside is the subtext – the cottage will be a sanatorium. He keeps apologising;

she keeps telling him everything is OK. She doesn't push him on the details of his addiction, but over the next few days he will begin to tell her. Fifteen years on and off, which seems extraordinary. There have been whole periods when he was clean, he says – during law school, when he first met Emily, IVF. Despite the infection and its scarring he is relatively healthy – middle-class living has prevented the worst version of it. At night he sleeps poorly, she can hear his nightmares, then insomnia that has him walking the house.

In the coming weeks, there will be moments of temper, moods, and the ironclad choreography of well-being that will come to replace the habit itself, but this first morning back from hospital, he makes her a promise.

I don't want it in my life any more, Rachel. I won't do it, I swear. I know you'll be worried about me being around Charlie –

It's going to be fine, she says for the hundredth time.

She does trust him, or wants to. She must trust him if they are to make it work, and, though she cannot say when he might have been using in the past and whether Charlie was exposed, she never thought of him as a danger to the baby; and he never was. After he has eaten some toast, she brings Charlie into the room, bathed and dressed in clean clothes, pure-looking. Lawrence takes his nephew's hand.

Hello, Bup, he says. You're a sight for sore eyes.

She passes the baby into his arms.

Here. I could do with a bath.

Really?

I won't be long. You know where everything is.

She leaves them. It is hard, but her brother has held the baby a hundred times. In the bath she thinks about all the occasions she let Lawrence down as a kid; she knew she was letting him down, even though there were no real solutions to offer. All he wanted was her kindness, her company, assurances that things would be OK. She did not give enough. Half an hour later, she finds them in the living room. Charlie is sitting like a juvenile king in the middle of the rug, lobbing the toy lion away, while Lawrence fetches it back obediently. We can do this, she thinks, the three of us.

He arranges personal leave from work. Emily, to Rachel's surprise, agrees to send some of his things north, though for the last few weeks he has been staying with Sara and a lot of his possessions have been abandoned there.

Have you broken things off with her? she asks her brother.

They are outside in the garden, sitting on plastic bags on the damp wooden bench, sunlight bouncing around them, the trees dripping. Above, the rain clouds have dispersed; there are contrails from Atlantic-bound jets. The baby is sleeping in the carrier by their feet. He shakes his head.

No. I sort of walked out the night I called you. But she knew what state I was in, it was obvious.

Do you want me to speak to her?

The idea of intervention gives Rachel some pleasure. To confront the woman she imagines as some sort of enabler, a wrecker of homes. But then, who is she to judge? She, of all people.

Thanks, he says. I'll do it. I doubt it'll be a surprise. She didn't really believe I was going to stay with her. She kept asking me if I still loved my wife.

Do you?

I don't know. Yes. I don't know.

He rises from the bench and goes slowly inside the cottage, a man condemned. She hears him speaking on the phone, then a long silence. A minute or two later he comes back. His eyes are sheened, but he is done crying.

She called me a cunt.

Well, Rachel says. In some cultures that's a compliment.

The faintest glimmer of a smile from her brother, the first in days. He looks down at Charlie, whose head is lolling to one side, his cheek podging as it presses against his shoulder.

I feel like I've come crashing in. Your life is going so well. You don't need me here.

That's not true, she says. Who's going to save me from the Penningtons?

She reaches for his hand, which is curled tightly in his lap like the hand of an anxious little boy.

*

They are born, blind and deaf, in the warm, fusty alcove of soil that has been lined with their mother's fur. A few weeks later, Gregor's motion-sensor rig catches their first foray into the world. Rachel has been coming into the office every morning in the hope of good news, leaving Lawrence to babysit. As soon as they are caught on the live feed, Gregor messages her. She and Huib review the footage. Ra is standing on a hummock near the den; lean and patient, his head slung low, the pale hind fur blazing around the shuttle of his penis. He yawns, bends, stretching through the front legs and then the rear. Downward facing: the pose looks yogic. He rights himself, shakes his ears, and continues watching the entrance.

He's definitely expecting something, Rachel says. And just

look how trim he is. He's been working hard.

Ja. I need to go to the gym.

She glances at Huib, who has no discernible fat anywhere on his body, has a monastic diet, and cycles miles across the mountain passes of Lakeland on his days off.

I know. You've really let yourself go, my friend.

Come out, come out, he says. It's a beautiful day.

He is staring intently at the screen. This is the moment everything has been resting on – the fight to change the law, the expense, the surrender of national parkland. Suddenly they are there, emerging on the den run, blunt-faced and clumsy. Their eyes are slatey and opaque; eerily unfinished. They can only just see.

OK, how many have we got? Rachel murmurs.

They count them out – one, two, three smoky heads, a pause, and then a fourth. The last is smaller, more tentative, gets jounced about by the others. The slope is sheer below the opening, quite a challenge. The first skids down, almost tumbles, manages to brake with its front paws. The others follow its lead – the runt losing control and swinging round, bottom-first, then rolling over in the dirt. Nearby, Merle is lying in the grass, panting, unconcerned. Her mate is on duty; she need not intervene.

Where's Sylvia? Huib asks. She's going to want to see this.

She's got the morning off. Studying, I think.

He takes a still of the film, converts the image and sends it to her phone.

Can you send that to Alexander too? And Stephan in Romania.

Sure. What about Thomas? He won't be back for a few weeks, will he?

She is about to say, and not without bitterness, No, don't bother. Thomas Pennington has not shown any interest in the project for months; he has not attended any of the team meetings since Christmas. But he is their benefactor, the man to whom everything is owed, and owned. She nods.

If you like.

It is an important day, after all, a landmark – he will surely want to know. She tries to get a good view of each pup, makes notes on their appearance, size, and sex, speculatively. They are all dirty grey, black-snouted, as if having riffled in soot, with dark tufts along their backs. Once out in the open, their father approaches. They surround him, lick his muzzle and wag frenziedly, trembling, craning upwards. The joy of recognition. Two have classic white stars on their chests. Names come to mind but she resists attaching any. They do not venture far; they follow their father, and then make their way over to their mother, nudging into her side and vying for milk. The fourth – already Rachel feels extremely interested in its plight – scrambles hard for position, is squeezed out, tries again and finally makes its way in. Merle blinks slowly, sensually, as the pups suckle. After a time, they are encouraged back inside the den. Ra lifts the runt by its scruff and it swings from his jaw. He deposits it with the others safely in the underground chamber.

Rachel turns to look at Huib. He is glowing with satisfaction.

We have our pack, she says.

Yes, we do. Let's go and find Sylvia, he suggests. I think she should be the one to speak to the press. How do you want to handle it? Think they'll be any trouble?

We'll get the footage out. It'll be fine. In fact, I think it's just what the project needs. Everyone loves a baby.

Sylvia is not in the main part of the Hall. Honor directs them towards the lake – she has gone for a walk to the boathouse, of which she is very fond, and perhaps over to the island. They're welcome to go and find her. She lets them through the private rear door. They walk down the long steps towards the water, the edifice of the Hall rising magnificently behind, its windows glinting. Thomas has recently had the Victorian iris water feature reinstalled – either side of the steps purple spears are flowering and small rivulets trickle and spill. The lawns leading down to the lake are exceptionally green and manicured – a lush jewel in the rough patchwork of the region's terrain. This is not a part of the Hall Rachel often sees. She's reminded once again of the level of luxury she lives in proximity to. How does one confront the real world after such a place? she wonders. How must it have been to grow up here? Remarkable or ruinous; either way she cannot conceive of it. They follow a stone footpath down the rolling tiers and along the shoreline. The Reiki platform looks stranded and out of place, like a climbing frame or a watchtower. Does Thomas still use it, or has that fad passed?

How's your brother? Huib asks as they walk.

The exact details of Lawrence's illness are not known by everyone, but she has confided a little in Huib.

He's doing better. Still a bit emotional.

I thought maybe I would ask him to come on a hike with me. If you think he's up to it? I'm going to go up Catbells this weekend.

That would be great. He'd like that.

The male company will be good for her brother, she thinks. Huib's company will be good for him – so far he has seen no one but her and Charlie since his discharge. They make their way to the boathouse. It's another beautiful construction, made of jutting stone, with a day room above the wet dock and a balcony overlooking the reflecting water. A long sloping roof, almost Swiss-looking. The door is unlocked. They call, but there's no answer. On a table upstairs is Sylvia's iPhone, her laptop, and a thick law textbook. Were this another location, less hermetic, less protected, the casualness of leaving expensive possessions around would be ludicrous. The quilted daybed near the balcony is rumpled. There are fresh-cut flowers in a vase, used teacups stacked by the sink. The place looks inhabited – perhaps Sylvia uses it as living quarters. In the corner is a small wood-burning stove, a wine rack, and refrigerator.

Have you taken the boats out before? Rachel asks Huib.

A couple of times, he says. It's nice to go out with a sandwich. Shall we try the island?

She has not yet ventured out to the folly, though staff members are entitled; nor has she accessed many of the perks of the estate – the horses, the sauna. They launch one of the varnished wooden rowing crafts moored below the day room. There are cushions for the seats. The oarlocks have been recently tallowed. Huib rows expertly across the water. The land falls away, and the boat glides steadily across the cloudy surface. From the mid-point of the lake, Pennington Hall looks like a ship itself, afloat above breakers of grass, an improbable pink-stone galleon. It is very, very quiet on the water, just the sound of the oars washing. She watches Huib rowing. He seems contented, overall. She has been socialising with the project team less and less, and is out of the loop. He must still go to the pub, but with whom? Perhaps a girlfriend on the staff here, or someone local? The seclusion of the estate seems not to affect him. Cumbria is not inaccessible, she knows, not compared with some of the areas where Huib has worked, but the county somehow manages to preserve its cut-off atmosphere, selling its vision of farness and loneliness, its Romantic psychology.

Do you ever miss home? she asks him.

You mean South Africa? I haven't considered it home for years.
I probably miss the idea, but not the place. Do you miss Idaho?

She shakes her head.

I don't. Well, maybe a few things. Corruptions – steak sauce, you
know. And the straightforwardness. People say what they mean.

I love it here, he says. It's easy. It's easy to breathe.

There are those for whom the Lakeland spell works, she
thinks, and those for whom there is no spell. Huib turns and
glances at the island, pulls a few strokes with his right arm to
realign the boat's trajectory, and aims for a small shingle beach,
where a wooden jetty runs into the water. Another skiff is tied to
the pillars, lying almost motionless in the shallow inlet. The folly
is lost between trees. As they approach, the sound of birdsong
grows louder, an avian chorus. They moor the boat and follow
the path through the woods. The trees are old, deciduous, possibly originals. The island feels incredibly peaceful, a botanical
biosphere dense with insect life – almost too lovely to be invaded.
No wonder Huib has brought picnics. As they pass through the
briar, the singing stops, then starts again.

In a clearing, on a buttress of rock, the mock-Gothic tower rises
– a theatrical ruin with cross-loops and arched windows, false
cracks, and a half-built flanking wall. They walk through the
doorway and a flock of large birds bursts raucously into the sky.
Rachel looks up. There's no interior, just a shell. It is a joke building, constructed in an era of aristocratic whimsy. Perhaps there
was once a bearded hermit employed to live nearby, to maintain a
grotto and issue riddling Delphic wisdoms to any visitor arriving
on the shore.

They continue round the circumference of the island and are upon Sylvia before they realise. She is sitting by a small, enclosed plot, next to a monument – a modern, stylised angel, cast in corrugated metal. She is looking into the woods as if expecting an approach from that angle. She stands and brushes her jeans down.

Hi. I thought there was someone else here. I heard the jackdaws in the tower going. I was just visiting Mummy. It's the anniversary of the day she died today.

She looks at the statue – Carolyn Pennington's memorial. The angel is corroding to burnished rust, the same colour as autumn bracken. Moss is growing in the ripples of the wings. It is a very tasteful piece, fitting in its environment, no doubt commissioned from a well-respected artist. A fresh posy of flowers has been laid at the base. There's a small bottle of spirits – vodka, perhaps – and two glasses in the grass.

Sorry to disturb you, Rachel says. I had no idea.

She feels awkward to have intruded upon the moment, and whatever ritual was taking place. But Sylvia is smiling and looking into the woods again, as if seeing something there they cannot see.

No, you aren't disturbing me at all. Everything's fine.

Suddenly, the Annerdale project is big news: both local and national television run pieces; Rachel is interviewed on Radio 4 and international shows. Letters pour in, expressing positive wishes, overtaking the naysayers. These are the first wolf pups born in the wild for centuries, the significance is not lost on the nation. They become almost like mascots, for what exactly no one is sure, a beleaguered England, an England no longer associated with Scotland's great natural resources. The project has pluck, and scope. Requests for interviews keep coming. Thomas hires a publicity company and throws another party, a promotional event for the media and supporters of the scheme. Though it is another occasion she would prefer to skip, Rachel must attend. There's the usual hoopla – dignitaries, fancy food, and drinks, more in keeping with an award ceremony or junket. The hall buzzes with reporters. Vaughan Andrews puts in an appearance, keen to capitalise on the good news in his constituency. Yes, it is a Tory-backed initiative, Rachel hears him say. Sebastian Mellor himself is involved and has visited the site on numerous occasions.

Thomas assumes a florid style of mingling, and Rachel tries not to hold his recent disinterest against him. Let him puff and pander. She is singled out lavishly in the Earl's address, as the Cumbrian who reintroduced wolves to Cumbria, the usual rubbish; she grits her teeth, smiles. Immediately after the speech, she finds herself swarmed by journalists, portable microphones thrust her way. Is she proud? they ask. Does she feel protective of the pups? It is as if she is some lupine mother figure, expected to give an emotional account. Did the country always treat its women experts with such sexism and reductionism? she wonders. She looks at the sea of rumpled shirts and high-street tweeds, hipster accessories; the reporters range from charmingly stupid and urbane, to slick, eelish, and presumptuous. No one, it seems, has researched the subject with any care or read the press release. The great capital–countryside divide. How to explain to those unused to rural issues, to Londoners surprised by the fast trains north and the relative proximity of the Lake District to the Great Wen, surprised, it seems, that anything outside their own experience exists? There's a misunderstanding about the transmitters – she explains the purpose. She explains the size of the enclosure, the ratio of biomass. No, this is not Scotland, she explains, Scotland lies forty miles to the north. Then, one reporter who has researched, into her at least, or has simply been listening to the idle chatter in the room, catches her by surprise.

You've given birth yourself this year, haven't you, Rachel? he asks. So are you considering this the lucky double?

She stares at him, and a small flare of panic fires internally. The shutters come down. She ignores the question, begins to lecture the listening crowd on the development of the pups.

Once they're weaned and are taking regurgitated meat, the next phase will be learning to hunt, she says. That's when they're taught all the skills they need to survive. It's called the hunting school.

The reporter steps in and moves the microphone disconcertingly close to her face; he is about to repeat the question, far more interested in that which is personal than in animal behaviour. She glances at his name and company lanyard – a glossy celebrity magazine. Why is he even here? She keeps talking, mentions predation rate and digestive systems, even scat, verging on scientific bore, until his eyes begin to flicker and he looks down at the recording device. Denying a son – she wonders if this is a crime that will be forgiven. Finally, he moves away, towards Sylvia, and Rachel is glad of the girl's photogenic qualities. The whole experience feels slightly unsavoury – the bald assessing of what is newsworthy, what is inflammatory, or titillating. Is the achievement not enough? Are such beautiful creatures not enough? After another fifteen minutes, she excuses herself, steps into a side room, and calls Lawrence to check on the baby.

The party begins to wind down. The last of the champagne is swilled, too fine and expensive to let it go to waste. A convoy of taxis arrives to take guests back to Kendal, where they have hotels booked, or to catch the last train south. Thomas has disappeared, but Sylvia gives out gift bags to the departing, containing a project pamphlet, badges, and some of the estate's paraphernalia. The gathering takes on an air of *fin de siècle*, but not simply for its curtailment. Some kind of aftermath or anticlimax pervades. Rachel begins to feel depressed.

On the drive back to the cottage, a strange, heavy sensation overwhelms her, like fatigue. She parks for a few minutes on the verge, next to the main gate of the enclosure. Rain falls through the beam of the headlights with extraordinary grace. Despite the vulturish atmosphere of the evening, the tipping point of public opinion will be a good thing. There's much to celebrate, not least the fact of the litter. And yet. Rather than expanding, the project feels as if it is moving towards a conclusion, a dead end.

She stares out into the rain. The steel frame of the fence glows in the headlights. The estate is lost under darkness, its valleys and loaded mountains, its forest. Even the exuberantly blazing lights of the Hall are masked behind trees. Nature has ratified itself, as expected. The experiment has worked. There are pre-existing limits – space for one pack only inside the enclosure, one breeding pair. The pups will grow and form a society, but they will remain sexually inactive, unless one kills a parent, or a parent dies. The landscape will become healthier and more diverse, but outside the enclosure barren fells will remain, ditches dredged by machinery, booming and sickening deer populations, sheep, and evergreens. She knew all this when she took the job, and she took it anyway. Still, the project is a good thing, real under its falseness, intensive in its smallness, and unusual, in this country, for its vision.

For the first time in her life, work is not the primary concern; work is not in full possession of her soul, as it has been for more than a decade. She cannot hide in it. All those years in which she was safe and exempt, focused on the management of another species. Now, a different sphere has ascended. The qualities of human reward and failure rest with her. *There's more to life*, Binny had said on the last day Rachel saw her alive, even as she was plotting to end her own existence. And Rachel had thought, But you've never seen a wolf, standing against the skyline in profile, you've never seen a wolf running alongside an elk, seeing through the flurry of back legs to the single, perfect moment of the strike. There is no greater beauty.

She wants to get back to the cottage. She wants to hold Charlie, feel his warm skin, or look at him in the cot. She wants to tell her brother she is proud – of his days, his weeks of sobriety, his determination. She might forgive the journalists for their callow versions and enquiries, because she too is looking away, at this other self, at her own kind. Ahead, the steel gate drips with rain. There is no going back. She starts the car and reverses off the verge, follows the lane through the woods to home.

THE HUNTING SCHOOL

Spring gives way early to summer, the foliage thickening, the light over the western mountains shedding its dullness. Six wolves are silhouetted against the Cumbrian fells. They are no longer aliens: they never were. She is nameless to them. They have everything they need. The herds swell with the arrival of the calves, so spindle-legged and spastic it seems they are defunct, tamping and flailing on the ground in an effort to stand, but capable of running within minutes, leaving their wet sacs strung behind them on the grass. And they do run – the deer no longer linger on the moorland or in the long valleys; they avoid areas where entrapment is possible, where many of their number have already fallen. They have been fully reprogrammed and obey the laws. Their sentries sniff the wind and scan the horizon. There is a form ghosting between the trees, skirting round the heather, perhaps nothing, or there is simply a scent drifting, with menacing association. They graze and quickly move on. When it happens, it happens like an explosion: a fuse lit at the corner of the herd, a burst of fear across their number. The closest kicks hard, for it has likely been chosen and senses it, setting the herd in motion, a terrestrial murmuration. They flush across the lowland, pursued without full exertion, but with a terrible evolved stamina, and are driven up a gradient. Degrees of weariness, the victim begins to struggle slightly and slow. The wolf closes, closes. Even after the pursuit is over and the calf is brought down, rump-first, back legs skittled, the herd still runs. Only its mother pauses to look back, then runs on with the rest. Merle has made the kill, independently, as if on principle.

From the top of a hill, the pups watch. Two females and two males. It will not be long before they begin to chase after their parents, part of the hunting squadron. They grow in radical bursts, quarrying small prey in the grass around the den, mouse-pouncing, venturing further into the enclosure as their endurance grows. Despite the distinguishing features – one with a striped grey back like a marsupial, one with a tipping ear, one honey furred, and the smallest darker than the others – they remain unnamed. This is Rachel's idea, but the team has agreed. There's some kind of wish fulfilment to it, she suspects – that they should remain as far from domestication as possible, because they are so close to it.

She comes into the office twice a week, works remotely otherwise. In her absence, Huib is a reliable project manager, updating her on any developments: the court case with The Ramblers, another email from Nigh, observations from the fieldwork, and any new film footage. Sylvia leads a team of four new volunteers. In the autumn she will start law school.

In the cottage, they coexist surprisingly well: Rachel, her rehabilitating brother, and the little master of the household. She concentrates on the baby, aware that this time will be irrecoverable, gone in an instant. She tries to savour the moments but everything rolls forward at an alarming pace. Some amazing, nuclear energy blazes in the baby, not related to food or diurnality, but simply of its own source. One might worship it easily. He is a learning machine. He meets her gaze, dark-eyed, wants to know what she knows, wants to converse. He is aggrieved that she will not fully, fluently learn his language, though her understanding of his inchoate English is adequate. The phenomenology of another human – there is so much shared, so much they will never share. Days of tossed bowls and food up the wall, and it is she who feels inarticulate, a foreign traveller in her son's realm.

What is it? What do you want? I don't know what you want.

He points: that, or more, or Roary, or Lawrence. His muscles get him into trouble, powerful as they are without the refined technology to walk or balance. Heaving himself up on the coffee table, on chairs. Pitching over. He moves impressively quickly across the floor on all fours, like some species fallen out of the canopy, disabled, but extremely dexterous on its secondary parts, and determined to escape. Lawrence hoists him up by the waistband of his little jeans, inches from the door. He squeals, flails. Outside is what he wants: the vibrant colours of the garden, the cacophony in the woods around the cottage, and the wind, the wind, which he adores, which he tries to qualify, hands held out to grasp and hold it, unable to, vexed. If only Rachel were as tolerable an element. He is frequently angry with her, for reasons unknown. His tantrums are galactic, often inexplicable; purple and glossy and howling, he throws himself against the chair back, or skulls her in the face, splits her lip open. She takes a deep breath, holds him away from her, licks the blood.

Don't take it personally, Lawrence says. He freaks out with me, too.

He doesn't. Not like this.

Well, you're the one he thinks of as the boss, when he wants to rebel.

Nice try, she says.

Here, give him to me. Go and take five.

They are a good team. Lawrence is patient, willing to give up an inordinate amount of time on childcare. She is aware that the baby is in part therapy, is giving him a reason to be sober. He goes to the meetings in Workington twice a week. Mitch, the group leader, is his personal sponsor; Lawrence speaks about him with enormous respect, though he is an ex-dealer, spent seven years in prison, beat up his wife. Her brother does not linger in the town after the sessions, where there might be temptation. He follows the steps. He has a checklist of danger signs, things to avoid.

And every day, he walks. Since his hike with Huib – she does not know what occurred or what was said on the trip – he has become obsessed. He walks before breakfast, even before dawn some days, if he cannot sleep. He arrives back at the cottage famished and eats an entire pan of porridge. Then he makes boiled eggs for Charlie. Some days he will be out until dusk, fasting for fifteen or twenty miles, like a pilgrim. He walks regardless of the weather conditions, lashing showers, brooding skies. The porch floor is mucky with smears and divots of dirt from his boots, pools of water from his dripping anorak. His fleece jacket and gloves wilt like pelts on the radiator.

Some days he borrows the Saab and drives into the heartland to tackle the proper peaks – Scafell, Helvellyn. He reports back, which route he took, how long to the summit. There are other lone walkers – retired crag-rats, men of persistent vitality, libidinous, perhaps unsatisfied by their arthritic wives, spending it instead on the mountain. Bearded, weathered, vowed to silence, or nodding at him and passing by on the scree, brisk and nervy as goats. The language of the uplands.

He walks after dinner, down to the lake, around the lake,

where trout rise and kiss the surface, then flicker away. This is also an addiction of sorts, Rachel thinks, but harmless – wholesome even. He is becoming fit; the worry spots on his arms are healing. She makes him sandwiches, flasks of tea – something she never willingly did when they were children. The gentle, demonic action is saving him; she hopes it is saving him. Still, she worries when he is gone too long, and on the days when he is dour, depressed, when he talks of Emily, and all that has been lost, and says the best part of his life is gone. Will he relapse? Not under her jurisdiction, she is determined.

You're going to find someone, she says. You can still have children. You're doing really well.

All of which is true, though probably not while he is sequestered at Seldom Seen, living with his sister and her child. Alexander comes to dinner once a week and stays the night. They are careful, quiet, considerate of the other adult in the household. It is companionable, this male grouping, and suits her sensibilities. Everyone gets on. Just occasionally she senses envy or frustration – something Alexander says or a look, subtly different to his response when she mentioned Kyle. A brother is greater and lesser than a sexual rival. A lover can be given up, but a sibling is a lifelong fixture, if the relationship is good. She knows he enjoyed having her to himself, being free to walk naked around the house, the lack of restraint, possibly even the potential role of father. The redefinition is not always easy to parse. It is true: she and Lawrence have found a kind of unity, a compatibility. They crawl across the floor, flanking the baby, like great doting pilots. They are perhaps reliving an era, or living an era that never existed, a childhood where they got along. She suddenly has a family, on her terms, and without antagonism.

She eats out with Alexander in L'Enclume on her birthday. It is just the two of them and they will stay the night, perhaps his way of marking territory, benignly. The restaurant is expensive and has flagrantly excessive courses. They indulge in particular intimacies in the luxurious bedroom. The sex is good, as good; he punishes her with pleasure. She thinks about but does not call home. The next morning the night's gluttony is forgotten, and they indulge in a colossal breakfast. Venison sausages. Passionfruit and rosewater salad.

How's Lawrence getting on? Alexander asks.

Really well, I think.

Yes. He seems back on his feet now.

Which means, perhaps, when will he be going back to Leeds? Of course, he does not say it, would not say it. Nor is his domestic set-up wholly conventional – the living arrangements with Chloe. She notes it, makes a point of inviting him over for the weekend while Lawrence is climbing Great Gable. He is happy enough, her boyfriend, the boyfriend of her brother's sister. Life is not straightforward: relationships bifurcate; there is nothing more complicated, more confounding, than love.

*

At the next project meeting, rather surprisingly, Thomas makes a late appearance. Before his arrival, they discuss whether or not to implant the pups with tracking devices, which will involve darting them – the same procedure as before. It's not strictly necessary, Rachel argues, given their range and the ease with which they might be located. But the data gathered would be interesting. There's also the question of sterilisation. This would need to be done before the females reach two years of age. The phenomenon of extra breeding couples in packs is rare, she explains, and all the studies relate to larger territories than Annerdale, but a surfeit of food might foster multiple breeding, and deer on the estate are plentiful. It's a possibility. The volunteers dutifully make notes, as if in a lecture hall.

What would happen then? Sylvia asks.

We'd have to control numbers. It might lead to in-fighting. There just isn't enough room.

She can see the idea of invasive sterilisation this early in the scheme makes Sylvia uncomfortable, but it must be considered. A reminder that the enclosure is governed, that it still requires management. Sylvia nods and frowns.

Did Daddy know about this at the start?

I've talked to him about it, yes.

That's odd. He didn't say anything to me.

The faintest glimmer of annoyance in Sylvia's voice. Rachel wonders whether her father sold her the project unrealistically, a boil-in-the-bag Eden, with no human interface, though she has read enough over the last year to know conservation is not without difficult choices, and sacrifices. Huib makes a round of tea for them all and tries to reassure her.

It's a common procedure, Syl. It's used in the wild as well, like the elephants in Kruger. Kinder than letting things get out of control in a given population. And much better than destroying the animals.

She nods again.

I know. It just seems a shame, that's all. It's an awful thing to have done to you.

Rachel does not disagree with her, but this is the price of partial freedom, and the girl knows better than to make emotional human connections with the animals. Sylvia seems out of sorts, unlike her usual self. She is pulling at a loose thread on her shirt.

We'll come back to it, Rachel says. We don't need to decide yet.

By which point, the Earl's daughter will no longer be at Annerdale. They move on to other topics. The BBC documentary Gregor is filming has been scheduled to air the following spring; Attenborough has agreed to narrate. The estate's legal team is working on an insurance-cost document relating to possible wolf-watching tours. The security report is good, though Michael is absent; Rachel has not seen him in weeks. His son, Barnaby, has been patrolling the fence and taking care of other duties around the estate.

Towards the end of the meeting, Thomas arrives. He is brusque as he greets them, lacks his usual bombastic charm.

Hello all. Sorry to parachute in. If you don't mind –

Instead of taking a chair, he stands at the head of the table, fingers locked together, chin tucked in – a politician's demeanour. A serious announcement is coming, Rachel thinks. Bad news. Thomas glances at Sylvia; she looks away, nurses her cup of tea, thumbing the rim. She already knows something, Rachel thinks. Or is she cross with her father?

I'm afraid to say, there's been a very sad development.

Thomas pauses, seems to stall before he has properly begun.

Oh, dear. This is really very tough. Very tough.

Surely it cannot be something to do with the project itself, Rachel thinks. The Earl may have been expressing dwindling interest, but he can't possibly have decided to abandon the scheme, not without speaking to her first. Thomas clears his throat, composes himself.

Last month, Lena Stott was diagnosed with cancer. The prognosis is not good, I'm sorry to say – it's particularly aggressive. We don't expect her to recover.

He pauses, swallows, then continues.

As you know, the Stotts have been at Annerdale for a very long time. It's a terrible blow. We'll be offering them all the support we can over the coming weeks. I'm sure you understand how difficult this is for Michael and Barnaby.

The room remains quiet. The volunteers shift awkwardly in their chairs, still new to the estate and not yet comfortable around its major players, not least the Earl, whom they have seen little of. Sylvia stares ahead, unblinking. Her father looks about at the group, waiting for a response perhaps.

Please pass on all our sympathies, Rachel says.

Yes, Huib agrees. We're all terribly sorry.

Thank you. Now, I'm afraid on this unfortunate note I must leave you.

Another trip across the border, where secession negotiations are still taking place and Thomas is embroiled. On the way out he leans towards Rachel, asks quietly if today's notes could be sent to Honor. There are matters on the agenda he would like to discuss with the team – he does not specify which. She nods – the minutes are always sent, though he often doesn't read them. Then he is gone. The meeting is concluded. The volunteers quietly disperse. Huib gives Sylvia a hug. She is suddenly teary and leans against his shoulder; he talks to her quietly. Rachel is surprised by her discomposure and their closeness. Talk of interfering with wolves and terminal cancer has upset her. Rachel recalls the way Michael and Lena helped steward Leo at Christmas – covetously, as if no pedigree separated them, as if they were related. Sylvia has known them since birth. Or there's possibly more to it – the underlying anxiety about her career, some other trouble. She stands back and lets Huib comfort her, at a loss.

Over the following days, Rachel learns the extent of Lena's illness, from Huib, who is privy to the Hall staff's gossip. The diagnosis came late, by which point the endometrial cancer had metastasised throughout her system, into her bones. A radical surgery was performed, pelvic evisceration, removal of her organs and bowel, followed by plastication – still experimental, ultimately palliative, but designed to give her as much life as possible. Barbie doll treatment: controversial, perhaps not even ethical, and paid for privately by the Earl. Suddenly Sylvia's reaction to the idea of sterilising the female pups, the intimate barbarity, makes sense.

The next time Rachel sees Michael, it is outside the Hall, getting into the utility vehicle. They are in plain view of each other – their eyes lock. She approaches, feeling she must say something, and he steps back out of the van, swinging the door closed. Tess, the ever-present lurcher, looks through the window inquisitively, tongue out. Michael squares himself and nods at her.

Mr Stott.

Mrs Caine. How's the little one?

Since Charlie came along, Michael has used him as a way of seeming to greet her civilly, while avoiding pleasantries that actually include her. Still, it is progress of a sort.

Yes, he's OK. Getting big. How is your wife?

He stares at her, assessing the question, not replying. He looks bleary-eyed, thinner; perhaps he has been cooking for himself, or missing meals; caring for the terminal patient is taking its toll. His hair is greasy at the roots; his cockerel chest has sunk. He seems now to inhabit his age: a man in his seventies, old enough to suffer under extra physical and mental burden. But he still has on a tie and jacket for going into the big house – the old ways of the estate prevail.

I don't mean to pry, she says. It's not my business.

It's not.

I just wanted to say I was sorry –

She stops short. She does not want to offer pity, nor would he accept any from her. They are not friends. She will do him the courtesy of not simpering. The approach was ill-judged, and she can see he suspects her, thinks her nosy or callous.

Anyway, my best wishes, she says, and turns away.

I heard your brother was sick, Michael says. Heard he'd moved up here permanent. There's a lot of bad business about.

She turns back. Now it is she who regards him cautiously, wondering whether he is genuine or goading her, quid pro quo. What has he heard about Lawrence? The whole sordid mess, or only an outline? No doubt he has his opinions about drug users, and they are unforgiving. Michael's face is set like granite. She holds her own expression in abeyance. They are as guarded as each other.

He was ill, she says. He's on the mend now.

That's good. Nice fellow. And good to have some young folk moving in, cut up the pastures a bit.

This surprises her. She would not have thought him keen to have any more of her associates on his turf. But then, he has more to worry about than the march of liberals or a petty dispute with a colleague, even wolves. He makes a noise, halfway between a grunt and a sigh.

Lena's putting up a fight. She's making mine and her sister's life a bloody nightmare. It is a bloody nightmare – all of it.

His voice is flat, and open. There is not much more to say; they both know it. He offers her his hand, willingly, for the first time, as if this is their true introduction, or they have agreed something. She takes it and they shake. The dog barks inside the van.

Good luck then.

And you.

He gets into the utility vehicle and starts the engine, pulls away, the tyres crunching gravel as he circles the drive. She stands for a moment, watching his departure. He is as ornery as he ever was, she is under no illusions. But the idea of him returning to a house of suffering, to a wife crippled by disease and exenteration, boluses of painkiller and colostomies, biding Macmillan nurses, would not be wished on anyone.

She continues towards the office. She passes Thomas Pennington, who is walking with the local bishop and Barnaby Stott in the gardens of the Hall, the three men engaged in reflective discussion. Thomas waves to her as she passes, a small, sombre acknowledgement. It occurs to her that they were all discussing Lena's funeral. You are lucky, she tells herself, don't forget it. In the blur of her new life, there are raised moments and memorable episodes – good and bad, she has been learning to fix what can be fixed, learning to accept what is broken. There is no other way.

*

Lawrence quits his job. He has savings, is paying half the mortgage in Leeds, but the house is to be sold. He will find work here in Cumbria, he tells Rachel, in one of the southern Lakeland practices. Or he will do something different for a while, reset his brain. She is nervous, but supports the decision. He needs a new chapter. He and Emily have managed several brief, polite phone calls to discuss matters, namely the divorce. He has not tried to win her back, though his recovery is going well, and he might have asserted such. Either he does not want a reunion, or he considers himself unworthy, the damage too great. It's the right thing, he keeps saying, and perhaps it is. Binny always maintained there was a wrong dynamic to the marriage, though, in the end, Rachel has come to respect Emily – even to like her.

She watches her brother for danger signs. He seems to have built tight defences. He keeps going to the centre in Workington, calls Mitch and people from the support group from time to time, and is called by them. He reads around the subject – a book about impulse control, a book about attachment disorders, a book about neurons; all this is in order to understand the physiology of his problems. He eats well, does not drink, not even beer – those who think they can merely moderate vices usually fail, he tells her, get stuck in a cycle of binging and quitting, as he did, for years. He meditates, in his room, in the garden, cross-legged, his head held erect. And he walks. He has walked himself lean, looks like a man who has crossed deserts, who has lived on figs and goat's milk. He looks both older and younger, like the scrawny boy he was and the bypassed man he might have become, under different circumstances. He offers to move out, repeatedly, but she tells him there is no hurry.

It's selfish, in a way. The support at home is a boon. The shared childcare gives her enough time to maintain a role in the project, go on dates with Alexander. Though what is selfish about an uncle adoring his nephew? They are happy in each other's company, have developed their own systems. Lawrence slathers sun cream on Charlie's arms and legs when they go outside, changes the most atrocious nappies, mashes baby food, a hundred thousand bananas pulverised under the fork.

Bup, where's this nom going? he says, patiently administering the substance. Four more and you get a fruitsicle. I'm going to count – ready?

She is a little in awe. The idea that paternal care is lesser, or secondary, seems ludicrous. She might have gone a little mad were it not for her brother's help. It is not the sleeplessness or the constant drill of infant duties, but the lack of privacy that has been hardest. With Lawrence on hand she can take a long bath, go out for a few hours, court, then re-enter the atmosphere of motherhood refreshed. One never knows how spoilt, how wanton with time one was, until those hours are disqualified. The closer Charlie and Lawrence get, the closer she too is to her brother. Underneath it all is a remedial feeling. She and Lawrence have survived; better, they have succeeded. No rush, she says, when he offers to leave again. Though she knows, soon, he must, for his own benefit if not hers.

Summer does not really get going, not in the voluptuous golden way of the previous year. Any heat is quickly extinguished by clouds or rain, the temperature barely reaching the twenties. Nevertheless, it is the season of plenty on the estate. The pups grow rapidly, become coordinated and swift. Rachel and Huib listen to recorded vocalisations, their high little wails and yips, barks, attempted howls. For the first time she leaves Charlie longer than twenty-four hours with his uncle, to camp in the enclosure and observe, work she has not undertaken for over a year. It is a test for all three – mother and son, and Lawrence, who is still a little sheepish about her trust, deferential, unpresumptuous. Only if she is sure, he says. He can cope, she knows. It is she who lingers, repacking a bag, hugging the baby. In the end, while Lawrence and Charlie are engaged in loud antics with the plastic drum set, she slips out of the cottage unseen, like a fugitive.

They stay in one of the hides that Gregor has been using, which is cold overnight, and damp, smells of utility and the chocolatey rusk of power bars. It is a thrill to be back out, to see the juveniles first-hand, gaining courage and endurance. They maul and tumble and ambush each other, more playful than dogs. The littlest male shows no signs of deficiency; he jumps on his father's back, harasses Ra until Ra stands over him demanding submission. Rachel feels peculiarly light, misses the smell and weight of Charlie, the sense of him close by. But this too is second nature; she has missed seeing wolves, missed waiting to see them. During the night their human presence in the enclosure sets off a volley of howling. She and Huib lie side by side and unmoving in their sleeping bags, like vegetables, making notes.

When she arrives home, it feels as if she has been in exile for a decade; she allows herself the indulgence of exaggeration, she is partially qualified: unwashed, weary, hungry. And she is rewarded. The immediate recognition and delight on Charlie's face is intoxicating, he leans steeply out of Lawrence's arms, towards her. Mamamama. She gathers him in and he clings on, his strong, monkey-ish arms throttling her.

Had a good time? she asks her brother.

He is smiling and looks pleased with himself – nothing untoward has occurred, no midnight meltdowns, tumbles, or other accidents. A victory.

Great. How about you? Good to get out there again, I bet?

It was wonderful. Am I allowed to say that?

Of course you are. Hey, wild woman, you've got something in your hair.

He brushes out the attached item.

Want some tea?

Oh God. Yes please! So much for doing without field comforts. Is there hot water? We want a bath!

She kisses her son on his hot fragrant neck.

Loads. How's the pack doing?

Oh, brilliantly.

It's true. There is no real danger to the litter. Not even the buzzards would have attempted a raid when the pups were smaller. The golden eagles, burly enough to have managed a steal, are long gone from the county. Regardless, Ra and Merle have created a protectorate, moving the pups from the natal den to a rendezvous site. They are closely watched and fed with regurgitated meat. They follow their parents, trotting alongside, noses up-tilted, at heel, keen little followers. They are brought to carcasses, allowed to tug at the ribcage of a deer. They make their own way back while their parents scout, sometimes roaming too far. Ra arrives hastily in response to any distress call, escorting the lost pup home. Soon they will be taught to hunt properly, beginning with the madcap chase of a brown hare. None of the pups land it, but their father does. At the ungodly screams of the kill, all four retreat over the brow of a hill. Ra carries it back to them, a shaggy, amber-eyed pelt, swinging between his teeth. Edible. Fresh. Ever after the association is made.

*

Lena dies soon after. The funeral service is very well attended, by the estate staff, family, and an older, rustic set, extending up through the borders – Michael's associates, those who worked the previous century's agricultural landscape, attending horse shows, common ridings, hunts. Rachel also attends with Charlie and Lawrence; it seems the right thing to do. The service is held in the old Annerdale church near the lake, accessible only by unmade track, so the guests must park along the roadside and walk in a long, dark, realist procession to the grounds. Thomas and Barnaby greet the mourners, handing out service sheets and printed copies of the eulogy. Saint Mary's is newly roofed and the cemetery is neat. Inside, oak polished to a dense shine, urns of cut flowers, soft organ music, and stiff black hats. It is perhaps inappropriate to bring the baby, but Rachel feels she cannot put in an appearance without him, given Michael's fondness. Binny never protected her from such things when she was growing up; she was made to face death, to understand its common occurrence. They find a pew towards the back, try to keep Charlie entertained and quiet.

The body is brought in via traditional horse and carriage over the lake road, two squat fell ponies straining against the harness, the leather creaking, their tack tinkling. The coffin is wicker, covered with floral cuttings. Six men, including the Earl and Barnaby, shoulder it off the trap and walk it to the altar of the church, where it is set on a stand. Rachel is reminded of her childhood – the processions, gates locked at weddings until coins were flung, first-footing, harvests, and carlin suppers. There was no nostalgic irony in any of it; it was simply current practice. Michael does not greet or speak during the service, but leans fatally on the front of his pew. The music plays out and the bishop prepares to conduct the ceremony. Rachel turns to Lawrence, and says, finally,

I'm sorry about missing Mum's funeral. I should have come.

Lawrence smiles sadly and shakes his head.

Don't worry. These things happen. Besides, it wasn't like this. I don't remember much of it anyway.

She wonders if he was using then. The bishop drones through the rituals. Barnaby takes the lectern and talks about his mother's endurance and loyalty, her love of the western valleys where she was born and lived out her life – her maiden name, Prowle, a signature of belonging, her people old-settlers, harbour masters. He thanks the Earl for the years of service, as one might thank an institution, or presiding deity. Rachel is surprised to see Leo, standing next to Sylvia in the front row, dressed this time in a black suit and tie, tidy, composed, behaving with dignity. She thinks again of the suited, wolf-headed man at the early protests. It was not him, she is sure, nor would he have cut the enclosure wire.

The hymns are sung at moderate volume. 'Abide with Me'. 'Lord of All Hopefulness'. There are no modern twists, no pop songs. Charlie begins to get restless in her arms, he wants down, to try his new stepping skills, wants to be hung touching the ground so he can walk with a stabiliser. She moves into the side aisle with him, holds his arms while he pigeon-steps on the flagstones. She looks at the plaques on the outer wall, the name Pennington repeated over and over, war memorials and honours. The smell all around is of stone kept fractionally damp by the seasons of rain, though outside it is warm; the second half of summer has dried the earth.

Then, suddenly, Michael does speak. Midway through the bishop's address, he releases his grip, and walks from the pew, forward to the front steps. The bishop steps to the side. *My* wife, Michael says, as if claiming her back. *My wife*. There's a pause.

Then he gives a short, bitter tirade against a God who would dole out such punishment to the undeserving. Such suffering, a plastic cunt, her bags of shit. The congregation winces and looks away, but no one intervenes, the embarrassment must be borne. His face is a mask of disgust. Whatever symmetry he found during Lena's illness has been abandoned. There's the sound of female crying from the front pews – Lena's sister, perhaps. It is all horrible to watch and hear, but surely he is entitled, Rachel thinks. She almost admires it. Lawrence glances over, makes a jerking movement with his head – does she want him to take Charlie outside? But Charlie can't understand. He leans backward in her grip and looks up at the painted bosses in the roof of the church. She shakes her head. Michael stands silently facing the congregation, and is led away by Barnaby, down the aisle and out of the church. He looks old. She sees him take a hip flask from his inside pocket as he passes. The bishop resumes, says such anger is understandable, we are all tested, we are all profoundly hurt by such seemingly senseless loss, but his starched cassock and talk of afterlife seem faintly ridiculous after the authenticity of the bereaved husband.

The wake is held at the manor. Whisky and sandwiches in the main hall, a room not often used for social events, but the only one large enough to fit the hundreds of mourners. It is a grand venue, dark woods, with the Pennington coat of arms above the door, but a less chic and glamorous affair than usual: traditional, northern. Lena's wishes perhaps – no fuss, quotidian fare. Lawrence takes Charlie back to the cottage and Rachel puts in an appearance, though it seems a cruelty to have the Stott family go through another public showcasing of grief. The son works hard to accept the condolences of everyone, shaking hands, thanking,

saying yes, yes, agreeing over and over with their kind or erroneous pronouncements about his mother. Michael remains in the
shadows, steadily taking the whisky. He rebuts Thomas' offer of
a plate of food. A few older gentlemen stand close to him making
cordial conversation – the social, thick-skinned drinkers – but
his condition is radioactive, mostly people veer away. Something
has come undone in him. He loved his wife. He loved her. Losing
her is unendurable, or the catalyst for other dangerously built-
up angers. Rachel mills, says hello to a few recognisable faces,
Neville Wilson, Vaughan Andrews, but talks to no one in particular. Huib seems stuck with a group of elderly ladies. Sylvia
is with her brother, near Michael, the steeply affected end of the
room, unapproachable. Now in civilian garb, the bishop steps
towards Michael, perhaps another attempt to mitigate the darkness, bring comfort, a format for acceptance. Leave him be, she
thinks. She decides to leave. There's an air of impending disaster
– she does not want to witness it.

On the way out she hears a commotion. People close in around
Michael. She can hear his voice, hard and drunken, Cumbrian,
*Fly to her in fucking heaven, you pious twat, I can no more fly than
this stupid little bastard here can. Can you fly, son?* She glances
back at the gaggle of players. Thomas looks mortified, and
Sylvia is trying to get between her brother and Michael, who has
Leo Pennington held by the lapel, a grip so strong the suit and
shirt underneath are riding high up his torso. *Come on then, let's
see, lad. Let's see if you really want to waste your life.* He hoists the
young man across the room and towards the nearest door, the
two of them locked together in a close wrestle that seems almost
erotic. Leo calls out to those following to get back, to leave them
alone, this is their business. The room has gone silent; the old

men continue to sip their drams.

Rachel gathers her coat and makes her way out of the Hall, to the Saab, parked amid the ranks of guests' cars along the driveway. Whatever is happening, there is no good way to intervene; it is certainly not her place. These are old troubles rearing. On the drive back to the cottage, Michael's words echo. *Can you fly, son?* Only later will she hear about the incident – a version of it anyway. But not from Sylvia or Thomas, whom she will see very little of in the coming weeks – the former preparing to move to London, the latter as absent from his house as God – but from Huib, who did follow and did try to help. A gun taken from the locker room. The two men in some kind of crazed dispute on the grounds of the estate. The firearm going off, and a flesh wound to Leo's shoulder. No prosecution was sought; the event was reported to the police as an accident. And according to Huib, Michael was pulling the shotgun away, he held the heir of Annerdale down and doctored him roughly as he bled, and held the young man's head against his shoulder as he wept. In the office, the following Monday, Huib tells her all this and tries to make sense of it.

They were arguing like dogs. About responsibility and death wishes, and Michael was challenging him to go ahead and do it. I don't know what it was about.

I think I might know, she says, quietly.

She does not go into detail, and Huib does not ask. She could be wrong, but Sylvia's account of Leo being present at the microlight crash in which his mother died, and Michael's drunken words, seem too revealing. The plane was a three-seater. Perhaps Thomas was not flying it, and Leo, barely a teenager at the time and with no licence, was. The untouchable Penningtons. Their reckless playfulness, their invincibility. His father would have covered for him – not even the power and connectedness of the Earl could have protected his son from the charges, perhaps even manslaughter. Michael would surely have known. And Leo's life since has been hell. Who would not loathe themselves for killing their own mother? She does not give Huib her theory; she does not know if it is simply speculation, a flight of fantasy on her part. Either way, Michael, loyal to the family, keeper of its land and perhaps its worst secrets, has watched the boy spiralling, trying to escape, self-destructing. There is no motive as great as the death of a loved one to make a person insist that others should live.

*

Lawrence gets a job at a solicitor's office in Kendal. He finds a flat in a converted wool yard, overlooking the graphite roofs of the town, and signs the contract. The Lakeland sabbatical is over. In late August, he moves out.

You'll be just down the road, she says, trying to be upbeat, though part of her regrets his decision and is conflicted about his departure.

Will he cope? Will she? No, she's pleased. The move will be good for him: a forward gesture. He must re-enter the world, leave the monastic security of the District behind. Much of his excavated life has yet to be refilled. He is not dating. In the counselling sessions he has agreed to avoid sex for a year – part of the untangling of addictions. Such doctrines make Rachel wonder about herself – might she have fallen into such a category at one stage? Is she past it now or simply stymied by single parenthood? Sometimes her thoughts move past Alexander, to the possibility of others – a destructive feeling, old ways.

Lawrence cooks a lavish meal the night before he moves out. They eat in the garden, with clear skies overhead, the pipping of birds in the woods, and a warm breeze. A last summer evening. He has made lemon chicken, herb potatoes, salad.

Who would have thought? he says. You and me back in the same county.

It does seem unlikely, she agrees.

I didn't think you'd ever come back.

That makes two of us.

He tilts his head, asks softly,

Do you think you'll stay?

For now. It depends on work, I suppose. Things can only go so far here.

There have been enquiries, from Europe, the Scottish Wildlife Trust, Mexico, mostly consultancy work. She pauses.

I should take Charlie to America at some point.

Because of his dad?

They've skirted the subject in the past; Lawrence perhaps too respectful to ask, and she not feeling it right to unburden herself. But the soft, grassy evening feels loose and permissive. They are friends now. Her brother is well and she is less restricted.

Yes, because of his dad. I keep thinking it's the right thing. I don't know why. I'm not under any obligation. That's not true – I feel I am in a way.

There are days she is sure Kyle knows: the tenor of his emails, the enquiries, nothing particular – perhaps she's paranoid and imagining it. He would come and say it, if he knew. There are times she's sat down and written, in emails and letters, a revelation, and an apology. *You have a son, I'm sorry I didn't tell you.* Reading back, it always seems too blundering, too belated. And

[355]

her motives are foggy, she's not sure why – why tell him now? Is it simply a confession, or a request for involvement? Her brother puts down his knife and fork, issues her with a moment of full concentration – something he has become disciplined at. The gesture often seems too intense and conspicuous, but is a tactic that works wonders with Charlie.

You know what I think, he says. They should give you an instruction manual when you're born. How to navigate all this shit. It's like running headlong downstairs in the dark otherwise.

She smiles and nods.

That's true.

Can I ask you something?

Sure.

Is he called Charles because of your dad?

She was not aware Lawrence had known; Binny excised Rachel's father from the family dialogue long before her second child was born. There is so much of their upbringing still to unearth.

He is. I didn't know him, she says. But he's on my birth certificate.

If it's an unknown quantity you can choose your approach, Lawrence says. It's a great name. Mitch keeps telling us to make the past positive. You can tell me to shut up, by the way. I know I sound like a fanatic.

I don't mind. I like the name, too. What I worry about is the lack of everything else.

What do you mean?

Lack of a dad. Whether I did alright without mine. Whether Charlie will do alright.

You did fine, Rachel. What about Alexander? He seems keen.

Oh, I don't know.

You'll be fine, Lawrence says, again, definitively. So will Bup.

He picks up his cutlery. He is, once more, the brother of restored optimism, at least where she is concerned. But she cannot allow herself to imagine the full happy scenario, not yet. They continue with dinner. She wonders how her brother will fare, back in the real world, whether the new policies will hold. The first stars are seeding brightly above the horizon – Venus, Vega, the North Star. From upstairs in the cottage, Charlie's long unsettled wail begins. She stands, but Lawrence tells her to sit back down.

I'll go. We're leaving the lights off and not picking him up, right?

Right. Thanks. Thank you, Lawrence. This is really delicious, by the way.

You're going to miss me, he says.

After he is gone, Seldom Seen falls back into gentle disarray – toys scattered, crockery crusted in the sink, soggy bath mats and towels left in heaps. Charlie looks around for his uncle, confused by the sudden absence. He asks for him in the morning and at night before bed, *Lor? Lor?* Then, as if a magnificent feat might summon him back, he lets go of the coffee table he has been using as a ballast for the last month, and walks towards the sofa, several steps, before falling onto his bottom. He gets up and tries again. The biped age has really begun.

Rachel employs a part-time minder, in her fifties, very experienced, with excellent references, and not cheap, but the woman does not seem to bond and she cancels the arrangement. She brings Charlie to the office again, but he's too big, too restive, in need of stimulus. Sylvia has gone south, to start her legal training. They have exchanged a few emails, but otherwise the relationship looks destined to fade. One of the volunteers offers to help with the baby, temporarily, giving her an hour or two each morning to catch up. It's not enough. She's missing the development of the wolves. She's failing to respond to enquiries and phone calls. She has not found time to meet with Thomas, who suddenly wants to discuss aspects of the project – the neutering – after months of indifference. He seems averse now to the intervention, and she wonders if Sylvia went to work on him before leaving. *The decision is irreversible and might be regretted*, he writes. They agree on a Skype meeting while he is in London. In the video link he is tying his tie, preparing to go out. He glances at the image of himself in the corner of the screen and adjusts the knot.

Is it absolutely necessary? he asks.

She again explains to him, as she did to his daughter, what the issues are.

Alright, he says. All I ask is that nothing happens too soon. You never know what the future might hold.

The sudden interference is annoying – it's a polite request but she senses the weight of the boss behind it. The future will hold exactly what I've outlined, she thinks. Unless he means expansion of the enclosure and the introduction of new males, separate packs, which will not be possible. He cannot encroach further into the national park – even he would be unable to acquire the land needed. She agrees to revisit the subject later in the year, but offers no further concession. A junior aid says something to the Earl and he nods and the call is finished.

There's a belated bloom of summer. The first weekend Alexander stays after Lawrence's departure, he walks around nude in the cottage and out into the garden, like a Scandinavian on holiday. The cottage windows are flung open, and giant white moths flicker round the climbing honeysuckle. Charlie is pleased to have another man in the house; he's sociable, prattling, boyish already. Alexander hangs him by his chubby fists from the washing line, tips him upside down, makes him scream giddily, and vomit. He liquidises beef hearts for him, gives him a tiny, early taste of honey. She gets used to sharing the bed again. Alexander's back is a giant slab of muscle, disproportionate to his waist, his cock flops between his legs as he strides about. He likes sex in the mornings, before she is even properly awake, before the baby is.

There's been trouble with Chloe over the summer – hormones, early pubescence. He has not been sure how to handle it all, he confesses. She's been moody, embarrassed by the irregular show of blood, the flowery folded packages she must now keep in her bag, and the starter bra, which she refuses to wear. She's been fighting with her grandmother and staying at Alexander's house more. The previous month the family of her friend Lucy took her on holiday to Portugal for three weeks – on her return, she was sullen, did not go into detail but said she hated it, hated swimming, the sun, and hated her friend.

I don't know what went on, he says. I don't suppose you might want to see her for a bit? I think she thinks you're cool.

Me? Ha!

You are pretty cool.

She does not feel confident about her feminine communication skills, which are all but non-existent, but Alexander has been generous and supportive over the past year; she owes him the favour.

OK. Shall I take her to see the wolves again?

Yes! That would be great.

He kisses her.

I don't know, he says. I thought I was New Age. I thought I was a bloody feminist. All she wants to do is hang out with her horse and tell me I don't understand anything.

What should I say to her?

Nothing. Just talk shop. Just let her talk if she wants.

Rachel has not seen Chloe for several months, and the time has been transformative. When they go into the enclosure – only the two of them this time – the girl is less vivacious and uninhibited, though still sweet and clever. She has a layer of fat, proper, cupped breasts under her T-shirt; even her face is a different shape. Gone is the floral mac and crocheted animal jumper; she has on jeans, a white shirt, conservative high street items. She walks up the grassland slowly, as if aware of her body and its limitations.

It's nice of you to do this, she says. I know Dad asked you.

He did. But I thought you might want to see how they're getting on.

I do.

They take signal readings from the handheld device, locate Ra and Merle, and situate themselves on the hillside near the rendezvous point. Rachel sets up the portable telescope in the hope of getting a clear view. The juveniles are probably too big to interest a typical young girl, no longer puppyish and scruffy, getting on for two-thirds the size of their parents. They are now more guileful than playful. But Chloe is still interested, and not typical. The high definition of the telescope is enough to impress her – she can see their eyes, their whiskers. They do not remain in view for long, but run off, casting glances up at the hill.

I like how they move, she says. Sort of floppy but fast. Can they live without their parents yet?

It's perhaps a loaded question. Should the subtext – *I'm not getting on with my dad* – be addressed? Fall back on what you know, Rachel thinks. On the hike back to the car, she talks about the notion of intelligence and problem-solving. She tells Chloe about a wolf in the rescue centre in Romania that learnt to open its cage door by watching its caretakers.

How?

She pulled on the mechanism. A rope.

That's really clever.

Maybe. But how can we know it wasn't a reflex action? I mean, wolves and dogs tug on things. I bet you've seen them do it with slippers and anything dangling.

Yes. Our old sheepdog used to.

Chloe pauses, thinks for a moment.

But just because they do that doesn't mean it isn't clever to do it right then, on the lock. It doesn't really sound like an accident. She figured it out.

Rachel nods and smiles.

I think so too. It's called application. Some people think intelligence is learning to do new things using acquired skills. Do you still want to be a geneticist? she asks.

Chloe shrugs.

Maybe. I don't know. I'd quite like to be a singer.

Ah, right.

I'm not very poppy, though. I don't really look like a pop star. No sex appeal.

I've heard you sing. You have a great voice.

Thanks.

Don't, Rachel thinks. Don't succumb. She gets the sense Chloe would talk to her, intimately – that the grandmother has been somewhat practical on the subjects troubling her granddaughter, but has fallen short: the generational gap. She feels for the girl, for her predicament. She is ahead of her school friends physically, the boys are commenting on her figure, there are embarrassing things going on she cannot control. It is a stormy, lonely place to be. She tries to remember what Binny did. Noticed the row of rinsed underwear on the washing line, bought a box of Tampax, and left Rachel to her own devices, probably. There were no heart-to-hearts. They walk in silence, and then Chloe asks, out of the blue,

Are you going to marry Dad?

Whoa! Well, I don't know.

There is, of course, no other answer. Rachel panics internally, tries to formulate a better explanation, but Chloe doesn't ask anything more on the subject and Rachel has no idea whether such a thing would be considered good or bad. They walk back to the car and drive to meet Alexander in The Horse and Farrier, where the girl orders salad for lunch and looks longingly at her father's plate of chips.

After come cool days, and glazed white skies. The swifts, late-leaving, migrate to other continents. Enormous spiders come into the cottage – a couple of times she gets to Charlie only just before they are inserted into his mouth, their legs thrashing in his little fist. The wind gets up, hurricanes over the Atlantic that disperse before reaching the edge of Europe. Autumn crackles in the air in the mornings and evenings, and the canopy of the woods begins to smoulder, yellowish.

The Annerdale project is officially a year old, as is her son. She throws a birthday party for Charlie, attended mostly by adults – Lawrence, Alexander and Chloe, Huib, a few similarly aged children from the area whose mothers she is linked to but rarely sees. Rachel tells herself she must do better at finding playmates for Charlie: a local crèche, a baby swim group, something. She must do better at making friends herself, with mothers who are at a similar stage, wrestling similar problems. But the times when she has met them the conversations always seem awkward; once the subject of babies is finished, there is little in common. She doesn't watch television, she has no husband, her work is bizarre. She watches Charlie smear chocolate cake across his mouth, his heels pounding against his high chair, mumbling some kind of happy eating song, eyes huge. They have each other – is that enough? It's hard to remember a time when he wasn't hers, the central part of her life. At other moments she looks at him and he seems like an alien, randomly dropped from the sky – unrecognisable and incredible.

The weather finally breaks. A week of proper rain and wind, thunder. The lull is over. With the blusters and the change of pressure comes a strange cycle of dreams. She dreams of the baby, worming on the blanket when he was first born and she barely knew how to hold him, and a world after catastrophe; she is looking for his buried hand in the rubble. Then she dreams she is still pregnant, she feels him moving in her, the slippery jutting of his legs. The next night, a dream where she cannot stop the white, surprising milk, litres of it, soaking through her shirt, though she is old and grey-haired and her breasts are atrophied. She wakes, goes back to sleep, and has a nightmare: her abdomen is gaping open like a damp red purse – she cannot find the surgeon to stitch her, she limps around holding it closed. Alexander shakes her awake.

Hey, it's alright, it's alright.

What time is it?

Little after three.

Is he crying?

No.

Wind in the branches outside. She sleeps again and dreams of wolves. There are dozens, loping across the fields, not Merle and Ra and the Annerdale litter, but wolves of the past – Tungsten, Left Paw, Caligula, the Belarus scavengers. They are part of an impossible number, a super-pack, like a modern fable. The fields are full of black water. The body of a cow floats, its ribs lathed raw, like the beams of a boat. Then they are in a town, running through deserted buildings, scrambling over walls and fences and tables. The dream becomes tortured. There are snarling fights; they inflict terrible injuries.

She wakes hot under the covers and with a headache – the heating has kicked in overnight with the sudden drop in temperature. Alexander has left for a conference in Northern Ireland. A cold cup of tea sits on the bedside table. Someone is banging on the front door. She glances at the bedside clock. Six-thirty: dawn is barely firing and the cottage is murky.

The banging continues. She gets up, pulls on her jeans and a T-shirt from a pile on the chair, looks in on Charlie. He is gripping the toy lion and sucking his thumb, asleep. She goes downstairs and opens the door to a neon-jacketed police officer.

Miss Caine?

His high-visibility jacket is garish against the grey trees. His features are hooked and hollowed by shadow. Parked in the lane behind him is a police Land Rover, the top light silently flashing, sending blue arcs wheeling into the woods. In the passenger seat another police officer is talking on the radio.

Rachel Caine?

Yes.

After the turbulent night, the morning seems oddly weather-less. Stillness ascends skyward. The day does not feel cold. Lawrence, she thinks. Lawrence is dead. He's overdosed.

I'm Sergeant Armstrong. Sorry for the early hour. We were hoping you could come with us. There's been an incident.

She doesn't brace, though her arms cross automatically over her chest. I wasn't expecting it, she thinks, I'm not ready – though in part she was and is. She begins, in those few seconds, to try to un-love her brother. She didn't love him once, as a child, and it was easy then. The police officer waits for her to respond. Under his hat, shadows, she can't see his face. He has no eyes. The surrounding stillness is immense, as if they are both standing at the bottom of a vast structure. She didn't love Lawrence once. She can un-love him now. But it's too late. There are ectopic beats in her heart and her throat is clenching. On the kitchen table, her phone is ringing, vibrating against the wooden surface.

Yes, she says. OK.

Can you come down to Pennington Hall?

To the Hall? Why the Hall?

You are in charge of the wolf enclosure?

She shakes her head, then nods.

Yes, I am. Is Lawrence alright?

Lawrence?

My brother Lawrence. Sorry. I'm not really awake. Is he OK?

The officer nods, slightly baffled; he is also tired – the end of a night shift, or the beginning of an early one. Now, after all, there is movement, in the branches nearby, a fluttering, a fast wing. She still cannot see the man's face properly. She reaches out and turns on the porch light, and he appears, an ordinary man in his late forties.

Miss Caine, are you alright?

Yes. I'm sorry, I thought you were – What's happened?

Are you in charge of the wolves?

Yes.

We received a report last night. A man near Sawrey driving home said he saw a wolf crossing the road in front of him.

OK, she says. There have been a few of those kinds of sightings, since they were released last year. It's usually a big dog off a lead. Was this person drunk?

Not to my knowledge. We might not have been so concerned, but there was another separate report this morning. Near the Galt Forest.

The feeling of weakness is still in her legs, but her heart has levelled, and the meaning of the officer's presence is registering. Upstairs the baby begins shouting from his cot. He can hear her voice; he knows she's up.

Right. You're taking the calls seriously?

We're following up. At this stage, we don't believe they're hoaxes. We need you to verify the location of the wolves. The Animal Protection Officer is on standby in case, he says.

Her phone is ringing again. Charlie is shouting louder.

Yes, fine. Come in. I've got to see to my son.

The police officer follows her into the cottage, bending under the low doorframe. He removes his hat. He is tall, has straight grey hair like a heron, and is beginning to develop jowls. One eye sits a fraction higher than the other. The uniform does not suit him, though he must have worn it for decades.

I won't be a minute, she says, heading for the stairs.

She goes up to Charlie. He is standing holding the edges of the cot, his sleep-suit askew, Roary turfed onto the floor. The tone of his crying changes when he sees her, downgrades. She stands for a moment within arm range, looking at him as he reaches out. She steadies herself, breathes. Not Lawrence. Lawrence is alive. She lifts the baby. She dresses him, then sets him back into the cot, at which he protests loudly. She goes into the bedroom and quickly puts on a bra under her T-shirt. Sergeant Armstrong is standing in the hallway, waiting, when they come downstairs.

I just need to – she says, moving past him to the kitchen.

Charlie twists in her arms to get a better view of the strange man, standing ominously in the hallway, clad in yellow and black like a great biding wasp. His wail borders on uncontrolled; soon it will be a turbine of calamity. She pours some milk in a bottle and puts bananas and biscuits in a bag. The routine is all wrong, but what can she do. She feels harried and resentful, drops things clumsily; a plastic plate clatters on the tiles. Who was it? she wonders. Some short-sighted grandfather on the way to get the paper? The hysterical mother of Nancy, from the protests? She gathers up the bag, looks down at her phone. There are three missed calls from Huib. The police have obviously woken him, too. She pockets the phone, picks up the car keys and her coat, and walks the policeman out of the cottage. The second officer is getting out of the Land Rover, adjusting his hat. The blue light is still going. Such dawn theatrics seem ridiculous.

Need a hand? he asks.

I'll follow you down, she says.

She opens the Saab door, straps Charlie in, and gives him the bottle, which he holds expertly by the handles up to his mouth, tipping his head back. He is calmer. The uncommon development of the car and the sippy cup this early in the morning are enough to distract him for the time being. She half peels and puts a banana on the passenger seat.

The Land Rover wallows slowly down the lane, pauses at the fork, turns onto the estate road, and speeds up. She takes a bite of the banana. It had to happen again sooner or later, she thinks. They're probably lucky to have had so many months without serious trouble on the project, just the odd griping madman quoting obscure biblical passages. She glances behind. Charlie is looking out of the window at the yellow trees, the empty bottle held loosely in one hand. He drops it into the footwell behind the passenger seat.

Uh-oh, he says.

Uh-oh, she agrees.

THE EXPOSED

A golden, industrial sun is on the way up, gilding the low clouds. October, the month of riches and mutability. The long driveway to the Hall smokes with light and mist. Rising along the verges are the ancient oaks, cast like thrones along the wayside. She knows the story of the oldest now, which is elaborately underpinned with struts – its health superstitiously tied to the fortunes of the estate, it cannot be allowed to die. Annerdale appears like a myth out of the haze, a holy land, artificially made but gloriously convincing.

Another police vehicle is parked outside Pennington Hall – two more officers are standing with Huib. Here we go again, she thinks. Honor's blue MG is in the usual spot, tucked under the willow tree by the walled garden. It's early, even for her. The Land Rover pulls up; the policemen get out and confer with their colleagues. Two consecutive sightings: they are clearly taking it all very seriously. The uniformed gathering has an air of malfeasance to it, like a posse about to ride out. They're just doing their job, Rachel tells herself, but the talk of an Animal Protection Officer has made her nervous. She opens the back door of the Saab, unclips Charlie, and lifts him out. He hides his face coyly against her shoulder as she approaches the uniformed group. There's a brief discussion; Sergeant Armstrong asks about access to the enclosure – how can they get in, where the wolves might have got out.

Let's just make sure first, shall we? Rachel suggests. They're tagged. If we can get a radio signal, we'll know it's a false alarm. If we can't get one from the office, it usually means they're on the other side of the estate, but it doesn't take long to find them.

This is the truth, more or less. The signal range is five miles. Weather and hills and broadcast anomalies notwithstanding, it is rare that Ra and Merle cannot be found reasonably quickly with the quad bikes and the handheld receivers.

Actually, I already tried, Huib says. No go from this end, I'm afraid.

OK, she says. We'll try from another point.

What about GPS? the sergeant asks. Can you track them that way?

Rachel moves Charlie to the other arm – he's becoming a dead weight. He ducks his head again and remains quiet, but the placid shyness is not going to last. He needs to eat something proper, and soon. So does she. She is in no mood for a discussion about telemetry.

Implants are problematic with satellites, she says. We can get some data from ARGOS, but it's delayed. It's more for research than anything else – activity, temperature, heart rate, that kind of thing. We don't use the mapping software: it's not reliable.

The sergeant frowns slightly, as if an oversight has already been exposed.

I see.

They have a limited home range, she says, her tone a fraction curter. They aren't free-roaming. We don't need GPS.

She shrugs Charlie upward. He puts his hands on her face. She is not paying him enough attention.

Ma-ma.

When was the last time they were actually seen by anyone here – I mean, seen by one of your staff? the sergeant says.

She moves Charlie's hands away. You really don't understand, she thinks.

I was inside the enclosure about ten days ago, Huib offers. Listen, I'll go and try the receiver again; sometimes it's just the antenna. I can take a quad bike around the enclosure if there's still no signal.

How long will that take?

No more than an hour.

It's really the best approach, Rachel says.

Huib heads back towards the office, a young officer escorting him. The rest of the group waits on the driveway, ready for deployment. The specifics of this call-out might be slightly unusual, with a note of wild glamour, even, but they are probably used to freak animal incidents, she thinks, it being part of rural policing. Bulls blocking the road. Horse trailers overturned. Llamas on the A66 from the exotic farm nearby.

How many wolves are there? Sergeant Armstrong asks.

Six. Two adults, four juveniles.

She does not mention that the litter hasn't been implanted with tracking devices.

I understand my colleague was here last year looking into an attempted sabotage? Have there been any more such incidents?

No. It's been very quiet.

The main door of the Hall opens. Honor Clark approaches, heels crisp in the gravel, as if she has been awake and working for hours. She offers coffee inside the Hall while they wait. Thomas Pennington is away, she tells them, but is aware of the situation, and will of course cooperate in any way he can. She stewards them inside. There is a slight, almost imperceptible strain in her manner, Rachel notices; her scarf is loosely knotted, the hair underneath erupting in loose strands. She has rushed to work, rushed here to mediate. It's bad for the estate's profile to have the police on site, yet again. One attack on the enclosure and one accidental shooting, within a year.

Where's Thomas? Rachel asks her, as they make their way along the corridor towards the drawing room.

He's away.

Where?

I'm not sure at the moment.

Honor does not meet Rachel's eye. It's possible she has not even talked to him yet, if he is AWOL, and she is covering. The usual goose-chase will go on behind closed doors, unseen, until he is found. In the drawing room she pours a round of coffee into fine china cups. The sergeant moves to the corner of the room and radios back to the station. The officers remove their hats.

Please help yourself.

Honor gestures to a tray of fresh pastries.

You know where I am, she says to Rachel. Do keep me in the loop.

Rachel takes a croissant from the plate, pulls it into pieces, and gives some to Charlie. He chews it, but is unsure and spits out a damp wad, which she wraps in a napkin. The police mill round the room with their tiny cups and then sit on the various designer chairs, the silk chaise longue, the leather Bauhaus, each looking out of place, as if having stumbled into the wrong stage play. Nor is Rachel any better suited, two years on, since she sat here waiting for the Earl, having just flown in from Idaho. Her phone pings – a text from Huib. *Out on quad.* Sergeant Armstrong is looking through the French windows towards the lake, at the spectacular, picturesque view. One of the junior officers is researching on his smartphone. He begins to question Rachel informally.

So, you surgically implant the radio transmitters in them?

Yes.

And each has its own frequency.

Yes.

Do they have tranquillisers fitted in the devices, in case of emergency?

He has found the Telonics website, which offers the most advanced form of wildlife tracking. She can see where the line of questioning will probably lead. Can they be controlled remotely, if necessary? Can they be destroyed if they are on the rampage?

No, she says. Tranquilliser cases are too big for our implants. They're usually only installed in radio collars.

Why choose implants over collars?

Collars are bulky. They get damaged. The animals can pull them off. Even the weather can affect them.

He nods. He looks barely twenty years old, close-cropped, spotty, and cadet-like. She cannot imagine him in an action scenario. She thinks of the Idaho state troopers, their swagger, the antagonism every time they had reason to come onto the Reservation – their guns seemed brazen to her; she never got used to it. The sergeant helps himself to another cup of coffee – no doubt a cut above the usual refreshments offered during call-outs. He seems more relaxed than when he knocked at her door, teases the junior.

That your auxiliary brain, Tom? What else does it say? Brush your teeth?

For all the grand showing of force, there seems to be no state of alarm. Extra precautionary measures, perhaps. Charlie begins to act up. He smells soiled. She excuses herself, slips into the library, and changes him. He rolls about, squirms and kicks on the change mat, and threatens the plush carpet beneath.

Knock it off, kiddo, she says quietly, we can't afford the dry-cleaning bill.

He fights the new nappy. Too much sugar, the wrong routine; he senses her stress. She cleans her hands on a wet wipe. Attended to, Charlie performs a wobbling circuit of the room, past the bookcases – she stops him from pulling off and demolishing the expensive first editions – past the elaborate fireplace. She picks him up and shows him the bronze Capitoline sculpture on the mantel.

Look, she says. This is a Mrs Wolf. And two little boys, like you.

Charlie reaches for a china vase next to the statue.

Nope, she says, and swiftly turns away.

Thwarted, he begins to cry. Hurry up, Huib, she thinks. The situation is only going to get more unmanageable the longer it goes on. She must take control. She considers waking one of the volunteers, asking them to babysit for an hour. Or perhaps Honor could mind Charlie – though that seems unlikely and undesirable. When she returns to the drawing room, there's a stir of new energy. The officers are all on their feet, hats in hand, primed. Sergeant Armstrong is talking on his PTT again, asking his correspondent to repeat something, the cause of injury. *Say again, Samantha.* He is looking ahead at the wall, concentrating, his forehead buckled in the middle. *OK, OK.* He turns back into the room.

Right. There's been another sighting on the Galt Forest road.

A cyclist – said he saw a pack of wolves. He's come off his bike, has a broken wrist and a fractured cheekbone – he's about to go into surgery.

The sergeant glances at Rachel.

He managed to get a picture on his phone – they've sent it through. Tom, pass me that thing a minute.

He takes the iPhone from his colleague, fiddles with it, then shows Rachel. The image is slightly blurred; the animal is retreating down the forest track, looking to the side. It could be mistaken for a husky or some other kind of big, heavy-coated dog by anyone else. White fur. Long legs, a long, thin nose. Ra.

I can't be certain, Rachel says. But, yes, he could be ours.

They don't confirm their point of escape until later, when Huib finds the north gate standing open. The digital lock is undamaged – the mechanism has been triggered, or overridden. There are paw prints in the nearby soil, either side of the fence and the barrier. He measures them. At least four different wolves are out, possibly all. Officers are dispatched to examine the scene; the volunteers are brought over from their quarters for questioning. More police arrive at the Hall – spilling out of cars – minor, dark-clad Lucifers. The entire county force is put on immediate alert.

Rachel has several brief phone calls with Huib. He confirms both Merle and Ra's tracks. They do not speculate about what might have happened; there will be time for that later. She tells him to take the quad bike to the old den site and the rendezvous points, to check the enclosure as best he can for any sign that they have not all gone – a faint hope. There are still no radio signals; most likely they have passed by without detection and are now out of range.

Her patience quickly wanes. She must get to the broad expanse of the Galt Forest, a preserved stretch of national parkland in the heart of the Lakes, and soon. They may linger where there are red deer, and the tree coverage is dense. Other than cyclists and orienteers, there will not be many people at this time of year. First she must make sure the situation is under control – she will insist on leading the search – and that any police involvement is restrained.

She leaves Charlie with one of the volunteers – he's still acting up and shouts, but she has little choice. She sits with Sergeant Armstrong in a quiet corner of the drawing room, which has become an informal operation hub. He seems unperturbed, is old enough to have seen a myriad of unusual incidents, though perhaps not quite like this. He calmly walks her through operating procedure, hands splayed on the table, leaning forwards.

What we need to do is coordinate a joint search effort. Get them back as soon as possible.

She's heartened by his phrasing – *get them back* – but still not convinced extreme measures won't be taken – a marksman.

Rachel – do you mind if I call you Rachel?

No.

OK, I'm David. Rachel, do you have any idea what their movements might be, where they'll go?

Probably north, she says, though maybe not directly. They might stay in the forest a while, if there's prey.

She looks him in the eye.

Deer, I mean. They aren't a threat to the public. They'll try to avoid people wherever they can. You don't need any guns. That guy came off his bike because he was shocked. He probably braked too hard.

The sergeant holds up his hand, fending off her anxiety, her hostility.

I know, Rachel. He wasn't attacked. I know that. I understand what you're saying.

I don't want them shot, she says. These are precious animals. They belong to the estate.

She surprises herself by invoking the power of the Pennington realm. But she is determined, and will use any method to keep them unharmed.

I understand, he says. But this is a big county, as you know. If they can't be located quickly, then they might be at risk. We need to warn and inform the public, prevent panic, and ask for help. It's standard procedure for anything like this, even a missing child. That's the system – it works well, so we tend to stick to it. We'll use existing networks like Farm Watch, Mountain Rescue, all the neighbourhood networks. OK?

OK. Sorry.

She needs to get moving, but sits back and tries to feel less combative – the police want to help and she may need their help. The reality of the situation begins to sink in. The phenomenon is nowhere near standard, she knows. One wolf would be difficult enough, but a pack?

We'll start with a bulletin on local radio, Sergeant Armstrong is saying. You'd be surprised how much of the county listens. So. What, in your opinion, should the message say?

It seems to her that common sense should simply lead people, but then common sense is often the last thing the public employs. England is without predators; it is, or was, a de-mined zone. There will be those looking to face down the new invader, for kudos, for glory.

Don't approach them, she says. Don't try to interact; don't leave bait out or anything to attract them. They'd rather hunt, but they'll scavenge if there's an opportunity. They're not tigers, but they're not poodles, either.

OK, good. So, we'll reassure first and foremost, say they are wild creatures, but not harmful to humans. They should not under any circumstances be approached. Don't attempt to interfere with the animals. Just notify us.

She pauses.

That's fine.

So, you think they might stay in the forest? We'll cordon off the Galt roads anyway.

She shakes her head.

It's possible they will. But not certain. They don't need to hunt, not immediately.

Meaning?

They're well fed. They could pass through the forest and keep on going. For quite a while, and without stopping.

Sergeant Armstrong nods, but looks slightly alarmed by the information. This is not what he wanted to hear, she knows.

How far can they travel in, say, a day or two?

In forty-eight hours? To the border. Across it.

He recoils a little.

Even with the young ones?

They're not quite mature but they're big enough to travel now. If they were in the wild, they'd be migrating.

He considers this for a moment. She does not mention, though it has crossed her mind, that whoever let them out – if they were let out – perhaps understood this. If it is another sabotage, it has been elegantly executed; it is beneficent.

Right. I'm going to contact police headquarters in Dumfries and Galloway, the sergeant says. They should be aware. We might need to formally hand over control at some stage.

He lowers his tone, attempts to be tactful.

Also, I'm assuming Lord Pennington will have connections. We need to liaise with anyone from the private sector involved, OK? Will you let me know once you've talked to him?

Rachel shakes her head again.

I'm going to track them, she says. I'm licensed to carry barbiturates and a gas-projector. Do you need to see the paperwork?

No. That's OK. You'll be registered on the system.

Then I should get going.

She stands up. Sergeant Armstrong collects his hat from the chair next to him.

All right. Stay in touch, Rachel. You've got my number, and we can arrange transport. Last thing for now – we'll need a full list of names – anyone with access to the enclosure, anyone agitating against the project, anyone you might suspect. Perhaps your colleague can help when he gets back?

Yes, he can.

She tries not to think beyond the present, to a phase of accusations and recrimination. But already her mind is at work. She's sure the timing of the incident is not random. But talking with Sergeant Armstrong has been somewhat reassuring: she had conceived of a far worse scenario, the county grinding to a halt, aerial spotters and thermal cameras, a race to save them from execution. It is clear the police don't want to own the situation. At least not yet. She pulls on her coat. An hour has passed since the last sighting. There's still Charlie to manage. She has tried Lawrence but his phone is switched off, and his office line has been going through to voicemail.

Rachel is about to take her leave when Honor enters the drawing room and makes her way over, a tight smile on her face. She's neatened herself – the chignon is smooth and there's a waft of newly applied perfume.

I've just been speaking with Thomas, she says. He'll be here by this evening.

She glances at Sergeant Armstrong.

He'd like it to be known that he is offering a substantial reward for anyone assisting with their safe return. I won't disclose the figure at this stage. There's also the matter of compensation, for any natural damage.

The phrasing is very tactful. Damn it, Rachel thinks, did she have to flag that up? She turns back to the sergeant.

OK to say that in the bulletin, too? he asks.

Just the reward part, Rachel says. But it might be an idea for farmers to bring flocks indoors for the time being. I mean indoors, not penned. Just as a precaution, there's no need to get dramatic.

I understand, he says. We'll mention it to the union.

I better go.

He nods.

Good luck.

She excuses herself and heads to the office to collect Charlie. Damn Honor, she thinks again. She did not want to be explicit about the negatives in the first stages. But this is Cumbria; there's a high possibility of agricultural loss. In tracking the pack she may indeed be following a trail of carcasses. Most animals will instinctively avoid the path of wolves, but the sheep, lame motif of the Lake District, corralled in their walled fields and scattered across the moors, won't stand a chance. Nor will the famous republic of shepherds remain peaceful about their plight.

*

The Galt Valley is on fire as she makes her way in. The planta-
tions blaze with autumn colours – copper, mustard, a hundred
reds. The heather has bronzed; worked over by bees all summer,
it is dying back. Higher on the slopes are industrial stands of coni-
fers, not yet stripped out, oddly artificial-looking in the anatomy
of the forest. The summit of Galt Fell rises above the yellow and
green skirts, hairpins looping the mountain pass and the broken
face of the crags. There's no traffic on the forestry road, which has
been cordoned off by the police; Rachel's is the only car. The Saab
bounces over potholes, tracks gamely upward. In places the lane
has deteriorated to shingle, small landslides moving the concrete
surface downhill. There are no passing places; were she to meet
another vehicle, she would have to reverse for miles.

Charlie is asleep in the child seat in the back, serene now,
thankfully. There seemed no choice in the rush to leave the Hall,
after the abortive search for a trusted sitter. She will keep trying
Lawrence – he is her best bet and she does not know how long
she will need to be out searching. Until then, better to keep him
with her; she will contend with any problems along the way, as
women have always contended. En route to the forest she has
bought supplies – fruit, yogurt, cheese slices, and crackers from a
garage, plenty of water and milk. The baby bag is stocked. There
is no plan beyond simply finding the wolves. On the dashboard is
one of the handheld radio receivers, tuned to Merle's frequency,
the antenna out and adjusted. In the boot: eight slim tranquilliser
darts and the gun. Even if found, there will be difficult decisions
to make – she is under no illusions. Dart the pups first because

they are not radio-traceable and are green hunters, or prioritise the valuable breeding pair?

She has not talked to Thomas, though there are several blocked calls listed on her phone, which are probably from him. She cannot call back. The satellite signal keeps cutting out. The estate will be making arrangements, no doubt – but for now, she has a head start. If the animals stay off the main roads and are not hit, if they keep to cover and away from the farmsteads, perhaps they will all survive. They will move skilfully between more efficient manmade routes and secretive pathways. Much will be left to chance.

She looks west. There's a slight red tint to the sky, above the blaze of the canopy. Two hours of daylight left. Her phone rings. The number is again withheld. This time she catches it before it cuts out. Thomas. The reception is terrible, crackles on the line, and his voice drifts in and out. *All under control; don't worry, Rachel.* A wave of static, and then silence. She thinks she has lost him, until his voice cuts in again: *Metcalfe is working on it . . .* There's a rushing sound, engines; he is on a plane, or the helicopter. Metcalfe: the head of his legal team. Trust Thomas to be concerned with the legalities – probably covering his arse, she thinks.

Where are you? she asks, pointlessly.

He does not hear her. The line is dead. Reception has gone as the trees thicken, or his aircraft has sped out of range.

The road climbs upward, the tower of the first rock bluff looming above, a lone buzzard circling, up-tipped wings. It is annoying, but hardly surprising that Thomas is working a top-down policy. No doubt he is putting in motion a hefty compensation package. Or perhaps he is securing some kind of special emergency status for the pack. She is more concerned with the problems of the here and now – the awed, anxious public, the motorways.

She checks on Charlie again in the rear-view mirror. Still asleep. The forest closes behind her, the road tapering and disappearing. The chassis of the car scrapes over a series of craters, the exhaust clunking. Either side, the ground is soft, pitted. There's no choice but forward. She releases her seatbelt, opens the window. The cedarish, earthy smell of the woods blows in; fresh, cool air. In places the branches knit tightly over the road, roofing it; dry husks rain sporadically on the car and the light flickers and strobes.

Very faintly, a sound on the handheld receiver as it picks up Merle's signal. A few beeps, then silence again. She stops the car and takes the device from the dashboard, looks at the reading, and turns up the dial. The pulsing starts again. She is to the northwest, within five miles, still in the Galt. Rachel tracks to Ra's signal frequency – the reading is the same. The relief is almost overwhelming. Now she has a chance. She takes the Ordinance Survey map out of its plastic sleeve and studies the forestry road and the bridleways. She will need to take a left fork, clear the pass, and then walk – she tries not to dwell on the latter part of the plan. She puts the car in gear and drives on towards the summit, through the crags. In the rock ledges are withered sprays of ferns, trickling brackish water. The road curves steeply to the right, then banks left – the first of the hairpins. She concentrates on steering. The sun is below the trees, and the lane is shadowed. She drops into second gear, then first, each bend is steeper and tighter than the last. The car almost stalls, and she revs the engine. It judders forward. The noise and the motion wake Charlie. He whimpers and then blurts a protest.

I know, I know, she says. Sorry.

Mama.

He struggles against the buckles of the seat and starts to cry. She tries to distract him with a song he likes, but it doesn't work and it's hard to concentrate on the vertiginous road at the same time. He fusses behind the harness, kicks the rim of the seat, his face set in an expression of upset. The car swings and pitches round the bends. Don't be sick, she thinks. She puts all four windows down. Air buffets around inside the car. Charlie's fine, dark hair flutters and laps against his head. He stops crying, assesses the sensation, and smiles. Then he laughs.

Yes. I know what you like, she says. Windy. We're very high.

Wee-dee, he says.

That's right.

Wee-dee.

Yes.

She doesn't know if he understands, whether the words he says have meaning or he is now just a good copyist.

Wee-dee, he repeats.

The transmitter signal is still there, weak, but no weaker, though the road is veering slightly east. Something flashes at the side of the road – a deer's rump – a white flag, like semaphore. There is a new state of emergency in the woods.

Did you see? she asks Charlie. Did you see the deer?

He is too low in the seat.

Wee-dee.

She is glad of his company, no matter the levels of comprehension and the fact that he may make everything come unstuck. The Saab grinds up the last incline and reaches the granite shoulder of the pass. Below, a spreading arboretum – the sharp vanes of the quadrant pines, and deciduous forest stretching out in every direction, in bright lungs. The sun is becoming bloodied and is sitting close to the horizon. She will have to stop soon and get Charlie out, change him, walk him around, give him something to eat. She starts the descent, slowly, the bonnet of the car nose-diving and disappearing under the first sheer tilt downward. She hits the brakes. Driving begins to feel like an act of faith. But she must make it over the Galt pass before dark, and get close to the pack — as close as she can.

By dusk, there's a strong reading, near the northern border of the forest. She parks, changes Charlie by the side of the road, lying him in the grass. A great arc of pee as the nappy is taken off. She leaves the car radio on, tuned to the local station. They have been featuring the story all day. The bulletin wording is sensible enough, delivered flatly by Sergeant Armstrong himself, though the evening show host's response is giddy; he is excited to have something meaty to discuss instead of the usual mundane parochial events. The item also makes the national news. She is surprised to hear Huib on air, interviewed by the BBC. He is clear and calm, reiterating that there is no danger, that the animals are not a threat and should be left alone. He does not answer questions about who might be responsible. It is probably better to have him at the Hall for now, she thinks, managing everything. He has sent through a few texts. No group has claimed responsibility for the gate yet. The lock system is being re-examined. The police have interviewed the staff, the volunteers, Michael. No one has been arrested; there are no immediate suspects.

She and Charlie picnic on the verge: cheese and crackers, yogurt, bananas. Charlie has taken to resisting her help, grabbing handfuls and crushing the food across his face. He wants to do it all himself. He sits in the grass and yanks at the blades. She takes a clump from his hand before he can eat it.

No. Purgative, she says. Yucky.

She gives him another piece of banana. While he is occupied, she takes the small, aluminium case from the boot of the car, and checks its contents, checks the expiry date of the drug, again. When she can get reception, she calls Lawrence, leaves him a message.

I've a huge favour to ask. You've probably heard already. Can you call me back as soon as you get this?

He will know what she needs. She sits for a few minutes with Charlie between her knees, looking at the handheld receiver. They are close, close enough. She should probably call the police and give them the coordinates in case she needs a transport van. The light is fading, but there is perhaps half an hour. She thinks for a moment about leaving Charlie in the car. What are the penalties for abandoning a bawling or sleeping infant in a locked, secluded vehicle, on a defunct road? But the decision is already made – she knows what she is going to do, and speculation is academic, a kind of decoy of the mind. She sets the baby down, attaches the papoose, and fits him snugly inside. She takes the dart case from the boot of the car, picks up the receiver, and walks into the Galt.

She takes her bearings, follows an animal track through the trees. It's cool and dim and high, like being inside a dense, overgrown cathedral. Guttering seraphs in the leaves as the last of the sunlight lifts through the canopy. Charlie gabbles away in front of her – narrating the journey, the shapes, the sights, some unknowable part of the experience. There's a slight buzz to her nerves – she should probably not be doing this. She continues on, softly along the forest floor, following the signal. Moss and drifts of burnt leaves underfoot. Fading light. The ground begins to create difficult shadows, the occasional looped root is thrown up, and there are illusory corridors between the trees, false pathways. She takes her bearings again. The smell all around is of the organic world dressing for evening: earthen, amberish. The signal is strong, but she knows, deep down, that she will not find them; and she would not be able to see well enough to aim the gun. Still, she walks for another few minutes. Now and then she stops, listens. There is immense quiet to the hardwoods but no real silence – rustles, pecking, the ripple of underground water. A bird on the cusp of night, its trills almost desperate. Charlie is quiet, too, thinking his own thoughts or mesmerised by the gloom, falling asleep. She strokes his hair. It was not a glitch in the locking device of the gate, she is sure of that, though it may never be proved. Someone let them out. Only a dozen people knew the codes, Michael among them, but it was not him. The certainty surprises her, but she is sure. Who, then? It doesn't matter now. What matters is that they are found.

At a small clearing, she stops again. The light is thin and pouring away fast. She turns and looks behind. A smirr of shadow. Bark the colour of grey and white fur. Nothing is there. It is better not to allow the imagination liberty, she knows; twilight senses will assist with any lurking conceit. She's not in any real danger. That is to say, the risks are very low. She adjusts the receiver's antenna, but she is on borrowed time. The forest is extinguishing itself all around her.

You OK? she asks Charlie, and strokes his hair again.

He mumbles something, shifts a fraction.

Me too, she says. Time to go back, I think.

She follows the path back through the trees. Dusk, the time of border patrols. She half expects to hear them somewhere close in the forest – a declarative chorus, in minor key, sounding the new territory, but there is just the great, imperfect silence of the trees. She is not lost, but when she encounters a piece of fence with an old checked shirt attached to the wire, looming like a man, her heart lurches. She stumbles a little and gasps. She is in a different part of the woods. Shit, she thinks, this is stupid; this is reckless. She takes her bearings again, starts forward, walking as quickly as she can without tripping. Can she hear voices? Men talking? It is then she begins to panic a little; not because of the dark or the wolves, but because there might be humans – and they are far more likely to do her, and the baby, harm. She is just a moving shape. A hunter might mistake her for something else.

She breaks onto the road a few hundred yards short of the car and walks up the track, a little breathless, relieved.

Look, Charlie, she says. We're back. We made it.

Speaking more to sedate her own nerves than to calm the baby. A new moon hangs above the forest. Despite the modern shine of the paintwork, the car looks as if it has been parked in this place forever. An artifact or caravan left stranded in the Galt by some older tribe. She opens the boot and puts the aluminium case inside. She takes out a bundle of blankets. It is not very cold and she has slept in far less comfortable places.

Home sweet home, she says to Charlie. What shall we do now? Have some milk? Read a story?

She changes him again by the light of the open car door – there are three clean nappies in the supply bag. She talks to him, tells him the plan, trying to convince herself at the same time.

We're going to camp. We're going to snuggle up and have a nice time. You'll see Uncle Lawrence tomorrow.

He resists being put in the car seat again, so she sits with him on her lap on the back seat, telling the same stories from the two books in the baby bag, over and over until he is asleep. She sits for a while thinking, then sleeps, upright, leaning against the door, with Charlie in the crook of her body – the rough, musty blankets drawn around them both. Outside, uniform blackness, the moon has gone and there are no stars. At 10 p.m. – which feels like the middle of the night – her phone flashes. Reception enough that a series of texts have arrived. Several more from Huib and Thomas. One from her brother, saying, *No problem. Tell me where to be and when.* One from Alexander: *Saw on the news. Hope you catch them.*

Dawn wakes her, cold legs, and stiffness through her back. The car is cool inside and the door moulding feels damp with condensation, but against her side Charlie is a little engine of heat. The windows have misted with their breathing; she wipes the nearest one, looks out at the misty citrine light filtering through the woods. Small flocks of birds break above the canopy and disperse. She reaches onto the parcel shelf for the handheld tracker and switches it on. The battery is on half charge. There's no signal. She switches to Ra's frequency, but it's the same. They have moved on.

She slides carefully from underneath Charlie, inch by inch, as if he's a bomb she doesn't want to detonate, and lays him flat on the back seat in the blankets. He stirs but doesn't wake. Several times in the night he came round, confused, and she had to coax him to slumber again. She opens the car door quietly and gets out, stretches, walks about. The air feels newly laundered, fresh and green. She eats a banana, walks about to find reception, and calls the police number on the card given to her by Sergeant

Armstrong, asks to be put through to the officer manning the enquiry. There have been no more reported sightings.

She opens the OS map fully and lays it flat on the dewy ground, charts the position from Annerdale to the point in the Galt where the signal was strongest, then continues the trajectory on into farmland and the hills beyond. Their tendency to travel in straight lines might help her to find them. There are few settlements on the other side of the Galt, mostly small lanes and B roads, until the A66, and the town of Cockermouth. After that, they will have to traverse Bassenthwaite and the North Western Fells. The rural tracts between towns will suit them, might give them cover. They will continue through Greystoke and Hutton, towards the border and Carlisle, the county's only city. At the Solway Firth, they would be forced to follow the estuary inland and cross by road, where the water narrows, or perhaps at a shallow swim. Then, Scotland.

She plots a route on the closest roads, waits again for the wandering phone reception, and texts Lawrence, gives him a rendezvous point to meet and pick up Charlie. He is already up and texts back. *There in one hour.* It's an ambitious timescale, almost heroic; if he makes it, he will not have observed the speed limit.

She hears Charlie murmuring sleepily and lifts him out of the car, hugs him, and talks quietly to him. He is clingy in the morning these days. She wipes his crusty nose, gives him some formula, and changes him. She walks him around for a few minutes – he is still unsure on his feet, likes to make stumbling rushes towards her, then collapse into her arms. She tries not to hurry him – she will need cooperation for the ordeal of the car seat. They examine some notable things on the verge – curling bracken, a puffball, which she sets smoking with her foot, some spindling toadstools.

After ten minutes, they set off along the bumpy forestry road. It's a brilliant October day, with a flawless sky. The summit of Galt Fell rises behind her, the north face of its crags dark and fissured. Charlie begins an invented song; a tuneless string of noise with emphatic peaks and murmuring rests. He's in a good mood; he likes travelling. He reminds her of Kyle that way. She begins to feel hopeful. Perhaps it will all work out. She keeps the receiver next to her on the passenger seat. The ruts begin to even out, and she picks up speed. At the forestry commission gate there's an official warning sign set up – *Danger, Please Do Not Enter*. Too late, she thinks.

The car breaks free of the trees; she turns onto the road and heads into rolling pastureland, a stretch of fallow fields surrounded by drystone walls. The receiver begins to sound. She notes the coordinates. She keeps checking the map, follows a series of single lanes, lonnings that all look the same, webbed with brambles on either side. As she passes a gate, she notices three horses gathered in the corner of a field. She stops and reverses, looks through the wooden bars. The creatures are visibly upset. Their heads nod up and down, and they push against each other and vie for wall space. One rears up, a white crescent cupping its dark eye. Something has spooked them, and not long ago. She dials Sergeant Armstrong's number, but does not get through, then drives on. When her phone rings, she pulls over.

Morning, Rachel. I was on the other line. Where are you?

Near Priest's Mill. I think I might be close to them. We need to think about getting them back to the estate, if I can dart them. The sedative lasts about two hours.

OK. Listen. We just had a call from a farmer at Mire Hall Farm. He said one of his dogs was going crazy this morning, barking and growling. When he went out to investigate, he saw one of the wolves in the field where his sheep are.

There's a pause.

And?

Her mood of levity begins to fade. She knows what's coming. Charlie is burbling louder, singing away, fighting for her attention now that she is on the phone.

Hush, hush, darling, she says, over her shoulder.

I'm afraid he fired a shot off, Sergeant Armstrong says.

What?

He fired at it.

Did he kill it? she asks.

Well, he says it's not in the field any more. He thought he hit it. How he described it is: its back end sort of dropped to the ground, but then it ran off.

Bastard, she thinks. Not even a clean shot. She wonders which is the unfortunate one: possibly a juvenile opportunistically trying its luck with the flock.

Any other information? Size? Markings?

No. I'm sorry. The farm is about four miles from Priest's Mill. Are you near there now?

I think so. Mire Hall, you said?

Yes. The farmer's name is Jim Corrigan. We're sending someone out, but I thought you'd want to know. We've told him not to go looking for it, in case it's injured.

Good. I'll go there now.

She hangs up, grips the wheel tightly for a moment. Charlie is still burbling; she looks at him in the rear-view mirror. She checks the signals from Merle and Ra's transmitters – they are still in the area, have not moved far. She won't know whether it's one of them until she finds the pack, or a body.

Mama, Charlie says.

Yes.

Mama.

Yes.

She tries to think positively; nothing has been confirmed yet. The dropped rear might have been a cowering flinch, a reaction to the noise of the shotgun. She checks the map, finds the farm, turns the car round in the next gateway, and sets off. She stops again almost immediately and calls Alexander. It's still early – the conference in Belfast will not have begun yet. He picks up straight away; everyone, it seems, is on standby. Briefly, she fills him in.

I haven't got the means, she says, if it's badly hurt. I've only got the dart case.

I know someone in practice round there, he tells her. I'll call and let her know what's happening. She's good; she'll take care of it. Are you OK, Rachel? Are you out there by yourself?

Yeah. I'm OK, just pissed off.

Have you spoken to Thomas? Sounds like you could use some help.

Not yet.

Maybe call him.

I will.

Charlie, who has been fussing for the last few minutes at her inattention, begins to wail.

Is that Charlie?

Yes. Lawrence is on his way to get him, though. I've got to go.

OK, he says. Let me know how it pans out. I'll call Justine and give her your number. Rachel, don't do anything crazy.

Like?

Just take care.

She finds the farm: a dirty whitewashed building in a courtyard of dilapidated barns and asbestos sheds. A dog is barking inside one of the bothies. Slurry and spilt straw on the cobbles as she pulls up. She half expects to see the wolf strung from a hook, but there are only farm vehicles, a rusting tractor and ancient threshing machines, an agricultural reliquary. A scruffy herd of sheep is penned inside a wooden enclosure – their fleeces trail, in need of shearing. In the window of the farmhouse is an anti-Europe poster, left over from the by-election. She leaves Charlie in the car, which he is not happy about, writhing and shouting, and knocks on the front door. She tries to dismiss her preconceptions, but the man who answers is latch-faced, suspicious, and rude, an old-school Cumbrian belligerent. At first he does not believe her – she is not the police, and he is expecting the police. How does she know about the wolf? Is she a reporter? She tells him again who she is and who she works for, that she is here to track and recapture the pack. He tuts, and frowns. She asks which direction the one in the field headed. He points to a nearby copse, standing half a mile away on the horizon.

Up there. They say not to go. Fucking thing was in on my ewes. Had one of them dangling by the neck. You should see the state of it.

Where is it? she asks. Do you want to show me?

It's in the range, he says, it's been incinerated.

Of course it has, she thinks. She holds her tongue, nods. He is angry, aggrieved. He also seems pleased. But then, he has shot an escaped wolf. He will dine out on the fact for years, retelling the story in the pub for a free pint.

Are you a reporter? he asks again.

No. I'm not.

She makes her way back to the car. Charlie is howling; his eyes screwed tightly shut and streaming wet, his fists clenched, furious at being abandoned. She opens the back door, and the wail escapes, ringing all round the courtyard. She hushes him, but does not release him from the car seat. The man is watching from the farm doorway, scowling – a crying baby in her possession, sinister proof that she is not who she says she is.

They said not to go up there, he calls. It's a big fucker.

She gets into the driver's seat and pulls away up the slippery cobbles. The petrol light has come on – less than a quarter of a tank. She heads towards the copse, finds a gateway clearing a few hundred yards from the farm, and parks the Saab. She gets Charlie out, soothes him, puts him in the last clean nappy – he is developing a rash – gives him some soft fruit and a jar of baby food. He struggles a little as she attaches him in the papoose. He is reaching the end of his tether, needs to get back to normality or there will be a huge meltdown, but she cannot let the creature suffer, if it is suffering. She takes the dart case out of the boot, and her binoculars, checks the handheld receiver, climbs the stile into the field, and walks towards the copse. The signal is strong. They are within close range, perhaps hesitating over the wounded member of the pack. If the bullet is in the hind area, the animal might have limped a mile or two, at best, and she will have to crisscross the fields and woods to find it, or get back in the car and wait for the police searchers. There's a slim chance that it could be darted, taken to the local vet, and saved, but she doubts it. If it has been hit anywhere critical, it'll be lucky to have come further than the top of the paddock. She makes her way uphill, scanning the area. The grass is empty, rutted and hummocked here and there, lost whorls of dirty wool caught on stalks. Charlie swings his legs, more content to be on the move and outside again, but it will not last.

The copse is sparse; once part of the greater Galt Forest, now a denuded cluster of trees, an island stranded in farmland. In the treetops, a few solicitous black crows caw, hopping down the branches, cautiously, peering below, then hopping back up again. It's here, she thinks. She checks the receiver again. The signal is still strong – they are very close, unseen. She moves carefully, searching for tracks in the softer earth. Single paw prints, a spattering of dark blood. She turns and looks back at the farm, which is clearly visible: a huddle of pens, low chimneys, and a bowed roof. Jim Corrigan will have watched the animal's departure, might even have fired more shots as it took off, just to be sure.

She begins to circle the copse, keeping back a reasonable distance, trying to separate the undergrowth from a camouflaged body. She makes a full circuit of the trees, moves in closer, and begins again. She sees it, thirty feet away. It is lying on its side, unmoving, head tucked down, legs straight and stiff. The paler of the male juveniles; its ruff is indistinguishable against the pale birches. It looks dead. It has only just made cover, will have limped painfully to a spot where it might be hidden.

She retreats a few paces, kneels, and sets down the aluminium case. She lifts Charlie out of the papoose and puts him in a deep swale of grass, facing back down the hill towards the forest.

Look at the pretty colours, she says. So pretty. Red and yellow and orange.

But he looks all around, at the field, at her.

Mama.

Yes.

Mama.

Yes.

She gives him another piece of fruit. While he is distracted, she steps back over to the case, opens it, and loads the gun with a dart. She picks up the case and approaches the wolf, glancing back at Charlie. She inhales, exhales, thinks of her instructions to the Chief Joseph volunteers every year. *Do everything calmly, do everything confidently.* The animal does not lift its head or stir, but its side moves very slightly, up and down, still breathing. She turns to look at Charlie again and to scan the vicinity. Only the top of his head is visible, a burr of black hair in the depression. He is secluded by the grass, like a leveret inside a form.

She continues towards the animal. There's not much blood on the ground, but the honey fur is stained along the torso and back legs. The trauma is to the side of the lower abdomen, likely always fatal – there's no time to save it, or call Alexander's colleague; even fresh, the best surgeon would have struggled. There are tread marks in the earth around the animal and flattened grass; it has been turning, probably licking itself, trying to bite out whatever is lodged. She leans over the body. The eye is open, pale and bright in the sunlight, the pupil a small dark point. The jaw is slack, the black pleats drawn back over its teeth. Just enough life left to growl – its eye rolls a fraction, the muzzle ripples upward, but it can do nothing more. She aims and fires a dart. The muscle barely flinches as it hits. She fits another dart and fires again. The drug will only hasten what is inevitable, and it is perhaps a waste, but she will not leave the animal like this. The eye closes to a black slit.

She squats down, looks properly. The coat is blended and tawny, thickening for winter. It's better that he remained unnamed, she thinks, though the loss is the same with or without. She puts her hand on the warm head, moves it down the body, parts the matted fur to find the red os of the entry wound. The feeling isn't anger, just disgust. It is a pointless waste. She takes her phone from her back pocket, and switches to the camera setting. She will leave it to the police to remove the corpse, but the image might go to work for them now and help the others, horrible and unnecessary as the death is.

The crows clamour above her. She is invading. They have guarded the prize and want it back. From the paddock she hears a thin wail. She rights herself and walks towards Charlie. He is standing up in the hollow looking at the copse, his head and shoulder unburrowed. He is trying to climb out but the sides are too steep, and he cannot get traction. For a second she expects to see Merle appear behind him, pick him up, the straps of his dungarees clasped between her teeth, and carry him off, her abandoned, beloved son. The vision is so clear that she almost panics, almost shouts. His cries carry across the field. The pasture is empty. The sky is enormous above him. The wolves are watching or have already gone. She walks quickly to him, saying his name, telling him she is coming, everything is OK. It's OK, it's OK. She kneels at the edge of the hollow and takes the packet of baby wipes out of the papoose pocket and cleans the blood off her hands. Then she lifts him up and kisses him, holds him tightly. He won't remember this, she thinks. He won't think it really happened.

*

Lawrence is waiting for them in the little car park by Priest's Mill, leaning against the bonnet of his car – a small nondescript hatch-back. Behind him, a swift-flowing river and the mossy ruin of the old bobbin mill. He waves and stands up as she pulls in. She's never been more pleased to see him. He has on slacks and a pin-stripe shirt – a semi-corporate version of the wild man who was living with her a few weeks ago. He looks healthy, is still trim. He comes over to the car and opens the driver's door for her.

Morning, he says. Thought you might be knackered, so I brought you a flask of coffee. It's gone a bit tepid. There's some nosh as well. How's Bup?

Charlie makes a noise from the back seat, pleased to see his uncle.

Sorry to get you out of work, she says. I owe you.

Hardly. Besides, if this doesn't constitute an emergency, I'm not sure what does.

One of them's dead, she says.

Oh, Christ! Sorry. How?

Shot.

Sorry, Rachel.

She shakes her head, gets out of the car.

It shouldn't have happened.

How did it happen? he asks. The news just said there was an escape.

I don't know. Looks like someone let them out.

On purpose? Why? Who?

No idea yet.

This is not strictly true. Plenty of ideas have been forming in her head in the last twenty-four hours – not all of them realistic. They unload Charlie and his paraphernalia. Lawrence lifts him high in the air and swings him about.

Ready for some fun, little one?

I'm sorry – he's out of clean nappies, he needs a bath and some cream. And he didn't sleep much – it was a bit of a strange night. Expect him to be cranky.

That's OK.

Did you get a ticket?

No.

Did you?

He shrugs.

I'll do the speed-awareness course. Hey, it was an emergency! I'll pay the fine.

Don't worry about it. Right, get on and do what you need to do. We're fine. Aren't we, Bup?

Lawrence carousels the baby in a wide arc, makes him squeal. A heavy weight seems lifted in her brother's presence; how much easier it is to think clearly, to focus. She checks the receiver for a signal, but the wolves are once again out of range. The device is losing power, needs to be charged. She calls Huib. She gives him the bad news. He's disappointed but accepting. Probably he expected it, and has encountered far worse in his time: mass slaughter, sawn-off horns – the worst poaching imaginable.

I'm going to send through a picture, she says. Get it to the media as soon as possible. It'll gain some sympathy.

OK, good idea. Listen, I'm here with Thomas. We're going to come and meet you and broaden the search. Where are you now?

Priest's Mill. But I won't be staying here. I know where they are, roughly. They'll be almost to the northwest foothills.

OK, he says.

He repeats the location to Thomas. There's a pause. She can hear them talking on the other end of the line.

OK, Rachel. We need to find a good place nearby and get

clearance. Thomas says with luck we'll be with you in the next twenty-five minutes.

What? Twenty-five minutes?

Yes, about that, Huib says. We have to get clearance and permission to land – it can't be too close to any structures. I'll call you back once we're up with a rendezvous.

She realises then, not without a small thrill, that they are coming in the helicopter. Thomas Pennington has the means to traverse the entire county privately, by air.

OK, she says. Bring some more darts.

Yes, we are. We got lucky with the weather, Rachel. I think we'll find them very quickly now.

She hangs up. She does not know about luck; the day has issued none so far. She looks up at the sky. A shale-blue expanse, light cloud cover, feathered cirrus. It is a beautiful window between the storms. Even the climate favours the Earl when he needs it to, she thinks. Now he is paying attention of course, now there's reason, excitement. But she must quash the bitterness. Whatever advantages are at their disposal must be accepted, for the sake of the pack.

Got a plan? Lawrence asks, when she comes back over.

Yeah. You're not going to believe it, she says.

She hurriedly eats the pastries her brother has brought and finishes the flask of lukewarm coffee. Ten minutes later, Huib calls back. The sound of the helicopter almost drowns him out, a rhythmic thrumming, the whine of the rotor; they are already airborne or about to take off.

Go to Arthur's Seat, he shouts at her, on the Ullswater road. Thomas says the field beside the monument. Can you hear me, Rachel?

Yes, just about.

She checks the map book – the round table is about ten miles away. She needs petrol, but will make it. She kisses Charlie good-bye, thanks her brother again, and is about to get in the car when he stops her.

Wait, hold up. Won't it be better to leave your car here? I'll drive you. I know the place he means.

There's no time to argue and no good reason. Nor, if she's honest, does she want to be parted from her family just yet. Lawrence quickly transfers the baby seat. She takes what equipment she needs from the boot of the Saab and they start out. Her brother drives fast, but not dangerously, through St John's Vale, past the small greenish mere, soupy with reeds, to the broadland before the northern fells. There is little traffic on the roads, only a few late-season tourists. Lawrence overtakes a caravan, accelerating with determination, pulling back in and reducing speed.

Is he asleep back there? he asks.

Yes, spark out. Poor thing, he's really tired.

I bet.

I had to take him with me.

I know. Sorry I wasn't around. I was in a deposition all day.

How are you? she asks.

I'm alright. Good days, bad days.

You look well.

Thanks. Rachel, don't worry; he'll be safe with me.

I know that.

As her brother drives, she texts the picture of the dead wolf to Sergeant Armstrong, and to Alexander. *Thanks for Justine's number. No joy.* She looks out at the landscape, moors burnished along the base of the mountains, furze, sedge-coloured fields. They are out there, somewhere, and moving fast. As they near Arthur's

Seat, she checks the sky for the Gazelle coming in to land, but there's only empty drifting blue.

Lawrence parks near the monument. They get out, leaving Charlie asleep in the back. The landing site is not so much a field as a slightly raised plateau of common land, covered with flocks of rush and grass. From the south, they hear it coming. The sound bends around the nearby fells, makes locating the helicopter difficult. She sees it down the valley, a dark blue insect suspended between the brown withers of the mountains, ominous-looking, dropping altitude slowly. The helicopter circles, begins its descent towards the ground. The noise of the engine and the blades fills the valley. A hundred feet from the ground, the grass begins to flutter, then to billow in the strong wash, and is crushed flat as the craft puts down. The turbulence tugs at Rachel's clothes.

Charlie's going to wake up and freak out, she shouts to Lawrence.

He nods.

Maybe I should go now?

I think so.

He gives her a quick hug, releases her.

Take care of him.

I will! We'll watch you go up from down the road. Good luck! It'll be alright.

He makes his way to the car, gets in, and drives back along the road. She cannot see her son. She suddenly feels unwilling to leave, but she has no choice now. The helicopter door opens, and Huib beckons to her. The blades have not been cut; the wind coming from the machine is extraordinary. Her clothes flap and twist as she approaches. She bends low and runs towards the helicopter. Huib takes the case and the tracker from her, and she climbs in. The door is shut and secured. Inside, the racket is only slightly milder. The body of the craft judders, seems too lightweight, too frail for the power of the rotor. Huib puts his thumb up. She takes a seat and fastens the belt. He passes her headphones with a microphone attached. She fits them and hears Thomas talking, saying, *Hello, Rachel, glad you could join us*, and she realises, with a feeling of dread, that he is piloting. Sylvia is sitting next to him up front. She turns, reaches back, and takes hold of Rachel's wrist, smiles, mouths something. Why is she here? Rachel wonders. All fools together? On the headphones, Huib is talking about the signal, the last reading, but her heart is flurrying and she cannot concentrate. She is not afraid of flying. But this feels like madness, an event choreographed to put an end to it all, to conclude the entire, year-long fiasco. She's never going to see her son again. She will never see him grow up or be able to tell him anything that matters – what he meant to her, who his father is, that he was a gift, the greatest of all gifts, and she could hardly believe he was hers.

She closes her eyes. The pitch and roar increase. There's a swinging sensation. When she looks, the helicopter has lifted off, is nodding left and right, tilting hard to the side, and gaining altitude. The ground slides away beneath them at a sharp angle. She feels incredibly sad for a moment, almost resigned. *Everything tends towards iron.* They lift up, up. The monument grows smaller – the outline of the architectural site appears, a deep barrow in the earth. Down on the road, she sees her brother, holding the baby and waving. Please, she thinks, love him like I do, and then they are gone, and the Gazelle is moving swiftly across the landscape. The moorland blurs. A slow version of the blades is visible through the glass roof, an illusion created by speed. They

pass along the valley, the space melting away as if it were nothing, fields and upland enclosures, three white wind turbines on
a sacrificed hill, and the river like silver rope, unwinding. She
looks down. Over a low summit is a hidden ghyll, running from a
mountain tarn, the waterfall deeply channelled, wound-like. The
upper crags of the fells draw level, weeping with grey and blue
scree. And higher, they are above the peaks; there are contours
that she has never seen before – that very few have or ever will – a
land suddenly revealed, as if in a dream.

The geography of the northwest mountains makes it impossible
to find them on the first day. The peaks veer into the sky and
must be given a wide berth. The helicopter cannot pass too closely
in the tight glacial valleys. Thomas obeys the regulations; he is
not an unsafe pilot, in fact he is skilled, and she thinks again, It
wasn't him who crashed, though the stigma has been with him
for over a decade. Occasionally, the transmitters' signals are
faintly read, then disappear. They are following the route, more
or less, that Rachel predicted. The helicopter circles and tracks
back, circles and tracks back, looping one valley, then the next.
She scans the ground for movement, a migrating formation.
The search method is efficient, but they will have to get closer to
the ground if there's any chance of tranquillising them. She has
tracked in planes several times before and knows the animals are
very good at evading pursuit, chicaning, doubling back, even on
open ground. Space in the Gazelle is limited – they will not be
able to transport the bodies back to Annerdale and it would be
too dangerous to try. She imagines wolves tumbling from the sky,
like some kind of Roman myth. But there is a ground unit on
standby, she learns from Huib – a private company. The police

and the mountain rescue centres are also ready to assist.

After an hour she gets used to the tipping and shuddering sensation of the helicopter, the intermittent rocks of turbulence. Thomas and Sylvia converse calmly, about the fast-acting protection grip Metcalfe is trying to arrange. There are problems on the English side of the border – no real precedent has been set; the law is antiquated, murky. Another sighting is called into the police, near Mungrisdale, which seems improbable – too far east. They follow the lead anyway, flying around the vast hulk of Saddleback, and over the windswept brown moors, not finding them. They pass lower, set a herd of wild fell ponies galloping, slaloming through the gorse, their ragged tails trailing behind them. Thomas communicates regularly with air-traffic control, but other than one medi-vac heading from Whitehaven to the brain-injury centre in Newcastle, the skies above the District are clear. Another hour, two. The gauge reads low, and they land at Cockermouth heliport to refuel. At the hub, several private and military helicopters are parked. The paperwork is completed; they wait for permission to take off, their business no more important than anyone else's.

The search resumes, but clouds begin to flow in; the air becomes choppier, the ride uncomfortable. There are jolts and sudden drops. Their good fortune with the weather is running out. The signals are picked up again above a quiet valley west of Lorwood, but a blanket of scrub and trees obscures the pack. Rachel's legs feel numb from the vibrations through the seat; she wishes she were on land again.

They abort the search. The Earl sets down at the Sharrow Bay Hotel on Ullswater, where there is a helipad for its more salubrious guests. They have been booked in for the evening. They might be millionaire tourists, Rachel thinks, putting down for a luxury weekend in Romantic country, not trackers, conservationists. In her lake-view room, she takes a long hot shower, washes her underwear, and lies down for an hour before dinner. She is extremely tired, but cannot sleep. The noise of the rotor echoes demonically in her skull. She can still see the fells rolling below. She thinks about Charlie, what he is eating and whether Lawrence will remember to find the toy lion before bed – she texts him, *Call you later; don't forget Roary.* She looks at the picture of the dead wolf. Then she thinks about Left Paw, whose collar was posted back to the Reservation, and whose body they never found. The Chief Joseph pack will soon be heading north, too. She thinks again about phoning Kyle. *You have a son.* The thought is like a splinter. Can she really go on not telling him? She pictures Charlie as a man, how she imagines he might look. He is tall, his hair is long and dark. His quarter heritage.

Dinner is a contrite affair. No one is in the mood to savour or celebrate, though Thomas remains upbeat.

Do leave the bottle, he tells the sommelier, and don't worry, we aren't in need of your usual superb level of attendance this evening.

A polite euphemism that is interpreted and obeyed; they are mostly left alone during the meal. No doubt there is discreet speculation in the kitchens – they are an odd group. Huib is dressed in shorts and a flannel shirt, as usual, though the dress code at the Sharrow Bay is deeply formal. Perhaps they think him an eccentric African millionaire. Rachel's day-old, slept-in clothing is rumpled; the Earl and his daughter both look passable, blazered, eternally prepared. They all know who Thomas Pennington is, she thinks, and will surely be following the events.

Is there any news about the gate? she asks.

We're still trying to figure that out, Thomas says. The company is looking at the computer system. It might just be one of those things, I'm afraid. A technological blip.

A blip, Rachel thinks. His tone is casual and oddly accepting. He made a very good case for the unassailable security of the project to her in the beginning, she recalls, which she herself has often repeated. Now that they are not directly engaged with the search, she wants some answers. She does not want to be fobbed off.

So nobody has claimed responsibility? Nobody has a theory?

No, Huib says. If it was a group or a single activist, they're keeping schtum.

What about this loon, this Nigh, who's been in touch? Thomas asks, sipping his wine. He sounds like a good candidate, doesn't he?

So Thomas has stayed up to date on the project and read the meeting notes, she thinks.

It's doubtful, she says. We never thought of him as a serious threat. He seems too chaotic.

Well, sometimes the chaotic characters are the most surprising and dangerous, Thomas suggests. Lord knows, I see enough of them in the House, always upsetting the apple cart, but they can be very effective.

There's also the guy in the mask, Huib suggests. Remember him? We never really figured that one out, did we?

Maybe, she says.

She is not convinced, not by any of the obvious suspects.

Halfway through dinner, Thomas excuses himself to speak

with the environment minister – the call he has been waiting for all afternoon. He is gone half an hour. The jus on his plate congeals, but none of the waiting staff dare remove his plate.

It is good to see you both again, Sylvia says, warmly. I'm just really sorry about the circumstances. And I'm so sorry we lost one. It's absolutely dreadful. Sometimes I really dislike this county. People can be very backward.

It is the first negative thing Rachel has ever heard her say about Cumbria. The apology sounds so heartfelt and sincere it is as if she herself committed the crime, as if she is Cumbria, or its representative. She seems older and more knowing from her months in the city: grit in the pearl. Her hair has been cut stylishly: a kind of sharp, bevelled bob.

It's good of you to come back, Syl, Huib says.

Daddy asked me to come home and help, she explains, so of course I did. Never mind exams. I do miss the project. Some days I'd love to jack in the law and work with you both again.

A nice sentiment, but there may be no more project, Rachel thinks. She does not say it. There's no point in taking her mood out on Sylvia.

Let's order pudding. Daddy won't mind. He might be ages anyway. David Uttley is a bit of a gas-bag, I've heard.

The menus reappear. Rachel looks out of the dining-room windows. The lake is dark but shining under the evening sky, a looser version of what lies above. Night will offer some reprieve. She suspects they will continue to travel under the cover of darkness, like a raiding party, responding to the new level of human activity encountered since leaving the estate. They might even clear the northwest range and head for the border by morning. The outer district offers only a partially adequate environment;

they will certainly not linger, or return to Annerdale. They will sense the greater uplands to the north, and will keep moving until they find the best territory.

When Thomas returns, he is visibly annoyed, muttering about the obduracy and lack of vision possessed by the environment minister, who has failed to give assurances on temporary protected status.

Well, that was a waste of time. He really is the most ludicrous appointment Mellor's made. Whoever heard of an environment minister from Solihull! Bloody ignoramus. I'll talk to Mell in the morning.

Sylvia attempts to mediate and calm her father, aware, perhaps, that he is sounding like a snob. Notes of petulance and belligerence in his voice – he is not used to being thwarted.

I checked on this, Daddy. They don't fall under the Endangered Species Act. They're simply not listed and will just fall between stools. It means they might not need or get authorisation because it wasn't a deliberate re-wilding.

A wolf between stools, Thomas exclaims. Preposterous!

He takes a sip of wine, then unfolds his napkin, composes himself.

Hopefully it'll be moot, anyway. Douglas will play ball. The Scots have a new environmental policy to uphold – they can't be seen to be conservative on this. No, don't worry, darling. The Highland estate owners are so worried about losing their subsidies, they'll do as they're told. There won't be any more shootings, I promise.

That's quite a difficult promise to make, Rachel says quietly.

Thomas helps himself to another large glass of red wine, adjusts the napkin across his lap, takes up his silverware, and tidily cuts the cold piece of meat.

Well, Rachel, you know better than I how the money works. You've already published a splendidly compelling paper on cull savings and tourist revenue for a potential reintroduction in Scotland, haven't you?

He glances at her and smiles. Rachel sets down her glass.

That article's ten years old.

Yes, but not much has really changed. Except that Westminster can't prevent anything, and now our free Caledonian cousins may actually have to put the theory into practice.

She frowns, says nothing, annoyed to have her work used as part of his presumptuous political argument.

So, what's your best guess, then? he asks her.

About what?

About our refugees seeking asylum in the newest European nation. Will they continue north, as planned, over the border?

She looks at him for a moment. *As planned*, she thinks. By who? He is forking up the veal, eating with relish. He is not concerned – in fact, he seems very sure of himself, speaking as if the damage control is effortless, assessing the odds. Real politic. She wants to take out her phone, put it on his plate, so he can see the picture of the carcass in the grass, the bullet hole. He glances up. She catches his eye.

Is that what you're gambling on? she asks.

Is it a gamble?

They'll go to Scotland, she says, stonily. Unless we catch them. Or they're killed.

He nods, and continues to eat.

Excellent.

In that moment she hates him. His calculation. His certainty, which is almost childish. And in that moment she is also sure that it was he who opened the gate. Though he was elsewhere, though he may never have keyed in the code; he was the one. He has not once mentioned recapture, reinstallation of the pack, for all the expensive aerial pursuit. The worthy investment, the millions spent building a trophic Eden, it is simply another grand scheme that he can choose to dismantle again, if he so wishes. There is a bigger, more exciting game – testing beyond the cage, wolves in the real world. You godly fuck, she thinks, you absolute maniac, this is what you wanted all along. She cannot bear to look at him. She looks instead at her dessert – created by the best chef in the best restaurant in the North. It all feels like a mockery. Her appetite has gone. The others continue with their meal, oblivious. Are they really so blind? she wonders. Sylvia, protecting her father, complicit in his scheme by virtue of her institutionalisation. Huib is reconciled, co-opted, too white of heart to suspect anything nefarious. She begins to feels sick. There is a conspiracy around the table, and they don't even realise they are taking part. Even she is implicated. Thomas knows she won't walk away, not now, not while the wolves are out and in danger, which amounts to capitulation. She stands, undramatically, and lays her napkin over her food.

Excuse me. I have to ring my brother.

The next morning, rain. The surface of the lake is stippled; its reflections hover and break apart. They stand in the lounge after breakfast, drinking coffee, looking out at the grey sky. On the helipad, the bowed rotor blades of the helicopter drip. Huib liaises with the police, checks the weather app, sits cross-legged, and waits for the cue – less a stooge than a sophist. Sylvia reads on her iPad in a plush armchair by the fire. She tracks through the papers and the blogs – there is a huge public outcry over the dead wolf; the picture is being widely circulated. So like the English, Rachel thinks: object, ignore, and then, late in the day, after a tragedy, rally. She has a strong urge to leave the hotel, get a taxi to her car, and continue with the search alone. At least she would feel useful, authentic, perhaps less like she had been played.

Thomas makes a series of private phone calls, and afterwards seems pleased, more humble than the previous evening, though his humility is in all likelihood due to success, things going his way. The desire to take him aside and accuse him has faded overnight. She can prove nothing; will probably never be able to prove anything. She will not give him the satisfaction of sounding like a paranoid hysteric. She speaks with Lawrence, and then with Charlie, who recognises her voice and exclaims loudly, but doesn't understand that she is not there in the room. He begins to cry, and she feels it like a barb in the chest. She speaks with Alexander, who is en route back from the conference, sitting in the airport waiting for a flight himself.

I've been thinking, she says. Maybe we can go on holiday.

On holiday?

Yes. I mean, all of us. Chloe and Charlie, too. Maybe even Lawrence. Can we?

It is a strange request out of the blue, and a strange time to be making it.

Are you alright? he asks.

Yeah.

She isn't, of course. She is weary, though she slept surprisingly well in the plush bed and without Charlie to attend to; she did not lie awake grinding over everything in the small hours, as she feared she might. When she woke, there was a sense of powerlessness, of it all being over. The Annerdale pack. The cottage in the woods. She got up, brushed her teeth, and sat on the bed, watching the sun rise and the rain on the lake, feeling the light of day translate notions of what is right and wrong – or expand those notions.

By mid-afternoon, the weather clears – breaks appear in the clouds and hard, wet sunlight glints through. There is a moderate wind, not ideal but not prohibitive for flight. They prepare to leave. In the interim there have been two more sightings, both in the farmland between Aspatria and Wigton. A woman riding on a bridleway, whose horse bolted with her clinging on to it, and a child on a school bus, disbelieved by everyone at first, the boyish fantasy of seeing White Fang running alongside. It means they have left the Lake District national park and are nearing the metropolis, with its heavy traffic and intersections. If they keep to the salt marsh and estuary belt to the north of the city, they will be OK, she thinks.

They walk through Sharrow's lakeside gardens to the Gazelle. The last thing she wants is to be flown anywhere by Thomas Pennington, but she gives herself over to his methods. What else can she do? Her duty is to the pack. It is galling, and she dislikes herself for the surrender. But what matters, matters by degrees. That they make it past the city of Carlisle. That they are not vilified for their instincts and appetites. That Scotland, if it is the beacon of progression that Thomas challenges it to be, does the right thing.

There is no careful plan to get them back; she knows that now. She has the case of darts in her hand, but it's redundant. She will not get the chance to sedate them, she's sure of that, even if they are found. From the position of a deity, she will simply bear witness to their true, illegal release. She follows the others out to the helicopter, favourite words of Binny's trumpeting in her head: *It's easier to get forgiveness than permission, my girl.* Her mother's excuse for doing as she pleased, living as she pleased, selfishly, perhaps better than most.

There's a provisional meeting scheduled later in Edinburgh, Thomas tells them, should it be necessary. She knows what the arguments will be, what Thomas is currently negotiating with his Scottish peers and what she, too, will be required to say, expertly, in a roomful of law-makers. That study, conservation, and protection in the natural habitat are of utmost benefit to the public. That wolves are not only economically beneficial, but environmentally curative. That in the far reaches there are tracts of suitable land and Scotland should embrace them, cherish them. The truth will not be hard to speak. If they are harmed, she thinks, in between, anywhere, she will find a way of making Thomas Pennington suffer for the heedless experiment. No one is invulnerable. Not even him. But such a thing is fantasy, she knows.

The flight is uncomfortably bumpy, the helicopter lurches and swings in the stiff wind. Her anger keeps her focused and unafraid. They sweep over northern Cumbria, leaving the swathed massifs of the Lake District behind them. Villages. Small towns. There are passable rural corridors. They can slip through; she has confidence. The Solway shines on the horizon, and then is under them, patched by mudflats and sand. They are in range of Carlisle airport. The Gazelle flies lower than it should – she can see wading birds and geese, rivulets as water floods into and out of the neck of the former United Kingdom. Huib holds up the handheld receiver, talks to Thomas on the headset. She, too, has a signal on her device.

They find them a few minutes later, passing over the inter-mediate lands, the debatable lands as they once were. They are running over open moorland, the surviving five, driven hard by the noise of the helicopter. Ra leads them. She watches them run. She is rusty at targeting on the move, but could almost certainly tranquillise the breeding pair, were Thomas to hold the aircraft steadier. Instead, she watches and says nothing. They run in for-mation, arrow-shaped, the three juveniles keeping pace beauti-fully, strong now, and sleek. The helicopter flies above and then alongside them, and the animals disperse, each lighting out on an averse route. Separated, they run on across the moor, eyes ahead, grey fire across the border. There's no meridian to mark the inter-national crossing, no checkpoint, for all the rhetoric of the past year, just a smattering of whin and rowan, barren slopes and cut-tings. The unspectacular lowlands stretch ahead, taupe and tan, and just below the helicopter, painted on the gable of a lone croft dwelling, in welcome or defiance, is a blue and white Saltire. The helicopter banks east, towards the capital.

*

It ends, as conflicts and dreams do, in a government committee room. The Earl lands at Edinburgh airport, and they are driven through the tall, sooted city to Holyrood. The new parliament building glints at the bottom of the Royal Mile, pale and angular, wharfs of glass and stylised windows jutting: a modernist vision for a modern state. Rachel takes a phone call from the Dumfries and Galloway police chief before entering the building – the woman assures her the animals will be monitored and protected throughout the Borders, and that there is much public support.

Rachel thanks her. The words are reassuring but there will be other challenges. For all the reforms, and the possible protection, there are still powerful, absentee estate owners to contend with, sheiks and millionaires residing abroad whose compliance with the law is loose at best, who do not care about fines or penalties.

The others are waiting for her by the main public entrance. The views from inside Holyrood are spectacular – mountains, and the gothic pinnacles of the city. Huib and Sylvia take a seat on the benches nearby; Rachel and Thomas will have twenty minutes to address the situation, and find a solution. They are late and are ushered through to a light, pine-clad room. Around the table: representatives from the National and John Muir Trusts, the Forestry Commission, and the National Farmers' Association. Sitting at the head, leafing through papers and ignoring everyone, the Scottish Prime Minister, Caleb Douglas, and next to him his new environment minister. Douglas glances up.

Evening, Thomas.

Hello, Caleb. I do appreciate you seeing us at short notice.

The Prime Minister looks down again at his sheaf of papers.

Needs must. This is a live issue, unfortunately.

Rachel and Thomas take their seats. Introductions are quickly made. Caleb Douglas barely looks at her when her name is given, though he reaches across the table and pours her a glass of water from a decanter. He is a round-faced, heavy-chinned man with thinning hair, has the look of a retired boxer, once solidly built, now running to fat. He is curt, wastes no words, and she recognises shades of the hard-line bully from newspaper reports, *The Fife Fighter*.

Right, then. We should get on, should we not?

She has borrowed Sylvia's laptop, has accessed her own data

and files, and has prepared her best case at very short notice. There is no time for PowerPoint; she does not want to waste time setting everything up. Instead, she simply speaks. There is a particular site that many ecologists believe suitable for a wolf population, she explains, an 'abandoned area' where farming has failed, European subsidies have been stopped, and re-wilding is possible. From Rannoch, north of Loch Lomond, west of Ben Nevis, to the sea. The wolves may find their own way there, if left alone, she suggests, or could be sedated and transferred. This and other areas in the Highlands could support three or four packs. She outlines the rest of the argument hastily. The Highland deer population is once again out of control. There's sickness; the herds are damaging the environment, and are proving expensive to cull. She wishes she'd had another day to prepare. There's an excellent Romanian model for eco-tourism she could have used, demonstrating high-revenue potential, but she does not have the figures to hand.

She speaks for barely three minutes. The only protest, from the Farmers' Association representative, who says he cannot allow a new predator to ruin the old, cherished industries, is quashed by Douglas.

Stop your twittering, man, and let her finish. And you really should update your definition of ruin. The state of your hillsides after years of little yellow teeth bloody mowing them!

A bully indeed. After allowing Rachel another minute or so, and glancing at his watch, he himself interrupts.

This is clearly not an ideal situation, he remarks.

He glances around the table.

I take it the rest of you gentlemen have no objections to what Miss Caine is saying? Good. Simon, why don't you give us a brief rundown of everything and tell us the plan.

He gestures towards the environment minister, a young man barely in his thirties, who stands.

No need for formalities, Simon, let's get on.

The minister sits again and efficiently speeds through his agenda. Recent polls on the reintroduction of larger species have been favourable, in towns as well as in the countryside. There will be a public consultation, but for now a quick-acting environmental grip is being granted, and there will be a three-year authorised study, the same as for the escaped Tay beavers. Long-term protected status may follow. It is just as Thomas predicted. Rachel exhales quietly, feels her shoulders untense. The pack has been granted amnesty, which is not to say she wholly trusts Caleb Douglas. He clearly has strong opinions, suited to her needs or otherwise, and seems iron-fisted with his colleagues. The long, sometimes dirty fight for independence has certainly not made him popular. Now he must run his country, overseeing huge legal battles for fuel revenue, renegotiated European status, and a struggling economy. Wolves are not high on the agenda. Thomas is, of course, delighted.

This is really very sporting of you, Caleb. And very generous. A new era for Scottish ecology, I'd say. I hope we can follow your example one day.

The Prime Minister is in his own house; he is done with the Lords, the ethos of unelected exclusivity, and evidently has little time for fey earls – their simper or their gratitude. He stands up, gathers his documents together.

I think we'll leave the sports to you, Thomas. I never did see the appeal of wiping fox blood all over the faces of gay little princes. More notice next time, if you please.

Thomas smiles, enjoying the spar, or seeming to, though there is a remarkable degree of rudeness to it. The subtext is clear – *We'll take your carelessly lost wolves and mop up your English mess.* The Earl of Annerdale is being rendered club-less by a parvenu head of state, which is in some way satisfying, but Rachel doubts the old networks are truly gone. Thomas' committee meetings over the border during the last year, his friends in the lodges and the banks; she would not be surprised if he had sounded out the venture, if not arranged with a select few for the extradition of his wild pets. What are a few high-ranking insults in the face of his scheme's success? Of course he is smiling. She wants out from under him, as soon as possible.

The meeting is concluded. Caleb Douglas bids no one farewell as he leaves the room. Another meeting, perhaps several, before he can head home. The casualness of the outcome is surprising to her. There are no handshakes. No signature of transferred ownership has been required, though there will be paperwork, stamps, scheduled legislature, she knows, wilderness being as bureaucratic as anywhere else. The Trust representatives nod goodbye and file out. She closes the laptop and stands while Thomas waits, all smiles, but the environment minister stops her as she is leaving the room.

Ms Caine, if you've got a minute, can I have a word?

Before leaving Holyrood, she looks in on the main debating chamber – a cyclone of wood and glass, acres of air above the bisected seats. There is something medieval about it, too, redolent of cruick barns and meeting houses. She is impressed, far more than she thought she would be. The place did not exist when she was a child, is less than twenty years old, but in that time much has changed, the fabric of British politics, state definitions. It can be done, she thinks, if people want it badly enough, if they are tired, and hopeful. She stalls, wanders the hallway, reads a notice about the architect – a Catalan, controversially chosen at the time, though widely celebrated now. The result for the pack is good, as good as it can be, better even than their original situation, and yet she still feels conflicted, and as if she has been beaten. The others are waiting for her outside. It's dark, but sails of light arc from the parliament building. Huib and Sylvia are chatting excitedly with Thomas; they are all laughing. They clap as she approaches.

Superbly handled, Rachel, Thomas says, putting a hand on her back. And good that you had a private word with Simon. No doubt he wants you as chief advisor up here.

She does not fill him in on the private conversation she has just had, but he is not widely off the mark and she must think carefully about the proposal.

I was just saying to Huib, Thomas continues, that you and he mustn't worry about jobs and pay and accommodation or any such thing. This is absolutely unforeseen. We won't be seeing you out in the cold. You've both done a terrific job.

She nods and says nothing.

Shall we go?

Thomas leads the way across the grounds.

I've got a taxi booked to take us back to the airport. Honor's reserved rooms in the Sheridan. We'll get an early start tomorrow, but tonight we should celebrate!

She remains quiet on the walk to the rank while the others discuss the events.

This will suit Douglas very nicely, Thomas says. A new icon for a new nation. I wouldn't be surprised if the wolf ends up on the Scottish flag.

Sylvia laughs.

I'm glad they've gone to a good home. I think Mummy would have been so happy.

She would. I am, too, Soo-Bear. Very happy.

He kisses his daughter and opens the taxi door for her – Sylvia slides in. Their etiquette is flawless, as ever. Thomas Pennington is unfathomable, Rachel decides. He is not mad. Such a persona is a front that works well in the southern offices, and always will. The ebullient, boyish elite, which is anything but harmless, and masks, in fact, something very dangerous. He fits his position, or the position has created him to suit. But what is at the core, she cannot tell. Nothing, perhaps, a vacancy. Or the most ardent conviction – *I am right, therefore I have the right.* He is subject to different laws of gravity, that's all. No doubt she will be offered a generous settlement, a payoff. Her silence radiates dissatisfaction, and she feels sorry for Huib, though he seems in no way worried. Zen acceptance; he will move on to another job, thinking it fortuitous and an adventure, which, by virtue of his temperament, it will be. As she is getting into the taxi, Thomas leans towards her, and speaks softly, with the sincerity of the damned.

It's been super working with you on this, a privilege. I care very much about what happens to them, Rachel. That's really all I've ever cared about. I hope you can see that.

She shakes her head.

I can see exactly what's happened.

It is not a threat, and there's nothing more she can say. No doubt he believes what he says, but his tone is so equitable that she wants to hit him. Or is he to be congratulated? She wonders. Has he achieved something unarguably worthwhile, no matter the means? No other individual in the country was in a position to do what he has done. He is an accelerant in the world. An environmentalist, a master tactician, and a spoilt child. She gets into the taxi, and he closes the door behind her.

They drive through the tall, steepled city, the castle spot-lit and looming above, the new trams sounding their bells. After a few minutes, she tells them to let her out, that she would prefer to get the train home tonight. It sounds churlish, but she has the excuse of needing to get back to Charlie. She does want to see the baby, but she also wants to sit alone, quietly, in a carriage, with the blacked-out landscape flushing by, and think – or not have to think. Huib offers to accompany her, his comrade spirit undented by her mood, but she tells him, no, stay, enjoy the evening and the flight tomorrow. The taxi detours and drops her at Waverley station.

Keep your train receipt, Thomas tells her as she gets out.

The next train to Penrith is not for an hour; she has just missed the previous one. She finds a bench at the far end of the platform, away from the travelling throngs. She calls Lawrence and lets him know what has happened, what time she will be back, and that she will be coming north again the next day. A light aircraft has been arranged for her to monitor the progress of the wolves as they make their way up the country, and then she will be required to liaise with various local groups, smooth the way for Scotland's new hunter. The contract offered is temporary, with moderate government pay, but suitable, more in keeping with what she is used to earning, and she is not yet ready to let them go. First she must pick up her car, and her son, speak to her brother and to Alexander, explain what she has to do.

The station rattles and clanks with trains arriving and departing; the tannoy announces which are late, or boarding, or cancelled. Pigeons coo from the roof, flurrying between wrought-iron rafters, swapping positions between the metal spikes designed to deter them. She stares at the ground. A pile of feathers near the bench where a hawk has been at work. Sweet wrappers, crushed cans, the grey boles of chewing gum trodden flat. The wind on the platform is blissfully cold, and bears the consoling thought of winter, an end, or a beginning. She takes out her phone and dials the number of the office at Chief Joseph.

*

After takeoff, when the seatbelt sign has been extinguished, she unbuckles herself and Charlie and walks him down the aisle, past all the passengers he has offended with his yelling for the last fifteen minutes. He has stopped screaming and thrashing, his ears probably having equalised, but his cheeks are still flushed and damp. She tries not to feel impatient. It will be a long flight in a confined space, shortcutting over the polar cap, but still another nine hours to endure. She'll need to keep him occupied as much as possible, or try to get him to sleep. The plane tilts as it banks west. He parades gamely on down the aisle, stopping to look at various passengers, a large man already snoring, head back, a girl with a brightly tattooed arm. Rachel steers him onward, thinking about the chalky little pills Binny used to give her when they were driving any great distance. *To stop you being sick*, her mother always said, though Rachel was never travel-sick. The thought does appeal now, of doping her son. Perhaps it's cruel to subject a fourteen-month-old to such physical discomforts and tedium, she thinks, but the same might be said of the terms of existence.

A steward makes his way towards them and smiles as he passes by, shaking his head.

You were the one making all that noise, were you?

Charlie looks up at the man, all innocence and big dark eyes, and continues walking unsteadily towards the back of the plane.

We don't care, do we? Rachel says. We're doing our own thing.

If Binny taught her anything, it was exactly that. Don't be cowed. Live singularly, and without regret. Not always the best creed, but maybe now Rachel can put it to good use. It's going to be a very difficult, very strange visit. What will Kyle say when he sees her, and – more to the point – when he sees Charlie and learns who he is? Her phone call explained very little, just that she was coming with some friends to visit the Reservation and to say hi. He could be struck dumb. He may never forgive her. She would not blame him.

Well, he's probably not going to stove your head in, Alexander had assured her at the airport when he dropped them off. He doesn't sound the type.

I know. But still.

Hey, don't worry. Men love children. The more the better, scattered all round the world.

Oh shut up, she'd said, pushing him gently.

He'd grinned and kissed her, then leant down and kissed Charlie.

Go on, then. You get to board on the plane first with this one, you know. See you in a week.

Don't forget to do your visas online, she reminds him, and tell Chloe to bring some warm gear – it'll get very cold. I'll pick you up in Spokane. OK?

OK. Hey, Kyle might stove my head in. Men love that possessive stuff, too.

She'd laughed and wheeled her bag to the front of the security check, Charlie heavy on her hip.

Maybe.

She walks Charlie to the back of the plane, where he takes extreme interest in the handles of the cabin storage drawers, trying to open them one by one. She disengages him, wends him round the toilets, and down the other aisle. He stops to yank on the trailing wire of someone's headphones, drawn to pull-able things with almost narcotic intensity.

Nope, she says, untangling his hands, and to the lady whose film has suddenly gone silent, says, Sorry about that, he's a little monkey.

Oh, no, the woman says. He's a little angel.

The great debate, Rachel thinks, I'll go with monkey. Charlie steps forward. She is glad she's travelling ahead of Alexander; she owes Kyle that much, the courtesy of private explanation and some time alone with his son. She will plan what to say on the flight. Or maybe she won't. The subject is not going to be gentle on the palate: human beings are strong meat. Maybe she'll arrive at the centre and present the baby as a given, a thing that simply is, a boon – which he is. Perhaps there won't be too much shock. The world is used to reproduction, after all. Nothing seems to stop it – not war, not science, not humanity's own incalculable stupidity.

Lawrence's advice was just that – hold Charlie up, introduce him, and don't worry about the rest. Her brother's advice is usually simply put these days, often revolving around truth, exposing the root, squeezing out the poison. Fear of re-entering the labyrinth of self-deception, perhaps, and getting sick again. He did not want to come on the American trip, though she asked him several times, assured him there was no intrusion: he would be one of the gang.

No, no, you guys need to do this by yourselves, he'd said.

Meaning, perhaps, that he needs to do things by himself now, be confident of his borders again. He needs not to rely on her so much, not to call her drunk from the hillside above Kendal, crying, lamenting his past, his mistakes, all that has been lost: as far as she knows, his sole insobriety since he gave it all up. She did not mind the late-night call, was glad there was nothing worse happening; it was simply a boozy evening with work colleagues that had gone too far and knocked out a section of his carefully built scaffolding. At the end of the conversation, he'd told her that without her he would not have made it, would have given in.

Lawrence, she said, you're forgetting who you are. What would we have done without you, you dope?

Poor choice of words, but he'd laughed. She has, she knows, come to rely on him more and more, for support, and for solidarity, which is not fraternal, not sororal, but the curiously unnamed relationship of brother and sister.

Go and enjoy each other, he'd said. Send me a postcard.

He did come to Scotland. He was there to see the wolves reach the moors of Rannoch. He sat in the little plane with her, as it pitched and bounced, breathing hard, his hands gripping the seat. She'd not known he was phobic until then. But he'd known how much the moment meant to her – a victory amid all the exhaustion and chaos of the last few weeks. The outcome had never been certain. The pack had struggled through the Scottish heartland, another of the juveniles lost a few days after her return, this time to the motorways north of Glasgow. A miracle the others made it; just be thankful, is what she'd told herself, what she had to tell herself. It was the smaller grey that had been hit, the runt, the one she'd kept a soft spot for, and rooted for, against her better judgement. Mercifully quick, its death. The body had been handed in at the local police station – the lorry driver was mortified, she was told, he had been following the story and wanted them to make it all the way to Nevis; he was for them, a Yes voter, he'd tried to swerve but it was under the wheels before he knew it. A burly man from Aberdeenshire, weeping over a wolf pup.

Then the pack seemed to be veering too far east, and she had met with the environment minister again, the Wildlife Trust, and chairman of Wildwoods, the radical new group sponsoring the re-homing enterprise, to discuss intervention – tranquillisation and transporting them to the chosen location. In the end they'd resisted, held out, and hoped instinct would prevail.

It had. The wolves had doubled back, after three weeks' hard negotiations in the rich farmlands of the central belt, emergency cooperation projects with the farmers, and makeshift electric fences put up around flocks. Easy prey – there were days of excessive predation, slaughter, and outcry; the tide of opinion began to turn. It looked at one point as if they might have to be destroyed. But they'd finally gone west, towards the deer herds.

Lawrence got away from work as soon as he could, called upon once again in her hour of need. She had not liked leaving Charlie with the childminder at first, nor enjoyed the series of hotels, the hours spent apart, late evenings when her son would already be bathed and asleep in the travel cot when she came in, but it could have been worse. She'd felt like she was on the run, too – the cottage in the Lakes half packed up, promissory messages left for her boyfriend.

By the time her brother arrived, the situation was looking

less bleak, she was feeling optimistic, and the pack was in the Highland corridor. She did not want to lumber Lawrence with childcare duties, though she knew that's why he'd come. Instead, she'd urged him into the tiny four-seater with her, introduced him to Rob, the Hebridean pilot, with whom she had developed a silent rapport over the weeks, not noticing her brother's pallor, until he confessed.

Fuck it, Rachel. I'm usually high when I get on a plane.

Oh, God! I'm sorry, Lawrence, she said. Do you want to go back to the hotel?

No, no way.

He got in. He clenched his knees and gripped the seat as they took off, and tried not to panic as the choppy air of the mountains rocked them, the plane dropped like a stone, then bucked upward. Rachel had put a steadying hand on his shoulder.

You're doing great.

Am I?

At reconnaissance altitude the view was spectacular, distracting him from his fear. Snow on the Grampians, rank after rank of hard white peaks stretching out, a serious version of the Cumbrian uplands, steel-blue tarns and lochs, trout and salmon burns. Here and there, tucked-away settlements, a miniature white palace with towers, the old Glencoe ski lift looping up and over to the runs, and the winding roads made famous by song.

The transmitters were still working; the telemetry signal started beeping ten minutes into the flight and they were quickly found, cutting through a narrow valley, strung one behind the other. Dark-backed and long-legged, their tails shaggy. The plane flew over, looped round, following their trajectory. She and Lawrence watched as the four wolves loped onto the outskirts of Rannoch, its turf still bloody from autumn, as if battle-worn; the red bracken beginning to disappear under the first low-lying drifts. The pilot had looked over his shoulder and put his thumb up.

Fàilte, he'd said.

ACKNOWLEDGEMENTS

Thanks for assistance with research to the following: Andy Wightman, Land Matters – for helpful speculation about reintroduction and political scenarios north of the border. George Monbiot's book *Feral: Searching for Enchantment on the Frontiers of Rewilding* was also informative and inspiring. Vicky Allison Hughes, formerly of The UK Wolf Conservation Trust, for all things wolf-related and the tour of the sanctuary near Reading. *Wolves: Behavior, Ecology, and Conservation*, edited by L David Mech and Luigi Boitani, was vital reading. Stan Tomkiewicz, for advice about telemetry and transmitter implants. The Rosenwoods, Mike, Linda and Erik, for travels in Idaho. Olivia Pinkney, Deputy Chief Constable for Sussex Police, for procedural information and worst-case-scenario advice. Alan Bissett and Kirstin Innes, for some excellent introductions. Mairi MacPherson, for civil service and governmental information. Tony and Hilary Renkin, for their early recollections. Dr Frances Astley-Jones, for medical advice, and Dr Richard Thwaites, for psychology and Cumbrian advice. Anna Tristram, for linguistics. Stephen Brown, for architectural references.

Thanks for editorial feedback to the following: Lee Brackstone, Hannah Griffiths, Kate Nintzel, John Freeman and Ellah Allfrey. And for general literary discussions, aesthetic, poetic and metaphoric, to: Owen Sheers, Jarred McGinnis, Katja Sutela, Joanna Harma and Henna Silvennoinen.

Special thanks to Clare Conville and James Garvey, the fiercest of supporters.

About the author

2 Meet Sarah Hall

About the book

4 Reading Group Guide:
Discussion Questions for
The Wolf Border

Read on

6 Excerpt from *The Electric
Michelangelo*

Insights,
Interviews
& More . . .

Meet Sarah Hall

SARAH HALL was born in Cumbria in 1974. She received a BA from Aberystwyth University, Wales, and a master's degree in creative writing from St. Andrews, Scotland. She is the author of *Haweswater*, which won the 2003 Commonwealth Writers Prize for Best First Novel, a Society of Authors Betty Trask Award, and a Lakeland Book of the Year prize.

In 2004, her second novel, *The Electric Michelangelo*, was short-listed for the Man Booker Prize, the Commonwealth Writers Prize (Eurasia region), and the Prix Femina Etranger, and was long-listed for the Orange Prize for Fiction.

Her third novel, *The Carhullan Army*, was published in 2007, and won the 2006/07 John Llewellyn Rhys Prize, the James Tiptree Jr. Award, a Lakeland Book of the Year prize, was short-listed for the Arthur C. Clarke Award for

science fiction, and long-listed for the Dublin IMPAC Award. *The Carhullan Army* was listed as one of *The Times* 100 Best Books of the Decade.

Her fourth novel, *How to Paint a Dead Man*, was published in 2009 and was long-listed for the Man Booker Prize and won the Portico Prize for Fiction 2010. Her work has been translated into more than a dozen languages.

Her first collection of short stories, titled *The Beautiful Indifference*, was published by Faber & Faber in November 2011. *The Beautiful Indifference* won the Portico Prize for Fiction 2012 and the Edge Hill Short Story Prize, and it was also short-listed for the Frank O'Connor Prize.

"When you listen to something like that, there's no doubting the power of fiction to get to the grim heart of things."—Val McDermid, commenting on "Butcher's Perfume" on Radio 4's Pick of the Week. The story was short-listed for the BBC National Short Story Award.

Jonathan Ruppin, Foyles Web Editor, recommends books by Sarah Hall here: www.foyles.co.uk.

Sarah Hall is an honorary fellow of Aberystwyth University and a fellow of the Civitella Ranieri Foundation (2007). She has judged a number of prestigious literary awards and prizes. She tutors for the Faber Academy, the Guardian Foundation, and the Arvon Foundation, and has taught creative writing in a variety of establishments in the UK and abroad. Sarah currently lives in Norwich, Norfolk. ∾

Reading Group Guide
Discussion Questions for *The Wolf Border*

1. The title of this book is taken from the Finnish term *susiraja*, which describes the boundary between the capital region and the rest of Finland, suggesting the rest of the country is wilderness. How does this definition reflect the themes of the novel?

2. In what ways is Rachel very much like the wolves she studies? And in what ways is she different?

3. How does the author use language and description to define the different landscapes Rachel inhabits? How does her prose shape your ideas of Rachel's place in those landscapes?

4. What are some of the leitmotifs that appear throughout the novel and why are they significant?

5. The novel presents us with different examples of wilderness and preservation. Which version do you believe is the most authentic? Do you think the author comes down on one side or the other?

6. How do you think Rachel's ideas about sex evolved to become so wild and casual? How does this attitude affect other aspects of her life?

7. When Rachel visits her mother in a nursing home, she considers how "humanity's demise . . . is dreadful.

We eke it out, limp on, medicate. . . .
For humans there will be no final
status fights, no usurping, no
healthy death." Do you get the
sense that Rachel's character resents
humanity's tendency to prolong life,
and its fear of death? How does her
work reinforce or betray this point
of view?

8. The author pays particular attention
   to the body, and turns an even closer
   lens on the bodily sensations of
   pregnancy. Why do you think
   she made this choice? How did it
   change your conception of Rachel's
   character? ✒

Excerpt from
The Electric Michelangelo

– Bloodlights –

IF THE EYES COULD LIE, his troubles might all be over. If the eyes were not such well-behaving creatures, that spent their time trying their best to convey the world and all its gore to him, good portions of life might not be so abysmal. This very moment, for instance, as he stood by the hotel window with a bucket in his hands listening to Mrs Baxter coughing her lungs up, was about to deteriorate into something nasty, he just knew it, thanks to the eyes and all their petty, nit-picking honesty. The trick of course was to not look down. The trick was to concentrate and pretend to be observing the view or counting seagulls on the sill outside. If he kept his eyes away from what he was carrying they would not go about their indiscriminating business, he would be spared the indelicacy of truth, and he would not get that nauseous feeling, his hands would not turn cold and clammy and the back of his tongue would not begin to pitch and roll.

He looked up and out to the horizon. The large, smeary bay window revealed a desolate summer scene. The tide was a long way out, further than he could see, so as far as anyone knew it was just gone for good and had left the town permanently inland. It took a lot of trust to believe the water would

ever come back each day, all that
distance, it seemed like an awful
amount of labour for no good reason.
The whole dirty, grey-shingled beach
was now bare, except for one or two
souls out for a stroll, and one or two
hardy sunbathers, in their two-shilling-
hire deck-chairs, determined to make
the most of their annual holiday week
away from the mills, the mines and the
foundries of the north. A week to take
in the bracing salty air and perhaps, if
they were blessed, the sun would make
a cheerful appearance and rid them of
their pallor. A week to remove all the
coal and metal dust and chaff and
smoke from their lungs and to be a
consolation for their perpetual poor
health, the chest diseases they would
eventually inherit and often die from,
the shoddy eyesight, swollen arthritic
fingers, allergies, calluses, deafness,
all the squalid cousins of their trade.
One way to tell you were in this town,
should you ever forget where you were,
should you ever go mad and begin not to
recognize the obvious scenery, the hotels,
the choppy water, the cheap tea rooms,
pie and pea restaurants, fish and chip
kiosks, the amusement arcades, and
the dancehalls on the piers, one way to
verify your location was to watch the way
visitors breathed. There was method to
it. Deliberation. They put effort into it.
Their chests rose and fell like furnace
bellows. So as to make the most of
whatever they could snort down into
them.

There was a wet cough to the left
of him, prolonged, meaty, ploughing ▸

Excerpt from *The Electric Michelangelo* (continued)

through phlegm, he felt the enamel basin being tugged from his hands and then there was the sound of spitting and throat clearing. And then another cough, not as busy as the last, but thorough. His eyes flickered, involuntarily. Do not look down, he thought. He sighed and stared outside. The trick was to concentrate and pretend he was looking out to sea for herring boats and trawlers returning from their 150-mile search, pretend his father might come in on one of them, seven years late and not dead after all, wouldn't that be a jolly thing, even though the sea was empty of boats and ebbing just now. The vessels were presently trapped outside the great bay until the tide came back in. Odd patches of dull shining water rested on the sand and shingle, barely enough to paddle through, let alone return an absent father.

Outside the sky was solidifying, he noticed, as if the windowpane had someone's breath on it. A white horse was heading west across the sands with three small figures next to her, the guide had taken the blanket off the mare, the better that she be seen. As if she was a beacon. Coniston Old Man was slipping behind low cloud across the bay as the first trails of mist moved in off the Irish Sea, always the first of the Lake District fells to lose its summit to the weather. So the guide was right to uncover the horse, something was moving in fast and soon would blanket the beach and make it impossible to take direction, unless you knew the route, which few did in those thick conditions. Then you'd be stranded and at the mercy of the notorious tide.

—Grey old day, isn't it, luvvie? Not very pleasant for June.

—It is, Mrs Baxter. There's a haar coming in. Shall I be taking this now or will you need it again shortly do you think?

—No, I feel a bit better, now I'm cleared out, you shan't be depriving me. And if I need to go again I'll try to make it to the wash room. You're a very good boy, Cyril Parks, your mammy should be proud to have a pet like you helping her around here. Well spoken and the manners of a prince. Is it a little chilly to have the sash open today, luvvie?

The woman watched him from her chair. She resembled a piece of boiled pork, or blanched cloth, with all her colour removed. Just her mouth remained vivid, saturated by brightness, garish against her skin, and like the inside of a fruit when she spoke, red-ruined, glistening and damp.

—Yes, Mrs Baxter, I'm afraid it is. Would you like some potted shrimp? Mam made it fresh today.

—Oh yes. That would be lovely. I do so enjoy her potted shrimp, just a touch of nutmeg, not too heavy handed, salt and pepper, and never anything but fresh butter. Some of these places here leave their butter out of the pantry to spoil and use it all the same, I can tell. I've a delicate palate that way and can spot a cheap tray. Nothing worse than rancid butter, is there, luvvie? You tell your mammy I'm of the opinion that hers is the best potted shrimp in Morecambe. I won't mind telling her myself next time I see her. And is it her?

—Is what her, Mrs Baxter?

—You know. Is it her that King George gets his potted shrimp from? I know he has it sent specially to him from Morecambe Bay. I read it in the papers, that he's very partial to it and has it sent to him from a mystery person, a secret source. Would she be that mystery person? Because now that wouldn't surprise me, wouldn't surprise me in the least, I do so enjoy her potted shrimp.

—No, it's not her, Mrs Baxter.

He shook his head and picked up the basin. The trick was not to look down, to think of anything else other than that which was in his hands, but he always did look. He was self-torturing that way. He had eyes for the grotesque things of life, though in all fairness, given the current situation, he was provided ample opportunity to indulge his morbid curiosity. His mother said that human eyes saw no more nor less than the human brain commanded them to, a glass half empty or a glass half full, the Lord's leftovers or Satan's finest dining. In which case, he feared, he tumbled headlong into the realm of pessimistic and suspicious divination. Which, furthermore, left him swinging in a rather grave and hazardous position, influenced not just by the fair and graceful winds of heaven, but by a forked-tongued, red-hoofed, south-to-north blown breeze.

The consumptives in his mother's hotel coughed up blood into their basins and handkerchiefs hourly. They did it earnestly, ▶

Excerpt from *The Electric Michelangelo* (continued)

guiltily, as if each time fulfilling a pact with the Devil himself that in the matter of their failing health there would be those intolerable moments when the undersigned must bring up their monstrous, viscous, bloody end of the bargain, involving immeasurable discomfort on their behalf, for the Devil had his humorous perversions after all, before they were allowed future reprieve and life. And merciful breath. They looked at Cy with apology as they hacked and gurgled but also with a measure of determination on their ashen, bulging faces, which was at heart impersonal and informed him his presence mattered not in the affair. Whatever the Devil did with the by-product of the deal after it washed down the sink he did not care to know. He hated the pink wash of fluid that broke on their temples before the coughing began, for there were little giveaways of the disease he'd learned to interpret, and if he saw them in time and his mother was not around to prevent him, he would put down the fresh linens, the bars of pungent soap he was distributing, and back out of the room. Tuberculosis gave him the withering-willies. That and the other sick industrial legacies did not seem to bother his mother. She went about the hotel with no such trepidation. They needed the money to keep the hotel afloat and these guests were as welcome as any others, money was money after all. But Cy knew that Reeda Parks possessed a tolerance for these patients that went well beyond financial solvency and that many had lost their jobs due to poor health, so he suspected her rates must have been lower than those for ordinary folk. None of the other Morecambe boarding houses and hotels were as keen to take consumptives as Reeda. The Bayview Hotel had become known as a sanctuary, though it was not advertised outright in the papers as such. Even folk on their last legs often got room and board within, so that she acted as both bed-nurse and hostess. She was immune to the effluent, the slime, the smell and the sense of false hope that hung around their rooms like flies about finished with a corpse. She did not get that weak-kneed feeling when they coughed and spat. She didn't object to the proximity of mucus and fluid and damp spillage in her environment. She was toad-like in that fashion. Nor was Cy encouraged towards a better frame of mind by her resolve. It was distressing to him that she abdicated her common share of distaste, and it made her seem overly stern, even a touch Gothic. But if he took it up with her she simply lost her temper.

—What ails you boy! What a cold heart you have! Cyril, they did not ask to be struck with this disease. They received it for a lifetime's honest toil. I'm just looking after my own, as should you, my boy. We're not all born with our hands and feet above deck, port-out starboard-home, now are we? Manners to strangers, whether your equals or your betters, should be one and the same, young man. One and the same. That is to say equal to the courtesy you pay yourself.

Still, this did not change the fact that the consumptives coughed up blood and phlegm into basins like unholy spawn and he could not abide it.

—Now take this shrimp up to Mrs Baxter and inform her that the Territorial Band is marching at three o'clock if she cares to take a turn on the prom. I shall be available to take her arm if she's feeling wan.

The consumptives appreciated Reeda's immunity and mistook it for compassion or some kind of heightened sense of social duty, and for her kindness they would often take her hand in theirs and kiss it with their roe-red mouths.

—Reeda, Reeda. You're an absolute angel.

They sat next to the open bay windows of the hotel if they were too weak to stroll on the promenade with the rest of the summer masses in straw hats and with breeze-tugged umbrellas, letting the curtains blow in and eager for the wind on their faces. Their basins tucked like upturned helmets on their blanketed knees. They were desperate for air. More specifically, they were desperate for the air in Morecambe. They sucked it down in between their fits and held it inside their lungs like opium smokers in a den. They inhaled like they were performing exercises: loudly, with determination and regiment. They exhaled the way people sometimes did behind closed doors at night in the Bayview when all were abed and Cy was passing on the way to the kitchen for a glass of milk, letting out breathy noises as if their lungs were working a fraction beyond their control. Morecambe's air was renowned, if not nationwide then reliably in the north, for its ▶

restorative properties, its tonic qualities. It was soft. That was how everyone described it, including the Morecambe Visitor and General Advertiser. Soft, soft air. Healing. Medicinal almost, and if only someone had known how to bottle it, fortunes could have been made worldwide. Beautifully soft. This was, in large part, a tourism ruse, but of course the claim was a feature endorsed in every advertisement for every hotel or boarding house in the town. See Naples and Die, see Morecambe and Live! they read. When a white lie was told here, it was told in bold. So as far as the unwitting, desperate, industrially ravaged workers of the north were concerned the air possessed mystical, salving, qualities. It might even save them from Old Chokey if they were lucky. They wanted to believe it, and so they did believe it. And in the end, with the proliferation of the claim, year after year, season after season, even Morecambrians half-believed what they were issuing as truth, thus their maintenance of the fib took on extremely convincing proportions. Including Reeda Parks's.

—Cyril, if they ask for open windows, just open the windows, for pity's sake, and fetch more blankets if it's chilly. Best we let them have what they came for. Nothing like fresh air to improve the inflicted and we have plenty of it to spare, and it is very special.

Now Cyril Parks knew that this claim of miracle air was a fiction even at his age. The townsfolk of Morecambe were no more robust than anyone else he had met in England and they had access to it all the time. Locals still passed away in old age and were driven in carriages to the graveyard on Heysham Hill by men in tall black hats and horses with creaking black bridlery and sinister feather head-plumes. The consumptives sometimes died in the hotel while on holiday, if they had a sudden decline in condition and could not be transported to the sanatorium under Blencathra mountain, or home to loved ones in Glasgow, Bradford or the Yorkshire towns in time. Upon consideration the air was quite soft, he supposed; you didn't particularly notice it going in and out, though he had no idea what hard air was like in comparison. The air over in Yorkshire seemed about the same when Cy had visited his Aunt Doris there, two Christmases ago, though the wind on the Yorkshire moors had had something different about it, a spirit that was not coastal, a tone that was dry and dirge-like, and it had sent shivers down his spine as it fluted and lamented during his stay, haunting the rocks and trees and grass. Perhaps London had hard air. Perhaps it was what they called a city phenomenon. Or perhaps the lack of sea had something to do with it. No. Morecambe's air was not discomforting. It didn't make your lungs bleed, unless they were bleeding already. The consumptives liked it, trusted it, used it. They could obviously tell the difference between a soft and hard climate where he could not.

There were times his mother caught him backing out of the hotel rooms looking disgusted, and he'd find her hand on the back of his neck. A cool hand that might have been, of late, near the puckered mouth of a consumptive. A hand that told him not to move back another inch. A hand that felt as pale as the sick body it had been joined with. And he would shiver. He imagined if he ever touched one of the customers with tuberculosis they would feel cold like snow, even on their necks where they should be warm. Like a stone house already abandoned. Or a candle, since their appearance was deadened like the waxwork figures in Madame Tussaud's. But he was careful not to touch them, if at all possible. And he was careful to try not to look at the soupish mess in their basins, that substance with its disagreeable appearance which had led him to avoid eating stewed tomatoes and thick-shred marmalade for going on three years now purely because of the cursed similarities.

They were always so grateful. Grateful to have their basins emptied and disinfected so they could cough into them clean again as if to convince themselves that there wasn't so much blood and disease coming out of them, and grateful to be holidaying in Morecambe where there was soft air. All told, it was a sorry state of affairs. Especially as he knew that Morecambe's air wouldn't save them, these strange, pale, red-mouthed ghouls who smelled slightly metallic or like vegetables fermenting, who preferred their windows to be open and liked to consume potted shrimp almost as much as the King of England himself did. A very sorry state. ▸

13

Excerpt from *The Electric Michelangelo*
(*continued*)

Once, after catching him in the act of slipping his basin-emptying duties, having spotted a telltale sour-cherry glaze on the face of a customer as he had, Reeda sat him down at the kitchen table, and with the stern sympathy which was her calling card she instructed him to buck up.

—Look, love, I know it's not the cat's whiskers to have to care for these folk in this manner. But, honest to goodness, you're beginning to riddle my grate with your behaviour. I don't wish to judge you uncharitably, son, but I do consider it a rudeness. Now pull your socks up. I've not the time to tend to everything myself. Some might think us foolish for taking those we do. You might think us foolish. But these people deserve a little holiday as well as anyone. And some deserve it more. They've worked their lives away digging the coal that keeps you warm, and fixing the threads that bind your pant-seat, and I won't have you spoil their fun. You'll simply have to find a way to cope, please.

Her eyes, the colour of a smithy's anvil. She had, of course, a guilt-inducing and persuasive case. Also, if his mother had more than her fair share of consumptives in the hotel in the spring and summer seasons, compared with the other guest houses of the town, she also never complained about her gas bills, or worried that the present war would rob her of her best customers. ༄